Just for Show includes mentions of the past death of a parent and the grief and guilt associated with that event.

JUST FOR SHOW

Julie Hamilton

carina
press

carina
press®

Recycling programs
for this product may
not exist in your area.

ISBN-13: 978-1-335-47524-4

Just for Show

Copyright © 2021 by Julie Hamilton

This edition published by arrangement with Harlequin Books S.A.

For questions and comments about the quality of this book, please contact us at CustomerService@Harlequin.com.

Carina Press
22 Adelaide St. West, 41st Floor
Toronto, Ontario M5H 4E3, Canada
www.CarinaPress.com

Printed in U.S.A.

For all my writer friends who helped get me here.

JUST FOR SHOW

Chapter One

In less than five hours, Audrey Whitaker would get to take off her bra and change into her comfiest pajamas.

She couldn't wait.

She rode in silence to Boston's Logan Airport for her midmorning flight back to Chicago, making plans in the backseat of the taxi. The minute she got home, she was going to order a gigantic pizza, fire up Netflix, and turn off her phone. She would have blissful silence for the next three days—she hoped. Now that the conference was over, her boss didn't have a reason to text her at the ass-crack of dawn with some emergency only she could handle.

And wow, had she dealt with her fair share of emergencies over the past few days. Everything had gone wrong. She could figure out how to deal with a late freight shipment and audio-visual problems in the meeting rooms. Keynote speaker forgot his tie? Handled. Catering ran out of those delicious dinner rolls? On it. She could manage most things that were thrown at her in this business—until the water main break at the conference hotel yesterday morning.

The water went out while she was in the shower, because of course it did. Nothing like getting a screeching phone call from her boss at five thirty in the morning while under a trickling stream of water, desperately trying to make sure she got all the shampoo rinsed out of her hair.

She planned conferences for a living, figuring out logistics and anticipating what could go wrong. Even she hadn't considered *that* scenario.

Listening to her boss scream, the thought had come to her, so clear and sudden it had almost knocked her over: *I need out.* Any time she entertained the idea of quitting her day job, voices popped up in her head asking how she'd support herself. Why she thought she could start her own business. How she'd get clients.

For once, she'd shut those voices down.

Audrey had a plan. She had a plan for everything. At the moment, it was half-finished, but she would never jump into anything without one.

Tonight, pizza and Netflix. Tomorrow, business plan to change her life.

After an interminable amount of time spent in traffic, her taxi pulled up to the curb at the airport. Inside, she checked in at one of the kiosks, going through all the on-screen prompts she knew by heart after almost a decade of regular business travel. Before she could confirm her seat, one of those special offer screens popped up.

Would you like to upgrade to first class?

She paused, her finger hovering over the *No, thanks* button. She always said *No, thanks.*

She'd never flown first class before. It was an unattainable extravagance. Upgrades weren't covered under her employer's travel policy except in special circumstances. Gary would have a fit if she tried to claim this on her expense report.

Her finger still hovered over *No, thanks*. The flight was only a couple hours. She didn't need to spend money on an upgrade.

And then her shithead boss's voice played in her head, blaming her for everything up to and including the water main break. Screw it. She could afford a hundred dollars of her own money to treat herself for once.

I deserve it. She mashed her index finger on the *OK* button and inserted her debit card into the kiosk.

An hour later, she settled into a comfortable leather seat, sipping champagne and eating a warm chocolate chip cookie. Definitely the best hundred dollars she'd ever spent.

"Hey," said a deep voice, breaking her cookie-induced reverie. "Sorry, but I'm in the window seat."

She looked up at her seatmate, the guy giving her an expectant, almost apologetic smile. Her insides *whooshed* and she lost the ability to make words for a second. Good Lord. He was like a Disney prince come to life.

"Sure, no problem." She got up from her seat to let him in.

After an awkward shuffle in the aisle, he sat, glancing over at her as she settled back in. No, he wasn't a Disney prince—more like a movie superhero. He was tall and leanly muscular, with tanned skin, dark blond hair, and a strong jawline. When he looked at her again, he gave her a smile that crinkled the corners of his eyes.

Yeah, that upgrade charge was definitely worth it.

"There are free cookies," she said with a grin, "and free booze." She lifted her champagne flute and wiggled it back and forth.

What was she doing? Under normal circumstances on flights, she didn't chat up her seatmate. She certainly didn't flirt. She would have her earbuds in and Kindle out, a do-not-interrupt-my-reading-time look on her face. But under normal circumstances, she wasn't buzzed from champagne and sugar, and she never had guys this cute sitting next to her.

He shoved a duffel bag under the seat in front of him. "The cookies are good, but wait until you try the cheese plate."

"Oh man, there's free cheese, too?"

"Yeah, and it's better than you'd expect." He turned toward her, his lips quirked up at the corners, a hint of mischief in his eyes. "I'm up for splitting one, if you want."

"What if I want my own?" She was joking. Kind of.

"You can get your own," he said, "but it's a lot of cheese. A *lot*."

"Okay, we can split one." Audrey leaned back against the headrest and sighed. "If I knew I could have all the cheese and champagne I wanted, I would have flown first class sooner."

He laughed, a bright, rich sound, and her insides *whooshed* again.

"I know, it was probably obvious before I said anything," she said, moving her head to look at him. "I fly for work a lot, but I've never been up here."

"I'm usually back there," he said, tilting his head in the direction of the main cabin as more passengers began to filter on to the plane. "But if I'm flying for work, it's free cheese plates all the way."

He must have had some fancy job that ensured all the first-class perks he wanted. "What do you do?"

"I'm, um." His mouth opened and closed, and he rubbed the back of his neck. Was he nervous? What if he was an air marshal and he couldn't tell her and was really bad at lying? "I'm—I remodel houses. What about you?"

"I'm a meeting planner. I work at a trade association, and I handle all the logistics for our conferences."

"That sounds stressful."

Oh, he didn't know the half of it. "It is, but we just wrapped up the biggest conference of the year, so I get to relax. For like a week, until I have to start planning the next one." The mention of work made her skin itch. "You said you remodel houses?"

He did the neck-rubbing thing again. "Yeah. Mostly vintage homes. Modernizing them but still keeping the vintage feel on the inside and outside."

"That's awesome. I love old houses, but in Chicago a lot of them get torn down for new construction."

They chatted for a few minutes about what a shame that was. How when those old houses were torn down, all that character, all those things that contributed to a neighborhood's history, were lost. Audrey wasn't into home renovation and restoration or anything like that— she didn't binge-watch shows on HomeTV like her best friend, Natalie—but she couldn't help feeling passionate about it talking to…shit, she hadn't asked his name.

"We've spent all this time talking about cheese and old houses and we still haven't introduced ourselves," she said.

He stuck out his hand. "Luke."

"Audrey." She shook his hand, a twinge of awareness speeding through her body like an electric current. "Nice to meet you."

The flight attendant came over and offered Luke a drink. When you were in the fancy people section of the plane, you didn't have to ask for anything. People anticipated your needs, a point proven when a cheese plate magically appeared on her tray table.

"Amazing," she murmured, more at the fact the plate had appeared without her asking rather than at the contents of the tray itself. It was a nice spread, though—cheddar, Brie, Gouda, crackers, grapes, apple slices, and a few thin slivers of prosciutto.

"I told you there was a lot of cheese."

"And it's even on a real plate."

Luke laughed, and they ate. The side of his hand occasionally bumped hers, which sent a rush of heat to her cheeks every single time. Here she was, eating cheese on a plane with a stranger who was maybe an air marshal or maybe actually did remodel houses, and blushing every time their hands touched.

It was the most action she'd gotten in months.

She couldn't decide if that was pathetic or normal, but everything about this moment was outside her usual scope of reality. She should be back in coach, reading a book and looking forward to her evening of pizza and all the streaming TV her heart desired.

Luke's hand bumped hers again when they both reached for the same slice of cheddar. He let her have it and picked up the next slice instead. They talked about where they lived—they were both born and raised Chicagoans, but he lived in Boston for work—and polished off the rest of the cheese and crackers.

"Is this a work trip? Or are you headed home to visit family?" she asked.

"I'll be staying with my family, but I've got a job in Chicago for the rest of the summer."

Rest of the summer meant her brain heard *possibility*. She was getting way ahead of herself. She wasn't looking for a summer fling. She didn't *have* summer flings. Anyway, she would be busy working on that half-finished business plan. She also had her volunteer gig at the animal shelter on the weekends. And work, although it should slow down once she returned to the office.

Ha, right. Her job never slowed down.

Don't think about work.

"Chicago is great in the summer," she said, her voice sounding too cheerful. "I guess you'll be remodeling a house?"

"I am." His face lit up, and he gestured with his hands. "This big, old Victorian from 1891. It has tons of old woodwork and details I want to preserve. It'll be a lot of work, but I'm looking forward to it."

He was dorky about old houses the way she was about cameras. Definitely not an air marshal, then. She smiled to herself. "And the homeowners are flying you out here? You must be a pretty big deal."

He didn't look at her, focusing on their shared plate instead. "I guess I am." He popped a grape in his mouth and folded his hands on top of his tray table.

She glanced at his hands. When they shook hands earlier, she'd felt the roughness of them. They were hands that worked, hands that broke down walls and hammered things into place and made things more beautiful than they were before.

Those hands made her want to pull out her camera to photograph them, to capture the calluses on his fingertips, the light catching the faint dusting of hair close to his wrists.

When he spoke again, it startled her, pulling her out of her thoughts. "Do you want to see pictures of the house?"

"I'd love to."

While he showed her the pictures on his phone, she took the opportunity to lean in, to let the warmth from his body radiate into hers. She was shameless, but she didn't care. What were the odds she'd see him again? Might as well enjoy being around a guy this hot while she had the chance.

"Now that the big conference is over," Luke said, putting away his phone, "what do you do when you're not planning meetings?"

"I'm a photographer." She'd never said it like that before—she usually said *I like taking pictures* or *Oh, I do photography sometimes*. "Actually, I'm hoping to start my own photography business."

"And quit the stressful day job?"

"I hope so." God, she hoped so. That was the plan.

Luke didn't ask how she'd support herself. He didn't ask what made her think she could start her own business. He asked questions about what kind of photography she did and how long she'd been doing it. How she got started. His attentiveness to her words, the way he paused before asking her a question, drew her in.

"I'd love to see some of your work," he said. "Do you have any pictures on your phone?"

"I have some stuff, but it's not my best."

Mainly because it was all pictures of dogs. And yeah, the dogs were cute. Her photos helped a number of dogs get adopted. But she didn't want to be known as the dog photographer.

He didn't push to see the photos, instead rolling with it when she changed the topic back to home renovation. Before she knew it, the captain announced they'd be landing soon.

A funny sensation settled over her, something like

nostalgia for a moment that wasn't over yet. Luke would be a fun story, a nice memory. Yes, she could make a move and ask for his number, but that wasn't a good idea. Guys did nothing but hold her back from going after what she wanted. Neil certainly had.

He's not your ex.

Whatever. She wasn't asking him out.

Once they arrived at the gate, she grabbed her bag from the overhead compartment and turned to Luke, almost bumping into his chest. They stood, waiting for the door to open so they could exit the plane. She took a tiny step backward, enough so she wasn't up close and personal with his very broad, very solid chest. She was about to say it was nice meeting him, but he spoke first.

"Hey." He shifted his duffel bag onto his shoulder. "I don't want to put you on the spot, but what are your plans for the rest of the summer?"

Her heart thudded in her chest. Was he asking her out, or was she reading too much into the question? What if he asked to be nice? But the way he said it—*I don't want to put you on the spot*—made it sound like more than a friendly inquiry.

They'd spent an entire flight getting to know each other and not-so-accidentally touching. Of course he was asking her out. He wouldn't ask about her summer plans without there being some intention behind the question.

One of the flight attendants opened the door. The people in the rows ahead rushed toward the exit, carry-on bags in hand, like they couldn't get off the plane fast enough. A man from the row behind them moved around her with a murmured "excuse me," holding a baby, who started wailing. The enormous diaper bag on the dad's shoulder hit Audrey in the arm as he passed. A swell of people in the rows behind them surged up the aisle, grabbing bags from the overhead bins and anxiously waiting for their turn to get off the plane.

She rubbed her arm, glancing toward the exit. *Say something.* She stood frozen in the aisle, trying to pick an appropriate response, torn between what she wanted and what was good for her.

"I'm—" she started to say. This was not a hard question.

"Come on, lady," said an old man standing behind them. "Some of us want to get off the damn plane."

"Working, mostly," she said to Luke.

His eyebrows knitted together. He tilted his head to the side.

She squeezed her eyes shut for a second. Of all the things she could say, she chose that? When she opened her eyes, he looked like he was about to say something, but she turned around before he could. She hurried off the plane and up the jet bridge, dragging her carry-on behind her.

At least she would never have to see him again.

What the fuck just happened?

Luke stared at the space where Audrey had been a second ago. She'd given him go signs the entire flight. If she hadn't, he never would have asked her out. Or, you know, tried to. He'd been building up to that question when she said something about work and ran away. Clearly he'd misread the entire situation—every laugh, every blush, every time her hand brushed against his. He couldn't pinpoint what he did wrong.

"Aren't you going to go after her?" asked the same guy who had complained about people taking too long to get off the damn plane. "I had to spend the entire flight listening to you two flirt."

Luke shook his head, grabbed his other bag from the overhead, and took off. He would not be the creep who chased a woman through the airport, but they had to run into each other in the terminal, right? She couldn't have made it that far. He could ask if she wanted to exchange numbers, maybe get together for a drink or something while he was in town. No pressure.

And if she said no, that was that.

He hustled up the jet bridge. Hope built in his chest the closer he got to the end. Maybe he hadn't blown it. When he found her, they could try this again.

He emerged into the terminal, blinking in the bright afternoon sunlight pouring through the windows. She had to be around here somewhere. As he scanned the crowd, the hope that had been building in his chest sank to the pit of his stomach.

She was gone.

He moved forward in the sea of people streaming off the flight, still looking for her brown curls and teal suitcase. How the hell did she disappear so fast?

He swore under his breath. For the first time in a long time, he'd clicked with someone. Sure, their conversation had flowed easily, but it was her personality that had drawn him in. She was creative and ambitious in addition to being funny and beautiful. He couldn't keep his eyes off her. Couldn't stop thinking about seeing her again.

And he blew it.

He walked away from the gate, his steps quick and purposeful, like if he walked fast enough, he could catch up to her.

A tap on his back stopped him in his tracks. He slowly turned around, trying not to let that hope rise again.

The middle-aged woman standing there clapped her hands in delight. "Are you Luke Murphy? I love *Retro Renovations*!"

Oh, shit. Right. He was semi-famous. Four years ago, he'd been a carpenter running his family's remodeling business. Now people wanted pictures with him at the airport.

It was not at all how he'd expected his life to turn out.

"Hey, thanks." He forced some cheer into his voice. "Glad to hear you love the show."

"Could we get a picture together?" the woman asked.

"Yeah, sure." His moderate level of reality TV fame meant he got stopped sometimes by people who wanted a picture, or who wanted to ask if that one couple from the show were as terrible in real life as they were on TV. They were worse—not that he ever admitted that out loud. He kept things positive, said how every episode had its own challenges, and smiled in the fan photos.

Since most people were respectful, he was cool with the occasional selfie. But now? Now was a bad time. Right now, he could be missing his chance to catch up to Audrey. That sinking feeling intensified in his gut.

She's gone. You're not going to find her.

He shuffled out of people's way and waited while the woman pulled out her phone and got the camera ready. Once they took the photo, she thanked him and hurried off, calling out, "I'll tag you on Twitter and Insta!"

Hold on a second.

He *was* semi-famous. He had several thousand followers, not that he kept track or anything. It was a total shot in the dark, but...

He pulled out his phone and opened the Twitter app. He could throw something out there to see if Audrey found him. If she saw it and decided to reply, great. Or she could ignore it—although he hoped like hell she wouldn't.

He tapped the button to post a tweet and stared at the blinking cursor.

Okay, on second thought, this might not work. He'd kept the TV show thing to himself, and she didn't seem to have any idea who he was. Sometimes it was nice to be Luke, not *Retro Renovations* Guy. If he tweeted something, he would blow his own cover, but he was willing to take that risk. The tweet might end up in her feed if enough people retweeted it. She would recognize him from his profile picture.

Was he really doing this?

He stood there writing several tweets, backspacing on all of them before he could post. The last thing he wanted to do was put pressure on her. She needed to come to him. He just had to facilitate a way to make that happen.

Fuck it. He was overthinking this. He merged into the crowd of people headed toward baggage claim and typed something off the cuff.

Here's how things are going so far for me in Chicago:
1. Messed up my attempt at asking out the gorgeous woman next to me on the plane
2. Couldn't catch up to her at O'Hare
3. I'm hoping she finds me on Twitter
4. Maybe if she sees this, we can split another cheese plate sometime

He closed the app and stuck his phone back in his pocket. Now all he could do was wait.

Chapter Two

Luke checked his phone once in the cab from the airport to Mom's house. Once after dinner. Once before going to bed.

The tweet had started to gain some traction—a hundred retweets, a couple hundred likes, a handful of replies wishing him luck. But nothing from the one person he wanted to hear from.

Lying awake staring at his phone and hoping for a response was equal parts pathetic and ill-advised. Production schedules were brutal, and he needed to rest. He had plans the next morning to stop by the house he'd be renovating for the pilot of his new show, *Project Victorian*—its working title, since he was remodeling a Victorian. He planned to restore an older home in each episode if the show got picked up, and they probably wouldn't all be Victorians. The network could come up with a better title later. Although this was the same network that had a show called *Dude, Flip My House* on its schedule, so he might end up with something worse.

Construction and filming would start at the beginning of next week. Plus he had a charity thing to do over the weekend. He made the responsible decision, closing Twitter and plugging in his phone to charge, and promptly passed out.

The next morning, he woke to his phone buzzing. With a groan, he reached out in the darkness, his fingers fumbling toward the nightstand. He woke up early all the time, but he still had twenty minutes before he needed to get out of bed. If someone was calling before eight o'clock, it had better be an emergency.

He opened one eye and picked up the phone to look at the screen. Jessica. What would she want at this hour? He'd spoken to the HomeTV publicist a few times before, usually around the time a new season was set to premiere and the network forced him to do press.

He wasn't doing press right now. Not for a few more months, until he had to promote the pilot of *Project Victorian*.

He cleared his throat before answering, but his voice still came out rough and sleepy. "Hello?"

"I have a lot of interview requests for you," Jessica said. "I was wondering if we could discuss your schedule and figure out some good days and times. Obviously, *Good Day USA* would be top priority—"

"Huh?" *Good Day USA*? What the hell was she talking about?

"Should I call back at another time?" Jessica asked in a clipped tone.

"No, sorry. I just woke up. What's going on?" He sat up and swung his legs over the side of the bed. Coffee. He needed coffee.

"You sent a tweet yesterday." Jessica spoke slowly, like she needed to break this into smaller pieces for him to understand.

"Yeah, I did." What did the tweet have to do with anything, especially *Good Day USA*? He stood and headed into the hallway, then down the stairs into the kitchen. It was empty. Mom must have already left for work.

"It went viral overnight."

She had to be kidding. Cute videos of animals and kids went viral. His tweets did not.

"Is this like when *Retro Renovations* first started airing and people posted GIFs of my butt?" That had been mildly horrifying, first to realize the show had a lot of intentional shots of his butt, and worse when people tagged him in those posts. His family still made fun of him for it sometimes.

Jessica laughed and tried to cover it up with a cough. "No. Those didn't blow up like this did."

A throbbing started in the center of his forehead. He pulled the phone away from his ear and put it on speaker so he could look at his Twitter app. His mentions numbered in the thousands. The tweet itself had fifty thousand retweets. The likes were twice that. Jesus.

He set the phone down and peeked inside one of the kitchen cabinets. No coffee there. Staying with his mom was easier than getting temporary housing. Except for right now, when he desperately needed caffeine. "I don't understand. It had a hundred retweets when I went to bed last night."

"Never underestimate the power of Romance Novel Twitter," Jessica said, her voice full of reverence. "They started retweeting it, and it took off from there."

"Romance Novel Twitter? That's a thing?"

Jessica sighed. "Yes, it is. And whatever you were about to say next, please don't."

"I wasn't going to say anything."

He scrolled through his notifications. He'd never have

time to read all of them, nor did he want to. But what if something from Audrey was in there? He should probably go through them at some point.

He closed the app and rubbed his forehead with his free hand. Wasn't this what he wanted? For people to share it so it could end up in Audrey's feed? She'd definitely see it now. Whether or not she'd be cool with the attention if people found her, he didn't know. But he did know one thing: *he* wasn't cool with it, at least not at this level.

It seemed a little backward for a guy with a TV show to shy away from attention, but he wasn't super famous. Never wanted to be. He was happy doing his thing renovating houses and using whatever small bit of fame he had to help people. The whole point of taking the TV gig was so he could help his family. Send Erin to college. He would do interviews to promote his work, but his personal life was off limits.

Unless he tweeted the tiniest thing about his personal life and it got retweeted fifty thousand fucking times.

"Well?" Jessica asked, breaking into his thoughts. "Do you think you can be in New York tomorrow?"

"I don't want to do any interviews." He yanked open another cabinet. Where the hell was the coffee? "*Retro Renovations* is on its final season. *Project Victorian* won't air for months. I have nothing to promote." He'd already done interviews for the current season of *Retro Renovations* a couple months ago.

"Promotion isn't the point, at least not entirely. It's a human-interest story. People could use some happy news these days, and what's happier than people finding love?"

"Who said anything about love?" he grumbled, yanking open another cabinet.

"It would give you some great buzz for the new show," Jessica said, speaking faster now, "and *Today* is working to try to find this woman. They want to interview you together. It's a win-win. Don't you want to find her? Isn't that why you sent the tweet?"

"I sent the tweet so she could find me, not so we could end up on TV together." The idea of ending up on TV and dragging Audrey into it was enough to make him sick. "I'm sorry, but I'm not doing any interviews about this. I have to go."

He hit the button to end the call. Seconds later, his phone rang. Jessica again. He silenced it with a sense of nagging guilt. He'd hung up on her like an asshole, but he was not doing interviews. The tweet had been a low-stakes way to get Audrey's attention. Going on national television was definitely not low stakes.

He wasn't that desperate for publicity for *Project Victorian*. HomeTV had committed to airing the pilot, and if the response was good enough—which he hoped it would be, given his history with the network—he would get to film a limited number of episodes. This project would be a fresh start. A way to do the kind of TV he wanted to make instead of being the sideshow to a real estate agent and bickering couples. The focus could finally be on his work, and he could keep helping his family at the same time.

He should have considered all of this before hitting the Tweet button, but in the moment, all that had mattered was finding Audrey. They'd spent two hours together on a plane, but he couldn't remember the last time he'd enjoyed being around someone that much. He wanted to talk to her more. Get to know each other. Spend time together while he was in town. Have fun. It wasn't like he was looking for forever.

Neither is she. She ran away from you.

Now people on the internet were looking for her, along with a bunch of TV producers. A woman who froze up and ran off a plane wasn't someone who'd appreciate that kind of attention. If they found her, she wouldn't want anything to do with him.

He'd taken a chance and blown it again.

And he still hadn't found the fucking coffee.

Audrey enjoyed going full hermit when she returned from a conference. For the first day after she got home, she stuck to the plan: couch, pizza, Netflix, and absolutely no email or phone. By the second day, she caved. Avoiding her phone only made her want to look at it more. What if she missed an important text? Or what if her boss decided to call? While Gary was on vacation, too, that had never stopped him from contacting her before.

At least she had managed to unplug for an entire day.

When she turned her phone on, it buzzed with missed notifications—thankfully, none from her boss. Most of them were from her group text with her two best friends. She'd told them about her plans to turn off her phone once she got home from the conference, but the group text stopped for no one.

Natalie: AUDREY WE WANT TO HANG OUT

Grace: She needs time to decompress. Let her enjoy her time off!

Natalie: Why can't she enjoy her time off with us? We haven't seen her in like a month.

A month was stretching it, but with her schedule lately, she hadn't had much time to spend with them.

Audrey: Turns out I'm incapable of going without my phone longer than a day and a half. I miss you guys.

Natalie: I knew it. We're coming over.

Audrey glanced down at her T-shirt and sweatpants. She shrugged. She put on real pants for few visitors. Grace and Natalie were not among them.

An hour and some change later, the three of them had settled on the couch with bags of tacos, chips, and guacamole ordered from the place down the street from her apartment. This was their routine, the respite they all needed from work, family, and whatever else was going on in their lives. Every couple of weeks, they ended up at her place for a night of takeout and TV. Her apartment had become their go-to because she had cable and multiple streaming services, plus the only couch all three of them could fit on.

"What are we watching tonight?" Audrey asked. She took a chicken taco out of the bag and unwrapped it.

"Ooh, let's watch *Tiny Homes*," Natalie said, picking up the remote and turning on the TV.

Audrey groaned around a bite of taco. "Not that show again."

"But we had such a good time making fun of it last time."

"That couple had seven kids and a dog. It wasn't so

much making fun of them as pointing out the ridiculousness of that many people and a dog cramming into two hundred square feet and using a single composting toilet."

Grace scrunched up her face at the words "composting toilet" and shot a skeptical glance in Natalie's direction. "How do you know it's on right now?"

Natalie flipped her long, dark hair over one shoulder. "Because it's always on." She put on her favorite channel.

A commercial for one of the channel's other shows played on the screen. A white guy wearing a flannel shirt and safety glasses used a power saw to cut wood. In the next scene, a Latino guy in a suit stood in an empty room with two women and said, "You got the house." Then a quick cut to the tall, scruffy white dude using a sledgehammer to knock down a wall.

Audrey paused, her taco halfway to her mouth, and stared at the screen.

No fucking way.

Was that *Luke*? Sure, he'd been clean-shaven on the plane, but even the scruff couldn't hide that jawline. He said he remodeled houses, but he never said anything about being on TV. *Why wouldn't he mention that?*

Maybe she was imagining things. There were lots of tall, scruffy white dudes on this channel. Besides, it was hard to see the guy's face. The camera filmed from the side and behind, and in most of the shots he wore safety glasses. With all the quick cuts in the commercial, she couldn't get a good look—until the commercial ended with a shot of both guys standing next to each other.

Yep, that was the man she'd run away from two days ago.

"Holy shit," she breathed.

Luke didn't just remodel houses. He remodeled houses on TV. Which meant he must be a little famous. In all the hours of HomeTV she'd watched with Natalie, she'd never seen him—at least not that she could remember.

Audrey set down her taco. "Nat, do you ever watch that show?"

"*Retro Renovations*? Not really. When it's not people arguing, it's basically butt and forearm porn of the carpenter dude," Natalie said.

Grace's hazel eyes flashed with humor. "And you're complaining about that?"

"I'm not. Don't get me wrong, the other guy is cute, too. But the butt shots are literally the only reason to watch."

Natalie and Grace high-fived each other and dissolved into laughter. Audrey glanced between her friends. She had to tell them. She told them everything, and it was a good story.

She took a deep breath. Let it out. "The carpenter dude was on my flight home."

"*No*," Natalie said, grabbing Audrey's arm. Ow. For a small person, she had a strong grip. "Are you sure?"

"He was in the seat next to me. And he never said anything about"—Audrey waved her hand at the screen, even though the commercial had ended—"this. I asked him about his job, and—"

The neck rubbing. That was his tell. She'd *known* something had been up. Why hadn't he said he was on TV?

"And what?" Natalie eased up her hold on Audrey's arm.

"He said he remodeled houses. I guess he wasn't

lying. He told me he was in Chicago for the summer to remodel a house."

"Oh my God," Grace said. She wiped her hands on a napkin and reached for her phone on the coffee table. "I follow an author who retweeted this. You're hashtag TheOneWhoGotAway."

Audrey turned to look at Grace, who bounced in her seat with excitement, her blond curls shaking. "Hashtag? What are you talking about?"

"How long has your phone been off?" Grace asked.

"What does that have to do with anything?" She had social media accounts on all the major platforms, but she spent most of her time on Instagram. She didn't use Twitter often. She wouldn't have seen a tweet even if her phone had been on. And it wasn't like Luke could have texted her.

Natalie picked up her phone and started tapping and scrolling. "You *are* a hashtag. Wow, this is blowing up."

Audrey was ready to throw a taco against the wall. "Will someone please tell me *why* I'm a hashtag?"

"You said you were sitting next to him on the plane, right?" Grace shoved her phone at Audrey.

A tweet was on the screen from @LukeMurphy. She smiled as soon as she started reading it. At the mention of the cheese plate, a loud "Ha!" escaped her throat. She read the tweet again. And again. *The gorgeous woman next to me on the plane.*

Her cheeks heated. "He tweeted about me."

"In a self-deprecating way that appealed to the Twitter masses," Natalie said, nose still buried in her own phone.

"But there's no hashtag. What's the thing about the hashtag?"

"People started tweeting at him #TheOneWhoGot-

Away and it's a thing now," Grace said. "People are asking him if he's had any luck finding you."

Audrey glanced at the screen again for the retweets and likes—oh, wow. Seventy-five thousand retweets. Two hundred thousand likes. That was a ton of people. Those were viral tweet numbers.

"Is my name out there anywhere?" Audrey's stomach turned over. The tacos that had smelled and tasted so delicious a few minutes ago suddenly weren't appealing. If her name was out there, or God forbid, if her boss or coworkers saw her name out there anywhere...

"No," Grace said. "At least not that I've seen."

Natalie nodded. "People would be calling you."

"They'd be tweeting at you."

Audrey's stomach turned again. This could have been worse. "You think this will blow over soon?"

"Yes, unless he does an interview about it or something," Natalie said. "What's the story behind this, anyway? He tried to ask you out and you ran away from him?"

"Basically."

"Um, we want details." Grace dug into the bag of chips, and Natalie took another taco. Both women looked at her with their eyebrows raised.

Audrey hugged one of the throw pillows to her chest. "Okay, fine. I upgraded myself to first class—"

Natalie let out a low whistle. "How much did that set you back?" Grace shot Natalie a look.

"A hundred bucks," Audrey said. "Which was less than I expected, but I think I got some kind of frequent flier deal. I probably shouldn't have spent the money, but the conference sucked, and I was exhausted."

"Hey, you don't have to justify it to us." Grace raised her glass. "Treat yourself."

"Anyway, I take my seat, I'm enjoying some champagne, and this hot guy comes up and says he's in the seat next to me."

Audrey recounted the rest of the story, all the way up to her saying, "Working, mostly" when he started to ask her out. And how she ran away. She'd never hauled ass that fast in her life.

"But why did you run?" Grace asked.

"I don't know!" Audrey threw her hands in the air. "People were looking at us, and everyone was trying to get off the plane. I was overthinking what to say and how to react, and I couldn't get any words out. When I finally said something, I was so embarrassed all I could think was, 'You need to get off this plane right now.'" She picked at a loose thread on the throw pillow. "I locked myself in a bathroom stall until I was sure the coast was clear."

"Oh, Audrey." Grace grabbed her hand and squeezed.

"I love you, but sometimes I don't understand you," Natalie said, shaking her head. "He is *fine*."

"Trust me, I noticed."

Natalie gave her a sly glance and bumped their shoulders together. "You could slide into his DMs."

"I'm not sliding into anyone's DMs."

"He's looking for you. He clearly wants to see you again. And your little freak-out aside, it seems like you were interested in him, too."

"I don't want my name and face all over Twitter. I'm a hashtag!" Those were three words she never thought she'd say.

"You could reach out to him and say, 'Hey, I saw

your tweet, but I don't want to go public with this,'"
Grace said.

"It's not worth it. He's some guy I met on a plane."

"Who is into you. And wants to see you again. You
said he's in town for the summer. Hello, summer fling,"
Natalie said.

"I don't want a summer fling." Audrey had told herself that on the plane, and she'd had a good reason. "I
want to spend this summer trying to start my business."

She didn't need to get distracted by a guy, especially
a famous one who wouldn't be in town for long. Her
friends knew how important pursuing photography was
to her. They knew how Neil had made fun of the idea
and eroded her confidence. How he put doubts in her
head. But they'd broken up almost a year ago. It was
past time to get things moving—without anything or
anyone in her way.

Grace handed Natalie the bag of chips. "Here. Eat
these and leave her alone."

"I'm just saying." Natalie stuffed a chip in her mouth.
"She has a chance with a man who has one of the finest
asses in America."

Audrey burst out laughing. As her friends shifted
their attention to *Tiny Homes*, she grabbed her phone and
pulled up Luke's Twitter account. She scrolled through
some of the replies to his tweet. A few people mocked
him for not shooting his shot when he had the chance.
There were some bad puns related to sharing cheese
plates. But most of the replies were about her. People asking what her name was. People asking what she looked
like. People asking him to post if he found her.

Luke hadn't tweeted anything since the original tweet,

hadn't acknowledged any of the replies. That helped ease the weird feeling in her stomach.

She'd heard stories about people having their privacy destroyed when tweets or videos went viral. She had no interest in putting her name or face out there. No interest in letting this become what she was known for, not when she wanted to be known for her work.

Best to let it blow over.

Because it had to blow over, right? These viral tweets always did.

She set her phone down. Whether or not it blew over, she knew one thing for sure—she wasn't contacting him. Yeah, he was hot and seemed like a decent guy, but she didn't want a fling. She certainly didn't want a boyfriend.

This was the summer to pursue her goals. No man involved.

Chapter Three

On the list of bad decisions Luke had made in his life, the one he'd made four days ago to send that tweet was at the top of the list.

What the hell had he been thinking? A woman who ran away from him was not going to see a tweet and come running back.

He'd still kept an eye on his notifications in case her name popped up. After the hundredth bad pickup line about cheese plates landed in his inbox, he stopped getting the little fizzle of hope in his chest that the next notification would be from her.

Audrey hadn't reached out to him yet. Maybe she never would.

Every time his phone buzzed now, dread filled him, not hope. His inbox overflowed with so many DMs, he'd had to mute notifications and change his privacy settings. People he'd never met got his phone number and called him for interviews. He didn't answer any of the calls or messages, but his silence spurred more chatter, more interview requests, more articles wondering about the mysterious woman on the plane.

He couldn't blame anyone but himself for this shit-show. He sent the tweet, and now he had to deal with the aftermath. Spending the weekend on a charity project at an animal shelter was a good way to get his mind off things. Throwing himself into work hadn't failed him—yet.

"I don't think you should be allowed to use power tools right now."

Luke's head snapped up from where he'd positioned a circular saw to cut a piece of plywood. He glanced over at Aidan, holding his stare, and turned on the saw.

"Dude, what if you're so distracted by Twitter you chop off a finger?"

Inviting his cousin to help today was also on his list of bad decisions. After Luke finished cutting the plywood, he turned off the saw. "Seriously?"

"What are they calling you now?" Aidan asked, plowing right ahead. "Twitter Babe or something?"

Luke closed his eyes and prayed for patience. "It's TwitterBae."

With a noise like a cross between a honk and a laugh, Aidan repeated the word under his breath and hip-checked Luke away from the workbench. "What does that even mean?" Aidan said, picking up the saw.

An article with the headline "5 Fast Facts about Luke Murphy, Everyone's New #TwitterBae" had been posted online yesterday afternoon, and it was ruining his life. Actually, Twitter in general was ruining his life.

"It's not like I chose—"

The saw started up. Whatever. Aidan could joke around all he wanted. Luke threw up his hands and went to check on the progress of the crew remodeling the shelter's other meet-and-greet room.

He poked his head in, made sure things were going okay, and then stepped away from the construction zone.

He needed quiet. Having a minute to himself might help get him out of this mood, help him focus on the job. He walked past a couple of bathrooms and was heading toward what looked like a break room when he skidded to a stop.

A woman stood at the end of the hallway, her back to him. She wore a black T-shirt with the shelter's logo, but it didn't matter if she was an employee or volunteer. She shouldn't be in this area. It was a job site. What if something happened and she got hurt? He had to tell her to leave.

Wait a second.

She was curvy, not short but not tall, either, with pale skin and curly brown hair that fell to her shoulders.

Audrey?

He was imagining things. He had to be. The woman turned a corner, giving him a glimpse of her face in profile, too quick for him to tell if it was her.

Shit.

His chest grew tight with disappointment. *Let it go.* She was gone. She'd been gone since the moment she stepped off the plane and disappeared into the terminal.

But what if it *was* her?

He kept walking and rounded the corner, stopping midstride. She stood there fiddling with some buttons on the camera attached to a strap looped around her neck. Her hair fell into her face. His heart beat faster.

"Audrey?"

She looked up. Her eyes went wide and her head jerked back. "What the hell?"

"Sorry, I—"

"Did you track me down or something? Who told you

I volunteered here?" She took a couple steps backward and glanced over her shoulder.

What? She thought he'd stalked her and found her at this animal shelter? Someone else—someone who was an asshole with no boundaries—might do that. He wouldn't, but she didn't know that. "I didn't track you down. I had no idea."

"Then what are you doing here?"

"I—I'm remodeling a couple rooms for the shelter. It's a charity thing."

"For your show?" she asked, her eyes narrowing.

Well, he'd always known she would find out, especially once the tweet blew up. "No. It's—it's this—I do this thing where I like to, you know, give back to the community…"

He sounded like a fucking idiot. He should stop talking.

"What are you really doing in Chicago?" she asked. "It can't be just for this."

There was a note of accusation in her voice, an insinuation that he'd hidden something from her. And he had, but he also hadn't lied.

"Everything I told you about myself was true. I'm in town to remodel a house." He shook his head and swiped a hand over the bottom half of his face. "I left out the part about it being for TV."

She gave a short little "hmm" and tilted her chin up. "Why didn't you mention that?"

"Because sometimes it's nice not to be recognized. I don't have to be the guy from the show."

He sounded ungrateful. *Retro Renovations* had put Erin through college. It had paid off the balance on his own student loans. It had given him and his family so much. While he didn't always love the attention, he liked taking care of his family and being more comfortable financially. He also liked sharing his work with an audience—which *Project Victorian* would let him do more than *Retro Renovations*, where he was glorified eye candy. He'd get to show people more of his skills as a carpenter and make good money at the same time. He could save up. Buy a house of his own. Keep helping Mom and Erin. And even though he no longer handled the day-to-day at the family business, his fame helped Aidan get more jobs at Murphy Construction and Remodeling. If he got to do all that, being kind of famous wasn't so bad.

"It was useful to be the guy from the show when you decided to send that tweet."

He winced, but she was telling the truth. He'd leveraged his small amount of fame in service of finding her. "I'm guessing you saw it."

"Me and at least three hundred thousand other people. Good job working in the mention of the cheese plate," she said, a smile playing at the corner of her lips.

A surge of relief flooded him at the appearance of that tiny smile. Maybe he had a chance.

He smiled back. "I had to work in something specific."

"It was a good tweet."

"I wasn't expecting it to blow up the way it did." If his mentions had turned into a shitshow of epic proportions, what had her life been like these past few days? So far, he hadn't seen her name mentioned anywhere, but people were trying to find her—like the *Good Day USA* producers. "I hope no one's bothered you because of it."

"They haven't. I'm still just the woman from the plane." She shook her head, glancing down at her camera. "I didn't mean to run away."

Looking at her, a thousand questions raced through his head, questions he wasn't sure he deserved to have answered. Why she didn't reply, what made her run, how she felt about the whole thing. But she didn't owe him anything. Even as he sent the tweet, he'd known that. "You didn't?"

"I was tired and caught off guard. I got flustered, then I was embarrassed and thought to myself that I needed to get the hell out of there. Now here we are."

"You were embarrassed?"

"Well, yeah. We had an audience."

He did his best impression of the cranky guy on the plane. "'Some of us want to get off the damn plane.'" She laughed, and it did a lot to ease his nerves. Hers, too, he hoped. He switched back to his regular voice. "I shouldn't have put you on the spot."

"Thanks, but it's probably for the best." She shrugged. "I'm not looking to date anyone. I've got a lot going on, and it sounds like you do, too. But hey, now you can send a tweet saying you found me."

"Another tweet?" He didn't need more social media bullshit in his life. But if he tweeted that he'd found her, it could put a lot of things to rest. It could stop the avalanche of messages from random strangers. It might even stop more articles from reporters eager to dig into his personal life. "You know, that's a good idea."

"I was kind of joking."

"I don't know if it would work, but things have gotten out of control. Maybe it'll slow down if I post something."

Audrey tilted her head to the side. "When you say things have gotten out of control…"

"I mean I've gotten multiple calls asking me to do

TV interviews, people are writing articles about me, and my Twitter inbox is filled with explicit DMs about sharing cheese plates."

"Seriously?" She laughed and clapped a hand over her mouth. "Sorry, but that's so terrible it's funny."

"The DMs are annoying. It's all the other shit that's getting to me."

"You think saying you found me will get people to leave you alone? It won't make them want more?"

"It'll satisfy their curiosity. That's what they want, right? They want to know we found each other." At this point, he would do whatever it took for things to calm down. "All I have to do is say, 'Found her.'"

"You need proof."

His gaze snagged on her camera. "A picture of us together?"

"How else would you prove it?"

"Then let's take a picture," he said.

"It's interesting that you think I'm going to agree to this."

"You're the one who suggested it."

She pressed her lips together. "I'll do it on one condition. Tag the account I use for my photography, and if you have an Instagram account, share it there, too."

"Sure, fine." He wouldn't point out those were two conditions, not one. "Do we need to take this on one of our phones, or are we using the fancy camera?"

"Since this has to be a selfie, let's use my phone. It'll be easier." She pulled her phone out of the back pocket of her jeans. "I can send it to you. Here, come on."

He shuffled toward her. Audrey moved closer, pressing against his side. She fit perfectly underneath his arm. Her warmth seeped through the fabric of his shirt; her softness surrounded him. Her hair tickled his arm where he'd rolled up his sleeve. He breathed in something sweet and citrusy, probably her shampoo. Everything about her invaded his senses, put his nerve endings on high alert.

They needed to get this picture over with. Now.

She angled her phone to get them both in the frame and peered up at him. "Ready?"

He blinked, trying to come back to himself. "Yeah," he said, his voice sounding rougher than it had a minute ago.

She turned her face back to the camera and smiled, snapping a few photos. When she put down her arm and stepped away from him, he missed her warmth immediately.

"Here," she said, handing him the phone. Their fingers brushed for the briefest moment as he took it. "You can put in your number and send the pictures to yourself."

He typed in his number, pressing the wrong buttons a couple times. Fuck. His brain needed to get with the program. Finally, he hit Send on the pictures and handed back her phone. "Thanks."

"No problem." She raised her eyebrows. "Aren't you going to post now?"

"Uh, yeah. I'm just going to…" He pulled his phone out of his pocket. They'd stood pressed up against each other for less than a minute. He was losing it.

He downloaded the pictures and opened the Twitter app. Found her, he typed. Audrey gave him her handle, which he added to the post.

He showed her the screen. "How's that?"

"Very concise. No details." She fidgeted with the camera in her hands. "I like it."

Something about her nervous hands and darting gaze

made him pause. "I know this is a big ask. If you don't want me to post this, I won't."

His finger hovered over the Tweet button. She had to be on board with this one hundred percent, same as him.

This photo wouldn't end up as another item on his list of bad decisions.

If you don't want me to post this, I won't.

Audrey turned Luke's words over in her head. Putting conditions on his post had been a strategic move, but also an impulsive one. If he tagged her account on multiple platforms, it might get her clients. And the sooner she got clients, the sooner she could leave her soul-sucking day job.

The extra visibility couldn't hurt. She was doing this.

"Look at it this way," she said. "I'm helping you, and you're helping me. I want you to post it."

"As long as you're sure."

"I am. You can post it, and we'll call it a day, okay?"

"Okay." He tapped at his phone screen. "Posted."

They looked at each other, the silence stretching out between them. "I'm here for a volunteer shift, so I should…" she said, pointing her thumb in the direction of the kennels.

"Yeah, I have to get back, too." He stuck his hands in his front pockets, rocking forward on the balls of his feet. "Thanks for doing this. I hope it brings you some business."

"I hope it helps with your stuff, too."

"Thanks. I'll let you get to it."

He didn't make any move to go. Neither did she. Her stomach fluttered at his soft smile, the kind look in his eyes. The stubble and tight shirt didn't hurt, either. He wore a blue plaid shirt with the top two buttons undone and the sleeves rolled up to his elbows, jeans, and a tool belt slung low around his lean hips.

She should delete his number from her phone now. Otherwise, she might be tempted to use it.

"It was good seeing you again," she said, her voice soft and sad, a little wistful. It was the tight shirt and the tool belt, that was all. She would miss out on all of that deliciousness. "Well, you have my number now, right? Because I texted the pics to you."

Shut up shut up shut up. What was she doing? She couldn't afford any distractions right now, and Luke Murphy was one big distraction.

"You have mine, too," he said.

A tiny thrill worked its way down her spine. Her body was a traitor.

"Yo, Luke!" A dark-haired guy poked his head out of one of the rooms under construction down the hallway.

Luke muttered a curse. "I'll be back in a minute," he yelled over his shoulder. He turned back to Audrey. "That's my cousin. I left him alone with the power tools, which was probably a bad idea."

"I'll let you go then. Sounds like he requires super-vision."

"Sometimes."

They said goodbye, and he turned and walked away. That was it then. They ran into each other, he posted a picture, and now what? They'd never see each other again? Her chest and throat grew tight.

She should be glad, especially if she got some clients out of the whole thing. Enough people had held her back from starting this business already. She couldn't risk it happening again.

She stood there for a minute to gather herself. Then she headed into the kennel to photograph the dogs on her list.

No matter what she told herself about not needing any distractions, her phone burned a hole in her pocket. She wanted to look at the picture of them together. And check her notifications. And save Luke to her contacts. You know, in case she decided to text him.

Do. Not. Text. Him.

She put her phone on silent and got to work. Luke was a bad distraction. The dogs were a good one.

Thanks to the nice weather, she photographed the dogs outside. Mid-June in Chicago could be unpredictable—actually, Chicago weather was unpredictable year-round—but they'd gotten lucky today. No threat of rain, and it wasn't too hot outside. She loved photographing the dogs in natural light. It looked a lot better than the harsh lighting in the kennels. Out here, the dogs could run around, and their personalities shined through in the photos. She couldn't wait until they were posted on the shelter's website.

Once she finished a couple hours later, she packed up her camera and grabbed her purse from a locker. She stuck her phone inside her bag. Well…one peek at it before she left wasn't going to kill her. She pulled her phone out. The group text with Natalie and Grace had several unread messages:

Natalie: YOU RAN INTO HIM AT THE SHELTER?!

Grace: What's going on now?

Natalie: [link to Luke's tweet]

Grace: !!!

Audrey: Yeah, he's here remodeling our meet-and-greet rooms.

Grace: *thinking face emoji*

Natalie: I have so many questions.

Audrey wrote back that her shift had ended and asked if they wanted to meet up for dinner and drinks later. It would be easier to explain in person than through a text. Plus, she needed to get out. Blow off some steam instead of sitting at home trying to convince herself to delete his number from her phone and not look at his social media. Her resolve wasn't that strong.

Her phone buzzed again on her way out to her car. Probably the group text again.

Nope, it was a new Twitter notification. She'd been tagged in the replies to Luke about their photo from this afternoon. She'd missed the notifications on her lock screen a few minutes ago in her rush to reply to the group text.

Are you dating now?

Omg I'm so jealous of your girlfriend.

One good-looking couple. Congrats!

Dating? Girlfriend? Couple?
Shit.

Chapter Four

The photo was definitely on Luke's bad decisions list.

Audrey had asked if he was sure the follow-up tweet and picture would get people to leave him alone. He'd been so confident, so sure.

If he could go back in time, he would stop himself from posting anything in the first place. Knock his phone out of his hand at the airport the minute he decided Twitter was a good way to find her.

All weekend, more articles appeared ("#TwitterBae and #TheOneWhoGotAway: We Ship It!") and more replies came in to the picture of them together. He'd muted notifications, but that didn't stop him from checking to see what people said. The night before the pilot of *Project Victorian* began filming, the questions from fans—and his mom, who had gotten invested enough to start using her Google skills to try to find Audrey—raced through his head as he tried to fall asleep.

What's her name?

How did you find each other again?

Where's your first date going to be?

Will you post more pics together?

Going viral meant everyone was in your business all the time.

He hated it.

Sometime in the middle of the night, he'd worked out a plan to call Jessica, the publicist. She would know what to do, how to handle this. As long as she didn't try to put him on a morning talk show again, he wanted to hear her ideas. He knew how to fix houses. Jessica knew how to fix PR disasters.

The next morning, he walked down the street from his mom's house to the old Victorian on the corner, phone in one hand, travel mug of coffee in the other. He'd call Jessica before his workday started and get the conversation out of the way.

First, he had to stop and admire the house—the gabled windows, the columns on the front porch, the stained glass over the front door. All of these beautiful details he wanted to make even more beautiful. Embarking on a restoration was always exciting, but this one was special. He'd loved this house for years.

His phone chimed in his hand. Just a calendar alert, but it jolted him out of his thoughts and reminded him what he was here to do. He would have all the time in the world to admire the house later. If he didn't want this call hanging over his head all day, he had to make it now.

He headed up the walkway, sat on the front steps, and dialed. Jessica answered on the first ring. Once the pleasantries were out of the way, he got down to business.

"I was hoping you might be able to help me with something," he said, picking up the travel mug with his free hand and fiddling with the flap on the lid. "I posted over the weekend that I found the woman from the plane."

"I saw it. The picture was cute. Fans love this stuff. It's great promo."

He'd taken a swig of coffee and tried not to spit it out at the word *promo*. "I'll worry about promo once the new show airs. And my personal life won't be a part of it."

"You made your personal life a part of it once you tweeted. Now people are going to expect more."

"I thought if I said I found her, it would get everyone to leave me alone."

"What made you think that?" Jessica's voice was kind, although it held a note of *oh, you sweet summer child.*

"It would give them what they wanted. And once they got what they wanted, things would die down." It sounded ridiculous now. He set the mug next to him on the steps and stared down at his work boots. "At least that's what I'd hoped."

"But things haven't died down."

"No, they've gotten worse. I don't know what I'm supposed to do. Do I ignore it? Do I delete my account?"

Silence followed his questions. It went on so long he pulled his phone away from his ear to make sure he hadn't dropped the call. Nope, still connected. "Jessica?"

"Sorry, my boss just walked in. And your show's producer."

That was…strange. Having this many people on the call only made sense if they all had a plan to get rid of this mess.

Jessica's boss introduced herself as the head of publicity. And then the show's executive producer, Valerie, got on the line. They'd last spoken at the HomeTV offices several months ago when he'd pitched *Project Victorian* to her. He'd presented it as a show focused on restoring old homes around Chicago. She'd liked the idea but said a show set in the Midwest might be a hard sell. That it might have to travel around the country or move to a warmer climate for a shot at success. He'd tried not to think about that part. He wanted to stay put in his home-town for a while. She'd at least agreed to let him film the pilot in Chicago and see how it played out ratings-wise.

"Ratings went through the roof for the episode of *Retro Renovations* that aired last night," Valerie said. "They'll probably be even higher once we get the delayed viewing numbers. That said, I have an idea for you, Luke." She said it like the two of them were in on a secret.

"Um, okay." What the hell was going on here?

"We were wondering if you'd be willing to leverage this new relationship going forward."

She had to be kidding. "I'm not leveraging anything."

"Sharing your relationship is a good way to promote that you're filming a new show," the head of publicity—he'd missed her name earlier—chimed in. "Behind the scenes content plays well on social media. So do cute couples photos."

His head pounded. He wasn't in a relationship. Audrey took one picture to help him out, and now in everyone's minds they were dating? "I don't care about any of that. We're not dating. Can't you stop this stuff?"

Valerie gave a short laugh. "We don't want to stop it. It's a great opportunity to get some buzz going. If you keep posting about this woman from the plane and the ratings hold steady for *Retro Renovations*, we'll pick up the new show. Ten episodes." She paused, allowing time for her offer to sink in. "You might want to ask her out."

He stood and nearly knocked over the travel mug. That wasn't how TV worked. He'd film a pilot. The net-work would air the pilot and decide whether or not to pick up the show. Instead, they were bribing him to share

details of his personal life for their professional gain—
and his, too.

"Are you serious?"

"Very serious. I'll put it in writing."

He didn't have what they wanted. They wanted more
photos with Audrey, and he had no way to provide them,
at least not at the moment. He had her number. He could
text her. What would he say, though? *Hey, I need you to
pose for another picture with me so my new show can get
picked up*? It made him sound like a shithead. It made
him sound like he was using her.

He hadn't used her on Saturday. She'd suggested the
picture. If it were up to him, he would've written *Found
her* and left it at that. But she saw an opportunity and got
something out of it. If he could help her get even more clients, and get this show off the ground at the same time…

He wasn't dating her. But he could pretend to.

"How long would I have to do this?" he asked.

"If you start dating this woman, I don't see how it
would be a problem to post a photo or two per week
while you film in Chicago," Valerie said. "*Retro Renovations* will finish airing its final season around the same
time you're done filming the pilot of *Project Victorian*.
And if things go well, maybe she could even appear on
the show. Wouldn't that be fun?"

The rest of the summer. Around ten weeks. At one or
two posts per week—hell, was he actually considering
this? If he could buy himself some time, he might have
a shot at sitting down with Audrey to talk about it. He
could come up with a plan to benefit them both.

"Could I get back to you by the end of the week?"

"Absolutely. I look forward to hearing from you."

He'd text Audrey later. Right now, he had a show to film.

* * *

Audrey sat at her desk at work on Monday morning, sneaking peeks at her phone every couple of minutes. She was a genius. Asking Luke to tag her Instagram and Twitter accounts in his posts was the best thing she could have done for her business.

Correction—her almost-official business. She'd hunkered down and finished the business plan. Her website had been up and running for a while thanks to Grace's genius web design skills. All she had left to do was register her business with the state, which shouldn't take too long to process if she did it online.

Her phone dinged with another email from someone wondering if she did engagement photos. She bounced in her seat. It was all finally happening. She would have her own photography business. She would have clients. And if the clients kept rolling in, she could implement her plan to quit her day job.

Right on cue, Gary yelled her name from his office.

She threw her head back and suppressed a groan. She got up and dragged her feet the few steps from her desk to his office, where she stopped and stood on the threshold.

Gary had once sent a company-wide email to all one hundred and fifty employees that said, Please don't walk right into my office, even if the door is open. Knock on the door and say, "Excuse me," and then wait for me to acknowledge your presence. I will then tell you whether or not you may enter. I understand many millennials may not understand this concept, but it's common courtesy! Ever since, she'd refused to set foot in his office. He never told her to enter, so it wasn't a problem.

"Yes?" she asked, doing her best to keep her voice measured.

"The attendee evaluations for the meeting are starting to come in. People are upset about a lot of things."

She crossed her arms and waited for him to elaborate, but he didn't. "Like what?"

Gary clicked something on his computer and read off the screen. "The temperature in the meeting rooms, the coffee being taken away at ten a.m., the number of push notifications on the mobile app—"

"I don't handle the mobile app."

He breezed past her comment. "The water main break, not having enough time between sessions to use the bathroom, having to wait a long time for the elevators—I'm sure there are more, but that's the preliminary list."

She sighed. "We can't please everyone. Someone will always have a complaint about something. Aside from the water main break, I thought this meeting ran as smoothly as it could. A lot of these things, like the coffee and elevators, are the hotel's fault, not ours."

Gary continued to stare at his computer. "Did you talk to the hotel staff about any of these problems?"

"I mentioned multiple times they shouldn't take the coffee away so early, but they said it was their policy not to leave it out past ten. And there was nothing they could do about the elevators."

He kept scrolling through whatever was on his screen while she spoke, not looking away once or making any effort to show he'd listened. Typical Gary. "I'm going to send you a link to the evaluation site. You'll need to email a personal apology to anyone who complains."

Was he kidding with this shit? "If I have to do that, I won't have time to work on other things. Are you sure we need to respond to everyone? Can't we just respond to people with legitimate issues?"

"Yes, we need to respond to everyone. I guess you'll have to stay late. Maybe answer some emails over the weekend."

"I'm already staying late most nights—"

He cut her off. "Don't you think you owe people an explanation? As the main contact with the hotel, many of these things are your fault. I'm sure the attendees would appreciate a personal apology."

"They're not my fault, and I'm not staying even later to go through hundreds of evaluations looking for complaints," she said, her pulse pounding and ears ringing. She tried to swallow, but her mouth had gone dry.

Gary finally flicked his eyes away from his screen to look at her. "Excuse me?"

She'd put up with this crap for the past two years, grinning and bearing it through all the toxicity for the good salary and excellent benefits. But she'd had enough. "I'm not doing it."

"I'm your boss," Gary said, making those three words sound evil. "If I tell you to do something, you do it. I don't know why you have to be so difficult. You should be grateful you have a job."

Grateful? For putting up with him?

"You should be grateful for *me*," she said, struggling not to raise her voice. "I worked twelve-hour days in the weeks leading up to the convention. Sixteen-hour days when I was on-site and you were nowhere to be found. I kept things running, and for the most part I kept people happy."

"You did your job," Gary said with a sneer. "Congratulations, here's your trophy."

"I'm not asking for a trophy, Gary. I'm asking for some appreciation and respect."

"You're not going to get it by complaining." He turned back to his computer. "Don't you have work to do?"

She ran some numbers through her head, doing the calculations of whether or not she had enough money to live on, at least for the next month or two. She wouldn't be homeless any time soon. There was the issue of health insurance to figure out, but she'd already planned on that as part of having her own business.

Potential clients were rolling in. She had the privilege of having people in her life who could help if she needed it, even though she didn't want to rely on anyone but herself. She would be fine—she hoped.

"I'm not doing it." She walked right into Gary's office and stood in front of his desk.

Slack-jawed, he stared up at her.

"Not now. Not ever. If you care that much, write the damn emails yourself. I quit."

Gary spluttered, but she didn't wait for him to get any words out. She turned around, went to her desk, grabbed her phone and her purse, and left. She had nothing of value at her desk, nothing personal aside from a stash of emergency chocolate in one of the drawers. Her co-workers could have it. They'd need it.

With every step she took toward the parking lot, the ball of stress she carried around inside her loosened. She got in her car, hands trembling on the steering wheel, and gripped it tight.

And then she laughed.

Holy shit, she'd done it. She'd stood up for herself and told Gary off. She'd had a mic-drop moment right there in his office.

She could do *anything*.

* * *

She got home a half hour later, still riding the high of quitting. She sent a message to the group text with Natalie and Grace, getting all-caps messages and party hat emojis in return. While she changed out of her work clothes, her phone pinged again. She picked it up once she'd pulled on her favorite comfy T-shirt and lounge pants.

Hi, Audrey. It's Luke. I was wondering if we could meet up.

She stared at the screen and read the message a second time. What would he want to meet up for? They'd agreed on Saturday to take the picture, post it, and call it a day. That knowledge didn't stop a delighted little shiver from making its way down her spine at seeing his name pop up on her screen.

She should probably be more concerned about that shiver. Oh, well.

Her phone chimed with another text from Luke: It's not a date.

Audrey: I like that you felt the need to clarify.

Luke: I thought it was important.

Audrey: Why do you want to meet up?

Luke: It's about the picture we posted. Are you free tonight?

Her mind flashed to him wearing a tool belt, looking mind-meltingly hot. She groaned. Meeting up with him was a bad idea. She needed to respond to potential clients and complete the online application to register her business. Although now that she didn't have a job taking up the rest of her day, she could take care of the registration application this afternoon and send those emails tomorrow.

Before she typed a single word, she'd talked herself into it. Her curiosity—and okay, her attraction to him— won out. Even though she wouldn't do anything about that attraction, he was fun to look at.

Anyway, it wasn't a date. He said so himself.

Audrey: I am. Does 7:00 work?

That night, she walked into Old Irving Brewing Company. Luke sat at a table along the wall. He was still rocking the scruff and plaid, and he had his shirtsleeves rolled up.

You knew this was a bad idea. Yeah, but did she care? Looking didn't hurt anyone. And oh, did she look.

His forearms were a thing of beauty. One corded arm rested on the table as he looked at his phone. The white bulbs strung across the length of the room bathed the space in a warm glow that brought out the lighter strands of blond in his hair and shadowed his chiseled jawline.

This lighting was made for him.

Her fingers tingled. If she had her camera, she'd frame the shot from a distance, capturing the blur of people around him with Luke in focus at the center. She was still composing the image when his head jerked up. Their eyes met from across the room.

She shook off the buzz of creativity and attraction. Forcing herself to move, she hurried over to the table. "Hi." She pulled out the chair across from him.

"Thanks for meeting me here."

"Sure." She hooked her purse strap over the back of the chair and sat down. Up close, he had dark circles under his eyes. He looked like he could use a nap and something stronger than whatever beer he was drinking.

They made small talk while she flipped through the drink menu. She'd already checked it out online, but looking at it gave her something to do while they eased into the reason why he'd asked her here.

After the server stopped by the table and Audrey had placed her order, she got to it. "You said this was about the picture you posted?"

"I don't know what it's been like for you, but it definitely backfired for me."

She had a feeling that might happen, but she bit her tongue. "How so?"

"People want more." He sat back, his shoulders slumped. "Including the network."

"So, basically the exact opposite of what you wanted to happen. And what do you mean, the network wants more?"

"Ratings went way up thanks to my tweets. They want to know if I can post more pictures of us together."

She laughed, a short, staccato burst that made Luke squint at her and tilt his head to the side. He looked exactly like the puppies at the shelter when they got confused. She laughed harder.

"I'm not sure what to do with that reaction," he said, his eyebrows drawing together.

"You asked me here to take another picture with you? Come on, it's kind of funny."

"Not just one picture." He shifted in his chair and

took a drink. "The network people think we've started dating."

"Oh, dear God." What the hell had she gotten herself into by coming here tonight?

The server dropped off her Moscow mule. Good, because she needed it. She took a sip. Ginger and lime hit her tongue, sweetness with a hint of spice. Fortified by her drink, Audrey spoke again. "What do they want?"

"Listen, I regret ever tweeting anything," Luke said, briefly closing his eyes. He let out a long, slow breath before opening them. "But now I'm deep in this shit, and they offered me a deal."

This kept getting more absurd by the minute. "What kind of deal?"

"Something that will benefit us both." He smiled, but it was a wary one. It didn't take over his whole face like his other smiles did. "They're driven by ratings, and they saw an opportunity."

She tapped her fingers on the table. "You still haven't told me what they want you to do."

"Before I tell you, I want to say I know how ridiculous it sounds. I won't blame you if you get up and leave."

"Just tell me before I actually do get up and leave," she said, going for a jokey tone, trying to erase the wariness from his expression.

He didn't laugh. "They want me to keep posting pictures of us together until the end of summer. If the ratings stay high for my old show, they'll pick up the new one. They called it 'leveraging my new relationship.'"

Wow. She had no idea TV worked that way, but it didn't surprise her. "You need my help."

"All I need is for you to take one or two pictures with me every week until the end of August. You can tell me no, you can walk out of here, but…" He shook his head, abandoning the rest of the thought, and stared down at his hands clasped together on top of the table. When he spoke again, he raised his head and met her eyes. "My old show—*Retro Renovations*—is ending. If the new one doesn't get picked up, I'm not sure what I'll do next. And I'm finally getting a chance to do the kind of work I want to do, all on my own. I've never really had that."

"And this is important enough that you're asking me to have a fake relationship with you for social media."

He wrinkled his nose. "It sounds bad, but yes."

It sounded bad, but it also sounded perfect—for both of them. She leaned in and lowered her voice. "If you're getting professional advancement out of it, I am, too."

"I'll tag you. I'll share your posts. I'll do whatever I can."

"I've been getting lots of emails from potential clients since we posted that picture at the shelter. This is only going to help." She ran a finger along the handle of the copper mug in front of her. Should Luke know how much it could help? Hell, she might as well go for it. They were both desperate for this plan to succeed. "I need to keep getting clients. I quit my job today."

"What? Why?"

"It sucked. My boss was an asshole. I was going to wait until I'd built things up a little more and had a safety net, but I couldn't take it anymore."

"This is a good thing? You're okay?"

"I'm relieved. It was a toxic situation. Just understand I need this to work more than you do."

"I feel like I put you in a bad spot asking you to do this."

She shrugged. "It'll be good for me. If the reaction to the first post is any indication, I'm all for it."

He gave a shaky laugh and flopped back in his chair. When he smiled, it was still tired around the edges, but it reached his eyes this time. "You don't feel like I'm using you?"

"Nope." She grinned and raised her mug in a toast. "We're using each other."

Chapter Five

Two days after sharing his plan with Audrey, Luke still couldn't believe his luck. She had more than agreed to go along with it—she'd taken an active role in orchestrating the whole thing.

They'd exchanged a couple emails since meeting up, both coming to the conclusion they needed some ground rules before they posted anything. What landed in his inbox after he wrapped filming and headed home for the day went beyond ground rules. Fake relationships, it turned out, had a lot of stipulations.

1. We won't tell anyone this is fake.

2. One to two posts per week (minimum) on Twitter and Instagram.

3. Both parties shall agree to the date, time, and location where photos are taken.

4. Touching is only allowed in photos.

He walked in the door and kept scrolling through the list, which took up half a page. The phone went back in

his pocket while he greeted Mom and Erin. By the time
he sat down to eat the pizza Erin had brought over, the
temptation to finish reading the list proved too strong to
ignore. His family was engrossed in some British baking show anyway.

He opened the email and clicked on the link to the
document again.

5. No dating anyone else as long as this agreement is
valid.

No problem there. He didn't have time for a fake relationship as well as a real one.

6. No sex with anyone else either. We have to keep up
appearances.

7. No sex with each other.

Jesus. He backed out of the document. The words on
the screen were an invitation for his mind to go there.
The sooner they weren't in front of his face, the better.

He went to text Audrey to tell her he was fine with all
of it. Especially the last one. He could make it through
an entire summer without wanting to touch her. Or he
could want to, but he just…wouldn't.

"Hey, no phones during dinner," Mom said, interrupting his thoughts.

He startled, his face growing hot. "Sorry. It's work
stuff."

Erin craned her neck from her spot next to him on the
couch. "What about work?"

"Nothing important."

"Well, that's convincing." Erin was seven years younger and delighted in her role as annoying little sister. She'd moved out and was busy with her job as a nurse at a hospital downtown, but she'd made time to come over for dinner a couple times since he was back in Chicago. "Is it your girlfriend?"

"No." She was one to talk. Before they sat down to eat tonight, he'd caught her more than once grinning at her phone and typing fast. "Who are you always texting? Do *you* have a girlfriend?"

She got all shifty eyed and picked up another slice of pizza from the box on the coffee table. "No," she said, shoving the pizza in her mouth.

"Liar."

"Knock it off," Mom said. "You're too old to tease each other."

True—they were thirty and twenty-three—but that didn't stop them.

"What about the girl from Twitter?" Erin asked. When he shot her a look, she added, "You told the entire world about running into her again. Excuse me for asking, TwitterBae."

"Please never say TwitterBae again."

"What's going on with her?" Mom asked. Great, now he had both of them interrogating him about his favorite topic. "You looked cute together. Are you going to see each other again?"

We won't tell anyone this is fake. He hesitated, but they had to know he and Audrey would see each other again. Even if he didn't tell them, it was about to be all over social media. "Yeah, I think so."

The two of them peppered him with questions about running into Audrey at the shelter, what she was like, and how she felt about all the online attention, until Erin announced she had a pickup hockey game and had to get going. While she went upstairs to the bathroom, he helped Mom load the dishwasher.

"I'm happy for you," she said, placing a hand on his back. "Things are working out for you professionally, and dating someone new is always exciting."

His chest got tight. Lying to his family sucked, but he couldn't risk it. "Yeah, it is."

"If things start getting serious, I'd love to meet her."

"Ma."

"What? I'm not allowed?"

"We're—we just met, and we're both busy." He closed the door to the dishwasher and leaned against the counter, crossing his arms. "We'll see what happens."

Mom raised her hands. "No pressure. But if it does get serious, she's welcome here, and so is anyone your sister dates. If someone is important to my kids, I want to meet them."

She went off to see Erin out the door while unease settled over him. Would part of this fake relationship thing involve pretending it was serious? It was one thing to lie to his family about dating Audrey, but another thing entirely to make Mom believe they had a future.

Because they didn't have one. Their time together expired at the end of August. They'd make one last post, pretend like they broke up, and go back to their normal lives. That was what the rules said.

After grabbing a beer from the fridge, he headed out to the back deck and settled into one of the lounge chairs, his body heavy with exhaustion and guilt. He closed his eyes. The beer bottle dangled from his fingers. He'd gotten himself into this mess. He'd come up with this idea, and now he had to see it through.

His phone chimed. He set the beer on the side table and dug his phone out of his pocket. Audrey.

I saw that you opened the document. Do you have any changes?

He typed a few words, then deleted them. He hit the button to call her instead.

"Hi," she said, her voice surprised. "I guess you must have some significant changes if they can't fit in a text."

"I don't have any. You covered everything." Rule number seven flashed through his head at that exact moment. Good thing she couldn't see his face right now.

"I thought it helped to go into detail. Less room for confusion." After a few beats of silence, she said, "Was there something you wanted to discuss?"

Right, he'd called her for a reason.

"I don't have any changes, but I have some concerns." He let out a big sigh and scrubbed a hand through his hair. "I don't know how well I'm going to do with the part about not telling anyone."

"Telling people could mess up the whole plan. The more people who know, the more who can blab the truth, and then neither of us gets what we want. We can't."

"I know it's important to have rules, but this is—can't we meet up, take some pictures doing stuff around town, and have that be it?"

She chuckled. "Come on, Luke."

"What?"

"I know there's more to us pulling this off than that," she said. "I think you do, too."

He reached for the beer, finally uncapping it and

taking a drink. "I do. It's just gonna be harder than I thought."

"Pretending doesn't hurt anyone."

But what if it did? He was reading too much into this, making it a bigger deal than it had to be. All they had to do was take some pictures and tell people they were dating. How hard could it be?

"Yeah, I guess you're right," he said, after another too-long pause. "Anyway, thanks for doing this. I forget if I said that the other night, but I mean it."

"You're welcome. But remember, you're helping me, too." She cleared her throat. "Now, why don't we discuss where to have our first date?"

On Saturday morning, Audrey arrived at the Garfield Park Conservatory fifteen minutes early for her first fake date with Luke. She took a seat on a bench outside and let the sun warm her bare shoulders. Maybe he'd texted to say he was on his way. She pulled out her phone.

Nothing.

She sighed and slid her phone back into her purse. They hadn't talked in a few days, not since their call about the rules. Parts of that conversation kept coming back to her while she waited for him. *It's just gonna be harder than I thought.* He'd had a wariness in his voice that didn't bode well for their plan's future. If he let his worries get the best of him and bailed, she was screwed.

She wasn't thrilled about lying to her friends and family, either, but she'd do it for the right reasons. Both of their careers were on the line. And, like she told him, pretending didn't hurt anybody.

She needed to stop assuming the worst. She'd written the rules, but he was the one who came up with the plan in the first place. He would show.

A couple minutes after ten, Luke strode up the sidewalk to the conservatory. Thank God. She shielded her eyes from the sun and looked him over as he approached.

"Oh, come the fuck on," she muttered.

He wore aviator sunglasses, a tight gray T-shirt that did excellent things for his biceps, and jeans that hugged his thighs. Was this how he planned on looking for all of their dates? If so, she was in trouble—the kind of trouble the rules were designed to help her avoid.

"Hey." He came to a stop in front of the bench. His gaze swooped over her, making her cheeks grow hot. "You ready to do this?"

She bit back the comment she wanted to make about how he should ask himself that question based on their conversation the other night.

She squinted up at him. The light lit him from behind, glinting off his hair. "Yes. Are you?"

He raised his eyebrows and tucked his sunglasses into one of his pockets. "I'm ready."

She smoothed out the skirt of her yellow floral sundress and stood. The sundress wasn't something she usually wore for casual outings, but she wanted to look cute in the photos. It had nothing to do with wanting to look good for him. Nope, not at all. Maybe if she told herself that enough, it would become true.

They walked together up to the building's entrance, where he opened the door and gestured for her to go in.

"You're not worried about following the rules?" she asked, glancing over her shoulder at him.

"I'm an excellent rule follower."

"So you're not planning on breaking any of them? Not a single one?"

"Only if you ask me to."

Goose bumps broke out all over her arms. Which of the rules could they break? And why did her brain immediately go to the "no sex" rule?

Ugh, get yourself under control.

She breezed past him once they were both inside and tried to play it cool. This wasn't real flirting. Those goose bumps? An involuntary physical reaction.

In the lobby, she grabbed a map and they headed into the palm house. The warm, damp air in the room pressed in on them as they wound their way past palm trees and other tropical plants.

Luke's arm brushed against hers. He leaned down and said in her ear, "How couple-y are we supposed to be acting?"

She sucked in a breath at that brief moment of contact. His lips were so close to her ear. "What do you mean?"

"I mean those people over there keep looking over at us, and I think they recognize me. I'm wondering if we need to look like we're actually on a date."

"We *are* on a date." They stopped at a curve in the path and she looked around him, trying to get a better view of the people checking them out.

"A fake date," he corrected, "but we're supposed to look like we're on a real one."

"Rule number four says—"

"Touching is only allowed in photos. I know."

No touching kept things safe, uncomplicated. She'd put it on the list because she didn't trust herself, not the other way around.

"Do we really need to play up being a couple?" she

asked. "Doesn't it only matter as long as we look like one in our posts?"

"People are going to see us out and about. Shouldn't we sell it?"

Okay, he had a point. If people's eyes were on them, they needed to look like they were actually together. They had to sell it online and offline to make this work. If even one person suspected their relationship wasn't real and decided to tweet about it, they were both done for.

She looked around Luke again. Oh, shit. Those people were coming over here. The woman looked familiar, but Audrey couldn't place her. A vendor she used to work with? Someone she'd met at the shelter? Regardless of who the woman was, Audrey had met her before.

They needed to look like they were on a real date within the next thirty seconds.

"Hold my hand."

He stared at her open palm. "I don't want to do anything that makes you uncomfortable."

"What happened to breaking the rules if I asked you to? I'm telling you to hold my hand. So hold it."

"Yes, boss." He took her hand, sliding their fingers together. His rough hand enveloped her softer one, his thumb rubbing a gentle circle on one of her knuckles. The soothing motion gave her a strange sense of comfort.

Yeah, she wasn't going to overanalyze that.

He looked up from their joined hands. "Is this okay?" His voice dipped low on the question.

It was more than okay. It was fantastic.

"Yes. Yes, it's okay."

She pasted a smile on her face just in time for the woman to reach them. A gangly kid around nine years old and a tall man with dark hair followed behind. They both wandered off when the kid got distracted by one of the trees, yelling something about how cool the bark looked.

"Audrey?" the woman said. "I'm not sure if you remember me—"

"Career Day," Audrey said, the pieces coming together now that the woman was up close. Late last year, she'd presented at the career day at the elementary school where her mom taught fourth grade. This woman was a teacher there, too, and had organized the event. "Ms. Yang, it's great to see you."

They exchanged pleasantries, and Ms. Yang—Estelle—introduced herself to Luke, who shook her hand. "Hi, I'm Luke. I'm…"

"My boyfriend," Audrey jumped in, loud enough to turn some heads. "He's my boyfriend."

Luke's head whipped toward her, his eyes going wide. She gritted her teeth and squeezed his hand. He was the one who'd said they needed to sell it, and he wanted to give her that look when she called him her boyfriend? Please.

If Estelle noticed anything odd, she didn't show it. She and Luke did the whole shaking-hands-nice-to-meet-you thing, and then she turned back to Audrey.

"The kids loved your photography lesson. You should do it again this coming school year," she said, her tone kind and encouraging. "We'd love to have you."

"That would be great," Audrey said. She meant it. The kids had been enthusiastic and asked great questions. "I'll talk to my mom about it."

"Let me give you my phone number and email, too."

After Estelle made sure Audrey had her contact information, Audrey promised she'd be in touch and they said goodbye.

She nudged Luke and dropped her voice to a stage whisper. "Surprise—I'm the famous one."

He laughed, and the sound sent a pure beam of happiness straight to her heart. *Be careful.*

She brushed the thought aside. Fake date or not, she liked making people laugh. She couldn't help it.

They strolled together through the rest of the palm room, through the fern room and into the show house. The sweet, intoxicating scent of jasmine filled the air. Flowers in vibrant pinks, purples, and reds stretched along both sides of the path ahead. A deep sense of peace settled over her. She loved this room. It was her favorite in the entire conservatory.

It was also the perfect spot for a photo.

They found someone to take their picture and spent a minute trying to figure out a pose. This was weird. People on first dates didn't take photos like this. Then again, most couples on first dates didn't have an eager social media audience hungry for content. Or a TV network that wanted them to leverage their relationship for ratings.

"Maybe if I stand like this…" she said, standing in front of him and to the side. Why was this so hard? She was a photographer. She should know how to compose this shot and how to position their bodies. This was basic, Photography 101 stuff.

"That's a prom photo." Luke shot a glance in the direction of the guy patiently waiting for them to figure their shit out. "Stand next to me and turn toward me a little."

She did as he said. He wrapped an arm around her middle. One big hand rested at her waist, warm through the thin cotton of her dress. She would *not* react to the heat of his touch, no matter how wonderful that hand felt on her waist.

"Put your arm around me," he said, his voice gentle.

Right. They couldn't take a photo with his arm around her and her not touching him.

When she looped her arm across his back, his muscles tensed where she rested her fingers right below his rib-cage. His shirt was soft, so soft she had to resist the urge to rub the fabric. Her head swam, too aware of everywhere they touched, everywhere they weren't touching.

The stranger holding Luke's phone said, "Say cheese!"

Audrey startled, pulling herself together in time for the photo, smiling at the camera. Luke jumped away from her the second they finished posing. While he went to retrieve his phone, she sat on a nearby bench, trying to calm the thundering of her heart and the buzz in her fingertips.

If their plan was going to work—if she was going to get her business off the ground—she had to get her reactions to him under control. She couldn't afford to lose her focus.

He returned with his phone and took a seat next to her on the bench, close but not too close. He rubbed his chin and made a *huh* noise. That didn't sound good.

He turned the phone toward her. "What do you think? Are we convincing?"

"Convincing enough," she said, peering at the photo. "But somebody sure looks tense."

He shook his head. The corners of his mouth moved upward, but he flattened his lips. "Look who's talking. You look like I forced you to smile."

She elbowed him gently. "Hey."

"You called me tense."

She reached for his phone. "This is a terrible school dance photo. It's not even prom, it's the eighth-grade dance, and you're the tallest kid in the class everyone has a crush on."

They looked at each other. He did that thing again where he tried to flatten his mouth down to hide the smile threatening to let loose. She held eye contact. No way was he actually annoyed.

His smile started out slow before he broke into a rich, deep laugh. She gave up on holding back her own laughter, and pretty soon they were both cracking up.

"Okay," he said. "Should we post this one or try again?"

"Post it. We're looking at it more critically than other people will. And a little awkwardness makes it more authentic, don't you think?"

"I guess." He stood, slipping his phone back into his pocket. "I'll post it later. Where to next?"

Somewhere that involves us not touching each other. "Um." She consulted the map. She didn't need to, but it gave her something to look at that wasn't his face. "The Horticulture Hall."

They spent the next forty-five minutes wandering through the rest of the conservatory. Her mind stayed in a haze as thick as the humid air in the palm house, caught somewhere between the present and the moment Luke wrapped his arm around her.

Something told her she'd spend a lot of time this summer lying. Not just to others, but to herself, too.

Chapter Six

The day after his first date with Audrey, Luke spent the morning at the Victorian putting up drywall. It was a good way to spend a Sunday. Hammering or drilling the shit out of something was always preferable to worrying about things he couldn't change or fix.

Like this whole fake relationship.

He'd fallen asleep the night before, reading the Twitter replies to their photo at the conservatory. He'd also spent more time than he cared to admit staring at the picture itself.

According to one of the gems in his mentions, lol this looks like a staged photo shoot. The person had a point—he and Audrey didn't look natural. The longer he looked at the photo, the more awkward they seemed.

Funny that it looked stiff and awkward when the moment had been heightened, electric. Everything in his body had to fight the urge to pull her closer, to brush her hair away from her bare shoulder and let his fingers linger on her skin.

There was a thin line between selling the relationship to their followers and taking advantage of the situation. He would never do anything to cross that line. She wasn't his girlfriend, their relationship wasn't real, and lingering touches were different from posed photos and holding hands.

While the camera crew filmed, he screwed in a sheet of drywall, then another. Maybe he and Audrey needed to try something else, something that didn't make them look like they were trying so hard. The pictures needed to look like actual pictures a couple would take together and of each other. Candid, not posed. Real, not fake.

Maybe he could ask for advice. Erin would know. She was on Instagram all the time.

Except for how he couldn't, under any circumstances, talk to anyone about how this was fake. It was in the rules.

Dammit. He'd have to do his own research.

By the time the director yelled cut, Luke needed to clear his head and get some food. He'd just set down his drill when he was sidetracked by an assistant producer who asked to go over that afternoon's schedule with him. She wanted shots of him knocking down walls. The HomeTV audience *loved* seeing walls get knocked down. Luckily for them, Luke enjoyed taking a sledgehammer to drywall.

"And," the producer said with a knowing glint in her eye, "if you could wear short sleeves while you do it, that would be great."

He didn't have it in him to protest. Give the audience what they want, he guessed. As long as the shots weren't gratuitous, it was fine.

Finally, he headed to the craft services table, where he ran into his cousin loading up a plate. Aidan had sweet-talked his way into what he called a guest role on the new show. The HomeTV producers took one look at him, heard "Luke's cousin" and "runs the family construction business," and hired him on the spot. And yeah, Luke put in a good word for him, because Aidan did excellent work.

Luke grunted a greeting and grabbed a plate, getting into line behind Aidan.

"Is that how you say hello to your new girlfriend, too?" Aidan said. "I'm sure she's charmed."

"She's not—" *Shit*. "She's—we went on one date. It's not serious."

"Her face is all over your social media."

"That doesn't mean it's serious. Anyway, there are two pictures of us together."

"That's more than you've ever posted with any of your exes."

"I didn't know you paid such close attention," Luke said, ignoring the sting from Aidan's comment. He dated a little bit, but he rarely got serious enough with someone to take pictures with them. For the past eight years, he'd been focused on work and doing whatever he could to take care of his family. It had to be that way since Dad died. Dating and love didn't matter in comparison, even after this long. Or that was what he told himself.

"Only because you show up at the top of my feed," Aidan said, turning Luke's attention away from those thoughts. "And no offense, but now that you're going viral, you need to up your Insta game."

"I'm not on Instagram a lot. I mostly use Twitter."

Aidan barreled on like Luke hadn't spoken. "Before those pictures with you and Audrey, your last post was from three months ago. It was this sad-ass picture of a Chicago-style hot dog with no caption. You never post anything about what you actually do, and you do some interesting stuff."

They finished fixing their plates and took seats in the big tent set up in the backyard with tables and chairs for the crew.

"I didn't think it was important," Luke said. "Who cares if I post pictures of food? And when did you become a social media expert?"

Aidan frowned at Luke from across the table. "I run the account for Murphy Construction and Remodeling. We have three thousand followers. That's pretty damn good for a local construction business."

"I didn't know."

Aidan shrugged and picked up his sandwich. Since Luke got the HomeTV gig and handed the day-to-day running of the family business over to Aidan, he didn't pay attention to their social media. Or anything else having to do with the business. He waited for Aidan to say something about that, to call him out.

That was his own guilt talking, though. He swallowed his pride, along with his distaste for the phrase *Insta game*. He needed advice. Aidan had given him an opening. He should take it, and also stop being a jerk to his cousin, no matter how annoying he was sometimes.

"Do you have any suggestions for my Instagram?"

Aidan's face immediately brightened. "Your girl's a photographer, right?"

Luke nodded, ignoring the impulse to say she wasn't his girl. Knowing what he knew about Audrey—which, admittedly, wasn't much—she'd balk at that description for multiple reasons.

"Why not have her come over here and take pictures of you working, or pictures of the renovation coming together?" Aidan said. "That would up the Insta game big time. Maybe help her out, too."

Luke almost said no, but he stopped himself. It actually wasn't a bad idea. If she stopped by and took some pictures, it would get the new show on people's radars and keep his followers interested. An entire feed of nothing but couples photos could get old fast. It didn't fix the problem of having more candid shots of the two of them together, but it was something. Plus, Valerie had mentioned possibly getting Audrey on camera. He wouldn't make her do anything she was uncomfortable with, but he could put the idea out there.

"I'll ask her."

"Whoa, I think that's the first time you've ever taken one of my suggestions."

"I've taken plenty of your suggestions."

"Work-related ones, sure," Aidan said. "Outside of work, not really."

Aidan had him there. Luke finally picked up his own sandwich to take a bite.

Aidan balled up his napkin and threw it into a nearby garbage can like it was a basketball. He even made a *whoosh* noise. "Anyway, I should get back inside. Lots of filming to do for my guest role."

Luke swore Aidan kept calling it a guest role just to irritate him, but he played along anyway. "It's not a guest role. You're building cabinets."

"Building cabinets and getting screen time," he said with a lazy grin. Aidan stood and stretched, calling out a "later" over his shoulder on his way out of the tent.

Luke turned over the idea again of having Audrey at the house, photographing his work. He should ask her before he talked himself out of it.

He took out his phone and opened a new text.

* * *

"He wants you to do what now?" Natalie adjusted her position in the corner of the couch and craned her neck to look at Audrey's phone.

In the middle of a Sunday afternoon of Thai food and rom-coms with her friends, Luke had texted. Because her friends were nosy—and because Audrey couldn't stop the "Huh?" from coming out of her mouth when she read it—she'd shared the message with them.

"I told you what it said." Audrey read the text out loud. "'Hey, I was wondering if you might be interested in taking pictures of the house I'm working on.' That's it."

"That's an interesting request from a guy you've been on one date with," Grace said.

"Agreed," Natalie said. "Is your free labor supposed to be a second date?"

"Well, he didn't say it was unpaid."

"It was implied."

"We don't know what this is for," Audrey said, although she had an idea social media was involved. Everything in her life revolved around social media now.

She turned off the screen and set her phone facedown on the coffee table, away from prying eyes. She hadn't hung out with Natalie and Grace since the day she saw Luke at the shelter. Before they came over today, she thought she was prepared to hide the fact she was in a fake relationship from her friends.

She most definitely was not.

Natalie took a sip of her sparkling water and gave Audrey a pointed look. "I thought you weren't interested in seeing him again."

"I said that before we ran into each other at the shelter. And before we went on a date."

"Then all of a sudden he's sending you random texts about doing stuff for his work and you're posting pictures of your first date."

"The picture at the conservatory was cute," Grace said. "Kind of odd for a first date, but cute."

It was weird and artificial because everything about their relationship was. The fear of being found out, of saying too much, threatened to overwhelm her. She took a deep breath and tried to recalibrate.

"Since he tweeted about running into me, his followers are interested in seeing us together," she said. "Anyway, it's nice spending time with him. Nat, weren't you the one who said something about a summer fling?"

If she told Grace and Natalie it was a summer fling, they wouldn't be surprised when it ended in a few months. They didn't have to know the fling wasn't real, that it never existed in the first place.

"I did, and you said you weren't interested," Natalie said.

"Now that she's seen that ass in person multiple times, though…" Grace raised her eyebrows.

They all burst out laughing, breaking the tension that had wedged its way inside her chest.

Luke did have a fine ass. He had a fine everything. She had to do her best not to notice, because those rules were not getting broken. If she let herself get distracted now, she might not be able to pay her rent next month. No one would stop her from doing what she set out to do.

"I know what I said, but I changed my mind. I can have fun with him and start my business at the same time." *Lies upon lies.*

"Good, because you need some fun," Natalie said. Her face lit up a second later, and she turned to Audrey. "Ooh, speaking of fun, you should invite him to the lake house for the Fourth of July."

That was less than two weeks away. She wouldn't commit to anything now, especially a trip out of town. Audrey's phone buzzed on the coffee table. She snatched it up, glad for the distraction.

Luke: You can think about it. It might help both of us.

Can you send me details about what you're looking for? she wrote.

"If you're texting him, tell him you want to get paid," Natalie said, pressing *play* on the movie they'd paused. "You don't work for exposure."

Damn right she didn't. This was different, though. Their plan was ridiculous, but it worked. Since posting photos from the conservatory on Instagram yesterday, she'd gained a hundred followers and a couple more potential clients. They were good jobs, too—engagement photos and a family photo shoot.

She got something out of this, even if it meant keeping secrets and telling lies. Looking at her friends and not telling them the truth was the worst. It made her insides twist into a tangled knot that kept getting bigger and bigger. They told each other everything and always had, since the day they met as teenagers on a website where they kept journals and wrote fanfiction.

They would have so much fun talking about the absurdity of her being in a fake relationship if they knew. Lying to them hurt for that reason, too. She trusted them, but all it would take for this plan to backfire was one slipup. If she told two people, inevitably she'd rationalize telling more people. Then those people would tell more people, and things would be ruined. She couldn't take the risk.

It's just until the end of summer.

And once it was over, she'd have a thriving business and everything would go back to normal—as long as everything went according to plan.

Chapter Seven

Luke stared at the cursor blinking in the empty text box.

Audrey wanted details.

He still owed her a response to the text from yesterday, but what details did she need besides an address, date, and time? They could talk about things like what to take pictures of when she got to the house.

He'd spent enough time trying to figure out what to say. He tapped out a message.

Do you want to stop by today? We can talk about it.

He included the address and said if she was able to come, to text him when she was on her way. The *swoosh* sound of an incoming text came from his phone a minute later.

I don't have time. I have a shoot with a client, and then a meeting with a potential client.

Her being busy was a good thing. If she had clients, that meant their posts were working. He stuck his phone in his pocket and got back to cutting pieces of wood to make a kitchen island. The repetitive motion of the task was soothing. He needed not to think for a little while, to focus on a single, simple task. It helped quiet his thoughts and allowed him to take pleasure in the real reason why he was here: to restore this house he loved.

At the end of the day, Darryl, one of the guys from the reno crew, poked his head into the kitchen. Luke had spent the afternoon there building the frame for the island. He'd just finished doing a retake of hammering the last nail in the frame. Which was kind of ridiculous, but the producer wanted him to "have a more satisfied look" on his face when he finished that part of the project. Luke never complained about retakes. He did what the directors and producers told him to do. He knew good construction, but they knew what made for good TV.

"Hey," Darryl said, "there's a lady here to see you. She's waiting on the front porch."

Luke stood, dusting his hands off on his jeans. "Thanks, man. I'll be out in a second."

Who would stop by to see him? Mom and Erin wouldn't have a reason to come by. Audrey said she was too busy. Probably someone from the city, then, although he'd made sure he had all the proper permits before construction began.

He walked to the front of the house and opened the door, stepping onto the porch. "Audrey?"

She turned around from where she stood looking out at the street. His heart leaped at seeing her again so soon.

"Hi," she said, tucking a stray curl behind one ear. "My meeting ended early, so I thought I'd stop by."

"We're wrapping up for the day. It's not the best time to take pictures." That sounded kind of dickish. She'd made a special trip here and made time for him in her day. He cleared his throat. "I'm glad you're here, though."

"I'm not here to take pictures." She adjusted the strap of the bag on her shoulder and stood up straighter. "You said we could talk about your idea."

"Yeah, that would be good." His stomach grumbled, and he checked the time on his phone. "Do you want to grab something to eat? I have to put some stuff away inside, and then we can go."

"Sure. Can I come in with you?" She bounced a little on her toes. "This house looks amazing from the outside."

He hesitated with his hand on the doorknob. She didn't have any safety equipment on, but given that work had ended for the day, it should be fine. He opened the door and let her walk in first.

"Careful," he said, placing a hand at her elbow as she stepped inside, more out of instinct than actual precaution.

She turned her head to look at him, amusement in her eyes. "I'm sure I'll be fine."

He let go of her elbow. They walked together down a hallway and back to the kitchen. The whole time, Audrey kept her head on a swivel, checking everything out. "You're not gutting the whole place," she said, more a statement than a question.

"We're not. We're updating the kitchen and bathrooms, refinishing the hardwood floors, finishing the basement, and making a bigger master bedroom upstairs. All while trying to preserve as many of the original details as possible." She hadn't asked about specific updates, but once he got started talking about the house, he couldn't stop. "I don't want the house to lose its character."

"You told me that when we met."

"I would never be able to gut something with wood-work this beautiful."

While she was here, she should see it. He motioned for her to follow him. He led her into the living room, pointing out the stained glass above the windows and the ornate crown molding. She hummed in acknowl-edgement and moved into the connected dining room.

She came to a stop in the middle of the room, staring at the enormous bay window that took up most of one wall. "Wow," she whispered.

Light flooded the room through the window, which looked out over a garden on the side of the house. She stepped closer to take in the view.

"This window is gorgeous," she said. "Is it original to the house? All of this?" She gestured at the molding above the window and the wainscoting on either side.

"It is."

"If I lived here, I'd put a couch in front of this win-dow—or one of those padded benches—and I'd sit here and read." She turned to look at him and smiled, backlit by the evening sunlight. "I know it's a dining room, but I don't care. This is a perfect reading nook."

A pleasant warmth spread through him the longer he looked at her, the longer she gave him that smile.

"You could make it into whatever you wanted. A com-bination dining room and reading room sounds great to me."

They wandered back into the kitchen, talking about the types of books they liked—thrillers for him, romance and mysteries for her. He wanted to show her the rest of the house and see her reaction to every room, but most of the construction wasn't as far along as it was on this floor.

Someday, though, he would show her the whole thing.

After he packed up his tools in the kitchen, they took a short walk to a twenty-four-hour burger and hot dog stand near Montrose and Elston. All he'd had to say was, "They're known for their milkshakes," and Audrey was in.

They got their food and took seats at a picnic table out front. It was late enough in the day—the time between the dinner crowd and the after-dinner ice cream crowd—that they didn't have trouble getting a seat. They opened their bags and spread out their food, a huge order of fries on the table between them to share.

"You asked me about taking pictures of the house," Audrey said, dipping a fry in a tiny paper cup of ketchup, "and I need to know exactly what you want me to do."

She had this way of getting down to business he admired even while it unnerved him. He finished chewing the first bite of his hot dog. Ah, crap. It was too late to get a picture of the hot dog for Instagram. Posting another captionless hot dog photo would have irritated Aidan, which would have been fun.

"I thought you could take photos as the renovation progresses. Maybe some of me working, too. I figured it could help, you know"—he turned around to see if he spotted anyone he knew—"the plan."

"Did you really just check to see if anyone was listening to us?"

"Hey, I grew up in this neighborhood. You never know."

"I'm sure they all suspect you have a fake girlfriend."

"Shit, don't say that out loud."

She grinned and took a sip of her chocolate milkshake. "Anyway, how does this help the plan, exactly?"

"We'll be posting more than photos of us together. We don't want people to get bored and unfollow us."

"I have actual paying clients now," she said. "I don't know if I'll have time. I also don't see how this fits in with our overall strategy."

"It'll give you more things to post, help drive some more business your way."

She raised a skeptical, perfectly arched eyebrow and ate another french fry.

He sighed. "I think it would add some authenticity. You know, you're my girlfriend, you're a photographer, so it makes sense that you'd be at the house sometimes taking pictures."

"But you're filming a show. I don't have to be part of it, do I? Because the answer," she said, doing the eyebrow arch thing again and tilting her head to the side, "is no."

"Back when my executive producer brought up this whole idea, she said it might be nice to get you on camera."

"I signed up for social media, not a TV show."

"There might be too many potential liability issues involved with that, anyway," he said. If he sat there long enough, he could come up with all of them.

"Although…" She brought the straw of her milkshake to her lips. "It could help get me some business. I don't know. I have to think about it."

He imagined her caught up in taking photos, tripping over something and breaking an arm. If she got hurt during construction, he didn't know what he'd do. Blame himself and wallow in guilt, probably.

"What did the network say about my photos?"

"Huh?"

"What if they want to use them on their accounts?"

"If they do, I'll make sure you get paid for them."

She took a bite of her burger and scrunched up her face as she chewed. "Promise?"

"Promise."

"Okay." She set down the burger and wiped her hands on a napkin. "I'll do it, schedule permitting. We can work out how often, but I probably can't do more than once a week at the most."

He smiled over the top of his milkshake. "You drive a hard bargain."

"It's why you're dating me." She shot a smile of her own back at him.

He liked being around her so much. Too much.

He pushed the thought aside, but it kept popping up as they cleared their table and left. It was like that old arcade game from his childhood, Whack-a-Mole. Only in this case, instead of moles, it was fond thoughts about his fake girlfriend he had to keep smashing down.

Her hair looks pretty. Smash.

She's funny. Smash.

She's strategic as hell, and it's kind of a turn-on. Smash.

Audrey's voice broke through his thoughts as they rounded the corner onto Keeler Avenue, heading back to the house and her car.

"This is a cute neighborhood," she said. "I haven't spent a lot of time in Old Irving Park."

"I grew up right down the street. My mom still lives there."

"Wow. You're renovating a house on the street you grew up on?"

"Yep." He chuckled. "When I was little, I called it the gingerbread house because I thought it was made out of gingerbread. I've always loved it. I know that's senti-mental and shit, but…"

She shook her head. "No, I think it's great that you love this neighborhood and this house so much. Being sentimental isn't a bad thing."

"I'm still filming it for a TV show."

"If you share how much you love this place, just think of the connection you'll make with your viewers." They both went quiet for a moment, then she asked, "Is there a reason you didn't stick around here? Why you moved to Boston?" She glanced over at him but quickly shifted her gaze away. "If that's too personal, you don't have to answer."

"It's not. I've been asked before."

It wasn't a complicated answer, but he didn't want to get into the reasons why. The explanation would involve too many things he wasn't ready to share. Best to keep it simple for now.

"It's where we filmed *Retro Renovations*. We did a season in Houston and one in Denver, but most of the episodes were filmed around Boston. Lots of older homes there."

"Do you think," she said, careful pauses between her words, "if this new show is picked up, you'll move back home?"

"Yes," he said. It wasn't even a question. "There's a chance the show could travel around the country, but I'm pushing for it to be a Chicago show. Being back here, I realize how much I miss it. The city, my fam-ily—everything."

"I hope you get to stay." She gave him a soft smile.

If he took half a step closer to her, he could brush his

fingers against hers. Take her hand. But he couldn't do that, so he returned her smile and said, "Me, too."

Their steps slowed as they reached the Victorian. Audrey pointed at a small black car parked a few doors down. "I'm parked right there."

Crickets hummed in the cool night air. Lights inside houses began to turn on. A siren started up in the distance and then faded away. A breeze blew through Audrey's hair. He had to resist the urge to reach out and move the strands away from her face.

He shoved his hands into his pockets. "I'll see you soon, then?"

"About that," she said, her tone turning businesslike. "There's an event at the shelter on Saturday. It's one of those 'clear the shelters' things where we have discounted adoptions all day. I was wondering if you'd want to come hang out and take pictures with puppies."

Who wouldn't want to hang out with puppies all day? "I could get there around one, if that works."

She clasped her hands to her chest and beamed at him. That rush of warmth he got around her spread through him again. "Great. It'll be fun."

He walked her to her car, watching while she got in and waving when she drove off. Once she was gone, he continued down the street toward home.

He'd told Audrey a lot about himself tonight—more than he told most people. He still didn't know much about her beyond her photography and volunteering at the animal shelter. And the scary part—the thing that made his pulse thunder, that made his head dizzy—was he wanted to know more.

She was supposed to be his fake girlfriend. Not a real girlfriend, or even a friend. They needed to be friendly with each other for the plan to work, but otherwise he couldn't get too close. He couldn't afford to. Not when so much of his future was riding on this new show. Not when he might be leaving town.

Later, while he got ready for bed, his phone buzzed. Audrey's name lit up the screen, along with a picture of her holding a tiny brown puppy in her arms. Underneath, she'd written, *This is the kind of cuteness you can look forward to on Saturday.*

I really fucking like her. Smash.

Chapter Eight

Four hours into the Clear the Shelters event, things were going great. Fifty dogs had found new homes, and they had a line out the door of potential adopters. If the crowds held steady, by the time the shelter closed this evening they might find homes for all the dogs.

It was one of the best days of the year. Audrey couldn't wait for Luke to get here and experience it for the first time.

In past years, she would wander around with her camera throughout the day. This year, she'd had the idea to take free portraits of the dogs with their new families. A shiny new app on her phone let her send the photos to people on the spot. She'd set up a makeshift studio in one of the meet-and-greet rooms Luke renovated. Other volunteers brought the happy pets and people to her.

During a post-lunchtime lull in activity, she scrolled through the morning's photos. Her heart grew about three sizes looking at the joy on everyone's faces. The single dad with two kids and their golden retriever. An elderly woman and the Maltese mix who would make a great companion for her now that she lived alone.

Audrey sniffled. She closed the app. It was about

to get real emotional up in here if she kept looking at these pictures.

"Hey."

Luke. She looked up from her phone. A different sort of happiness spread through her, a giddiness that fizzed and sparkled like the bubbles in the champagne they drank on the plane.

"Hi," she said. "You made it."

"Sorry I couldn't come earlier." Luke stood in the doorway, hands tucked in his pockets. Did he ever leave the house not looking good? She wanted to know. "What do you need help with?"

"Not much. I'm taking pictures of people with their dogs. If you want to make sure everyone gets a treat bag before they leave, that would be great." She pointed to a box on a table in the corner that held small gift bags with dog treats. "And if we get a line for pictures, you could help manage that."

He'd barely gotten out a "Sure, no problem" before one of the other volunteers led a woman holding a small black-and-white terrier mix into the room.

"This is Mindy," the volunteer said, gesturing at the woman, "and you know Felix."

Felix gave a yip at the sound of his name. Aw, Felix. He'd come to the shelter last month infested with fleas and underweight. Now the little dude was healthy, happy, and going home with a new owner.

After the other volunteer left, Mindy's phone rang, making them all jump with its loud, old-timey ring. She set Felix down to pull the phone out of her purse.

"I'm sorry, but I need to take this." She gave Audrey an apologetic look. "I'll only be a couple minutes. Could you watch him?"

Unless it was an emergency, was a phone call really more important than this lady's new dog? Audrey couldn't say anything, even though she wanted to. Good customer service and all that. She pasted on her best smile, the same one she used when she worked part-time at a clothing store in college and customers got snippy with her.

"Sure." Audrey smiled down at Felix, then looked back up at Mindy. "He's in good hands."

"I promise I'll be right back." Mindy stepped into the hallway, leaving the door to the room open.

Felix turned his head to watch her go, but he was more interested in sniffing things. First the photo backdrop, then Audrey, then Luke. After a couple sniffs of Luke's shoes and legs, Felix's tail wagged. He looked up at Luke with big, adoring eyes before rolling to his back.

"Oh, he likes you," Audrey said, taking a seat in a nearby chair and holding her camera in her lap. "He only asks for belly rubs from people he really likes."

Luke got down on the floor and indulged the dog, who kicked one of his little legs and wagged his tail as his new friend rubbed his belly.

"He's cute," Luke said.

"He's one of my favorites." She glanced over her shoulder at the open door and turned back to Luke, lowering her voice. "Mindy better treat him right."

"We'll make sure she gives you lots of treats and belly rubs," Luke said to Felix, who closed his eyes in belly-rub-induced ecstasy. The dog put his paw on Luke's arm to keep him there.

Something about the combination of big dude and tiny dog tugged at her heartstrings. Luke whispered, "Belly rubs" to Felix in a goofy voice, which only made the tugging stronger. Before she knew what she was doing, she'd snapped a picture.

"You taking my picture?" He looked up at her. Amusement played at the corners of his mouth.

Her cheeks grew warm. So much for the stealth pic. "Come on, this is Instagram gold."

He shook his head, but he still had that amused not-quite-a-smile on his face. "Do you think Mindy's coming back?"

"I can go check."

She got up and faced the door at the same time a family of four came in with a goofy senior Lab in tow. The dog's tongue lolled out of his mouth, and he flopped down on the floor.

Audrey greeted the family and got them set up in front of the backdrop. The moment she turned to look at Luke and Felix, panic set in. What were they going to do about watching Felix if more people came in for photos? More importantly, where was Mindy? She'd been gone much longer than the couple minutes she'd promised.

"Don't worry, I've got him," Luke said, reaching down to grab Felix.

The dog must have thought they were playing a game, because he wiggled his butt and dodged Luke. He ran behind the backdrop instead. The Lab got up and strained at his leash like he wanted to go check out what Felix was doing.

Luke went after his new best friend, stepping behind the backdrop and softly saying the dog's name. Felix didn't care, though—his paws scrambled on the floor, he turned tail, and he ran out into the hallway.

Oh, no.

Luke took off after Felix, leaving Audrey frozen in

place. This was bad. They should have had him on a leash. Why didn't they have him on a leash?

She needed to get that dog.

"Just give us a second," she said to the family, whose members shared a *What the hell is going on?* look. Well, she had no idea what the hell was going on, either. They were about to find out.

She grabbed one of the treat bags and stepped into the hallway. No Mindy, which she couldn't decide was a good or a bad thing. But there was Luke, trying to get Felix to come to him. That only made the dog turn more playful. He ran down the hallway. Luke jogged after him.

Felix stopped. He turned around, got down on his front paws with his butt in the air and barked, his tail wagging.

Luke turned toward her and let out a huge breath. "Where were you?"

"I had to deal with that family."

"It would have been nice to have some help."

"It took me thirty seconds to get out here. It's not like I left you alone."

Some grumbling, something that sounded like, "It felt like you did."

Her anger spiked. "You can't chase him and expect him to stop."

"How else am I supposed to get him back?"

"He thinks you're playing. Try using these." She reached into the bag and pulled out a couple dog treats. She took one and handed the other to Luke. "Felix, look! Treats!"

Hold up. She glanced from one end of the hallway to the other. Her hand fell back to her side. "Felix?" He'd been *right there* a minute ago.

Her heart pounded. She could not lose this dog. He had to be around here somewhere. He couldn't go far, but he was tiny and rambunctious. If he thought they were playing, who knew where he'd run off to?

She went after the dog, calling his name. *Shit.* Panic rose up and lodged itself in her throat. They'd lost Felix, plus she still had that family back in the room waiting for their picture—

"Great job," Luke said, throwing up his hands.

She whirled around, hands on her hips. "Excuse me?" Her voice was loud. Too loud. A person in a volunteer shirt walked past and gave her a look. "I don't need your sarcasm. Don't you dare blame me for this."

"I'm not—" He sighed and looked up at the ceiling before meeting her eyes again. "I wasn't blaming you. That comment was for both of us."

"Sure it was."

"Go back to the room," he said, clenching his jaw. "I'll find him."

"You weren't doing so great on your own." She knew it was unfair to put this all on him, but her frustration and fear had given way to anger and annoyance.

"I was going to get him before you showed up."

"What's that supposed to mean?"

He ran his hands over his face. "Can we not do this? We're both stressed out. I don't want to argue with you."

You started it was on the tip of her tongue, but she held it back. He was right. They were both stressed out. She didn't want to argue with him, either. They'd lost a dog—or almost lost him. He was around here some-where, wiggling his butt and not caring about treats.

Clack clack clack. Someone else was coming now, stomping with purpose toward them. She turned her head at the sound of the approaching footsteps…which belonged to Mindy.

Audrey's stomach dropped. This was officially a disaster.

Mindy looked between them. "Um, I went to the room we were in, and the people in there said you lost Felix?"

Yeah, because you left him, Mindy. Okay, maybe that was a little harsh. For all Audrey knew, that call could have been an actual emergency. And now they had another one on their hands.

"We didn't lose him," Luke said. "We're playing a game."

"A game? What kind of game?" Mindy narrowed her eyes.

"You know Felix!" Audrey said, trying for a happy voice, but it sounded frantic. "So playful!"

"Why don't you go out into the waiting room, maybe grab some tea or coffee?" Wow, Luke was much better at smoothing things over than her. "We'll be right out."

"What about the picture?" Mindy asked.

Audrey jumped in. "Don't worry, we'll get you taken care of. Luke, will you show her to the waiting room?" Some of Luke's confidence must have transferred to her, because she sounded way less frantic now.

"Sure. Follow me," he said to Mindy, who gave Audrey a wary look over her shoulder as she followed Luke down the hall.

Once they were gone, Audrey's shoulders sagged. They'd wasted a ton of time. If anyone found out about this, she'd never be welcome again at the shelter. Right now the family with the goofy Lab was probably complaining to the shelter's director about the unprofessional photographer who lost a dog and forgot about them.

No, she wouldn't think that way. She and Luke were going to find Felix, and return him to Mindy, and everything would be okay.

Her throat grew tight, but she managed to get out a half-hearted, "Felix?"

A little yip came from around the corner. She headed in that direction, only for her stomach to drop again.

No Felix. Maybe she was desperate enough to imagine she heard him.

Luke returned from getting Mindy situated in the waiting room. "Any luck?"

"I thought I heard him, but I don't see him anywhere."

Another yip. Luke raised his eyebrows and headed in the direction of the yips, which kept getting louder and louder. Audrey followed him into the break room.

There was Felix hiding under a table in the dark, his tail wagging.

All of the tension inside her released, and tears welled up behind her eyelids. What was up with her today?

Luke held out a treat. Felix came trotting out like they hadn't spent ten minutes that felt like ten hours looking for him.

"Thank God." She scooped Felix up before he could get away again and kissed the top of his head. "You little stinker. Let's get you to your new home."

Chapter Nine

"What do you mean, you lost a dog?"

Luke went silent, listening to Jessica's fingers clacking on her keyboard. He'd finally gotten a chance to call the publicist after seeing her email that morning (*This is bad. The fans are upset. Call me*). In the email, she'd included a link to an article and screenshots of tweets from angry fans.

Some of the fans wanted to kick his ass. Others claimed they'd boycott HomeTV. And some of them expressed plain old disappointment with what they'd seen.

None of it had to do with losing the dog. Why did he have to bring up Felix in this conversation? He should have kept his mouth shut.

"He ran off, and we couldn't find him," he said.

That made yesterday's shelter debacle sound even worse. He quickly added, "Don't worry, we found him and returned him to his new owner."

Felix was safe and happy with Mindy, and he was never in any real danger. But that was beside the point. Luke had a whole different problem to deal with now.

"No one can know about the dog." Jessica enunciated every word in the sentence. "Do not say a word. #TwitterBaeBreakup is bad enough as it is."

"I'm trying to explain the picture. You know, provide some context."

"I don't care about context. I care about fixing this."

The picture going around Twitter and various other corners of the internet showed them in the background of a pet adopter's photo. The pet owner proudly posed with her new dog while behind her in the distance, Luke threw his hands in the air and Audrey yelled at him with her hands on her hips. It didn't matter that they were in the background of someone else's photo, or that they were frustrated and panicking over Felix's disappearance. People had a good enough view of their expressions and body language to make their own assumptions and interpretations.

The article Jessica had linked to breathlessly detailed how their relationship was "on the rocks" and how Audrey "wanted more" from him. Where did people come up with this shit? There wasn't a relationship to want more from.

On the other hand, if they wanted to make people think they had a real relationship, maybe the picture was a good thing. Their argument added an element of believability.

He hated himself for thinking that.

"Here's what's going to happen," Jessica said, breaking into his thoughts. "I'm sending you tickets for tomorrow afternoon's Cubs game. You're going to look cute, take selfies from your seats, and assure everybody that you're still together."

"Do I have any say at all in this?"

"You're getting free Cubs tickets. Don't tell me you're going to complain."

* * *

When Luke met up with Audrey in the plaza in front of Wrigley Field, he took one look at her and said, "Are you seriously wearing a Pirates shirt to a Cubs game?"

"They're playing the Pirates, and my dad is from Pittsburgh. So yes, I'm wearing this." She glanced down at her shirt, emblazoned with the team's name across her chest.

He looked away before she could catch him checking out her breasts. He didn't do it intentionally, but it was still inappropriate. She was also wearing shorts, which—*goddammit*—drew his eyes farther downward to her thick thighs and shapely calves.

He looked away again, clenching his jaw. Was "no ogling" in the rules? It should be.

She raised her chin, a challenge in her brown eyes. "Do you have a problem with what I'm wearing?"

"Nope. I'm just saying if you get heckled, you're on your own."

"Thank you for your support. Anyway, it's not a Cardinals shirt. I'll be fine." She pulled her phone out of the small purse she'd brought with her. "Selfie with the Wrigley Field sign in the background?"

After they took the photo and she posted it, they headed inside the ballpark. They grabbed drinks on the way to their seats, and he also picked up a paper scorecard. For as long as he'd been going to baseball games, he'd kept score by hand. Yeah, if he wanted to, he could download an app. But it wasn't the same as getting a scorecard and one of those little pencils and doing it himself.

Once the game started, he pulled the scorecard out of his back pocket and began filling it out.

"Well, this is delightfully charming and nerdy." Audrey tapped a finger against the paper. When he looked up, she had a grin on her face. She leaned closer to him and lowered her voice. "Luke, are you a secret baseball nerd?"

He gestured at the scorecard. "I don't think it's a secret."

Her hair brushed against his arm. He caught a whiff of her shampoo. The sweet citrus smell made him want to bury his nose in her hair. He shook off the impulse and focused on the scorecard instead.

Wanting to stick his nose in her hair. Christ, he was losing it.

"How'd you learn to fill this thing out? It looks complicated."

It was, but like anything, once you got the hang of it, it made sense. There was an order to keeping score, a rhythm of interpreting what he saw on the field into numbers and symbols written in boxes.

"My dad taught me." He rolled the pencil between his fingers. "I also used to play baseball, so that helps."

He didn't want to sit here and talk about his dad. Losing a parent never got easier, no matter how many years went by. He and Audrey had known each other for three weeks. They were pretending to date. No point in putting a damper on the day or the fun and attraction buzzing between them.

Audrey shifted to face him. "What? No offense, but I can't imagine you doing anything but wearing plaid and hammering things."

"Thanks." He tried not to laugh. "Don't get too excited—it was just Little League, then high school and college baseball."

"Were you good?"

People always asked that question, and it was always strange answering. "Good enough to get a scholarship." He turned his attention back to the field. Before she could ask, he added, "To Vanderbilt."

"That's meaningless to me because I know nothing about college baseball. I'm going to assume it's impressive."

It had the best baseball program in the country, but he kept his mouth shut.

He picked up his beer from the cup holder in front of him. He took a drink and glanced over at her. "Okay, I shared a fun fact about myself. Now it's your turn."

She laughed. "Fun facts? Is that what we're calling this?"

"It can be anything."

"Let's see." She bit her lip and scrunched up her face in concentration. "I'm obsessed with organization and planning. Color-coded spreadsheets, binders, special pens, all that stuff. I think that's why I was a meeting planner for so long. And now I have my own business, so I can do photography *and* make spreadsheets and plan things. I realize this isn't as exciting as being a baseball player, but…"

"If it's exciting to you, it matters to me."

Her expression changed, a combination of surprise and confusion that morphed into a softness he hadn't been expecting. The words had slipped out without thinking, but he meant it—what she cared about mattered. *She* mattered. Their relationship might be fake, but that didn't mean he didn't care about her.

He cared about her a lot more than he let on.

Which was why what happened at the shelter on Saturday made him feel like a jerk. Neither of them had reacted well, and neither of them looked good in that picture. He'd been unfair to her. He owed her an apology.

The crowd around them erupted in a cheer even though nothing had happened on the field. He didn't turn to look for the cause of their cheers. Audrey had gone quiet.

She knew what people were saying online. She knew Jessica had gotten them these tickets in an attempt to repair their image. But Audrey was so silent, he must have said something wrong.

"Audrey—"

"We're on the Jumbotron," she said.

Oh, fuck. She had to be kidding. He turned away from her to look at the screen in left field.

Sure enough, their faces were inside a heart with a banner that said "Kiss Cam" right above it. On the giant screen, his eyes went wide, which got a chuckle out of the crowd. He looked back to Audrey. They stared at each other, the hoots and hollers around them growing louder with each passing second.

"Kiss her!" yelled a drunk person a couple rows down.

Someone else chimed in. "You're on the Kiss Cam, bro!"

Like he didn't already know.

If he didn't kiss her, it would only add to the rumors they were headed for a breakup. His pulse pounded in his ears. The seconds stretched out. He couldn't move.

Audrey saved his ass. She played off of his surprise and hesitation, an amused smirk on her lips. She raised her wrist and tapped it like she was wearing a watch.

People loved it. The crowd got louder, cheering them on. She put her hand on his arm. "Kiss me."

He leaned in and gave her a peck on the corner of her mouth. Careful and sweet. Something to get the camera off them and the crowd to move on. Not a real kiss at all.

Not the way he really wanted to kiss her.

What the hell was that?

A peck at the corner of her mouth didn't count as a kiss. Audrey had told Luke to kiss her, and he'd given her the most awkward kiss of her life. Which was saying a lot because she went on a date in college with a guy who thought sticking his tongue in her mouth and aggressively poking it around was kissing.

"You couldn't even pretend to give me a real kiss?" She kept her voice light to hide the crush of disappointment.

"I didn't—" He glanced down at his scorecard. "I didn't want to break one of the rules."

"I pretty clearly gave you consent to break that rule. It was a special circumstance."

He didn't say anything. He stared out at the field.

Whatever.

She'd been enjoying herself until a few minutes ago. Sometimes, there was nothing better on a summer day in Chicago than going to the ballpark. Today was one of those perfect days, the kind she looked back on during the winter months to remind herself why she lived here. The weather wasn't too hot, the sun was out, and there was a cool breeze coming off the lake.

The day had more going for it than baseball and good weather. Up until the minute they appeared on the Kiss

Cam, their flirting had made it hard to keep a smile off her face.

That smile was gone now. It didn't matter. This was all fake anyway and would be over before she knew it.

They watched the game and didn't speak. When she got up to go to the bathroom, she asked if she could get him anything while she was gone. He shook his head and said nothing. She came back with a pretzel and of-fered him some. He did the same head-shaking thing, his eyes on the field.

If he wanted to keep giving her the silent treatment, why stay? She could go home, and he could continue to sit here brooding and filling out his scorecard.

"I think I'm gonna go."

He finally looked at her. "What?"

"You're sitting here and refusing to speak to me, plus my team is losing. There's no point in staying." She looped the strap of her cross-body purse over her head and stepped into the aisle. Good thing they were at the end of the row for an easy exit. "Goodbye."

Luke scrambled to his feet and followed her up the steps. "Audrey, wait."

"I'm leaving."

"I'll go with you."

She looked over her shoulder at him. "Fine. But once we get outside, I'm going my own way."

"Can we talk?"

Now he wanted to talk? He could save his explana-tion. She didn't want to hear it. She kept walking down the ramp to the main concourse and the exits.

She'd spent a long time at her job holding back her anger and what she wanted to say. It had happened in her personal life, too. Now that she was going after what she wanted and making her own way in the world, she refused to keep burying her feelings when she was pissed and hurt. What might seem like overreactions to some people were the result of years of restraining her real emotions.

She reached the exit. Luke was still with her. He had approximately one minute until they got outside and she told him to get lost.

"Is this about the kiss?" he asked.

"It's not about the kiss. It's about the fact that afterward, you straight-up ignored me. You couldn't even look at me."

She stepped through the gates and navigated through the crowd of fans in the plaza, trying to get out to the street. Every time she moved, some new person or obstacle appeared in her way, making it impossible to find a clear path to the sidewalk.

"I fucked up, okay?" he said. "I'm sorry."

She stopped walking and turned around. Waited for him to expand on that thought. If he wanted to apologize, she'd hear him out.

Someone bumped her as they moved past. She needed to get out of this crowd. She couldn't breathe, couldn't relax.

"I was having a good time until..." Luke scrubbed a hand over his face. "The Kiss Cam threw me for a loop."

"It threw me for a loop, too, but I didn't ignore you afterward."

"I shouldn't have treated you that way."

"You're right, you shouldn't have." She twisted the strap of her purse between her fingers.

Another person bumped into her. She growled. This was the worst fucking place on earth right now.

"Look, we can talk, but I have to get out of here," she said. "Can we walk for a bit? There's nothing but bars in this neighborhood, and I need to not be around people."

"Whatever you want."

She navigated them through the Wrigleyville shitshow and down Waveland, where the crowd thinned out after a couple minutes of walking. They turned onto a leafy street lined with two-flats and a few newer condo buildings. Everywhere else around here was too crowded. Some random side street would have to do.

She slowed her steps before coming to a stop on the sidewalk. If he wanted to talk, she'd talk. "I know you didn't want to break the rules, but I would have let you break that one. I invited you to."

"It didn't feel right. All those people looking at us, yelling, 'Kiss her!'" He shook his head. "Audrey, I wasn't going to kiss you the way I wanted to. Not there. Not on a fucking Kiss Cam."

She went completely still. Kiss her the way he wanted to? What did that mean? "I don't understand."

His gaze darted away from hers. "Forget I said that."

"No. I'm not going to forget."

At that, he looked at her again, his eyes blazing.

She lowered her voice to a whisper. "How did you want to kiss me?"

"Do you want me to show you?"

He took a step closer. Her heartbeat went into overdrive, a steady pounding in her ears. He came even closer. Anticipation and desire mixed together, making her skin tingle and her stomach flutter.

Her lips parted. She drew in a breath. "Show me."

He gently took her face in his hands. She tilted her chin up, and then his lips were on hers. The kiss was a little searching, a little tentative. So soft it left her wanting more. He moved his lips a fraction of an inch from hers.

Was the kiss already over? What if she never found out what it was like to really kiss him?

She didn't have to worry.

He kissed her again, harder this time. She sighed, and he licked into her mouth, hot and demanding. One of his hands drifted to her waist, the other to the back of her neck, holding her steady while their tongues tangled.

Insistent. That was the word for this kiss. Every stroke of his tongue demanded more, and she met it with the same urgency. She curled her fingers in his shirt and pressed herself against him. She was basically climbing a six-foot-two man on a public sidewalk. And she was okay with it.

Insistent was one word for this kiss, but another was *inappropriate.* If they'd kissed like this on the Kiss Cam, they would have gotten kicked out of Wrigley Field.

It would have been worth it.

Luke pulled away first. He rested his forehead against hers. She ran her hands over his chest because she'd wanted to since their first date, when he'd shown up to the conservatory in that tight T-shirt. Today's shirt was a blue Cubs one and not nearly as tight, but it still worked for her purposes of feeling him up.

She moved her face away from his, looking up at him with a smile. "See, you should have kissed me like *that* on camera."

Luke dropped his hands from Audrey's waist and took a step backward. She had to be kidding. They shared the hottest kiss he'd ever had, and her only reaction was to wish it could have happened on camera?

She peered up at him. "Luke?"

You're in a fake social media relationship. Everything they did was just for show. It didn't count unless it was documented, posted, and offered up for likes and retweets.

He needed to say something. "Yeah. Yeah, you're right."

"Oh." Her eyebrows scrunched together. "Okay?"

This had gone from hot to weird in about two seconds flat. They should call it a day before it got even weirder.

"You know, I should probably head out," he said. "How are you getting home?"

"The Red Line."

"I'll walk you there."

The worst kind of awkward silence descended while they made their way to the Addison stop. The two-minute walk dragged on, weighed down by all the things they needed to talk about but didn't say.

Did they really need to talk about this, though? They should forget about the kiss. Pretend it never happened. It was better that way.

At the entrance to the train station, Audrey turned to him but didn't look at his face. She barely slowed her pace, moving toward the doors. "I'll text you sometime this week to figure out our next date?"

"Yeah, sounds good. Get home safe."

She nodded and walked inside the station. He watched her go, the taste of her kiss still lingering on his lips, his hands still aching to touch her again. Getting through the next date without kissing her again would be a miracle, but he'd have to try. Because if he had to kiss her on camera, he wouldn't kiss her at all.

They could share the fake shit online all she wanted,

but some things should be private. Like kisses that felt way too real. The way she'd sighed into his mouth, how she'd touched him and pressed herself against him—nothing about it had been fake.

He couldn't shake off that kiss. Her breathy little *Show me* would be etched into his memory for the rest of his life.

The buzz of his phone in his pocket brought him back to reality. Zoning out over one kiss with his fake girl-friend. What the fuck was he doing?

He checked his texts while he waited for a Lyft home. Jessica had texted him twice, the messages spaced a few minutes apart.

Good job with the Kiss Cam!

People on Twitter are saying it was cute and that you must have made up.

Right, because the entire internet thought they were headed for a breakup. They even had a hashtag devoted to it.

He wanted to take Jessica's word that people believed #TwitterBaeBreakup was no longer imminent, yet morbid curiosity had him opening the Twitter app. It didn't take long to find the video.

Jessica was right. Instead of comments about how shocked he looked or how he couldn't give Audrey a real kiss, there were a lot of heart-eyes emojis and people calling him a gentleman for not grabbing her and shoving his tongue down her throat. Kind of sad the bar for decent behavior was that low.

By far his favorite comment was "Kiss Cams are

gross but this is cute." Kiss Cams *were* gross and appearing on one sucked. But the outcome, at least from a publicity perspective, wasn't terrible. He could live with this.

What happened afterward…well, he'd have to wait and see how that played out.

Chapter Ten

Audrey hadn't spoken to Luke since they kissed. For the past day and a half, his name hadn't lit up her phone screen, and she held off on contacting him. Sure, she was busy with clients, setting up appointments and doing an engagement photoshoot at the boathouse in Humboldt Park. Between responding to emails and editing photos, she caught herself more than once wanting to text him but not doing it.

Every time she pulled up their text thread, the awkward aftermath of the kiss came rushing back. She'd clearly misstepped. As soon as he realized what they'd done, he pushed her away.

After that, she didn't want to be the one to reach out first. But she had to.

Audrey scrolled through her phone. Should she call or text? Texts were easier to ignore. But if she called, he could send her straight to voicemail. Maybe she should grab her camera and go over to his job site. She was supposed to take pictures there once a week, and she was due for a visit.

No. She would not drive over there unannounced, in rush-hour traffic, and show up to ask him to go on a last-minute vacation. That was absurd.

She sucked it up and called him. He answered on the second ring. "Hey, what's up?"

"Hi." She sat up straighter on the couch and set aside her laptop, where she'd been alternating between color correcting photos and scrolling through people's reactions on Twitter to the Kiss Cam video, which the official Cubs account—oh God—had tweeted. "What are your plans for the Fourth of July?"

"Uh, I don't have any. Sometimes my cousins have a barbecue, but that's about it."

"Do you want to come with me to Michigan?" Whoops, there went her plan to build up to the question. "My friend's family owns a lake house, and pretty much every year my two best friends and I go up there for the holiday. You should come."

Since their social media posting ramped up, Natalie kept bugging Audrey about inviting Luke to the Moretti family's lake house. Audrey had neglected to mention the trip to Luke when Natalie first brought it up. Now here she was, two days away from leaving and in a bind— and in an awkward spot with her fake boyfriend since their very real kiss.

The temptation to lie and tell her friends he couldn't make it was strong. But she'd done a lot of lying lately. Something didn't sit right with her about making up an excuse.

After a silence that went on for way too long, Luke finally spoke. "Are you serious?"

"I am."

"The Fourth is in a couple days."

"I know. Will you come with me or not?"

She leaned her head back against the couch and stared at the ceiling. Looked like she'd have to work to convince him. She couldn't blame him—if the roles were reversed and he called her with an invitation out of the blue to go on vacation together, she'd ask what was wrong with him. They needed this, though.

"We need social media content that makes us look happy and like we're not falling apart," she said.

"We had the Kiss Cam."

"Yeah, but we didn't post that on our own, and it's not enough." She held herself back from mentioning the kiss after the game. And the not-kiss captured on the Kiss Cam. Luke's followers, for whatever reason, had eaten that up. "What better way to change the narrative than vacation pics?"

After another too-long pause, he sighed. "Getting away might be nice. Production is shut down for the long weekend anyway."

"Is that a yes?"

"Yeah, I'll come. But I need to be back by Sunday."

Oh, thank God. They needed the social media content, but they also needed the people in their lives to believe everything was fine in order for this thing to work. Her best friends wouldn't go running to Twitter—she knew that—but she didn't want to have to explain why she and her supposed boyfriend weren't spending time together. *Yeah, we kissed, and we weren't supposed to because the rules say we shouldn't* wasn't a conversation she wanted to have.

Her life would be so much easier if she told Natalie and Grace this was all a ruse. But if she told them and they accidentally mentioned it to someone, or someone overheard them talking about it in public, everything could be over. Her business, Luke's show. Everything they were working to build in their careers. She was definitely catastrophizing, but that was how her brain worked.

She filled Luke in on the details and said they could make the two-hour drive together. She was about to say goodbye and hang up, but he got in one last comment.

"A lake house, huh? Sounds like a great photo op." He used a wry tone, but she didn't miss the sharp edge to his words.

"I'll bring my camera. Just think of all the potential content."

"Can't wait."

On the day they left for the trip, Audrey picked up Luke once he finished filming for the day. He opened the passenger door of her trusty Prius and poked his head inside the car. His hair was damp, and he smelled like whatever body wash he used, something clean and spicy. She held herself back from sniffing him like a weirdo.

Get yourself together. You have to spend two hours in this car with him.

He scanned the car interior. "You know, we can take my truck."

"Not gonna happen. Put your bag in the car and let's go."

Before he could argue, she popped the trunk. He left the car door open and went to throw his duffel bag next to her suitcase. The tiniest twinge of guilt pricked her conscience when he slid into the passenger seat and needed to push it all the way back to fit his legs, but he had plenty of room. He would survive.

Would she? That was the real question.

She'd been attracted to him from the moment he sat next to her on the plane. But knowing how he kissed and how she fit in his arms took that attraction to a different level. One where she would explode if she didn't get her mouth on his again.

Considering the aftermath of their first kiss, that wasn't about to happen anytime soon. He regretted having kissed her. They were both better off for it. Their relationship needed to stay fake, and she needed to follow her own damn rules so her business could continue to thrive.

No distractions. No more breaking the rules.

Aside from hitting traffic on their way out of Chicago, the rest of the ride to South Haven was uneventful. When they talked, it was mostly about things to do on the trip. Luke alternated between looking out the window and closing his eyes. He must've been tired. Or maybe he didn't want to talk to her. That was fine, but if he kept it up, it would make for a long weekend. At least she had her driving playlist to keep her company.

The opening chords of "American Girl" by Tom Petty and the Heartbreakers filled the car. Luke turned to her with a slow smile. A burst of hope expanded in her chest. He had such a wonderful smile. Seeing it again was a gift.

"I love this song," he said.

She found herself smiling back. "Me, too. Definitely up there on the top ten favorite songs of all time list."

"My dad was a big Tom Petty fan, and I played the hell out of that greatest hits compilation when I was younger."

"*Anthology*? I did, too. My first car had a CD player, and I remember having both discs in one of those CD binder things that clipped to the sun visor." She turned the volume up a notch. "Remember those?"

He chuckled. "Yeah, and I'm glad I don't need one anymore."

Just like that, the silence between them dissolved. Talking about music led to talking about other things. Luke asked about her friends, and she was more than happy to tell him all about them. How Grace was more tenacious than she gave herself credit for, and an incredibly creative artist and designer. How Natalie was funny and fiercely protective of her friends and didn't take shit from anyone.

Audrey loved them so much.

"Are you sure it's not going to be strange that I'm the only guy there?" Luke asked. "Or that you're the only one who's bringing somebody?"

She glanced over at him. "Natalie suggested it. They both wanted you to come, so I don't think it'll be weird." *At least I hope it won't.*

He rubbed his hands against his thighs. "Meeting the friends is a big moment."

"It would be, if we were actually dating." The words came out sounding harsher than she'd intended. She forced a laugh to try to take the edge off.

"They don't know, do they?"

"Hell no. Rule number one."

"The pressure's still on, then." He lowered the volume on the stereo. She resisted the urge to swat his hand away. "They think I'm your real boyfriend. I've gotta make a good impression."

"Worried they'll give you a hard time?"

"Nah," he said. "I'm sure it'll be fine."

Maybe. Possibly. She wouldn't put it past her friends to invite Luke for the sole purpose of making sure he was up to their standards. Guilt made her throat grow tight. They cared about her, and here she was, about to spend their annual getaway lying to them. It sucked, but if they ever found out, she hoped they'd understand why she did it.

After they exited the highway, they drove for a few minutes before she turned up the driveway to the lake house. The two-story cottage had white siding and light blue trim around the windows, and a huge deck in back that faced the lake. It was one of her favorite places in the world.

She pulled in next to Natalie's Jeep at the end of the driveway. Once she'd parked, Luke got their bags from the trunk and they walked up the path to the front door.

Closer to her friends. Closer to having to spend an entire weekend putting on a show. Closer to putting their fake relationship to the test.

Shit. She should have considered their performance sooner. How they would act, what they would do. They couldn't wing this.

"Wait," she said, stopping in the middle of the walkway. She reached out to put a hand on Luke's arm. Her fingertips buzzed where she made contact with his skin. She forced herself to pull her hand away. "How are we going to play this?"

He tilted his head to the side and squinted at her. "What do you mean?"

"Do we really sell it and act obnoxious and over-the-top affectionate? Or do things more low key?"

"Whatever you're comfortable with, but I'm pretty sure neither of us is comfortable with over the top. Let's be normal."

Normal? Was he kidding?

"We're not normal." She took her suitcase from Luke

and wheeled it up the walkway to the house. Under her breath, she added, "Nothing about this is normal."

The front door swung open. Natalie stood there in a fluffy pink robe with a sheet mask on her face, her dark hair piled on top of her head in a loose bun. She looked Luke up and down. As she assessed him, she crossed her arms over her chest. She might have been all of five foot three, and she definitely looked ridiculous with the sheet mask and the robe, but she didn't give a fuck.

She would still cut you in your sleep if you crossed her.

Luke looked from Natalie to Audrey, his eyebrows climbing toward his hairline. He took a step forward, a nervous smile on his face. "Hi."

"Luke, this is Natalie," Audrey said, moving to stand next to him. "Natalie, this is Luke."

Natalie didn't budge from the doorway to let them in. She gave Luke another appraising glance and tilted her chin up. "What are your intentions with Audrey?"

Here we go. A laugh escaped Audrey's mouth. She clapped a hand over it.

"What are you doing?" Grace materialized behind Natalie and hip-checked her out of the way. "I told you not to scare him."

Natalie grumbled. "I'm not scaring him. I want to know his intentions before I let him into my house."

"Should I—" Luke glanced over his shoulder like he was seriously considering making a run for it.

Grace looped her arm through Natalie's, moving her so Audrey and Luke could enter the house. Audrey closed the door behind them. Her friends were something else. If Luke wanted to run, she wouldn't blame him.

Grace gave a nervous laugh. "Did you guys eat yet? I know it's getting late, but we have leftovers."

Audrey opened her mouth to answer—she was starving since they hadn't stopped anywhere on the way up here—but Luke straightened next to her and met Natalie's stare head-on.

"My intentions are to treat her with the respect she deserves, and to be there for her however I can." He looked at Audrey for the next part. "And, I hope, to make her happy."

They held eye contact for a few seconds. Her heartbeat sped up. He wanted to be there for her and make her happy? Even after all the weirdness of a few days ago?

He broke their gaze first, and it sent her crashing back to earth. He couldn't possibly mean what he said. This was all part of the act they had to put on this weekend.

"Good answer," Natalie said with a curt nod. "You can stay. But I've got my eye on you." She used two fingers to point at her eyes, then pointed those fingers back at Luke.

He gave Audrey a look that said, *Is this chick for real?* Yes, Natalie was for real, and the sooner you realized that, the easier your life would be. Natalie turned around and headed for the kitchen.

"Ignore her," Grace whispered to Luke. "She'll warm up to you eventually."

"Eventually?" Luke asked. "How long are we talking?"

Audrey and Grace exchanged looks. It could be anywhere between a day and never.

"Soon," Grace said, giving Luke a sweet smile.

Luke gave Audrey a look that said he wasn't buying it. "Okay, now that we have that out of the way, let's take our stuff upstairs so I can change." Audrey wheeled her suitcase over to the stairs. "I'm in the usual spot?"

"Yep," Grace said. "Up the stairs and to the left."

Luke insisted on carrying her suitcase upstairs to the bedroom, where he set it on a bench at the foot of the bed. He dropped his duffel in a corner of the room. He let out a huge sigh. "Is Natalie always like that?"

"You mean overly protective and not ashamed about it? Yes." She unzipped her suitcase. "I know she's a lot, but she wants to make sure I don't end up with another asshole."

"Bad ex?"

The less said about Neil, the better. "Yeah." She found the packing cube with her pajama pants. She pulled out a pair along with a T-shirt. "I'm going to change and go back downstairs. We always do a movie night the first night. You're welcome to join us." She looked up at him and smiled. She was trying here.

He opened his duffel and riffled through it with his back to her. "You go ahead. Kind of seems like your special thing."

"Don't let Natalie scare you. You're totally welcome. You should get some food, too."

"I ate before you picked me up. And I need to take care of some things for work."

"The night before a holiday?"

"I want to get it out of the way." He turned around to face her. "I don't know how late you'll be up, but whenever you come back upstairs, you can take the bed."

"What are you talking about?"

He pointed at the bed in the middle of the room. "There's only one bed."

The words smacked her upside the head. How had she

not considered the sleeping arrangements until now? She had double-checked the route on Google Maps and triple-checked her packing checklist, yet not once thought about sleeping in the same bed.

Of course they would share a room and a bed. That was what couples did, even newer couples like them. There was an extra bedroom with bunk beds down the hall, but she couldn't tell him to sleep there without inviting questions and suspicion. Making people believe you were a couple in real life came with way more pressure than posting photos on social media.

She held the bundle of clothes to her chest. "Are you okay with that?"

"It's not a big deal," Luke said, shrugging. "I can sleep on the floor."

"You're not sleeping on the floor." How could he think that was an option? She'd rather take the chance of accidentally cuddling him in the middle of the night than have him sleep on a hardwood floor.

"Audrey…"

"This is what, a queen-size?" She flung out the arm not holding her clothes to gesture at the bed. "There's enough room. I mean, we're both adults. It doesn't—"

"I told you I'm fine with the floor."

If he wanted to sleep on the floor, she wasn't going to argue. "Suit yourself. There's extra blankets and pillows in the closet." With a glance over her shoulder at him, she headed to the bathroom to change.

She'd offered to share the bed. Offering was all she could do.

Although, if he changed his mind…

The mere idea of it made her pulse quicken and her

body crave his touch. And *that* was why they shouldn't share a bed. Maybe Luke had the right idea.

She wouldn't be tempted again.

Chapter Eleven

Luke's back hurt. Everything hurt.

He was the first one awake this morning, mostly because he couldn't spend another minute on the floor. Once he got dressed, not knowing what else to do with himself, he went downstairs to the kitchen. If he couldn't sleep, he might as well make breakfast for everyone.

Last night, he'd taken a blanket from the closet and folded it so he had some sort of cushion to sleep on. He'd added the blanket from a chair in the corner of the room and a pillow. Nothing helped make the floor more comfortable. At some point during the night, he passed out, exhaustion winning in the battle with discomfort.

He should have slept in the damn bed. It was for the best he didn't.

When he left the bedroom twenty minutes ago, Audrey was curled up on her side, still asleep. It took everything he had not to slide in next to her. She'd offered to share, but he didn't want to take advantage of the situation. He needed to stick to the plan. Not kiss her again. Not do any activity where he might be tempted to touch her.

He wanted to, though. Fuck, he wanted to.

But why should he? She only cared about getting everything on camera. Nothing counted unless their followers could like it or she got more clients out of it. She was focused on the business side of things and the ultimate outcome of this fake relationship bullshit. He should follow her lead.

He stood at the stove and stretched his arms behind his back. Footsteps creaked overhead. Someone was awake.

Please don't let it be Natalie. He wasn't scared of Audrey's friend—okay, maybe a little bit. She wasn't playing around. Within seconds of meeting him, she'd demanded he prove himself worthy of Audrey. He understood. Her friends wanted to vet him. Make sure he wasn't a shithead who would mistreat her.

Fake relationship or not, he meant what he'd said about respecting her and making her happy. Getting her friends to believe that might take some convincing, but he wanted them to like him. If they didn't, Audrey might have a harder time pulling this thing off.

But there was something more to it, too. Natalie and Grace were important to her. Their liking him, their approval, meant he was the kind of man Audrey deserved.

Not that it mattered in the long run.

He did his best to quash the ache in his chest as footsteps made their way to the stairs. Audrey wandered into the kitchen first, wearing a T-shirt and pajama pants. Grace followed close behind and immediately took a seat at the breakfast bar. Still no Natalie, who very well could be upstairs planning his demise.

He glanced over his shoulder. "Hey. Do you want pancakes?"

"Yes, please," Audrey said, walking over to him. She

stood on her tiptoes and kissed his cheek, which turned hot when she pressed her lips to it. "Good morning."

He ducked his head and concentrated on the pan in front of him. Watched the batter sizzle. Flipped the pancakes. Audrey tugged at the hem of his shirt, forcing him to look at her. She tilted her head in the direction of the breakfast bar on the opposite side of the kitchen.

Grace sat there, scrolling through her phone and muttering something about clients not leaving her alone on a holiday weekend. Audrey had mentioned on the drive up here that her friend was a web designer. Who needed website updates on the Fourth of July?

Grace sighed and looked up from her phone. Audrey tugged on his shirt again.

Right, they had an audience. A distracted one, but still. He slid an arm around Audrey's waist and pulled her against his side.

"Morning," he said into her hair, his voice rough.

She placed a hand on his chest and looked up at him, playing the part of the adoring girlfriend. "Sleep okay?"

"Fine. You?"

"Great. Do you need help with anything?"

"I'm good."

Audrey sighed and left his side. "I can make coffee."

Natalie made her appearance then, strolling into the kitchen and sliding onto the stool next to Grace's. Without the mask on her face and the flinty stare, she was slightly less terrifying.

"Ooh, he cooks," she said, placing her elbows on the counter. Her eyes lit up. "Pancakes?"

A point in his favor. "Yep. Breakfast will be ready soon."

Standing there in the kitchen with all of them watching him, he couldn't help feeling like he'd get a grade at the end of this. At least he made decent pancakes.

A few minutes later, they all settled in with breakfast and cups of coffee. Luke took a seat next to Audrey.

"Thanks for breakfast," she said, her gaze on him soft.

He almost leaned in to kiss her because of that look but held himself back. "Not a problem."

While they ate, Natalie and Audrey talked about their plans for the day. Audrey pulled up a spreadsheet on her phone with their tentative schedule. She had a document or a spreadsheet for everything. Wasn't the whole point of vacation that you weren't on a schedule?

"We can spend the day at the lake, and then we'll barbecue for dinner," she said. "And tonight we can watch fireworks from the back deck."

"What about indoor reading time?" Grace said. "This sounds like a whole lot of peopling."

Natalie wrapped an arm around Grace's shoulders. "Anytime can be indoor reading time if you just believe."

Luke stifled a laugh and caught Audrey's eye. She smiled back at him, sharing his not-so-secret amusement. A rush of affection swept through him, almost powerful enough to knock his ass out of his seat.

Where the hell had that come from?

She turned away first. He went back to his pancakes and tried to shake off whatever odd sensation had come over him.

In the silence that followed while they all ate and finalized their schedule, his attention snagged on a steady sound.

Drip.

He stopped chewing and listened. "Do you hear that?"

"Do you think it's the sink?" Audrey asked.

He pushed his plate away and went over to the sink to investigate. The drip wasn't coming from there.

Drip. Drip. Drip.

A drop of water landed in the center of his forehead, and he wiped it away. He looked up. Another droplet fell. "You've got a leak in your ceiling."

The steady dripping continued. If he had to guess, the source was the bathroom directly above the kitchen.

Natalie jumped up to join him. She squinted at the ceiling. "I can text my parents to ask which plumber to call, but I don't know if someone can come out here on a holiday."

"I can fix it."

"But you'll miss everything we have planned for the day," Audrey said. Maybe he was imagining things, but she sounded disappointed.

He shrugged. "Someone needs to work on this now before it gets worse." If something needed fixing, he would fix it. And he'd rather be here than tagging along as the extra person in their friend group. They would have more fun at the lake without him. "Besides, I'd hate to see the crown molding get ruined."

"I guess this means unlike some of the other people on HomeTV, you can actually fix things," Natalie said, walking back to her seat at the breakfast bar.

Audrey rolled her eyes. "He's an actual carpenter."

"I'm just saying, a lot of them don't do their own work. Have you ever seen Ryan from *Dude, Flip My House* pick up a hammer?"

Luke had met Ryan and Tyler, the stars of *Dude, Flip My House*, at a HomeTV party once. Nice enough guys, but kind of clueless. They'd started out as actors who, after a few too many failed auditions, got involved in flipping houses. They didn't know how to do any of the work themselves, but they looked good on camera.

"I'll fix the leak," he said. "I'll also do it for free. That way you don't have to pay double to get someone out here on a holiday."

"You don't have to—" Natalie started to say.

The other women sent her looks that said, *Shut up and say thank you.*

"Thank you," she said, "but I can pay you."

He waved it off. "Do you have tools around here somewhere?"

"In the shed. I'll show you after breakfast."

In the meantime, he got a bucket from under the kitchen sink to catch the drips from the ceiling and went upstairs to check out the leak. After he came back downstairs, Natalie showed him out to the shed, where he found a ladder and toolbox. He could only hope this wouldn't be a complicated repair. If that were the case, he would do his best to mitigate the problem until he could get to a hardware store.

While Natalie and Grace went to get ready for their excursion to the lake, Audrey stayed behind in the kitchen. She leaned against the counter and watched him open the ladder. "Are you sure you're okay with staying back here?"

He climbed up the ladder to take a look at the damage. "I'm fine. Go have fun with your friends."

"Part of the reason I invited you here is so you could have fun with us and get to know them."

He climbed back down. They needed to have this conversation face to face. "I thought the reason you invited me here was for social media content."

"Partly, but that also benefits you." She crossed her

arms over her chest. The motion made her breasts shift in a way that made it all too obvious she wasn't wearing a bra under her T-shirt.

He opened the toolbox and rummaged through it. Screwdriver. He needed a screwdriver.

"We have a deal," she said, "and I'm not going to let you back out of it."

Backing out of the deal wasn't an option. He looked up from the toolbox. "I'm not backing out. I don't know how long this will take to fix, but I do know if I let it go all day it's going to get worse."

She uncrossed her arms. "Thanks for taking care of it. But this doesn't mean you're off the hook for pictures."

"We'll get them later."

"I could also get some of you doing repairs and mention how great of a boyfriend you are, working on a holiday to fix my friend's house."

She gave him a knowing, teasing smile. It was ridiculous how much it made him want to kiss her. But they weren't doing that again.

"Go for it. Show everyone I'm nothing like the *Dude, Flip My House* guys."

She laughed and slowly backed out of the kitchen. "I have to go get ready. When I come back downstairs, I'll have my camera." She clasped her hands to her chest. "Ooh, maybe I can also get a quick video with my phone for my Insta story."

"Whatever you need."

For a second, he swore she was about to say something else.

She turned and walked away.

Chapter Twelve

"Luke seems nice," Natalie said later that morning, "but I also think he might be afraid of me."

"You barely let the poor man say hello before acting like someone's old-school dad and demanding to know his intentions," Grace said.

Audrey pushed her sunglasses back into her hair and turned her head to look at them. They sat in lounge chairs underneath a beach umbrella, the vast blue expanse of Lake Michigan in front of them. Luckily they'd gotten there early enough to stake out a good spot among the other Fourth of July beachgoers.

"I told him you're only looking out for me. I think he gets it."

Natalie pursed her lips. "Is it bad that I want him to be a little afraid? I mean, at least until he shows us he's not an asshole. Tell me if I'm being overbearing"—Audrey had to chuckle at that—"but I don't want you to get in another Neil situation where he seems great at first but is actually a piece of shit."

"First of all," Audrey said, "Neil never would have gotten up early to make us breakfast, and he sure as hell never would have lifted a finger to help fix something around the house. Luke's already got him beat in that respect."

"Let us know if he says or does anything bad," Grace said. "Because as soon as he does…"

"We will *end* him." Natalie balled her hands into fists.

Audrey loved that her friends looked out for her. She would do the same for them. "He hasn't done anything bad yet."

He'd messed up at the baseball game, but he apologized. Both of them had been thrown by the Kiss Cam incident. Neither of them had acted perfectly.

They still hadn't addressed what happened with the kiss afterward. Maybe they never would.

Grace reached out to pat Audrey's hand. "I know we come on strong. Especially this one." She sent a pointed look in Natalie's direction. Nat rolled her eyes. "But things are good?"

"They are. We're taking things slow and getting to know each other."

"Everything looks like it's going great on social media," Natalie said. "You never posted this much about Neil."

She swallowed hard. She couldn't expect them not to notice. It was out of character for her to share this much of herself online. Her friends were bound to bring it up.

"We're dating, but we're also…" Also what? She scrambled for what to say. Her brain ran through a jumbled mess of ways to end the sentence. She plucked out a phrase from the heap of words. "Helping each other."

Ugh, why did she have to say that? She'd dug herself into a hole, and now she couldn't get out. She should have said she shared their relationship online because she was happy. Or how dating someone semi-famous meant she had to post photos.

Natalie pressed her lips together. "What do you mean, 'helping each other'?"

Her honesty would get her in trouble sooner or later. Fudging the truth got her right up to the line of breaking rule number one. She wanted to tell them everything, but she couldn't. After taking a brief pause, she chose her words carefully this time.

"Remember how I told you his followers were interested in seeing us together?" Her friends nodded. "When we took that photo at the conservatory, I gained a bunch of followers and got some new clients. And he kept his followers happy, so it made sense to keep doing it."

There was more to it than that, but she knew when to shut up. She'd already said too much.

Grace grinned. "That's kind of genius."

"I respect it," Natalie said. "You're saying it's good for business."

Their responses should have eased her mind, but she couldn't help playing the *what if* game. Would they have the same reaction if they knew all the posts—and the relationship itself—were fake? She didn't have long to linger on that question.

"Changing topics slightly," Natalie said, "when you say you're taking it slow…"

"We didn't even kiss until a few days ago."

Both women yelled, "*What?*"

"It was after the Kiss Cam, and things have been strange ever since."

"Why would things be weird after you kissed?" Grace made a face. "He's your boyfriend."

Every time Audrey opened her mouth, she dug herself into a deeper hole. She definitely shouldn't have said anything.

"Walk us through what happened," Natalie said.

Audrey left out the incriminating details, but she mentioned what Luke said about how he wouldn't kiss her the way he wanted to on a Kiss Cam. How she asked him to show her.

That kiss was burned into her brain. His mouth, her hands. The way he'd started out slow. How it turned desperate and urgent and hot. Even after they pulled away from each other, the intensity of the kiss lingered between them in her touches and his stare.

And then she'd said…

Oh God, she'd ruined it. How hadn't she seen that until now?

She took a deep breath before finishing the story. Might as well get it out in the open, see if it was as bad as she thought.

"I said something like, 'You should have kissed me like that on camera,' and it was like he couldn't get away from me fast enough."

Cold prickled her skin despite the heat of the July afternoon. She'd meant it as an offhand remark, but her intentions didn't matter. She said a shitty thing.

Grace sat back in her chair. She pulled her swimsuit cover-up over her face so only the top of her blond head poked out. Through the fabric, her muffled voice said, "Oh, Audrey. Oh, no."

Natalie shook her head. "With all the social media stuff and the Kiss Cam, don't you see how he could interpret that?"

"I do now."

With that one comment, she'd reminded him their

relationship only existed for the cameras. That the kiss didn't matter because he didn't do it when it counted—when they had an audience. Unconsciously or not, she put up a boundary between them. He'd walked away because she hurt him.

She stared out at the waves crashing against the shore. "I messed up."

Now she needed to fix it.

Fixing it was easier said than done.

When they returned from the beach, Audrey found Luke in the kitchen, standing on the ladder. He drilled something into the ceiling and stopped when she wandered farther into the room.

"Hey," he said, sounding pleased to see her. That alone made her feel lighter. "Have fun at the beach?"

Sure, if having painful realizations about her own behavior could be considered fun. "Yeah, it was good."

She looked around the kitchen. He had a tarp on the floor and a can of unopened paint sitting on the counter. A paintbrush rested on top of the can. "Where did you get all this?"

"I got a rideshare over to the big home improvement store in town. Figured I might as well get most of the job done today." He set down the drill on a tray connected to the ladder. "Hey, can you hand me the trowel?"

"The what?"

"The thing with the metal scoop on the end."

Audrey scanned the tools he had laid out. She picked up one that looked like what he needed. "Is this it?"

"Yep."

She handed it up to him. "I know you're busy, but you

should eat with us. Natalie's going to fire up the grill after she gets changed."

He grunted in response.

She squinted up at him. "Did you just grunt at me?"

He opened a container of some kind of paste and started using his spatula-type thing to spread it on the ceiling. The repetitive movements drew her attention to the muscles of his forearm. Damn.

"It was a grunt of acknowledgement," he said.

"Okay, fine. But I want to talk to you about something."

"I need to tape and mud the seams first."

Would he ever stop working so they could *talk*? She grunted back at him and left him to his task. By the time she came back downstairs from taking a shower and getting changed, he'd finished doing whatever he needed to do. He'd also cleared his stuff out of everyone's way so they could start making dinner.

She busied herself with making a salad, eavesdropping while Luke spoke to Natalie a few feet away.

"The drywall mud needs twenty-four hours to dry. Tomorrow I can paint that part of the ceiling," he said. "It was a pretty bad leak coming from that bathroom, so I'm glad I was able to get it fixed today."

"Thank you. You've been such a huge help, and you've basically given up your entire vacation."

"I'm happy to help," Luke said. Out of the corner of her eye, Audrey caught his gaze darting toward her.

"Audrey is lucky to have you. We're all lucky to have you here."

Audrey scrunched up her face. Natalie had gone from vaguely threatening to sickeningly sweet with him. She was overdoing it with the compliments.

He mumbled something about getting cleaned up before dinner and went upstairs. The shower started a couple minutes later. An image filled her mind, one of water running over strong arms and a broad chest. And then the image panned lower...

She shook her head like that could dislodge those thoughts. What was she doing? Right, salad. Dinner. She grabbed a cutting board, a knife, and a cucumber.

Okay, maybe not the best vegetable to pick if she was trying not to think about Luke naked.

Natalie walked over and leaned her hip against the counter. "I think I like him. I'm leaning toward giving him the official seal of approval."

"Isn't it too early for that?"

"I haven't made a final decision, but he's got several items in the plus column." Natalie ticked each one off on her fingers. "He's competent, he's helpful, and he has a smokin' hot bod."

Audrey's face grew warm. Yes, he did. "Do people still say smokin' hot bod? That's a thing?"

"Shut up."

Grace walked into the kitchen. She'd been upstairs, getting in some reading time before dinner. Audrey thought of herself as a big reader, but Grace plowed through romance novels like nobody's business. "Are we talking about Luke?" she asked.

Audrey glanced up from the cutting board. "What tipped you off?"

"I heard 'smokin' hot bod' and figured."

She used the knife to point at them. "Both of you need to stop objectifying my boyfriend."

Natalie popped a cucumber slice into her mouth. "Oh, shit. Speaking of, have you even seen him naked yet?"

Audrey's cheeks burned hotter. She set down the knife. "I told you, we're taking things slow."

She had no plans to see him naked. None. Yeah, she thought about it sometimes because—because, well. Just look at him. But it wasn't going to happen.

"I have condoms in my suitcase if you change your mind," Natalie said, gently bumping her shoulder with Audrey's.

"Why do you have condoms?" Grace asked.

"Because, Grace, sometimes when two people like each other very much—"

Grace swatted Natalie's arm. "When was the last time you hooked up with anyone in this town?"

"There was that one guy a few years ago when we went to a bar." Natalie ate another slice of cucumber. "I like being prepared."

Audrey dumped the rest of the cucumber in the salad bowl before Natalie could eat any more. "We're not going to sleep together here." True in more ways than one.

Like they'd conjured him up, Luke walked into the kitchen, his hair damp from the shower. Everyone went quiet. He looked at the three of them, his eyes narrowed like he couldn't figure them out. "Can I help with anything?"

Audrey ducked her head. "No, I think we've got it. But thanks."

Natalie put on her apron with *MAY I SUGGEST THE SAUSAGE?* written in red letters across the front. She grabbed the plate of hamburgers and hot dogs from the fridge. "Let's get these on the grill. I'm ready to eat."

She headed outside to the deck through the sliding glass door. Grace trotted out after her, leaving Audrey and Luke in the kitchen alone.

"Are you sure I can't help?" he asked.

"I don't know, there's probably another leak some-where you can fix."

Shit. She winced. Saying stuff like that did nothing to mend their situation. But he was always trying to help. From the moment they'd arrived, he never stopped help-ing, and he never stopped finding new ways to avoid her.

He shook his head slowly. "You know what, I'm gonna go outside."

She couldn't blame him. She was being a jerk. He wanted to help, and she threw it back in his face. Before she could open her mouth to apologize for that comment about the leak, he was already opening the door.

Yeah, she'd fucked up.

That night, after dinner and fireworks, Luke stayed out-side on the deck while Audrey and her friends went in-side. She hadn't invited him to join them, aside from a half-hearted attempt when Grace nudged her. He was a third wheel and he knew it.

And you know what? If that was what she wanted, fine. He was only useful to her in the presence of a cam-era anyway.

Instead of dwelling on what he couldn't change, he enjoyed the nice weather and used the time to catch up with his family. Before he left for Michigan, his mom had been thrilled to hear he was going on a trip with Audrey. Her excitement only added to his guilt about not telling the truth.

Somehow, tonight's *How are you doing?* text turned into Mom saying she wanted to have Audrey over for dinner next weekend, along with *that nice girl your sis-*

ter is dating. He could find a way out of the dinner invite later. He texted Erin immediately.

Luke: I heard you're dating a "nice girl."

Erin: Who told you?

Luke: Mom. Is it the girl from the hockey team?

Erin sent a rolling-eyes emoji and said yes, it was someone from her hockey team, and if he had to know, they'd spent the day together at a Fourth of July block party. As her big brother, he couldn't resist teasing her about all those secretive smiles she'd made at her phone a few weeks ago. He'd known something was up.

Luke: At least someone's love life was going well.

His phone pinged with another text from his sister. How are things with Audrey?

Luke: They're fine.

Erin: Gosh, what a romantic.

He tried to think of a witty comeback and failed. Erin had him beat in that department. He yawned and slid his phone into his pocket. Time to call it a night. He went inside the house, put his empty beer bottle in the recycling, clicked off the kitchen light, and headed up to bed.

When he reached the landing at the top of the stairs, the door to his and Audrey's bedroom was open. She sat in bed reading with a pillow propped behind her back. He rapped his knuckles lightly against the door.

She jerked her head up and snapped the cover closed on her e-reader. A blush spread across her cheeks. "I was just getting to the good part."

"You can keep reading." He went to get a pair of pajama pants and a T-shirt from his bag. "I'm gonna get ready for bed."

"Sleeping on the floor again?"

"Yeah." No matter how much he dreaded it, he had to.

"You've got to be sore from working all day."

"I'm used to it."

He left for the bathroom across the hall before she could say anything else. When he came back, he gently closed the bedroom door behind him. She'd turned off the bedside lamp and was under the covers. He went to the closet to gather up the bedding he used last night.

"Luke," she whispered.

"What?"

"This is ridiculous."

He walked over to the side of the bed and dropped the extra comforter and blanket on the floor. "It's better this way."

"Do you think I'm going to touch you in the middle of the night or something?"

"You wouldn't. There's not a camera around."

She sat up and flicked on the lamp. "I know I messed up, but way not to sugarcoat things."

Well, fuck. He'd thrown down the gauntlet, and he couldn't take it back. Not that he wanted to. What happened after the kiss—it'd been brewing between them for days, the tension an undercurrent to every interaction.

Audrey angled herself toward him. "To be clear, I—"

Her words the other day had been clear enough. No explanation needed.

"When I kissed you, I did it because I wanted to. Because I wanted you. Because I couldn't go one more second without knowing what it would feel like." He ran a hand through his hair. "But all you cared about was how I didn't kiss you like that on the Kiss Cam."

She stared at her hands clasped together in her lap. "I didn't mean it the way you think. It came out wrong."

"How was it supposed to come out? How was I supposed to take it?"

"I meant it as something funny and light. Now I know I said the wrong thing at the worst possible moment." She looked up from her hands, guilt all over her face. "Like I said, I know I messed up."

Funny and light? More like a punch to the gut. "And you had this realization all of a sudden?"

"I had some time to think about it today. About why you've been avoiding me, and why you'd rather spend this trip doing home repairs than spending time together. That's what I wanted to talk to you about."

He didn't say anything. Didn't deny it. Yeah, the ceiling needed fixing, but it was also a convenient way to keep his distance. A way to do what he did best—work with his hands and ignore the problems in his life that couldn't be fixed with tools, drywall, and a new coat of paint.

Now it was time to fix things with Audrey. He couldn't avoid this conversation any longer, and he didn't want to continue it standing here hovering over her. It didn't feel right.

He also didn't want to spend another night on the floor.

Fuck it. He pulled back the covers and got in.

Audrey's eyes went wide, and she inhaled sharply. He kept his distance, careful to stay on his side of the bed. She lay down next to him and put her head on the pillow.

"Is this okay?" he asked.

"I told you I wanted you to sleep here. But now that you're in this bed, you're going to hear me out." She turned on her side to face him. "I wanted to kiss you. I'm sorry what I said made you think I didn't. Or that I didn't want to unless people could see it." Her voice was soft, barely above a whisper. "That's not true."

"You asked me to. I thought that meant you wanted me, too."

"I did. I still do."

He turned his head. Their gazes met. The light from the lamp glowed behind her, softening her face. He clenched the hand closest to her into a fist at his side. It was the only way he could resist reaching out to touch her.

"I know this is supposed to be fake, but me kissing you? That was real. That was you and me, no bullshit." He held her gaze for the length of one heartbeat, then two. "Just us."

Her breath hitched. "What are we doing?"

He shook his head against the pillow. "I don't know. We should get some sleep."

She blinked. Bit her lip. Sighed. She flopped to her back and turned off the lamp. The room went dark.

They lay next to each other, a few inches separating them. It would be easy to close that distance. To pull her close, brush her hair away from her face, and press his mouth to hers. To soothe his tongue over the spot on her lip she just bit. To feel the way their bodies fit together and ask how she wanted him to touch her.

His heart raced. His thoughts roared. They had eight more weeks of pretending to be a couple. She wanted him, too. Would it be that bad if they gave in to whatever this thing was between them?

He glanced over at Audrey. She opened one eye and then rolled to her other side so her back faced him.

"Good night," she said.

"Night."

It would be a long one.

Chapter Thirteen

Audrey woke up the next morning to an empty bed.

Not a surprise. Despite the tension crackling between them last night, Luke hadn't made a move. He'd slept as close to the edge of the bed as possible, which couldn't have been comfortable. Meanwhile, she'd held herself still and focused on her breathing until she fell asleep. She once had a therapist teach her about the 4-7-8 breathing technique—breathing in for four seconds, holding the breath for seven seconds, and exhaling for eight seconds. It turned out it was useful not just for stress and anxiety but also for when you were trying not to touch your fake boyfriend.

She should be grateful neither of them had made a move. If they'd kissed, they might have taken things too far—and she would have gone there willingly if given the opportunity.

She'd spent an inordinate amount of time drafting rules she kept breaking or thinking about breaking. She loved rules. She thrived on rules. Why were these rules so hard to follow?

You know why.

She rolled over and smashed her face into her pillow. Goddamn pants feelings ruining everything.

"Hey, you okay?"

She lifted her head and glanced over her shoulder. Luke stood in the doorway to their bedroom, already dressed in a T-shirt and jeans. He crossed his arms over his chest and leaned against the doorframe. His shirt pulled tight around his biceps. The tiniest, faintest pulse fluttered between her legs. She buried her face in the pillow again and cursed.

"Audrey?"

"Yeah, I'm okay," she said, sitting up and pushing her hair out of her face. He squinted at her, still looking devastatingly handsome. "What's up?"

"Grace says you've never been late for blueberry picking in your life. She asked me to check on you."

She jumped out of bed and grabbed her phone, turning on the screen. Ten forty-five. The last time she slept that late, she'd been in college.

"Oh my God, I must have forgotten to set an alarm." She never forgot to set an alarm, and she never forgot about blueberry picking. How embarrassing. Every year, she made the schedule of activities and ensured they stuck to it. "We were supposed to leave at ten. The schedule is all messed up now."

He walked over to her and put his hands on her shoulders. When she tilted her chin up, she found nothing but understanding in his eyes.

They were close. She could kiss him if she wanted to.

"We're not punching a clock here," he said, his voice kind. "You're on vacation. It's okay to sleep in."

Had they turned a corner after last night? Odd tension aside, she wanted to hope they had.

"But the schedule."

"It's not set in stone, is it?"

She frowned. It might as well be.

"They're not upset," he said. "Anyway, I'm gonna go back downstairs and let you get ready."

"Ugh. Tell them I'll be down in fifteen minutes."

More like twenty. She wasn't one of those people who could roll out of bed, throw on some clothes, and be ready to go. The only reason it wouldn't take her an hour to get ready was because she showered last night.

"I will," Luke said. "And I already made coffee. It's waiting for you."

"You're a good fake boyfriend."

She pressed a quick kiss to his cheek. The way he ducked his head afterward and smiled was already the best part of her day.

Maybe they had turned a corner after all.

They'd needed that conversation last night. She deserved the accusation about only caring about getting things on camera, no matter how tough it was to hear.

She'd apologized. He'd finally opened up to her. He'd let her know what was going on inside his head. They'd confessed things. To top it all off, they'd stared at each other like they wanted to rip off all their clothes and make out.

There were many, many reasons they weren't going to do that. She needed to keep reminding herself.

Well, we could kiss with our clothes on...

She made a frustrated noise and went to get ready.

Luke couldn't remember the last time he'd gone blueberry picking. Given an option, it wouldn't be his first choice for how to spend the day. But boyfriends did things like go blueberry picking, and Audrey had rightfully called him out on not spending time with her and her friends.

He turned off the part of his brain that told him he had no business tagging along. She wanted him there. He liked being around her. Her friends had warmed up to him. And her friends needed to believe they were a couple.

Anyway, he didn't have a decent excuse even if he wanted to get out of it. He couldn't paint the ceiling until the drywall mud had set.

After a twenty-minute drive, Audrey pulled into the parking lot of Bill's Blueberry Farm, *Western Michigan's Premier U-Pick Destination!* according to the sign on the highway. She got out of the car first, and he walked around to the front to join her while they waited for Grace and Natalie to get out of the backseat.

"Who's ready to pick more blueberries than they know what to do with?" Natalie singsonged as she walked up to them.

Grace gave a little snort. "I think I still have some in my freezer from last year."

"Is this an annual tradition?" he asked.

"Yes," Grace said. "Ask Audrey to tell you about that one time a few years ago we did a tasting of blueberry wine and she got so drunk we had to put her to bed when we got home."

Audrey rolled her eyes. "They were generous pours."

"And you drank every last one," Natalie said.

The three friends had a nice, easy camaraderie, even when they were teasing each other. He hadn't had that kind of friendship since he played baseball. The closest he came to it these days was the mutual ribbing he did with his cousins. His schedule the last few years meant a lot of friendships had faded away.

If he ended up moving back to Chicago, maybe he could try to get in touch with those old teammates. Some of them had moved to the city for jobs after graduation. They might still be around.

With the three women still laughing and teasing each other, they all headed to the farm's entrance. They grabbed plastic buckets and split into pairs.

He strolled with Audrey down a grassy path lined with blueberry bushes on either side. They maneuvered around a family with small children and a few couples, walking until they found a good spot to stop.

She steered them over to a bush and began picking blueberries while he held out their bucket. "I forget if I thanked you for coming today," she said, dropping a handful of blueberries into the container.

"No thanks necessary. I wanted to."

A smile teased her lips, but she flattened them down. She pulled more berries off the bush and dropped them into the bucket. "No home renovation projects today?"

"I still have to paint the ceiling, but it can wait."

"Okay, be honest—what would you have done if you didn't have that repair to distract you?"

"You ask pointed questions."

She laughed. "Is that good or bad?"

"Good, I think." He shifted the blueberry bucket to his other hand. "I don't know what I would have done. I should have talked to you instead of avoiding you."

"You were pissed, and you had every right to be." She dropped a few more berries into the bucket and looked up at him, her expression bright. "But we're good now?"

"We're good." With his free hand, he reached out

and laced his fingers through hers. Her words from last night ran through his head. *What are we doing?* Hell if he knew, but he'd keep holding her hand for as long as she let him.

She gave his hand a squeeze. "Let's walk down a bit farther. I bet we can find more berries away from the crowds."

They walked hand in hand, like they were on an actual date and it wasn't a big deal. They were just another couple at the farm picking blueberries and enjoying the warm weather. Holding her hand, being with her like this—it didn't feel like pretending. It felt like he was meant to be by her side.

Audrey glanced over at him. "Do you ever get recognized at places like this?"

"Blueberry farms? Never," he said, deadpan.

She bumped his arm with her elbow. "You know what I mean. When you're out and about."

"Not a lot. Once in a while I get a HomeTV super fan, but it's mostly little kids who mistake me for that one guy from all the superhero movies." He chuckled. "Which I guess is a good ego boost. And it's pretty cute having kids run up to me."

"You know, when we first met, I thought you looked like someone who should be in one of those movies."

"Really?"

"It's the jawline. You have a strong one."

He couldn't help teasing her. "Are you hot for my jawline, Audrey?"

"Among other things."

She said it so casually, it took him a second to catch up. Well, then. He hadn't expected her to be that direct, but he liked it. "That's, uh. That's good to know."

They'd reached the end of the row of blueberry bushes, and she tugged him over to one. "Here. You should get a chance to pick."

She dropped his hand to reach for the bucket, their fingers brushing as he gave it to her. That brief contact sent a buzz traveling through him. Like her touch gave him a superpower that made him bold. "What if I wanted to kiss you first?"

He wanted her. He wanted her last night, he wanted her now, he wanted her any way she would allow him to have her.

She smiled, looking up at him through her eyelashes, and took a step closer. She set the bucket on the ground. His chest filled with hope; his pulse skittered with anticipation.

"Then I'd say you should do that."

He put his arm around her waist and pulled her close. The first press of his lips to hers made her gasp. The soft exhalation had him sliding a hand into her hair and taking her mouth in a slow, gentle kiss, as lazy as a summer day and just as sweet. He pressed the tip of his tongue to her bottom lip, and—

"Hey, lovebirds!"

They broke apart so suddenly their noses collided. *Ow.* Natalie and Grace bounded up to them, each carrying a bucket of blueberries.

"We got all of our blueberries, so we thought we'd come find you guys," Grace said. She glanced at the bucket near Audrey's feet. "Looks like you didn't do much berry picking."

Natalie looked between them, beaming. Hard to believe this was the same person who refused to let him in the house the other night until he declared his intentions.

Audrey's cheeks flushed a pretty shade of pink. She snatched up the bucket from the ground. "We're getting around to it."

Luke put his arm around Audrey's shoulders. "How about we meet you in the gift shop in fifteen minutes?"

Audrey, Grace, and Natalie all exchanged looks. Natalie spoke first. "Sounds good."

Once her friends were gone, Audrey threw back her head and groaned. "I really wish they hadn't interrupted."

That made two of them.

They finished picking blueberries, took some pictures to post on Twitter and Insta, and headed to the gift shop with two minutes to spare.

He could have used that time to kiss Audrey again, but no way would two minutes ever be long enough.

That night after dinner, Luke took care of painting the drywall on the kitchen ceiling while Audrey and her friends watched a movie in the living room. Since the kitchen and living room were all one big space, he could be a part of things—kind of.

By the time he finished the job and put the ladder and tools back in the shed, the movie was almost over. The smell of paint and sweat clung to his skin. Rather than inflict that on everyone, he headed upstairs to take a shower. He could come back downstairs and join them later if they were still hanging out.

He might like that. They were a fun group.

After a quick shower, he wrapped a towel around his waist and walked across the hall to the bedroom.

He stopped in his tracks right there in the doorway.

Audrey stood by the side of the bed, pulling back the

covers. She had little white earbuds in her ears, and she hummed to herself, bopping her head along to the beat of whatever song she was listening to.

She turned in his direction. Their eyes met. She froze with one hand clutching the floral-patterned bedspread.

"Luke." Her voice was higher than usual, a little strained. "Hi." She looked him up and down, her chest rising and falling with rapid breaths.

He couldn't move. Could barely speak. But he had to say *something*. "I forgot to grab clothes to change into." After a beat of silence, he added, "I thought you'd still be downstairs."

She didn't say anything. Just stared at him with a wide-eyed gaze that made his skin grow hot with awareness.

Droplets of water dripped from his hair and down his back and chest. He tightened his grip on the towel at his waist and willed his body not to respond.

His dick got hard anyway. *Shit.*

He wanted to move across the room toward her. Let her touch him. Let himself touch her.

But he couldn't.

Audrey shook her head, the dazed expression clearing from her face. Her cheeks were bright pink. "I'll leave so you can get dressed."

"No, I'll—I'll just get my stuff."

"Um. Okay." She picked up her phone from the nightstand and turned her back to him while he shuffled over to his bag and grabbed his T-shirt and pajama pants.

"Be right back."

He did the same awkward shuffle across the hallway to the bathroom to get dressed. He should sleep on the floor tonight and save himself the embarrassment. A muscle in his back twitched in protest. Sleeping on the cold hardwood floor sucked.

They'd made it through last night without touching each other. They could do it again.

Something had changed between last night and today, though. When he confronted her about what she said after their first kiss, things had shifted. They'd shifted again at the blueberry farm when they walked hand in hand, when they'd laughed and kissed. All of it added up, and all of it meant he'd have a hell of a time staying away from her.

He needed to resist temptation. Kisses were one thing, but sex was different. He'd agreed to the terms and conditions set out in their rules—the same rules that said both kisses and sex were off limits. They had already crossed out the one about kisses. With every heated look and every night spent in the same bedroom, they were coming dangerously close to striking the "no sex" rule, too.

If she asked him to have sex, he'd have his clothes off by the time she finished the sentence. Which, now that he thought about it, might not be the smartest idea.

He might be leaving Chicago. Anything they did would have to be temporary. He wanted to believe he'd be back in the city at some point if they pulled off this fake relationship and *Project Victorian* got picked up, but he didn't know if or when. No matter how hard he pushed for the show to film in his hometown, HomeTV could decide to send him around the country. The network executives had to do what they thought was best for ratings. He might end up in Chicago for only part of the year, for a couple weeks at a time.

He gripped the edge of the sink and shook his head. He couldn't do that to her—or to himself.

After finally getting dressed, he came back to the bedroom. Audrey was in bed but hadn't turned off the lamp on the nightstand. He walked around to his side, pulled back the covers, and paused before he got in. "What's this?"

Throw pillows in different shades of blue were arranged in a neat line down the center of the bed, forming a barrier between his side and hers.

"A solution to our problem."

"Huh." He rubbed his chin. This could work. One of them should have thought of this sooner. These pillows could have saved him from having a sore back that first night.

She narrowed her eyes. "Is that a good 'huh' or a bad 'huh'?"

"It's a good one."

This was definitely good. They must be on the same page about trying to keep their hands—and other body parts—off each other. They each had a clearly marked side of the bed, and a barrier that would make it difficult not to stay on those sides. Genius, really.

"Oh, I'm so glad you're not offended," she said, sitting up and giving him a relieved smile.

"Why would I be offended?"

"Because it's basically like putting in flashing lights, 'Warning! Do not touch!'"

She said the last part in a robotic voice, opening and closing her hands to mimic flashing lights. A swell of affection rushed through him. She was so fucking cute sometimes.

And that was why he needed to stay on his own damn side of the bed.

"Is that a warning for me or for you?" he asked.

"It's for both of us."

Part of him wanted to laugh. They needed a pillow barrier to stay away from each other. Whatever worked, though, right? They both had to stay focused on what they wanted to get out of this arrangement.

It couldn't all fall apart now.

Chapter Fourteen

The next morning, the first thing Audrey registered was something warm wrapped around her, like a blanket but better. She burrowed into it and rubbed her cheek against her pillow.

She sighed. This bed was so comfortable. No way was she getting up yet.

An arm tightened around her shoulders, pulling her deeper into the warmth, closer. A hand drifted over her side before settling at her hip.

Wait a second.

She opened her eyes. Blinked a few times. Raised her head from where it rested on...

Oh, no.

Oh my God, *no*.

She was using her fake boyfriend as a pillow.

Her gaze traveled down the length of their bodies. She'd wedged herself in the sliver of space between Luke and the pillow barrier, making herself right at home. She had an arm stretched across his middle and one of her legs twined with his. He held her close. They touched everywhere they could possibly be touching.

Had they been like this all night?

She lowered her head back down to Luke's chest. He

made a deep, satisfied sound. That sound said he wanted her there. That she belonged there.

Did she?

"Shit," she whispered. So much for her great idea to keep them apart.

"Audrey."

The rumble of his voice vibrated through her, making everything tingle. When he put his other hand on the arm she had across his stomach, those tingles turned into sparks. She held her breath and stayed very, very still.

Okay, there were a few ways she could play this. She could enjoy being in his arms, at least for the next few minutes, then forget it ever happened. She could freak out.

Or she could put some distance between them right now.

She carefully extricated herself from Luke's hold and rolled over to her side of the bed, where she flopped to her back.

He dragged a hand over his face and opened his eyes. "Where're you going?"

"Back to my side of the bed." *Where I belong.*

"What?" Confused, sleepy Luke was kind of adorable. Adorable in a way that made her want to rub herself all over him. Preferably while neither of them had clothes on. "Is it morning?"

The room had thick, heavy curtains on the windows, but sunlight shone through the gaps. Audrey turned her head to look at the clock on the nightstand. "It's eight thirty."

"What time did you want to get on the road?"

He must have sleep-induced brain fog. He couldn't

have missed the part where they slept all tangled up in each other.

"My schedule has us leaving around eleven." When he didn't say anything in response, she glanced over at him. Maybe she needed to confront this thing head on. "Sorry about using you as a pillow."

He gave her a soft, fond look that enveloped her with the same warmth his body had. "You're a determined cuddler."

She covered her face with her hands. "I cuddled you against your will."

"Hey." He tossed a couple of the throw pillows on the floor and scooted closer, turning to his side. "It wasn't against my will. Not at all."

She peeled her hands away from her face and took a peek at him. "I basically rolled on top of you."

"And I remember pulling you closer."

"I guess that means both of us were determined cuddlers."

He shrugged. "I guess."

"This isn't going to be awkward, is it?"

"Why would it be awkward?"

She groaned. Was he being deliberately obtuse? "We have to spend two hours in a car together."

"You know what's exactly two hours long?" His face lit up in a way she hadn't seen in a while. "The *Anthology* album."

"True. But I don't know how that makes the ride less awkward."

"If we sing along, it'll be a good distraction. We could do a duet to 'Stop Draggin' My Heart Around.'"

Luke, singing along in the car? She couldn't picture

it. He was so quiet, so stoic. Every time he let down his guard even a little bit surprised her.

"I get to be Stevie," she said automatically.

"What if I wanted to do the Stevie parts?"

"You're gonna have to fight me for it."

The corners of his mouth quirked up with little dimples at the edges of his smile. She wanted to press her thumbs to the indentations and kiss him. He held her stare for a beat too long, like he knew what she was thinking. Like he was thinking it, too.

You can't.

They'd kissed yesterday at the blueberry farm, but that was vastly different from kissing each other in bed after they cuddled all night.

"I'm going to hop in the shower now," she said, louder than she meant to.

She slipped out of bed and grabbed her robe from the bedpost. She was not about to have a situation like Luke's where she stumbled back into the room in only a towel. Her face heated. When he caught her staring last night, the part of her that didn't give a crap about the rules wanted him to drop the towel, lower her to the bed, and do all kinds of delicious things to her.

Things they would never do in real life. Her fantasy had to stay a fantasy. She was building a business. That had to be her focus. She couldn't let herself get carried away over cute dimples and hard muscles.

She hustled to the shower, doing her best to think unsexy thoughts. By the time they'd had breakfast, said goodbye to Natalie and Grace, and got on the road, she'd managed to banish most of the images of half-naked Luke from her mind. No matter how hot those images were, she didn't need to think about him like that. Especially not when he sat a few inches away from her in the passenger seat.

They spent the drive home listening to music and talking about work. Normal things. Things that didn't allow her mind to stray. And then she'd catch a glimpse of his forearms when she reached down to grab her coffee from the cup holder. Or their fingers would accidentally brush when they both went for their cups at the same time, and whoops, her mind wandered again.

Her thoughts turned to this morning, and to last night. To the blueberry farm. To that kiss after the ballgame. Did he have trouble forgetting those moments? Did he fantasize about her, too?

She glanced over at him as they sat in traffic, inching closer to their exit. His face gave nothing away. Before she got distracted by how handsome he looked in profile, she forced her attention back to the road. He'd teased her yesterday, but she really was hot for his jawline.

Stop thinking about him like that.

She took the next exit for Kostner Avenue. The maps app guided her through a couple more turns to Luke's mom's house.

Any remaining sexy thoughts got sucked out of her head when she pulled up to the house to drop him off.

A middle-aged woman stood from her spot on a porch swing. She had the same dark blond hair and smile as Luke, right down to the dimples.

"Is that Audrey?" she called out, cupping her hands around her mouth so the entire neighborhood could hear her.

"Ah, shit," Luke muttered.

Her thoughts exactly.

Audrey gripped the steering wheel. She could hit the

gas and drive back to Michigan, right? That would be a perfectly acceptable thing to do. If she drove fast, she could be back there in no time.

Oh, no. The woman was walking down the front porch steps and approaching the car.

Luke froze with one hand on the door handle. "Uh, so, that's my mom. And I think she wants to meet you."

"Anyway, that's how I'm having dinner with Luke's family on Friday."

Audrey sat across a table from Grace, who had joined her for lunch at one of their favorite restaurants. Natalie had to work and couldn't make it, but since Grace was a freelance web designer, she made her own schedule.

She couldn't tell Grace everything that happened with Luke on the Michigan trip, but she could tell her about being ambushed by his mother three days ago. "Ambushed" might be too strong a word, but the woman had Big Midwestern Mom Energy and a lot of enthusiasm for meeting her son's new girlfriend.

Grace tilted her head to the side. "She came up to your window when you were dropping him off and asked?"

"Well, she introduced herself first." Audrey took a sip of her iced tea. "She also said I was lovely. I don't think anyone's ever called me that before."

"You *are* lovely."

Audrey did a little hair flip. "Why, thank you."

Grace smiled. "What does Luke think about all this? You haven't been dating that long. It might be too early to meet the parents."

"He's rolling with it. He said his mom is so excited he's finally found someone." Every time those words crossed Audrey's mind, her chest and throat grew tight. "And it's just his mom. He never mentions his dad."

Except for that one time at the Cubs game, when he said his dad taught him how to score baseball games by hand. Luke had changed the subject, and they'd moved on. She didn't have any business prying, so she didn't ask.

"Oh. Maybe meeting one parent is less pressure than meeting two?" Grace dragged a french fry through the ketchup on her plate.

"I don't know. His sister and her new girlfriend are going to be there, too. I have to worry about making a good impression on all these people." She got the anxiety sweats just thinking about it. "I've never met the parents of someone I'm dating. I have nothing to compare it to."

She'd never met Neil's parents in the two years they dated. They lived in Virginia, but they visited Chicago at least once a year. Her parents, who lived locally, had met her ex and barely tolerated him. They still referred to Neil as "that jagoff."

"You'll be fine," Grace said. "His mom already thinks you're lovely. And Luke will be by your side. He seems like a decent guy."

"He is."

"On that note," Grace said in a cheery voice, "Natalie and I talked."

So that was why Grace asked her to lunch.

"And?" Audrey took a bite of her sandwich and waited for their verdict.

Grace did a drumroll on the table. "We both think he's a keeper."

Audrey sat back against the booth, the words like a glass of ice water dumped on her head. They thought her fake boyfriend was a keeper. That he and Audrey were in it for the long haul. Wasn't that what she wanted, for her friends—hell, for the entire internet—to believe what they had was real?

But it wasn't. He was leaving in a couple months. What would her friends say about this "keeper" when he left? Or if they found out their relationship was fake? *What if, what if, what if.*

Her throat grew tight, that guilty, uneasy feeling making an unwelcome reappearance.

Grace leaned forward, giving her an expectant look. Audrey needed to say something. Anything.

"I'm glad you both like him," she said past the lump in her throat. "I hoped you would."

"I feel like we're overly invested, but…" Grace trailed off and looked out the window next to their table. When she turned back to Audrey a few seconds later, her eyes shimmered with tears. Oh God.

"We want you to be happy, and he's great for you." Grace flapped her hands in front of her face. "I can't believe I'm getting emotional about this. I think I'm PMSing."

"It's okay. I want you guys to be happy, too." Audrey reached across the table and gave her friend's hand a quick squeeze before letting go.

"I know." Grace picked up a clean napkin from the stack their server had left on the table and wiped away her tears. "I also know happiness isn't dependent on being in a relationship, but it's nice to have someone who treats you right and makes you happy."

"Yeah, it is."

"I hope Luke is that person for you."

He can't be. Audrey nodded and picked at the remaining food on her plate.

"Hey, are you okay?"

Audrey pushed her plate aside. "I'm fine. I was thinking about what you said. About him being that person for me."

Or not.

"He better be," Grace said. "Because if he breaks your heart, Natalie will come for him. And I'll be the getaway driver."

Audrey didn't doubt it. The only thing that stopped her best friends from going after Neil was the fact Audrey was happy when she dumped him.

Luke wouldn't break her heart. He couldn't. It was hard to have a broken heart when the relationship never existed in the first place.

Chapter Fifteen

Luke had done the meet-the-family dinner with a girl-friend before. Sure, it had been a while, but he couldn't remember ever feeling this much pressure to get things right as he did with Audrey.

Acting like a couple was easy. Somewhere between kissing Audrey after the Cubs game and waking up with her at the lake house, he'd stopped having to pretend. Since he got home from the trip, he couldn't shake the memory of her wrapped around him as they slept—the warmth of her skin, the way their limbs had intertwined, or how she'd held on to him.

He'd slept better than he had in a long time.

So, no, he didn't have to pretend. But he did have to deal with his mother's expectations.

Mom hadn't stopped talking about Audrey since they met earlier in the week. *I'm so happy you've finally found someone*, she kept saying. The words were a steady drumbeat in his head while he helped prepare that night's dinner.

This was a fucking disaster, introducing his fake girl-friend to his mom. He should have tried to get them out of it. Or tried to tell Mom things weren't that serious, no matter what his Instagram and Twitter feeds might have her believe.

Yeah, good luck with that.

Audrey would be here any minute. And he was taking out his nerves and frustration on the mashed potatoes.

"Honey, you're going to over-mash those potatoes," Mom said, coming over to him and gently removing the masher from his hand. "Can you find your sister for me? She put some vegetables in the oven and then disappeared."

"I think she's upstairs fixing her makeup or something. I'll get her to come down."

The doorbell rang. Shit.

"I'll get it," he said. That way, he could ease Audrey into this evening instead of having Mom greet her with a bunch of questions. He wiped his hands on a dishtowel and headed to the front door.

But it wasn't Audrey.

A beautiful Black woman around Erin's age stood there with a nervous smile on her face. She tucked a reddish brown curl behind her ear. "Um, hi. I'm Chloe." She held a bottle of wine in one hand and gave a little wave with the other.

"Nice to meet you." He shook her hand. "I'm Luke, Erin's brother."

Chloe's face brightened. "Oh! The Twitter guy."

Luke held back a groan and stepped aside to let Chloe inside the house. "Yeah, that's me."

Would he always be the Twitter guy to everyone from here on out? Well, better that than being known for GIFs of his butt.

Erin's footsteps thudded down the stairs. His sister, who never blushed or acted shy about anything, ducked her head and turned pink when she saw Chloe. She stared at Erin with so much adoration in her eyes, Luke's heart gave a tug in his chest. Erin looked up at Chloe from under her eyelashes and beamed.

After everything Erin had been through as a kid losing their dad, all he'd ever wanted was for her to know she was loved. To be happy. And she was. But this kind of happiness, this kind of love—this was what he always hoped she'd have.

He didn't need to get emotional on top of everything else. Erin would never let him hear the end of it.

When she reached the bottom of the stairs, Erin said, "Did you call my brother the Twitter guy?" The two women hugged. Erin whispered in Chloe's ear loud enough for Luke to hear, "I believe the official name is TwitterBae."

Erin pulled away from the hug and gave him a look of pure delight. He rolled his eyes, acting more put upon than usual for her benefit.

"That's right." Chloe bit her lower lip like she was holding back a laugh. Or maybe she was wondering what the hell kind of evening she was in for. Luke didn't blame her. "Is there somewhere I can put this?" she asked, lifting up the bottle of wine.

"I'll put it in the kitchen." Erin took the bottle and reached for her girlfriend's hand. "Come on, I'll introduce you to my mom."

After they walked away, Luke checked his phone to see if Audrey had texted and got distracted by Twitter. The doorbell rang, and he nearly dropped his phone on the floor. He fumbled with the device, shoving it into his pocket.

Mom, Erin, and Chloe all came out to the living room

at that exact moment, laughing and holding glasses of wine. The foyer was right next to the living room, giving them a view of the front door.

The doorbell chimed a second time.

"That must be Audrey!" Mom said.

Luke took a deep breath and opened the door.

Once they all sat down to dinner a half hour later, Luke finally let himself relax. Audrey got along great with Erin and Chloe, chatting about their hockey team and her photography. Mom hadn't bombarded her with too many questions. The lemon-roasted chicken was delicious, and his mashed potatoes weren't over-mashed. Things were going...well.

Turned out Mom saved all her questions for dessert. It would have been easier if she'd handed both Chloe and Audrey surveys to fill out. Chloe had just finished answering a question about her family (her mom was a lawyer; her dad was a high school principal; she had two brothers, one older and one younger) when Mom turned to Audrey.

"Audrey, what about your family? Any siblings?"

Luke had been fake dating her for three weeks and he had no idea what her family was like. What her parents did, what neighborhood or suburb she grew up in, if she had siblings, or cousins she was close to. Basic information you were supposed to know about someone you were dating.

"Nope. Just me, my mom, and my dad."

"And what about your parents? What do they do?"

"My dad was a reporter for the *Sun-Times* for a long time, but he took a buyout a few years ago and is retired now. And my mom is a fourth grade teacher."

"Did you ever want to follow in your mom's foot-steps? Or your dad's?" Mom looked at Luke, pride evident in her expression. "You know, Luke followed in his dad's footsteps."

Yeah, because I didn't have a choice. He liked what he did, but taking over the family business had been a necessity, not something he wanted. Anyway, he was doing what he wanted now—or he had a chance to, with the new show.

Audrey gave his mom a tight smile. "I always had my heart set on photography from the first time I picked up a camera."

"But weren't you some sort of event planner before this?" Mom asked.

Audrey slid a glance in his direction. Was that a *Please save me from this line of questioning* look? He could step in if she needed him to, but he didn't want to speak for her.

"I was a meeting planner," she said. "I planned conferences and other events. But photography was always my dream."

"What made now the right time to pursue it?"

Oh, Jesus. Their arrangement, and the resulting publicity, made it the right time. Audrey wouldn't say that out loud. If she didn't have another answer, he might have to make something up on the spot to save them both.

Audrey set her fork down next to the half-finished piece of apple pie on her plate. She inhaled sharply, her shoulders rising before she spoke. "I wasn't treated well at my job. I reached a breaking point where I knew I needed to quit and pursue photography full time. That if I didn't, I'd regret it. I'd gone way too long not doing what I really wanted to do with my life."

He knew what that was like. While her words hung in the air, he took Audrey's hand under the table. She let her hand slide into his and turned to look at him with her eyebrows raised. The silence went on a little too long—long enough for him, Audrey, Chloe, and Erin to look at each other like they all wondered who should talk first—when Mom spoke.

"Well, I commend you for it," Mom said. "Life is too short to spend your time putting up with assholes and not doing what you want."

Erin raised her wine glass. "Cheers to that."

Audrey laughed and picked up her glass. She extended her arm across the table to clink her glass against Erin's and Chloe's, then Mom's, and finally his.

"Clink," she said, tapping their glasses together.

The tension in his muscles eased, and he allowed himself to smile. "Cheers."

The whole time, she didn't let go of his hand.

When Audrey walked out the door of the Murphys' house that night with Luke by her side, she wanted to pump her fist in victory. She'd come through that dinner with flying colors. Things had been precarious for a few minutes during dessert, but everything turned out okay. Luke's mom even hugged her and said she was welcome back anytime.

Ah, there was the wallop of guilt she'd been waiting for all night.

She turned to Luke as he walked her to her car. "I feel bad about lying to your mom."

He glanced over his shoulder at the house, then back to her. "It doesn't feel like we're lying."

"What do you mean?"

"I mean we didn't have to put on a show tonight."

He was right, but that didn't make a difference. "I'm not actually your girlfriend, though, and your mom thinks I am."

"Which means when we break up at the end of the summer, she'll think things didn't work out. It happens."

She sighed and leaned against her car, letting the breeze blow through her hair and cool the back of her neck. He had a point. People got together, met each other's families, and broke up all the time. It didn't change the fact they were lying. It just made things more realistic.

"The two of us are jumping through hoops to make ourselves feel better about this," she said.

Luke pinched the bridge of his nose. "I know. But the important thing about tonight is that it went well. We got through it."

"Right."

She let that be her final word. If they continued this conversation, it would keep going in circles, both of them expressing their guilt and trying to reassure each other. Considering how on edge she'd been for parts of the evening, getting through it was all she could ask for.

Yeah, she had gotten through it, but that didn't stop her from replaying the dinner conversation in her head on the drive home.

Patti, Luke's mom, wasn't mean or rude. She asked pointed questions. Although they seemed well intentioned, they hit a sore spot Patti couldn't possibly have known about. Audrey had held it together, answering those questions while her ex's words unspooled like a roll of film.

You're going to give up a stable job and drop every-thing to pursue this?

Photography is a hobby, not a career.

I don't think you have what it takes to run a business. You're never going to make it.

She'd proven him wrong several times over. Yes, her relationship with Luke helped give her an initial wave of clients, but her business was thriving on its own. Maybe she'd taken the easy way out by using their relationship to further her career, but she preferred to see it as a stra-tegic move meant to ensure her survival.

Everyone found a different way to hustle. Hers just happened to involve an over-the-top plan.

After she got back to her apartment, she responded to a couple emails inquiring about booking her for photo shoots. Her calendar didn't have many openings left. Soon, she might have to be more selective about what jobs she took on, but she'd deal with that when the time came. It was a good problem to have.

She set the phone down on the coffee table and almost immediately it chimed with a text from Luke. What are you doing tomorrow?

Hmm, weird. She last saw him an hour ago, and he didn't mention anything about getting together tomor-row.

Another text popped up on the screen. There's a place I want to take you.

Her pulse sped up. Luke had introduced her to his fam-ily and held her hand under the table, and now he wanted to take her someplace special? How…boyfriend-y of him.

The lines between real and fake kept blurring. Not once tonight did she worry about making anyone believe what they had was real. She didn't need to anymore.

They liked each other. They were attracted to each other. They didn't have to convince anyone. It should have concerned her more than it did.

Audrey: Doing a shoot with a client in the afternoon, but I'm free after. Where do you want to take me?

Luke: Did you know there's a photography-themed bar in Albany Park?

Audrey: I DID NOT. Clearly I need to get out more. How do you know about it?!

Luke: Erin heard about it from someone but couldn't remember the name. I did some googling.

Audrey: Well, sign me up. I'm there.

She could worry about what it all meant later.

Chapter Sixteen

Luke stood outside the bar, keeping an eye on the foot traffic coming from the nearby Brown Line stop at Kedzie. He'd offered to pick Audrey up, but she insisted on taking the train and meeting him there.

Picking her up would have made it seem too much like a date, but this *was* a date. He hadn't thought that through when he texted her last night. When Erin mentioned hearing about a photography-themed bar from someone at work, he jumped on Google. Minutes later, he was texting Audrey. He couldn't believe how fast she'd agreed.

He checked his phone. Put it in his pocket. Glanced up the street again.

The train roared into the ground-level station and screeched to a halt, letting out passengers. Relief swept over him when she exited the station and headed in his direction. Then his jaw promptly fell to the fucking sidewalk.

She wore her curly hair loose around her shoulders with one side pinned up and pulled away from her face. Her dress, which was dark red with tiny white flowers, tied around her waist and hugged her curves. The front of the dress dipped into a V, hinting at cleavage. Damn, what he wouldn't give for that V to dip a little lower.

Get a grip and stop ogling her.

She walked up the street toward him, smiling when their gazes met. That smile was like seeing the sun come out after a stretch of cloudy, rainy days. She was beautiful.

"Hi," Audrey said once she reached him. "I hope you weren't waiting long."

"No, not at all." He wasn't sure if he should say the next part, but he did anyway. "You look really pretty."

She beamed at the compliment. "Thanks. You look nice, too."

He reached for her hand, and she slid it into his. Inside the bar, they grabbed a table toward the back of the long, narrow room. The overhead lights were turned down low, and each table had a small candle in the center. Along with the round lanterns strung over the marble-top bar, the candles gave the room a soft glow.

Everything about this place screamed romance. When he heard photography-themed bar, he imagined old-fashioned cameras and archival photographs on the walls, maybe a photo booth in the back. Not dim lighting, candles, and small tables meant for intimate conversation. What did Audrey think? That he'd brought her here to woo her or something?

She picked up one of the menus the host had left on the table. She opened it to the first page and laughed. "Oh my God, this is great." She clasped her hands to her chest and wiggled her shoulders back and forth. "Look at the signature cocktails."

He picked up the other menu on the table and flipped it open. *Rule of Thirds. Tilt Shift. Shutter Speed. Exposure.*

"I'm guessing these are…"

"Photography terms!" She looked up at him and grinned. "I love it. Thank you for bringing me here."

Whew. She wasn't freaked out by all the candles and shit. "You're welcome."

When their server came to the table, they ordered drinks. Audrey chose the one called Shutter Speed, which had gin and lime in it. He went with a beer. She would probably give him shit for it in three, two, one…

"Not feeling adventurous enough for a signature cocktail?" she asked once their server had left.

"I don't know what half of the ingredients in them are. Better to play it safe than get something I don't like."

"You can always have a sip of mine if you change your mind." She picked up the menu again. "Do you want to get an appetizer?"

They looked over the menu and decided on the charcuterie board. "It's kind of like a cheese plate," he said, closing the menu and smiling at her.

"But fancier, and with meat."

She pulled out her phone to snap pictures of the charcuterie board once it arrived at the table. She took a photo of her drink, too, and finally, she aimed her phone at him. With his elbows on the table, he leaned in.

"Are you taking my picture?" He meant to tease her, but the question came out sounding serious.

"Is that okay?"

"Yeah, it's fine." He kept his eyes on her. "Is this for social media?"

"No," she said, pursing her lips. She glanced at him over the top of her phone. "It's for me."

Goose bumps prickled along the back of his neck. His

chest expanded with hope and pleasure and some other emotion he couldn't name.

"Okay," he finally said.

"Ready?"

He nodded. With a tap of her finger, she took the photo. She lowered the phone and stared at the screen. Her face softened with a smile.

"Oh, this is nice," she said. "It's a good picture of you."

"Can I see?"

She turned her phone toward him and slid it across the table. Their fingers brushed as he reached for the device. Audrey exhaled softly at the brief moment of contact. Warmth spread through his fingertips and up his arm, a pleasant buzz that traveled through the rest of his limbs. He looked up at her, and her face flushed when she met his eyes.

"Well, look," she said, nodding toward the phone.

In the photo, he leaned toward her, his head tilted to the side. One corner of his mouth quirked up. He gave her—and there was no other way to describe it— an adoring stare.

That was how he looked at her? Shit, he had it bad. And he didn't care that she knew.

She picked up her phone and put it back in her purse, which she'd hung on the back of her chair. "Um, anyway. Thanks for indulging me."

They stared at each other for a long moment. He wanted to touch her again. Do more than just brush his fingers against hers. Kiss her mouth, her throat, the skin exposed by the neckline of her dress. Hear her make that soft little exhalation again, right in his ear.

"No problem." He reached for his beer and took a drink to quench his suddenly dry throat.

She grabbed a plate for herself and passed one to him. "What do you say we dive in?" she said, gesturing at the charcuterie board. He nodded and set down his beer. Food was a good distraction from this tension building between them. From the thoughts racing through his head about how much he wanted to touch her.

They shared their food while he asked how her photo shoot went today, and she asked about his progress on the renovation.

"I should stop by next week," she said. "I promised you pictures. I got sidetracked by the holiday and coming back to a bunch of work."

"You can stop by whenever you have time."

"I have to check my schedule, but it'll be sometime next week. I'll let you know."

They switched to talking about their other plans for the coming week. Once they'd polished off the rest of the charcuterie board, Audrey insisted on checking out the dessert menu. They shared a plate of donut bites, all dusted with sugar and served with chocolate sauce on the side. He rarely got dessert, but ordering it tonight meant more time with her. She lit up as she talked—about her clients, about photography, about whatever show she was watching. He couldn't take his eyes off her.

He hadn't had a date this good in a long time. Long enough he couldn't remember the last time.

"What do you think?" Audrey asked, breaking into his thoughts. "Another drink, or do you want to get out of here?"

Whatever they did, he didn't want the night to end. "I'm good either way."

She huffed out a wry-sounding laugh. "I had a feeling you'd say that."

"Why?"

"Because you tend to go along with whatever I want to do. But Luke," she said, the flame from the candle flickering across her face, making her brown eyes sparkle, "what do you want?"

You. I want you.

"Let's get out of here."

Chapter Seventeen

All night, Luke had looked at her with fondness, admiration, and a hint of nerves. When he used that voice—that deep, no-nonsense voice—to say he wanted to get out of there, something clicked into place in Audrey's head. It hit her so fast and so hard she had to stop herself from saying *holy shit* out loud.

He was leaving next month, but that didn't have to be a bad thing. She could have her cake and eat it, too, as long as the bakery was open.

She'd taken risks and gone after what she wanted for the past month. Why stop now? They wanted each other. And they could have each other, rules be damned.

Yep, she was doing this.

"My place?" she asked.

"Yeah. Yeah, your place is great." His face almost relaxed into a smile, but at the last second, his forehead creased. "Are you sure?"

"I'm sure. Are you?"

"I am." He rested his elbows on the table. His voice went low and serious. "But you know whatever happens, this has to be temporary."

"I know. I like temporary."

Something clicked into place for him, too. His face

finally relaxed into that smile she loved, the crooked, knowing one with the dimples. He nodded once like her affirmation settled things.

After they took care of the check, they left the bar holding hands and walked down the street to where he'd parked his truck. He pulled her close to him before he unlocked the doors. She rested a hand on his chest and looked up at his face.

Sometimes, she was struck breathless by how handsome he was. Eyes as deep blue as Lake Michigan in the summertime. Stubble on his cheeks that was a shade darker than the blond of his hair. Those dimples on his cheeks, the jawline that looked like it had been carved and chiseled with a sculptor's precision. She reached up and cupped the side of his face in her hand, touching him just because she could.

"I've been dying to kiss you all night," he said.

Her heartbeat stumbled over itself. "So kiss me."

He lowered his mouth to hers, giving her a kiss so sweet and slow it made her legs shake. When she opened her lips to him, she tasted cinnamon and chocolate, anticipation and desire. She shivered, pressing herself against him, and clutched at his shirt.

They had a real knack for public make-out sessions, but she was ready to take this indoors.

He pulled away with a dazed expression. "Your place?"

"Yeah," she breathed. "Now, please."

He tucked a piece of hair behind her ear and gave her a quick kiss before opening the passenger-side door. He helped her up into the truck and closed the door once she got in. She watched him walk around to the driver's side, her lips still buzzing from his kisses and the taste of what was to come.

She couldn't wait.

When he slid into the driver's seat, the clean, spicy scent of his soap brought her right back to that night at the lake house. Luke, wet from the shower and wearing only a towel, with the outline of his cock clearly visible underneath. She had to bite back a grin and squeeze her thighs together. Tonight she'd get to see and touch all of *that*.

She didn't live that far from the bar, and she'd never been so glad to live so close to a place.

But she forgot about parking.

Luke turned onto her street, driving past rows of parked cars. He continued onto the next block, past more cars parked bumper to bumper.

Seriously? The universe was conspiring against them. At this rate, he'd have to park illegally somewhere and risk a ticket, or they'd have to park far away and walk. She would combust from horniness before they made it to her apartment.

"There's nowhere to park," he said, sounding like it pained him. It pained her, too. "Where do you park when you get home late?"

"I have a spot behind my building."

"You're incredibly lucky."

They drove past more parked cars. *Walking it is.* Either that, or dealing with the side effects of unresolved sexual tension. And she wouldn't stand for that—not tonight. She'd waited long enough.

"I know it's three blocks away, but there might be spots on Lawrence," she said.

That street was full of businesses, most of them closed

by this time of night, which meant they had a better chance of finding somewhere to leave Luke's monstrosity of a pickup truck. Who the hell thought it was a good idea to have a truck in this city? It made sense for his job, she guessed.

"Three blocks?" he said. "That's nothing. Let's give it a shot."

By some miracle, Luke found a parking spot shortly after they turned onto Lawrence. He put the truck in park and turned it off, but he kept his hands on the steering wheel, gripping it hard. He glanced over at her. A muscle in his jaw twitched. Even his jaw twitching was hot.

"Do you have condoms at your place?" When she didn't say anything right away, he rushed to fill the silence. "Because there's a pharmacy right there."

"I think I do, but they might be expired. Stopping at the pharmacy is an excellent idea." She unbuckled her seatbelt and grabbed the door handle.

"We could do other stuff, but I figured—" He swallowed. "It's been a while."

Was he nervous? A rush of affection moved through her.

"Hey." She reached out to touch his face, to turn it toward her and press a soft kiss to his lips. He let go of the steering wheel to slide a hand into her hair, to kiss her back. Before they could take the kiss too far, she pulled away. If they kept it up, they'd never make it back to her place.

"Condoms," she reminded him.

He grinned at her, the tension gone from his face. "Hell yes."

After they ran into the store and got what they needed—and after they hustled their way down three very long blocks—finally she had him inside her apartment. She walked in first, flipping on the light switch and dropping the bag from the pharmacy and her purse on the floor. While she stepped out of her shoes, Luke stood in the entryway. Was he…running his hand over her door?

"This place has nice woodwork," he mused, inspecting the wooden doorframe and nodding with approval. "What year was this built? It looks original."

She laughed and took a step toward him. "Do you want to get laid, or do you want to talk about woodwork?"

"Both. Hazards of being with a carpenter, I guess." He grabbed her by the waist, tugging her toward him until she was flush against his body. His hands settled at her hips. "But if I have to choose, woodwork is definitely going to lose."

He dipped his head and pressed his lips to hers. When her lips parted on a sigh, the kiss turned deeper, their tongues sliding together. Each stroke made her dizzy, eager for more.

She got lost in the kiss, in his touch. God, she'd been craving this. Wanting him, and trying to deny herself. That ended tonight. She wouldn't deny herself anything, not anymore.

With her hands on his chest, she urged him to move, giving him a push in the direction of her bedroom. She broke the kiss long enough to pick up the bag containing the condoms from the floor.

"Bedroom," she said, giving him another shove, which earned her a sexy as hell smile.

"Yes, boss."

He'd used that line on her during their first date at

the conservatory. She liked it a lot then. She especially liked it now, when it meant she got to be in control of her own pleasure.

He let himself be pushed into her bedroom and onto the edge of her bed, where he sat down and pulled her into his lap so she straddled him. She dropped the box of condoms on the bed and wound her arms around his neck.

One of his hands clutched her hip, holding her steady. The other crept under her dress, pushing the fabric aside to touch her bare thigh. She whimpered at the contact, at his rough hand against her soft skin.

His hand might have been rough and work worn, but his touch was gentle, his thumb moving back and forth in a soothing motion. She looked down to watch, mesmerized.

He had big, thick fingers. If she had a camera right now, she'd want to capture the flex of those fingers pressing into her thigh, the way he'd pushed up her skirt, the movement of his thumb. The column of his throat, mid-swallow. His heavy-lidded gaze, serious and intense, and how it had latched on to hers.

He moved her skirt up a little more, his hand sliding along her skin. Her breath caught in her throat.

"I like that," she whispered.

"Yeah?" He moved his hand higher, his fingers dancing upward, closer to the juncture of her thighs. "What about this?"

If he slid his fingers inside her… Her brain short-circuited at the thought. His thumb swept along her inner thigh, dangerously close to where she wanted him. Sparks flew across her skin.

"I like that, too."

"How do you want me to touch you, Audrey?" He pressed a kiss to the side of her neck. "How can I make you feel good?"

She shifted in his lap. Through his jeans, she could feel how hard he was. Want scorched through her, out of control and in need of release. Had she ever wanted someone this much? When she rocked her hips forward, seeking some relief for herself, he groaned.

"Tell me," he said, his voice strained.

"I want you to keep moving your hand until it's between my legs. And then I want you to use your fingers to make me come." Warmth spread from her cheeks down to her chest. She'd never talked like this with anyone, but she could with him. She took a deep breath before she said the next thing. "And get me ready for your cock."

"Fuck."

He watched while she climbed off his lap and reached under her dress to take off her panties. She stepped out of them, kicking them aside. While she was up, she flipped on the bedside lamp, bathing the room in golden light. She wanted to see him, wanted him to see her.

A few seconds later, she straddled him again and pushed her dress all the way up her thighs. Luke's arm came around her, holding her tightly to him. He brushed his nose against her neck, kissed the spot where her neck met her shoulder. Her clit thrummed in time with her pulse.

"Touch me," she said.

His right hand moved between her legs. He glanced up at her face, a silent check-in. She nodded for him to keep going. He teased along her folds, slick with her arousal. The rough pads of his fingers against her sensitive flesh made her gasp.

He kissed her neck, the hollow of her throat, her chest, all the while continuing those gentle touches. When his thumb circled her clit, she grabbed his shoulders, her body jolting.

"Is that good?" he murmured, kissing her collarbone.

"Y-yes."

It was more than good—it was perfect.

"Do you want my fingers?"

"*Yes*. Please."

She tilted his chin upward, toward her face. Their mouths met in a fierce kiss. He touched and teased, still working her clit as he slid a finger inside her, and then, slowly, another. She tightened her arms around his neck and held on, each touch, each stroke, bringing her closer.

The pleasure built, making her muscles tense and her limbs tingle. Her thighs trembled. Her breathing faltered. Everything became a blur of sensation: his body hard and hot beneath her. His lips pressing kisses to her neck and throat. His thumb on her clit, keeping the same rhythm as his fingers.

Oh God, his fingers. They worked inside her, filling her, hitting the spot that made fireworks explode behind her eyelids. She bucked her hips, turning desperate, riding his fingers until she came.

When it was over and the last spasm had passed, she slumped against him. One of Luke's hands moved up and down her back. Her dress stuck to her skin.

"We didn't even get undressed," she said, lifting her head to look at him.

"You know, we can change that."

That was the greatest idea she'd ever heard.

She tugged at the hem of his shirt, pulling it up. He took it off the rest of the way and tossed it on the floor. She'd seen him without a shirt on before, but holy shit, he was absolutely delicious—broad shoulders, lean muscles, and those biceps she'd admired in all of his tight T-shirts. She ran her hands over his chest, the dusting of hair there tickling her fingers.

Could she spend the rest of the night touching his muscles? Probably. There were a lot of them.

He shifted underneath her. "I gotta get out of these pants."

She laughed and undid the button. Their hands bumped each other, both going for the zipper.

"I'm gonna…" He grabbed her by the hips and lifted her off his lap. He set her on the bed and stood to take off his shoes, socks, and jeans.

Once he was undressed down to his underwear, she beckoned him toward her with a finger. "Don't get me wrong, I'm all about efficiency, but can I?"

"Yeah," he said in a gruff voice.

She slipped her thumbs into the waistband of his black boxer briefs, lowering them down his hips, letting them fall until he could step out of them.

And then he stood there naked in front of her, sporting a very impressive erection. She stared—she couldn't help it. As an artist, she had to take a moment to appreciate aesthetic perfection.

"So that's what was under the towel," she said, the words slipping past her brain-to-mouth filter.

They both laughed. He reached for her where she sat on the bed. "Can I take this off?" He tugged at the tie at her waist, letting it fall through his fingers.

"That's just for decoration," she said. "You can pull the dress up."

Once they'd gotten the dress over her head, she tossed it aside. Her bra came next and joined their other clothes on the floor. Luke had the same problem with her breasts that she had with his cock, staring slack-jawed like they were the best things he'd ever seen.

She couldn't blame him. They were pretty great.

"Come here," she said, scooting back on the bed and lying down.

He crawled onto the bed to join her, bracing himself above her and lowering his head for a kiss. "You're beautiful," he said right before their lips met.

The way he said those words—full of awe and reverence—made her chest expand until she wasn't sure it could hold this much happiness.

She should be worried about that. Right now, though, she couldn't bring herself to care.

He left a trail of hot kisses down her neck and throat, her collarbone, the tops of her breasts. His mouth lingered, each brush of his lips on her skin lighting her up from the inside out. One thing became clear quickly—he would take his time worshipping her, kissing and licking every inch of skin.

And she was here for it.

She sank into the mattress and closed her eyes, giving herself over to the pleasure of Luke's tongue circling each of her nipples and taking them into his mouth. His hands skimming along her sides and gripping her hips. His lips kissing their way down her stomach, all the way to the spot where she ached for him.

He licked her pussy, his tongue working some kind of magic that had her trembling. When he took her clit into his mouth, she gasped, her back arching off the bed. Too good. So good, it was on the edge of painful. She couldn't take it. Sliding her fingers into his hair, she tugged on the strands and forced him to look up.

"Wait," she said. "I can't—"

He immediately stopped, moving up her body until they were face to face. "Everything okay?"

"Yeah, that was just…" She trailed off, her fingers sliding through his hair again. "That was a little too much."

"We can stop."

She shook her head. "I don't want to stop." She'd waited way too long for this. Wanted him way too much. And there were other things they could do. She lowered her voice to a whisper and spoke into his ear. "If you want to go down on me, you have to start with that."

He shivered at the press of her lips to his skin. When he pulled back to meet her eyes, the desire in his gaze sent a new rush of heat through her.

"Yeah? I'll have to keep that in mind for next time."

She grinned. *Next time.* She moved her hands over his shoulders and down his back, over smooth skin and muscles, relishing the feel of him.

He kissed her neck and across her collarbone. "What's gonna make you feel good right now?"

She writhed underneath him, pressing against the hard length of him. "Right now? I'd really like it if you fucked me."

The moment Audrey asked Luke to fuck her, his brain stopped functioning. They were naked in her bed. She'd come on his fingers a few minutes ago. He'd had her clit in his mouth. But until she said those words, the reality of the situation hadn't sunk in.

"What did I do with the condoms?" she asked, raising her head to look around.

Condoms. Right.

He grabbed the box from where it had ended up behind her pillow and took out a foil packet. With trembling fingers, he ripped it open. Usually he was a lot smoother than this in the bedroom, but Audrey had him turned inside out. Her curves, her gasps, her taste—they all unraveled him.

Once he'd rolled the condom on, he positioned himself between her legs. There was no going back after this. A month ago, they'd agreed not to touch, not to kiss, not to fuck. The rules had blurred a long time ago, but this was the big one, the last rule on their list. The one that tempted him—tempted *them*—more than any of the others.

He was ready to break it, as long as she was, too.

"Ready?" he asked.

She gazed up at him. "I want this, Luke. I want you."

He didn't need to hear anything else.

He pressed forward, entering her inch by inch, her slick heat surrounding him. She felt so fucking good. Tight and hot and perfect. He resisted the urge to thrust, to fuck her senseless. He wanted to take his time, make this good for both of them.

She spread her legs wider, lifting them to lock around his hips. That changed the angle, made him slide deeper inside her. "Fuck, Audrey."

He raised himself up on both hands and stared down at her. He knew this would be good, but she was incredible. All he could do was hold himself steady, try to gather himself before he completely lost it.

"Don't hold back on me," she said, rocking her hips.

His vision damn near whited out. Her hands moved over his back and down to his ass, bringing him deeper, closer.

And he let go.

He withdrew and pushed back in, again and again until he'd built a steady rhythm. As he drove into her, he relished her gasps and moans. Every exhale, every whimper, every murmur of his name spurred him on. He bent his head to kiss her and lifted her knee higher on his hip. He never wanted this to end.

His thrusts grew slower, deeper, coaxing more of those moans out of her. Just to see if she'd like it, on his next thrust, he ground against her. She broke their kiss to say, "Yes, like *that*" and made a desperate sound into his mouth.

He ground against her again. "That feels good?"

"So good. But I need more."

"Yeah?"

She tugged on his hair. "Faster. Harder."

He gave her what she asked for. What she needed. He pounded into her hard and steady, his cock grinding against her clit with every stroke. She made those noises that drove him wild, but he wanted to give her more. Make her get loud.

"Do you want me to touch you?"

"Please," she gasped.

He slid a hand between their bodies and rubbed her clit in time with his thrusts, tight little circles that made her raise her hips and push into his hand. When he slammed into her and pressed down on her clit at the same time, she exploded. Her back bowed and her pussy spasmed around him, gripping him tight. He kept fucking her while she gasped and shook, giving her every last bit of pleasure he could. She was gorgeous—her hair spread over the pillow, her cheeks flushed and her lips parted as she came crying out his name.

The sight of her all blissed out and well fucked was his undoing.

A prickling sensation started at the base of his spine. He drove into her one last time, his hips jerking. Seconds later, his orgasm tore through him, white hot and blinding. He gave himself over to it, shuddering as he came harder than he had in a long time. Maybe ever.

Holy *shit*.

Was this a one-time thing? He sure as hell hoped not.

When it was over, they lay side by side, trying to catch their breath. They both got up eventually, him to deal with the condom and Audrey to use the bathroom. Once they were back in bed, he pulled her into his arms.

Wait a second. He froze.

Before he could say anything, she placed a hand on his chest and raised her head to look at him, like she knew exactly what he was thinking. "Stay."

He stretched out on the bed, his muscles relaxing. "Is it gonna bother you if I need to get up early for work?"

She shook her head and lowered it again. "You're not getting up at five in the morning, are you?"

"Not that early."

She burrowed deeper into his embrace. He couldn't think of anything more perfect than falling asleep with her all soft and naked in his arms. That didn't mean he could resist teasing them both a little.

"Hey," he whispered into her hair.

"Hmm?"

"We're sharing a bed and we forgot to build a pillow wall."

She swatted at his chest. "It's a pillow barrier, thank you very much. I'm never going to live that down, am I?"

"Nope. But I'm one hundred percent into you using me as your personal pillow, so it all works out."

She smiled and pressed a kiss to the spot on his chest she'd swatted. He ran a finger over her arm and down her hip, making her sigh.

No, once definitely wouldn't be enough.

Chapter Eighteen

The next morning, Audrey went into the kitchen to make coffee while Luke took a shower. They weren't quite at the taking-showers-together stage of things. She didn't know what stage they were at. She didn't even know whether or not he wanted to do this again.

I do. Oh my God, I do.

While she waited for the coffee to brew, she also waited for the dreaded second thoughts to pop into her head. They didn't come. She couldn't regret anything that good. She shivered, images from last night flashing through her head like photographs.

No one else had ever focused on her that much in bed, been that attentive. No one else had ever been that dedicated to her pleasure.

In addition to those things, sex with Luke had been really fucking hot. She grinned to herself and did a shimmy as she pulled the half-and-half out of the fridge.

The shower turned off, and the coffee machine gurgled to a stop. Perfect timing. She pulled two mugs out of the cabinet and filled up hers, adding a splash of half-and-half and some sugar. Cupping the mug in her hands, she leaned against the kitchen counter, trying to go for

Look, I'm so casual and sexy, I'm not at all wondering what happens next.

Luke walked into the kitchen—fully dressed, unfortunately—and smiled at her. The smile bloomed over his face. The dimples came out. His eyes lit up. And she was so, so gone.

"I made coffee," she said, because what else could she say? *Take me now right here on the kitchen floor?*

He ignored the coffee and came over to her, looping an arm around her waist and pressing a kiss to her temple. "Thanks. And thanks for letting me use your shower. And the extra toothbrush."

She took a deep breath of him. He smelled like her shampoo. "You're welcome."

When he let her go to fill up his coffee mug, she stifled a groan of protest into her own cup. If she had her way, they'd stand there a while longer with his warmth surrounding her. He could hold her, and she could keep sniffing him—which, yes, was weird. He smelled like her citrus verbena shower gel and shampoo, but it smelled different on him. Earthier. It kind of got her going. Then again, everything about him did.

He poured a cup and put the coffee pot back into the machine. Was she imagining things, or was the set of his shoulders a little looser this morning? He usually held himself so tight around her, like he was holding something back. He'd even tried to last night before she told him not to.

When he let go, it was glorious. She wanted to watch him unravel again and again.

He turned around to face her, leaning on the opposite counter. They both sipped their coffee. Something hummed between them—desire, attraction, curiosity.

Unsaid words. She set her mug down on the counter. They needed to have this conversation, preferably before he left for work.

He beat her to it.

"I really enjoyed last night," he said.

Relief swept through her—perhaps too soon, but she didn't care. "Me, too."

A teasing smile played at his lips, and he set down his cup next to hers. He reached for her, his big hands wrapping around her waist. She held back a shiver.

"How many rules do you think we've broken at this point?" he asked, his lips grazing over her ear.

She tilted her head to the side, trying to encourage him to move his mouth lower. "I don't know. All of them."

He pulled back and stared down at her. "I can think of one I don't want to break."

"Which one?"

"No seeing anyone else. If we're going to do this, I don't want anyone else. Just you."

Just you. The words reverberated in her head, in her heart. "When you say 'if we're going to do this,' you mean 'sleep together for the rest of the summer,' right?"

"Yes." He gave her an indulgent smile, and she couldn't help kissing it right off his lips.

"We're on the same page, then."

"Okay, good."

They both laughed.

He played with the belt on her robe, letting the ends slide through his fingers. Last night he did the same thing with her dress right before he took it off. A steady thrum started between her legs. It only intensified when he bent his head to kiss her neck. She slid a hand into his damp hair.

His next words came between kisses pressed to her neck and throat. Her collarbone. The space between her breasts. "When can we see each other again?"

"Tonight?" *But you can fuck me right now if you want to.*

He chuckled, all low and sexy. "I can do tonight."

Wait, did she have other plans? And could she cancel them for sex plans?

Oh, crap, she did have plans. If she backed out of them, she'd feel like such a shithead she wouldn't be able to enjoy herself with Luke. Rescheduling wasn't an option, either.

With a sigh, she took a step backward. "I just remembered I'm supposed to get together with Natalie and Grace. Natalie got a promotion at work, and we're going to celebrate."

"Tomorrow?" he asked.

She pulled her phone out of her robe pocket to check her calendar. All clear. "How about you come over after work? We can order food. Maybe watch a movie."

He reached for her free hand and pulled her toward him again. "That sounds perfect." He gave her a quick, soft kiss, as chaste as can be. Her pulse sped up anyway.

"It's a date." When she kissed him again, she had to force herself to break the kiss. He'd told her last night before they fell asleep that he had to start work at eight, and it was already seven thirty. She stepped out of his embrace. "You have to go to work."

"I do. Doesn't mean I want to, though."

"I don't want you to, either," she said softly.

Reluctantly, she walked him to the door. In her fantasy, he would untie her robe and drag her back to bed, but he had a TV show to film and construction-type things to do. She had her own work, too.

He gave her another kiss. "See you tomorrow."

After he left and she'd closed the door behind him, she stood there for a moment with her fingers touching her lips.

She couldn't get the smile off her face even if she tried.

Luke left Audrey's apartment with memories of last night seared into his brain. Morning-afters could be awkward, but they'd done okay. That conversation in her kitchen went easier than anticipated. Not that he expected her to freak out, but she was all about boundaries. He figured she'd want to set some after last night.

In the shower, he'd run through several different scenarios as to how things would go. He'd landed on her saying, *Hey, you know last night was a one-time thing, right?* as the winner.

But she didn't say that. She wanted to see him again. Well, get naked together again. They did plenty of seeing each other already. He could do with more getting naked. He'd have to wait until tomorrow night, but hey, he had enough things to keep him busy in the meantime.

After a quick stop at home to change, he went to the Victorian and got to work. The house buzzed with activity—camera people getting shots of the construction crew carrying new countertops for the bathroom vanities into the house. Crew members installing new tile in the guest bathroom. Producers milling around, bleary eyed and filling up coffee cups as they started their days. One of them approached Luke to go over that day's shooting schedule. Bathroom renovations in the morning, then talking head interviews in the afternoon.

The renovation was coming together nicely. They'd finished the kitchen and moved on to the bathrooms. The network executives loved shots of him lifting heavy things and hammering shit, so the camera crew filmed him installing a vanity in the master bathroom. He'd just finished the installation when Aidan showed up to inspect his own handiwork with more camera people not far behind.

Technically his cousin's guest role should have ended once Aidan finished building the vanities and cabinets, but he kept showing up and trying to make himself useful. As far as Luke could tell, Aidan's idea of "useful" was eating free food from craft services and wearing a T-shirt emblazoned with Murphy Construction and Remodeling's Instagram handle. When Luke had pointed out maybe he didn't need to wear that specific shirt, Aidan said, "Gotta get more followers, cuz" and shoved another Pringle into his mouth.

Aidan stood in the bathroom, opening up the cabinet doors and looking pleased with himself. He was good at woodwork, and he knew it.

"Didn't trust me to handle the installation myself?" Luke said.

"You did a nice job. I wanted to stop by to check it out."

Or he wanted to try to get on camera again with his Instagram shirt.

"Did you know you're all over Twitter this morning?" Aidan asked, which was a hell of a non sequitur.

"Again? What now?"

With the short shelf life of most viral tweets, people should have calmed down with the #TwitterBae stuff by now. He and Audrey still had enough people interested to get attention, but nowhere near the peak of three weeks ago.

Aidan pulled his phone out of his pocket and tap-tap-tapped at the screen. "You got caught making out with your girlfriend, and people are losing their shit."

Dammit. Wait—being all over Twitter was a good thing. That was the whole point of the fake relationship. But being part of the latest viral tweet could go downhill quickly, depending on people's reactions to it. Luke waved off the camera people. This part didn't need to be filmed, no matter how much the producers would love it.

"Uh, define 'losing their shit.'" Luke walked down the hall, out of earshot of the crew. Aidan followed.

"They're all screaming about couple goals and how hot you both are."

Oh, Jesus Christ. "How do you even find this stuff out?"

"It gets retweeted into my feed. You'd know this if you spent more time on Twitter." Aidan shook his head, his mouth creased in a frown. "And here I thought you upped your social media game."

"I upped it," Luke said. What was his life that he had to get defensive over how often he used Twitter? "I don't have a ton of time to spend scrolling my feed. What's this about getting caught? People took a picture of us?"

"Yeah." Aidan handed his phone over. "I guess some fan saw you outside a bar last night."

The image was blurry, but yep—someone had caught him and Audrey kissing by his truck. He tried not to bristle at the invasion of privacy. They'd created their relationship for public consumption and to get people invested in them. Maybe not invested enough for fans to snap these kinds of pictures, but if this could help Audrey's business and she was okay with it, he didn't mind.

He should check to make sure she was okay with it. Just in case she wasn't.

Swallowing hard, he looked at the picture again. Would Audrey really be okay with it, or would she feel the same way he did right now? His heart sped up looking at the photo, at how he held her and kissed her. Last night was special. Last night was theirs. And now one of his best moments in recent memory was out there for everyone to see. His *feelings* were out there for everyone to see. And they were realer than anything he'd posted since this whole thing started.

Fuck. Maybe he did mind after all.

Luke gave the phone back. "I don't know what to say."

"I thought you'd look at this and growl at my phone or something." It would be like Aidan to show him something with the express purpose of pissing him off.

Luke shrugged, trying to tamp down the surge of protectiveness and irritation he'd felt seeing the photo. "People can post what they want. And it's taken from far enough way that it's not that bad."

"Something's up with you."

"Nothing's up with me."

Aidan glanced at the picture on his phone screen, then back up at Luke. Recognition dawned on his face. He looked like the GIF of surprised Pikachu that Erin used in her texts sometimes. "You're getting laid."

Thank you, Captain Obvious. Luke sighed.

Aidan scratched at his jaw and glanced at his phone again. "I guess the picture makes that pretty clear."

He did not want to talk about anything having to do

with his sex life with his cousin, now or ever. "Do I need to check my mentions?"

He'd turned off notifications at the start of this whole thing after too many tweets and DMs from people sending him cheesy pickup lines—pun intended. If he needed to see something, it would make its way to him eventually. Erin would tell him, or Aidan, or Jessica the publicist, who had been surprisingly quiet ever since the Cubs game.

"Nah. The reaction is all positive. You're the sweethearts of social media."

"We are?"

Aidan gave Luke's arm a gentle punch. "Yeah, you are. Shit, you guys should get Sweethearts of Social Media T-shirts. Or Social Media Sweethearts. Which one do you think sounds better?"

Neither, but Aidan didn't wait for an answer. "The guy who made my Insta shirt will give you a discount if you put my name down as a referral," he said.

"No."

"No to the shirts? Or no, you don't want a discount?" Aidan shook his head. "I can't believe you want to pay full price."

"No to everything."

"Your loss. It would be a great marketing opportunity. You could make a website and sell those shirts."

"Aidan."

"Yeah?"

"Never mention the shirts to me again."

Aidan scoffed. "You should see what Audrey thinks. I bet she'd want to do it."

There would only be one way to get Aidan to drop

this topic: distract him with something else. Like his desire to appear on camera.

"I have to get back to work. Wanna stick around and help?"

"Yeah, I will. But man, I'm telling you, you could have a nice side hustle if you got those shirts made."

Luke's phone dinged. He pulled it out of his pocket. A notification for a new email. Huh. Most people who needed to get in touch with him called or texted. After reading the first line in the preview, he clicked into the message.

Valerie's assistant wanted to know if he had time for a phone call next week to discuss "some exciting news."

It better not involve T-shirts.

Chapter Nineteen

Since Audrey got back from the Michigan trip, the rest of July had sped by on fast-forward. Between photography jobs, social media, and spending time with Luke, the takeout and TV hangouts with her best friends had fallen by the wayside. Trying to juggle everything was becoming a challenge.

Working for herself was supposed to mean having more work-life balance, not less. Her business was still new, though, and she needed to make money. That meant taking as many jobs as she could and using social media to increase her visibility. Things would even out eventually.

Tonight, she needed to chat, relax, and hang out in her pajamas with her favorite people—even if it meant she had to wait until tomorrow to see Luke again. Natalie's promotion deserved to be celebrated. She'd been working for a while at a marketing agency and just gotten a bump up from marketing coordinator to marketing manager. The title change meant more money and that she got to supervise people. Audrey loved seeing her friends succeed. Their success was important. Her friends were important, period.

Once Natalie and Grace each texted to say they were

on their way, Audrey ordered pizza. It showed up right before Grace walked through the door. Natalie arrived ten minutes later.

"Sorry I'm late," she said. "I was writing a nasty note to my new neighbor."

Which was easily one of the most Natalie reasons ever for being late to something.

"Why?" Grace asked. She opened the pizza box Audrey had set on one of the kitchen counters and put a couple slices on her plate.

"Do we want to know?" Audrey handed a plate to Natalie.

"Because he's the most annoying human who's ever lived, that's why. He has no concept of an inside voice. Or that most people go to bed before midnight." Natalie huffed. "Anyway, I said what I needed to say, and now I'm going to enjoy being away from him. Let's eat and watch some drag queens."

They took their pizza and drinks over to the couch, where they settled in and turned on the TV. Audrey clicked through the menus on the screen to get to her DVR, where she had the newest episode of *RuPaul's Drag Race All Stars* saved for this occasion. Before she could start the episode, the show playing in the background on her TV made her freeze.

"Now it's time for today's viral tweets," the show's host said. "HomeTV hunk Luke Murphy has been spotted getting hot and heavy with his new girlfriend in Chicago. Check out this picture posted by a fan on Twitter."

She immediately exited the screen with the DVR recordings. *Hollywood Tonight* was one of those too-bright, too-cheery shows full of celebrity gossip and interviews.

She never watched it except when she happened to turn on the TV at the time it aired. Like now.

"What the actual fuck are they talking about?" Audrey said.

A blurry picture of her and Luke kissing outside the bar last night flashed on the screen. Whoever took the photo had zoomed in too far, but it was unmistakably them standing next to his truck. She was up on her tip-toes, her fists in his shirt as they kissed. One of his hands rested at her waist, the other on her lower back, low enough it was almost on her ass. Hot and heavy, indeed.

They really needed to stop making out in public.

But again—what the actual fuck?

"Damn," Natalie said.

"Oh my." That was Grace.

"Am I legitimately famous now?" Audrey gripped the remote hard enough she might break it. "Also, do I not have a name? I'm just some famous guy's girlfriend?"

Natalie gently pried the remote from Audrey's death grip and changed the channel, even though the show had already moved on to something else. "That show is garbage. You know that, right?"

"Objectively, yes. But that was—that was *private*."

Audrey's phone, which sat on the side table next to her, lit up with a new text. Mom. She picked up the phone.

Mom: Audrey! You're on TV kissing a very attractive man. Why haven't you told us you have a boyfriend? And he's famous!

Great, her mom had seen the picture. She suppressed a groan. The screen went dark for a few seconds before it lit up again.

Mom: Dad says he better not be a jagoff like the last one.

She turned the screen off. She'd deal with that later. Thank God her parents didn't do social media. Technically, Mom was on Facebook, but that was only to keep track of what various aunts and cousins were up to.

"It was private," Grace said, her voice serious. "It sucks someone had to take a picture and post it on the internet."

Audrey picked at her pizza. "I guess it's part of dating someone in the public eye."

"It shouldn't have to be," Natalie said. "And, no offense, but it's not like he's a megastar. I don't know why they're even showing that."

"TwitterBae," Grace said. "That's why."

"Slow news day if you ask me," Audrey grumbled.

Grace poked her arm. "I have a question."

"Yes?"

"Are you still taking things slow?" Grace did an exaggerated eyebrow wiggle.

"I think she wants to know if you've seen him naked," Natalie said, taking a bite of her pizza.

Grace gasped theatrically, all mock offended. "Natalie Marie, how dare you." She turned to Audrey. "Yeah, we need to know if you've seen the smokin' hot bod."

She couldn't help smiling. "I have. Shortly after that picture was taken."

Her friends whooped. They were weirdos. But they were her weirdos, and she was theirs.

With the mood lightened after all the whooping and talk of smokin' hot bods, they ate their pizza and started *Drag Race*. She'd been looking forward to the episode, but she couldn't focus.

What did Luke think about that picture? Did he even know about it? It could be all over Twitter, and he might have no idea. She'd changed her notification settings to only get alerted when people she followed tagged her. Luke might have a similar setup. She didn't need to get a push notification every time someone liked a tweet or mentioned her. People who wanted to contact her for legitimate business reasons could go to her website.

Anyway, she and Luke wanted publicity. They'd gotten it. But publicity she controlled—like their fake dates and cute selfies—was different from some random person taking their picture and posting it for the world to see. Yes, they'd been in public, but it was still an intimate moment. It wasn't meant to be splashed all over the internet and TV.

At least people moved on fast these days.

She tried to forget about it and enjoy the queens' eleganza extravaganza. But she couldn't get that picture—or Luke—out of her mind. Something rose up from deep inside her, a desire to see him, to talk to him. To find out how he felt about the picture being everywhere.

Later, after her friends had sashayed away, she picked up her phone, bypassing the notifications on the lock screen to open her text thread with Luke. She stared at the blinking cursor.

Are you up? she typed.

No. No no no. She backspaced immediately. He'd think she was booty-texting him. As much as she might welcome a repeat of last night, that wasn't why she wanted to contact him. It was way too late for him to come over, anyway. Too late for her, at least.

The cursor taunted her. She didn't know what she wanted, or what to say. Mostly she wanted to see his words on the screen and know he was on the other side reading hers. That kind of connection meant everything in moments like these.

But she couldn't say that. It was too real. They didn't do real.

Last night was real.

His touch, his kisses, the way he looked at her—that couldn't be faked. And she wouldn't want it to be.

They had plans for tomorrow. If she texted him now, she didn't want him to get the wrong idea, or to think she was getting attached. They'd decided this morning to have sex for the rest of the summer, not have an actual relationship. She intended for it to stay that way.

She should go to bed. Maybe by the morning, this feeling would pass.

As she brushed her teeth, her phone buzzed in the pocket of her pajama pants. Probably Grace or Natalie texting to say they made it home okay. They didn't always send those kinds of texts, but sometimes if they left her place late enough, they did.

After completing the rest of her bedtime routine, she checked her phone to make sure. Oddly enough, like he'd been thinking of her at the same time she was thinking of him, Luke had texted her.

Luke: Hey. I should have contacted you earlier, but I was tied up with filming most of the day.

Contacted her earlier just because? Or contacted her earlier because the entire internet, her mom, her best friends, and everyone who watched *Hollywood Tonight* saw them making out with his hand on her butt?

Another message popped up.

Luke: We went viral. Again. But you might already know that.

Audrey: We also made Hollywood Tonight. Yay. She added the upside-down smiley face emoji.

Luke: Shit. I'm sorry. I really should have texted you earlier.

Audrey: Having the picture all over Twitter is one thing, but my mom saw it on TV. So did my friends.

Luke: Are you okay?

Her stomach clenched at the question. She didn't want to have the rest of this conversation over text. Before she could think twice, she tapped the button to call him.

"Hey." Luke's voice rumbled down the line. "How are you?"

"I'm annoyed at having a private moment shared everywhere, but I'm fine. No one will care in a few days, right?" She laughed, but it came out sounding sad and tired.

"Probably not. It's this whole TwitterBae thing." He said the word "TwitterBae" with such disdain, she had to hold back another laugh. "I'm all for using social media if it's going to help us career-wise. I even thought this morning that maybe you'd be okay with the picture if it helped your business. But now…"

She burst out laughing for real this time. "I don't think it's going to help. For what it's worth, I don't think it's going to hurt, either."

"Like you said, no one will care in a few days."

"I wouldn't care if they photographed us having dinner or walking down the street, but *that*?" She closed her eyes for a second. The image flashed behind her eyelids. "Now I need to have an uncomfortable conversation with my mom. She texted to ask why I didn't tell her I had a boyfriend and called you 'a very attractive man.'"

"Oh. Uh. That's—"

She smiled. She could practically see him rubbing the back of his neck at that comment.

"Well, you *are* a very attractive man," she teased. She couldn't resist. "But I'm going to have to tell my mom about us."

"Is she going to want to meet me?"

Audrey flopped on top of her bed. Ugh. She should have thought of that herself. The minute Mom found out she was dating someone, meeting him would be the next step.

"Oh, she definitely will. My mom is cool, though. And my dad won't pull any of that overprotective stuff some dads like to pull, but he used to be a reporter. He'll have a ton of questions. He'll also thoroughly research you beforehand." When Luke didn't say anything, she added, "But let's cross that bridge when we get to it."

"You met my family. It only seems fair I meet yours."

"True." That didn't mean she was looking forward to it. "I'll let you know."

"I'll be there whenever you need me to be."

In the ensuing pause—the kind where both people wanted to get off the phone but no one wanted to be the one to say goodbye first—she almost asked him to come over.

Not for sex. Okay, mostly not for sex. But he had this way of quietly providing comfort she wanted to wrap herself up in. He cared. He wanted to make sure she was okay. He was good and kind.

"Thanks," she said.

"You know, we're in this together. You don't have to deal with it all by yourself."

She couldn't have picked a better person to fake date.

She just needed to remember not to get fake confused for real.

Chapter Twenty

The kissing picture wouldn't die. Two days later, it was still going strong.

Most of that was thanks to a person in the photo walking past Luke and Audrey with a bored look on their face. People had latched on to that look and were using it as a reaction to other posts. They photoshopped Bored Look Person out of the original picture and put them in famous works of art and iconic photos. The picture's virality had little to do with Luke and Audrey anymore, but they were still all over the place, making out next to his truck.

Bored Look Person identified themself on Twitter and seemed to love the attention. At least someone was happy about it.

Luke saw a few of the memes that morning, but for the rest of the day, he put it out of his mind and concentrated on work. There wasn't much he could do about Twitter. The picture and the memes would go away. It just might take longer than he originally thought.

After they finished at the Victorian for the day, Aidan talked him into going out for a drink "because we never get to hang out." They saw each other all the time, but he could stand to get out more. It was one drink. And

Colin, Aidan's brother, planned to join them. Luke hadn't seen him in a while.

That evening, they settled in at the bar at Old Irving Brewing Company and ordered beers. No sooner had Luke taken his first sip when his phone buzzed in his pocket. He took it out to make sure it wasn't anything urgent.

Audrey: Can I see you tonight?

A bolt of desire shot its way up his spine. He'd just seen Audrey last night for dinner and a movie they mostly didn't watch, but fuck, he wanted to see her again.

Luke: I'm at a bar with my cousins, but give me an hour and I can be at your place.

Audrey: I need to see you sooner than that. It's important.

Luke: Is everything okay?

Audrey: I'm fine!

"Who are you texting?" Aidan asked, his eyes lighting up. "Is it Audrey?"

"Mind your own business."

After Luke's dismissal, Aidan turned to Colin and said, "I keep telling him they should get T-shirts made, but he doesn't want to hear it."

I can leave now if it's important, he wrote back.

Audrey: Or I can come to you, if you're cool with that? I know you're with your cousins, but it'll be quick. It's nothing bad. Just something we need to talk about, and it's better to discuss in person.

Luke: I'm at Old Irving Brewing Company. You met me here once.

They came here the night he'd told her about the network's deal and this whole plan got set into motion. Hard to believe that was only a month ago.

Audrey: I remember. I'll be there in 20 minutes. 15 if traffic isn't bad. She put a crossed-fingers emoji at the end of the text.

"How are things going with her?" Aidan asked.

Ah, shit. If she came here, she'd have to meet his cousins. What had he been thinking?

He hadn't been thinking. She said she needed to see him, and he forgot about everything else.

"Things are good. Kind of casual," he said, setting his phone face down on the bar. He took a drink and looked up at one of the TVs. A Cubs game was on. They were playing the Pirates, like at the game he and Audrey went to. Everything reminded him of her. "She's going to stop by in a bit, so please don't act weird or mention T-shirts."

Aidan sat back from the bar and crossed his arms over his chest. "I'm trying to help with your branding. Colin said it's a good idea, and he has an MBA."

"I did not say it was a good idea," Colin said. "I said it could be a potential revenue stream with the right marketing."

"Same thing." Aidan waved a dismissive hand in his brother's direction. "Anyway, what's Audrey coming here for?"

"She's nearby and wanted to drop in to say hi." What

was one more lie at this point? Over the past month, he'd become a pro at telling them.

Aidan and Colin both looked at him with raised eyebrows.

"What?"

"Nothing," Colin said quickly, turning his attention to the game on TV.

Aidan clapped his hands and rubbed them together. "Let's get some food." He picked up a menu from the bar.

Well, that was strange. Had he missed something?

He didn't have time to think about it, because a few minutes later, Audrey walked into the bar. Their eyes met, and he held her gaze as she walked over to him. She didn't look as distressed as he'd expected based on her texts. A little tense in the shoulders, and twisting the strap of her purse between her fingers. Otherwise, she was as sunny and beautiful as ever.

Damn, he wanted to touch her. Maybe he'd get the chance to later tonight.

He hopped off his barstool and met her halfway across the room.

"Hey," he said, bending to give her a kiss on the cheek. "Do you want to talk here, or should we get a table?"

"Here is fine." She peered around him to where Aidan and Colin sat. "Are those your cousins?"

They walked over to the guys, and Luke made some brief introductions. Thankfully Aidan got distracted by baseball and didn't start asking Audrey about T-shirts.

"Actually," Audrey said, her voice low, "could we sit at the other end of the bar?"

Good idea. His cousins were nosy as shit. He guided her over to the other side of the room and they each took a seat. "Can I get you a drink?"

"A Moscow mule, please. It was amazing the last time we were here."

Once they'd ordered, she angled herself to face him. "I'm sorry if my text freaked you out. But that picture is everywhere."

"Does it really have anything to do with us now, though? It's all about the person looking at us."

"Still—we need to reclaim the narrative. Put our own picture out there."

He should have guessed. What did he expect? That because they'd had sex a couple times, she would stop caring about the performative aspect of their relationship? Stop caring about social media?

They were only hooking up. This was all still just for show.

He could probably use the reminder.

"I didn't want to crash your night out, but I thought if I stopped here we could take a quick picture together," Audrey said. "We need to get out in front of this."

"Right now?"

"I know my text made it seem more urgent than you probably think it is, but I was looking at Twitter and freaking out. I didn't want to wait, even if it was just an hour, or a day, to try to fix this."

"I thought you didn't care either way. That you were okay with waiting for everything to blow over."

"That was before it became a meme."

"At least we're not in the memes, as far as I've seen."

"It's made more people see the original picture. An old coworker sent me a Facebook message with a snarky comment about how she always knew I had a hidden wild side." Audrey sighed and shook her head. "She added that the entire department was surprised when she showed them the photo."

"Shit. I'm sorry." She had terrible former coworkers. Who did something like that? And who thought kissing someone in public meant a person had a wild side?

"I know I shouldn't care, but it was jarring to get a message like that, especially from someone I used to work with." The bartender set Audrey's drink in front of her, and she curled her hands around the copper mug. "Obviously I unfriended her. I should have done it a long time ago."

Audrey took a drink. After she set the mug back down, she pulled out her phone. "Take a selfie with me?"

"Yeah, sure."

They took a few pictures together. After Audrey was satisfied they had a decent shot, she also took a few pictures of the bar, her mug, and one of Luke's glass, which had the bar's name stamped on it.

"It worked out that you were here," she said. "When I post this, I can say this is where we had one of our first dates."

"Does it count as a date? I remember saying it wasn't one."

"Details." She rolled her eyes. "It counts."

She smiled, and he smiled back. He'd been so nervous that night, telling her about the network's offer, asking her to be his partner in this publicity stunt. And what had she said? *If you're getting professional advancement out of it, I am, too.*

At first he'd felt relief she agreed, and then a wave of admiration. This woman knew what she wanted. She had plans and ambition. And he should have known right then and there he wouldn't be able to keep this thing with her fake for long.

He wanted to kiss her so badly right now, he vibrated with need. Turning toward her, he took the hand closest to him and threaded their fingers together. "Would it be bad if I kissed you here?"

She leaned in close, definitely within kissing distance. "We need to stop kissing in public." Her voice had gone husky. That alone had him half hard.

"You're right."

Neither of them moved. His desire for her pulsed through him, made his whole body ache. They stared at each other, electricity and possibility charging the air between them.

Right at the moment where he couldn't take it anymore, Audrey slid off her stool. "I should go." She trailed her fingers across his back as she walked past him. His back tingled like she'd touched his bare skin. She leaned in close to say in his ear, "I'll be up late, though."

He'd leave with her right now if he could.

He turned to watch her go. Her jeans hugged her curves like they'd been made for her. The sway of her hips had him mesmerized. She glanced over her shoulder and gave him a wink.

She knew exactly what she did to him. And she liked it just as much as he did.

How soon could he get out of here?

"Are you the guy from the Twitter thing?"

Some guy a few seats down—some standard issue white brodude in a Cubs hat—had asked the question, breaking into Luke's thoughts.

Luke shifted in his seat. He was used to being recognized in public for *Retro Renovations*. Twitter, not so much. With a slight shake of his head, he picked up his glass and drank.

"Nah, man, you are. I saw that picture of you and your girl." Luke's head jerked in the guy's direction. Satisfied he had Luke's attention, he continued, "You tapping that? 'Cause, dude, I would. She's got nice big—" He started to raise his hands in front of his chest.

The rest of the man's sentence died on his lips as Luke stood up and stared him down. He clenched his hands into fists at his sides. This fucking prick.

The guy laughed. "What're you going to do? Beat me up?"

He had never beat up anybody in his life, but this dude might be the first. In a steady voice, he said, "Yes."

"Okay," the guy said. His bar stool screeched against the hardwood floor as he stood. "Let's go."

People were looking at them now. Luke knew he was swimming in the sludge of toxic masculinity, too much alcohol (on the other guy's part, not his), and irrational anger, and he still wanted to punch this asshole in the face.

Neither of them made a move for what felt like a long time but was probably only a matter of seconds. Then the guy reared back and took a wild swing.

A hand on Luke's shoulder dragged him backward and away from the guy before his fist could connect. Aidan said in Luke's ear, "Come on. What the hell are you doing?"

The noise of the bar flooded his ears again, like someone had turned the volume dial way down low and back up to full blast. With a hand still on his shoulder, Aidan marched him back over to his original seat. The asshole who'd tried to punch him stumbled out the door, his friends not far behind.

"You wanna tell us what that was about?" Colin asked.

"That guy was a jerk."

Aidan shook his head. "I thought you were gonna get in a bar fight."

"Luke, in a bar fight," Colin muttered, snorting into his glass of beer.

"What was he being a jerk about?" Aidan asked. "You looked like you were trying to murder him with your eyes."

"Audrey. Saying stuff about her body and 'tapping that.'"

"He's just some drunk asshole," Colin said.

Aidan slid back onto his stool. "If things with her are casual, why do you even care what some random drunk is running his mouth about?"

"Because he's fucking disgusting."

He'd been around other straight, cisgender men his whole life. He'd heard worse—not that it excused the brodude's comments. Something about that particular guy at that particular moment got under his skin.

"If he's making those kinds of comments, yeah, he's a jerk. But I don't think I've ever seen you react that way to anything," Aidan said. "That was intense."

Because…because it was more than some guy in a bar talking shit. It was some guy in a bar talking shit about Audrey. He'd only stared the other man down, but if Aidan hadn't pulled him away, Luke might have thrown a punch for the first time in his life.

He ran a hand through his hair. "Look, it's over. Can we forget about it?"

Colin and Aidan mumbled their assent. All three

of them turned their attention to the TV. At least they dropped the topic and now he could pretend to be interested in this game.

For all his bravado tonight, he was the one who felt like he'd gotten his ass kicked.

He had no idea what to do about it.

Chapter Twenty-One

Over the past week, Audrey and Luke spent more evenings together than not, eating dinner, talking, and ending up in her bed—sometimes in that order, sometimes not. In between, she did photo shoots, booked more clients, and tried to stay on top of work.

She hadn't seen Luke in a couple days when she stopped by at lunchtime on a Tuesday to get photos of the renovation. With his filming schedule and her appointments with clients, she hadn't had much of a chance to follow through on taking pictures of him at the house. Back when he first asked her, she did say "schedule permitting." Lately, her schedule was all over the place. Some things had to drop off her calendar. Like her usual volunteer slot at the animal shelter. She had to find time to go back soon. She missed it.

She went through the front gate and down a path along the side of the house, her camera bag knocking against her hip. Luke had told her to come around to the back door so she wouldn't have to traverse any hazardous areas inside. At the end of the path, she walked up a small set of steps leading to a deck and the back door. A tall, dark-haired white guy in his late twenties stood there checking his phone. Aidan, Luke's cousin. They'd met briefly that night at the bar last week.

"Hey, Audrey," he said, giving her a wave and a wide smile. He radiated easygoing charm.

"Hi. Is Luke around?"

"He should be in the kitchen, right through there." Aidan inclined his head toward the back door and reached out to open the door for her.

She thanked him and walked inside, stopping right in the doorway. Wow. It looked completely different in here from the last time. No longer a work in progress, the kitchen gleamed with a white-and-gray tile backsplash, white cabinets, and stainless steel appliances. An island with a stone countertop—marble or maybe quartz—stood in the center of the room. Three barstools were pulled up to the island to create a small eat-in dining area.

She moved into the kitchen and ran her hand along the edge of the island. The smooth surface of the countertop was cool under her fingertips. She opened her bag and took out her camera, pulling the strap over her head and removing the lens cap. After positioning herself in a corner of the room to get a wide view, she raised the camera to her eye. Her finger came down on the shutter at the exact moment Luke walked into the kitchen— and into her shot.

Oh, well. She'd never complain about having another picture of him.

She peeked at the photo on her camera's screen. Her breath caught.

His smile was bright and genuine. His eyes crinkled at the corners. That look was for her and only her. A strange sensation overtook her, a floaty kind of lightheadedness. *If he looks at me that way, how do I look at him?*

She exited the screen and glanced up from the camera just in time for him to greet her. He slid an arm around her waist and gave her a kiss on the cheek, his stubble gently scraping her skin. "Hi."

"This room looks incredible. Did you do all of this?"

"Not on my own."

"So humble."

He moved to face her, circling his other arm around her waist. She wound her arms around his neck, careful not to bump her camera against him. Ugh, silly camera. She couldn't get as close as she wanted.

"I have an amazing crew," he said. "No way could I do all of this on my own."

"But you designed it."

He ducked his head and smiled. He was so cute, sometimes she couldn't stand it.

She placed a soft kiss on his lips. Before she could get carried away—there was a camera crew around here somewhere, after all—she pulled back. She let her arms fall to her sides. "I'm going to get pictures of the kitchen, and then we can get shots of the rest of the house. It might also be good to get some of you in action."

"Yeah, of course."

Before Audrey could resume her position in the corner of the room, a young woman with a pink pixie cut walked into the kitchen. She wore a headset, a plain blue T-shirt, and jeans, and she held a clipboard at her side.

She gave Audrey a bright smile. "Hi, are you Audrey? I'm Katie, one of the assistant producers."

Audrey should have known if someone from HomeTV caught wind of her being here, they'd jump on the opportunity to get her involved in the show. She waited for the unease to creep over her skin. Instead her body tingled with excitement.

"Nice to meet you," Katie said, holding out her hand for Audrey to shake. Audrey took it and returned the greeting. "Since you're here, I was wondering if you'd be willing to appear on camera. Nothing major, maybe just you and Luke interacting."

If someone had asked Audrey a few weeks ago if she'd want to appear on national television, the answer would've been no. But now? As long as she didn't have to be part of some manufactured storyline for the show, it could be good for business.

Ha, manufactured storyline. Most of her life was one these days.

"Luke mentioned you'd be coming over to take photos." Katie pulled a piece of paper from her clipboard. "We could get some footage of you doing that." She smiled the same bright smile as before. "People are invested in you guys. It'd be good for the show."

Luke walked over to them from the other side of the room, where he'd been quietly observing their interaction. He stood next to Audrey. "What's going on?"

Katie looked between the two of them. "I was asking Audrey if she'd be okay with us filming her."

"Absolutely not," Luke said at the same time Audrey said, "I'm okay with it."

He turned to her. "I thought you didn't want to be on camera while you were here. Didn't you say you had to think about it?"

"I thought about it."

Luke said to Katie, "Can we have a moment, please?" Katie nodded and stepped aside, saying something into the microphone on her headset. Audrey didn't catch it, but she bet it had something to do with her.

"You don't have to do this," Luke said. "Just because Katie asked doesn't mean you need to say yes."

"I want to."

"But why?"

Audrey shrugged. "I'm looking at it as a business opportunity. Are *you* okay with me appearing on camera?"

He hesitated, his gaze darting over to where Katie stood, talking into her headset again. "It's your call."

"Luke." She let out a long sigh. He wasn't as into the public aspect of their relationship as she was, but if he didn't want her to do this, he needed to say so. "Do you not want me to be on camera?"

"I'm not saying that." He held up his hands. "I just wanted to make sure. I don't want you to do anything you're not comfortable with."

"If I didn't want to do it, I wouldn't." She turned away from him to address the producer. "Katie, is there anything you need me to do before we get started?"

Katie walked back over to hand the piece of paper to Audrey. "We'll just need you to sign a release."

Once she'd signed it, a couple camera people came in the room. Someone else—a director, maybe—wanted to get footage of her walking up the street to the house and going inside to greet Luke. They ran through it three times, the director telling her how to kiss Luke ("chastely—the HomeTV audience doesn't want a make-out session"), and that she didn't have to say anything because what really mattered was getting a kiss on camera.

"This is a little uncomfortable," Audrey whispered to Luke.

He looked down at her. "You know we can stop anytime you want."

"I don't want to stop," she said, staring up at him.

"Yes, keep looking at each other like that," the director said, clapping his hands. "Can you put your arms around her a little more tightly, Luke?"

He did, and they kept looking at each other for another minute, until she started laughing and pressed her forehead to his chest. She overheard Katie say to one of the camera people, "They're *so* cute. Please tell me you got that."

Their relationship was created for the public, but being in front of the cameras—having someone tell her how to kiss Luke, how to look at him, and what to do with their bodies—was something else. She was used to controlling every aspect of her image on social media. Having someone else direct her was strange, especially when it was something as intimate as a kiss.

A wave of relief swept through her once the director got the take he wanted. With the kiss scene finally taken care of, Audrey resumed her position in the corner of the kitchen, getting wide shots from a few different angles. Thankfully she wasn't micromanaged by the director when it came to her photography. She wouldn't have stood for that.

After she got her shots of the kitchen, the camera crew trailed behind them as she and Luke went upstairs to the recently redone bathrooms. Everything was updated and modern, but Luke had kept some of the old stuff and restored it—a clawfoot tub in the master bathroom he said was original to the house, a vintage mirror over the sink, the mosaic black-and-white tile on the floor. All tasteful, all elegant and beautiful.

They moved into the main bedroom, where he was in the middle of refinishing the baseboards and wood trim around the doorframe. She got a few shots of him doing that, although he kept looking at her and asking, "Did you get it yet?" He was not the most patient subject.

She still got decent pictures, though. In most of them, Luke was handsome and serious, his brows knitted in concentration as he worked. His followers would love these photos. If she wanted to bet on it, so would the network.

Seeing him like that was fun, and it got her going. Competence and craftsmanship were incredibly sexy. She tucked her camera back into its bag and gave him a smile.

"I can send these to you later," she said. "It looks like they came out really well. I don't think I'll need to do much editing."

"I'll keep an eye out for them."

The camera crew left them after that to break for lunch. She and Luke headed back downstairs to the kitchen, where Audrey skidded to a halt in the doorway. At the kitchen island, Luke's mom perched on one of the stools, a plastic bag full of takeout containers on the counter in front of her. Luke almost careened right into Audrey's back but steadied himself with a hand on the wall.

His mom likes you. It's fine.

She stood up straighter and walked into the room, approaching the island. "Hi, Mrs. Murphy."

"Audrey! I wasn't expecting to see you here. And please, call me Patti."

Luke came over to stand next to his mom. "What are

you doing here, Mom?" In a different tone, the question might be rude, but he said it with genuine curiosity.

"I worked a half day today, so I thought I'd stop by with lunch." She gestured at the bag.

"You didn't have to do that. They feed us pretty well here."

Patti reached out and patted his cheek. "I know, but I wanted to see you. You're never home anymore."

He lowered his eyes. "Sorry."

"Don't be sorry. It's about time you had a life outside work." Patti looked over at Audrey. Her face lit up with warmth and happiness. "And it's all thanks to Audrey. I'm so glad you're in his life, hon. He's a different person since you came along. I haven't seen him smile this much since before—well, since before his father died."

Luke's throat worked in a hard swallow. "Mom," he said, his voice a quiet warning.

"There used to be this…" Patti pursed her lips. When she spoke again, her voice was as quiet as her son's. "This heaviness that isn't there anymore."

Audrey had wondered about his family situation, but it wasn't any of her business. How long ago had his dad died? Did it happen when he was younger, or in the past couple years? Asking wouldn't be appropriate, so she said, "I'm happy he's happy."

"I hope he makes you happy, too," Patti said. "Because if he doesn't, I'm going to have to have a talk with him."

"I'm right here, Ma," Luke said, but there wasn't much heat behind his indignation.

Audrey laughed. "He does. No need for a talk."

She and Luke looked at each other at the same time. He put his arm around her, pulling her against his side.

She slid an arm around his back. Was he doing this for his mom's benefit, or was this just him being him?

It didn't matter.

"Oh, you kids are adorable," Patti said, beaming at them.

He really did make her happy. Seeing him was often the best part of her day, the part she looked forward to the most. No matter how busy her day had been or what problems she faced, he made things better. When he was around, she felt lighter, more relaxed, less tense.

It's the regular orgasms. They'll do that to you.

What was she doing, thinking about orgasms with his mom right there? Besides, what Patti saw wasn't real. She and Luke might be enjoying each other's company, but that was as deep as it went. Everything else was a construct designed for clicks and likes.

Patti's words echoed in her head—no, they didn't echo. They roared. *I'm so glad you're in his life, hon. He's a different person since you came along.*

Patti saw a happy son with a loving girlfriend who made him smile more than he had in a long time. She didn't just think this was real—she thought it was REAL, in all caps, surrounded by glitter and exploding cartoon hearts.

Shit.

While Luke and his mom took containers out of the bag, Audrey kept a smile on her face even as her insides twisted. For the past week, aside from the thing with the viral photo, she'd been in a bubble, having fun and getting laid on the regular. Now that bubble had been pricked, the air slowly deflating out of it. She and Luke knew what they were doing. They'd come to an agreement that allowed them to reap the benefits of being a couple in public while temporarily acting on their attraction in private.

But other people would get hurt eventually. If Luke was as happy as his mom said he was, he would, too.

Will I get hurt?

Audrey sucked in a breath. No, she wouldn't. She needed to keep her head on straight and stay focused. They were giving their careers a boost and having fun at the same time. That was it. What other people saw or felt was entirely out of her control.

At least that was what she told herself. Looking at Patti's kind smile and the way she adored her son, Audrey questioned whether she might be an asshole for helping him dupe his mother.

She struggled to meet Patti's eyes when the other woman pushed a couple containers across the counter toward her.

"I bought a lot of food," Patti said. "There's an extra pulled pork sandwich and a chicken sandwich. Stay and eat with us."

She should go. But it was thoughtful of Patti to invite her to join them, and Audrey needed to eat. "Sure, I'll stay. Thank you."

She took a seat at the island next to Luke. The lunch should have been awkward, but Patti kept the conversation moving. It went a long way toward helping Audrey ignore the guilt and dread roiling through her.

She had an appointment with a client in an hour. Working would get her mind off things.

It always did.

Out of everything he could have prepared himself for today, "Mom Showing Up Unannounced at My Job Site" hadn't crossed Luke's mind. He especially hadn't considered the possibility of her showing up while Audrey was there.

During their impromptu lunch, Audrey had picked at her sandwich. She sat there with a tight smile that didn't reach her eyes, nodding along to the conversation but not contributing much. When lunch was over, she left with a rushed goodbye and waved off his offer to walk her outside. Which left him in the kitchen with Mom, who kept darting worried looks in his direction while they cleaned up.

"I think I scared her off," Mom said.

You think? That was flippant. He didn't speak to his mother that way. But she had to know parts of their conversation crossed a line. "You laid it on pretty thick. Telling her I haven't been this happy since Dad died?"

"It's true, Luke. She brings out something good in you."

"That's putting a lot of pressure on her. You're making her responsible for my happiness. Imagine how she's gonna feel if we break up someday."

He needed to plant the idea now with Mom that he and Audrey wouldn't last. She was invested in their relationship beyond liking Audrey and being happy for him. Her eyes lit up when she saw the two of them together. She talked about how he was a different person now. He could practically see the wheels turning in her head.

She saw a future that didn't exist.

"I didn't mean it that way," Mom said. She threw the last of the takeout containers in the trash. "I wanted her to know how happy you are. And I hope you don't break up. You seem good together."

"We are."

The words came automatically. They *were* good together. But shit, it was the wrong thing to say if he wanted Mom to stop thinking he and Audrey were meant to last.

Mom gave him a soft look. "I'm sorry if I came on too strong. You're my baby"—he must have made a face, because she rolled her eyes before continuing—"yes, even though you're thirty, you're still my baby, and I want the best for you. I want the best for your sister, too. But I don't worry about her like I worry about you."

"Why not?"

"Erin doesn't carry around the weight of responsibility like you do. I know you felt like you had to take care of us after…" She trailed off, her eyes going glassy. Her shoulders heaved with a big sigh. "But you did your part. It's been eight years. It's past time for you to start living your life for yourself."

She took his hand and squeezed it. He squeezed back and swallowed past a lump in his throat. Dammit.

"I see you starting to do that," Mom said. "I know it's still new with her, but if you want a partner in your life and you make each other happy, I hope things work out. You deserve it."

"Thanks, Mom."

They hugged, and when he pulled back, he waited for the *you're lying to your mother* twinge of guilt and tightness in his chest. They didn't come. She wanted to see him happy, and he *was* happy.

What she said earlier was true. Since he'd started spending time with Audrey, he smiled more. For the first time in a long time, he had something to look forward to besides work—seeing her. The days he didn't see her, he missed her laugh, her touch, her smile. He would catch himself thinking about her throughout the day.

Wait.

Was he starting to have feelings for her?

He couldn't. She hadn't signed up for feelings, and neither did he. Audrey was his fake girlfriend who he happened to be sleeping with for another month. If he had feelings for her, they were "I like you and like having sex with you" ones. All the pheromones and endorphins and shit had him mixed up.

That had to be it.

When she texted him later and he couldn't hold back a smile at seeing her name on the screen? That was endorphins, too. His smile faded quickly as he read her text.

Audrey: Texting you because my mom texted to remind me—don't forget we have dinner with my parents on Friday. More parental interaction! Yay! She included a skull emoji and an upside-down smiley face.

Fake dating someone involved a lot of parental interaction. He'd signed up for it, though. Plus she'd met his mom—twice. Like he told her a week ago, it was only fair that he meet her parents, too.

More people to lie to. Great.

The more time he spent with Audrey, the less it felt like lying.

And that was a problem.

Chapter Twenty-Two

Audrey had to hand it to Luke. He knew exactly how to impress Mom and Dad without even trying. In fact, he put her skills at dealing with other people's parents to shame. Where she'd been on edge with his mom, he shined with her parents. He asked them questions about themselves, and handled their questions for him with ease. He talked to Dad about baseball, enduring some gentle ribbing about the Cubs' recent three-game losing streak. It turned out both Luke and Mom were devotees of the *New York Times*' daily Spelling Bee game, something Audrey didn't even know about Luke. They were bonding.

Her parents were much more chill about all of this than Patti had been. Not that she expected them to turn this into a big thing, but bringing him to meet her parents was still nerve-wracking. She wanted them to like him even though this would all be over soon. Even though he wasn't actually her boyfriend.

Sometimes, though, it felt like he was. Sometimes, she forgot.

She emerged from the fog of her thoughts when Mom said to Luke, "Audrey says you're renovating a house for a TV show. What's that like?"

The TV show. Right. One of the reasons why they were pretending.

Not only did he give Mom the rundown on what it was like filming a renovation for TV, he pulled out his phone and showed her pictures. As both of her parents peered at the screen, he made sure to tell them, "Audrey took these photos."

Mom *ooh*ed and *ahh*ed. Dad said, "Nice work."

Luke gave Audrey a smile full of so much pride her heart couldn't take it.

They were finishing dessert—she couldn't go to an Italian restaurant and not get the tiramisu—when Luke excused himself from the table. Once he'd disappeared in the direction of the restrooms, Mom turned to her with bright eyes and a huge smile. "I like him a lot."

"I like him a lot, too," Audrey said, her cheeks heating. Had she admitted that out loud to anyone else? She couldn't remember.

Dad set down his fork and leaned back from the table. Wait for it… "He's not a jagoff."

"I was hoping you'd say that. He's nothing like Neil."

"He's good to you?"

"He is."

"That's all I care about," Dad said. "That's all both your mother *and* I care about. We want you to be with someone who treats you right, not someone who puts you down."

The rest of the sentence went unsaid. *Someone like the last guy.* Someone who cared more about himself than others. Someone who would discourage her from pursuing her dreams.

Luke would never do that.

After he came back to the table and her parents took

care of the check—despite Luke's offer to pay—they left the restaurant. Outside, Mom gave Luke a hug and said, "It was so nice to meet you. I'm not sure when we'll see you again, but you should join us for Audrey's birthday next month."

Oh, hell no. He'd be gone a week after her birthday. Bringing him to her family birthday celebration was not a good idea.

He sent a look in her direction that said *Your birthday is next month?* before turning back to Mom. "Sure, as long as that's okay with her."

"August twenty-fifth!" Mom said, clasping her hands to her chest. "Mark your calendar!"

Audrey exchanged hugs with both of her parents. After she hugged Dad, he extended his hand to Luke and said, "Nice meeting you."

Luke shook his hand. "You, too. Thank you for dinner."

After a final goodbye, Audrey and Luke started in the direction of her car. She'd picked him up on the way out to the suburbs, and they'd already planned for him to come back to her place tonight.

They'd been spending a lot of time at her place. No wonder she kept forgetting he wasn't her actual boyfriend. He slotted into her life like he belonged there all along.

Should she be worried about that? Probably. She pushed the thought aside and started the car.

Once they were on the expressway headed back into the city, she said, "Sorry my mom put you on the spot like that. She's a little extra about birthdays. You don't have to come if you don't want to."

Because it wasn't just a dinner. It was a movie or some

other activity, followed by a meal. Afterward, they'd go to her parents' house for cake and presents, which included FaceTiming Grandma, who lived in Florida. Grandma loved watching Audrey open the card she sent, which always had a crisp fifty-dollar bill inside.

She was turning thirty-one, but her age didn't matter. Mom still went all out. Sometimes she even got balloons.

"I'll come as long as you want me there," Luke said. "When were you going to tell me your birthday was coming up?"

"I know this sounds bad, but it didn't seem important." *Not when you'll be leaving right after.*

"Of course it's important. I know you have the family thing, but maybe we could do something special for it, too."

Warmth bloomed in her chest. She tried to stop it, but she couldn't. "That's really sweet of you."

She should shut this down now. Tell him she didn't need him to do anything for her birthday—not her family party, and certainly nothing with just the two of them. But another part of her wanted to wring every last second out of their time together before he left.

She wanted the fantasy. She wanted to pretend, for a little while longer.

"Enough about my birthday. When's yours?"

"December thirtieth." He paused and looked out the window. "When I was born, my dad said I couldn't make up my mind about whether I wanted to be born on Christmas or New Year's, so I picked a day in between."

She smiled. "That's cute."

He turned away from the window and back to her. "Your dad reminds me of him. My dad had the same kind of no-nonsense attitude. You always knew where you stood with him. He was a hardass on the surface—not that I think your dad is—"

"Oh, he definitely is."

"But a total softie on the inside?"

"Yes. The biggest softie, especially where I'm concerned." She took her eyes off the road long enough to glance at Luke. "Can I ask about your dad?"

He nodded.

"What was he like? Besides being a secret softie."

"He was a good guy. A hard worker. And he always put my mom, Erin, and me first, no matter what. Didn't matter what else he had going on. If we needed him, he was there." Luke cleared his throat. "Until the very end."

"What happened?" When he didn't respond, she rushed to fill the silence. "That was insensitive. I shouldn't have asked. You don't have to—"

"No, it's okay."

He got quiet again, but she waited. He'd answer, or he wouldn't. She'd give him all the time he needed.

Luke hardly ever talked about Dad with anyone. Partly because it hurt too much. Partly because it brought up things he'd rather leave in the past or forget about entirely. He didn't like talking about the most painful moment of his life.

The weight of the grief had lessened, but it never went away. Neither did the guilt.

He didn't know if it was the way Audrey glanced over at him, her gaze soft and concerned, or the way she asked the question. But he wanted to tell her.

"He died during my senior year of college. Heart attack."

"I'm so sorry."

He could have left it at that. No one would judge him for not sharing more details. Now that he'd started, though, everything came pouring out.

"He came down to Nashville to watch me play in a big game—part of the College World Series. He went back to his hotel room afterward, and that's when it happened." He paused as the memories of that awful phone call telling him to come to the hospital came rushing back. "Somehow he managed to call 911, but by the time I got to the hospital, it was too late."

"Oh, Luke," she whispered. "That's awful. I'm sorry."

She took a hand off the steering wheel and reached to hold his hand. That simple gesture allowed the words to keep coming, a confession making its way past his lips before he could second-guess whether or not to say it out loud.

"I blamed myself for a long time."

"Why?"

This was the hard part. The part he tried not to think about.

"I convinced myself he wouldn't have died if he didn't make the trip. Or if I'd walked him back to his hotel room and had been there to help when it happened," he said. "Instead, I said goodbye to him after the game and went out with my teammates. I figured I could spend all of the next day with him before he went home."

What he wouldn't give to go back and make a different decision. He stared down at their joined hands and swallowed past the pain building in the back of his throat.

"You can't know if those things would have made a difference or not," Audrey said. "I don't think you should blame yourself."

"I talked to someone, about a year after he died. A therapist. I know it's not my fault. But I still wonder sometimes."

She squeezed his hand. "It's not your fault. At all."

He squeezed Audrey's hand back and kept talking. He hadn't talked this much about Dad in a long time, and now he couldn't stop. "Anyway, I moved back here after graduation. All my dad wanted was for one of his kids to take over the family business someday. I had to step up."

"On your own?"

"Erin was fifteen, my mom worked part-time, and we needed money, so yeah."

"Did you want to?"

"Not really. But someone had to."

Wasn't that the story of his life? Someone needed to do it, so he did. He took responsibility for everything at the age of twenty-two. Like Mom said, he'd carried that weight around for a long time. Part of him still did.

"Did you enjoy that kind of work at all?" Audrey asked.

"I grew up helping my dad."

She glanced over at him—a look that said, *you didn't answer the question*—then back to the road. "But did you like it? It sounds like you had different plans for your life right after college."

"I love carpentry and renovating, but I never wanted to run a business." He laughed, bitter and hollow. "Mostly I wanted to play baseball."

"You wanted to honor your dad's wishes, too."

It was more than that. A lot more. "I wanted to take care of my mom and my sister. Someone had to hold us together."

"And it was you."

It was always him. Therapy had helped with those feelings for a bit. Then he got busy and stopped going. Maybe he needed to go back. Talk about this stuff some more. Even talking about it right now helped.

When he didn't say anything else, she gave his hand another squeeze and then let go. They didn't talk for the rest of the ride back to her place. Fifteen minutes later, when she pulled into the reserved parking spot behind her building and turned off the car, she said, "I know that must have been hard to talk about."

"It helped," he said, echoing his earlier thought.

Audrey reached out and cupped his cheek. He pressed a kiss to her wrist. "I think your dad would be proud of you."

His throat grew tight again. "I hope so."

"You do a lot for your family."

He wasn't sure what to say to that. Taking care of his family was just what he did.

"You do a lot for me, too," she said, her voice quiet. "You're always there, trying to help. Trying to make things easier for me."

His fingers suddenly ached with the need to touch her. He wrapped an arm around her and pulled her as close as he could with the center console in the way. He still didn't know what to say. His actions would have to be enough.

With his heartbeat picking up speed, he lifted his hand to sweep his thumb over her cheekbone. Her eyelids fluttered closed, the lashes dark against her pale skin. He leaned in to press his lips to hers. The kiss started gentle and slow, sweet and undemanding. When she pulled back slightly and her tongue darted out to wet her lower lip, he couldn't resist. He licked that spot on her lip and took her mouth again. She opened for him, whimpering as he deepened the kiss. His tongue moved against hers, exploring, tasting, searching.

She skimmed her hands from his shoulders down to his chest. "I want tonight to be about you. What you want. What you need."

He touched her face again and stared into her eyes. "It's never going to be just about me. Not when we're together."

She kissed him then, a tender kiss that promised something more. "Upstairs?"

He nipped her mouth one last time before they both stumbled out of the car and up the stairs to her apartment, drunk on kisses and each other.

In her bedroom, after they'd undressed, he sat back against the bed's headboard. He pulled her into his lap. That first time, he'd loved the sight of her in that position, loved holding her in his arms while she fell apart. Now, he let his fingers fill her again while he whispered in her ear about how good she felt, how beautiful she was. When she came a few minutes later, she exhaled a little "Oh!" of surprise and shuddered.

He slid a hand into her hair, angling her mouth toward his. As they kissed, her fingers trailed down his chest to his stomach, then lower. His pulse jumped, picking up speed. She took his cock in her hand and squeezed around the base. At the first stroke, the back of his head thunked into the headboard. "Fuck, that feels good."

She tightened her hand around him. "Tell me what you want."

With her, he wanted everything. Anything she'd give him. He'd opened up to her in a way he hadn't with anyone else. For the first time in years, he'd shared a part of himself he usually kept locked down and hidden. He felt safe enough with her to do that.

"Tell me, Luke," she whispered. It took him a second to catch up, to get out of his own head. "Please."

That *please* turned him desperate. He needed her more than anything. He slipped his hands underneath her ass and lifted her closer to him. "Want you to ride me. You look so fucking hot like this."

She reached over to the nightstand for a condom and tore open the wrapper with her teeth. Holy shit, he was going to combust before he got inside her. He held himself still, clenching his jaw while she sheathed him. Seconds stretched out into what felt like hours. She positioned herself above him. Then, thank God, she sank down onto his cock.

They both gasped. He grabbed her hips, more to keep himself anchored than to keep her from moving. Slowly, she began to rock herself up and down, letting his hands guide her. The light from the bedside lamp highlighted her every curve, picked up the flecks of gold in her brown eyes. She closed those gorgeous eyes and threw her head back as she worked herself on his cock. Tingles traveled their way up his spine with every roll of her hips.

A month. He had one more month of this, of her. He couldn't imagine giving her up. How was he supposed to walk away? Did he even want to?

He'd think about it later. Right now, all that mattered was this. The movement of their bodies together, seeking release. Her soft sighs, the way she said his name on a breathy exhale as she took the pleasure he gave her. His desire for her, spinning out of control.

That desire grew wilder as her breasts brushed against his chest. He bent his head to lick one of her nipples and draw it into his mouth. She shivered and grabbed the back of his neck to keep him there.

"Yes," she said, arching toward him.

He moved to the other nipple, circling it with his tongue, teasing another shiver out of her and a low moan.

She was so responsive. He loved it.

When she began moving faster, he pulled away from her breasts and slid his hand down to where they were joined. He pressed his fingertips against her clit. Her rhythm faltered. She opened her eyes and sucked in a breath. "That's so good."

"You like that?" he asked, his gaze never leaving hers.

She nodded. "But I need more."

Who was he to deny her? He'd give her anything she asked for. With his fingers still moving in slow circles, he pumped up into her with short, determined thrusts, holding her against him with one arm around her waist.

"Don't stop," she gasped.

Need clawed at him, his own release dangerously close. He kept thrusting upward. Did that thing she liked where he pressed down on her clit at the same time he pushed into her. Her hips moved erratically. Her full breasts bounced close to his face. He couldn't resist taking her nipples into his mouth again, working his tongue over them.

"Oh my God, Luke." His name was a sharp cry as she jerked forward. She buried her fingers in his hair, pulling hard on the strands. He gritted his teeth. Pain mixed with the pleasure of her pussy squeezing him tight and spasming around him. She shook in his arms.

He couldn't last any longer.

The force of his orgasm ripped a raw, guttural sound

from his throat. Over the roar in his ears, he heard her say his name again before they both went still.

They clung to each other in the aftermath. He buried his face in the crook of her neck, breathing in the sweet scent of her hair and letting the curls tickle his nose. He pressed kisses to her neck, to her shoulder. She sighed and wound her arms around him.

I don't want to walk away from her. No fucking way.

The realization plowed into him with all the subtlety of a freight train.

This wasn't endorphins or whatever bullshit he'd told himself the other day. Try as he might, he couldn't stop denying it.

He had feelings for her. He might even be falling for her.

He was falling for a woman who definitely did not want him to.

Fuck.

She pulled back from their embrace first. He held the condom while she carefully moved off him. When he came back to bed after throwing away the condom in the bathroom, she was under the sheets, curled up on her side.

She smiled at him, all sleepy and sated, and lifted the sheet in invitation.

If he had any sense at all, he wouldn't stay the night. Because he had no sense and too many feelings, he climbed into bed next to her.

He kissed her. He held her. And he tried not to think about how this couldn't last.

Chapter Twenty-Three

Luke headed home early the next morning after kissing a sleepy Audrey goodbye. His Lyft had just dropped him off at his mom's house when his phone chimed with a calendar notification.

The call with Valerie, the executive producer from HomeTV. That was this morning? In—he looked at the time—fifteen minutes? He swore under his breath. This was the call they'd emailed him to set up last week, about the "exciting news." It could be anything. They should have put all the information in an email instead of making him set up a call.

He went straight to the kitchen, where he started a pot of coffee. By the time he'd fixed a cup for himself and sat at the kitchen table, he didn't have to wait long for the phone to ring.

After he greeted Valerie, she didn't waste time with small talk.

"We've been *so* pleased with your increased social media presence. The ratings for *Retro Renovations* are higher than they've been since the first season."

"Uh, well, that's great."

High ratings were part of the deal he and Valerie had discussed over a month ago, the one that would get his new show picked up in exchange for posting about his relationship with Audrey.

"We'll be moving forward with the ten-episode order on *Project Victorian*, but I wanted to give you some news," she said.

Relief washed over him. The show was getting picked up, but of course there was a surprise attached. He steeled himself before asking, "What is it?"

"We definitely want you to travel around the country to restore older homes. A new city in every episode."

He'd always known this was a possibility. For most of the summer, he'd treated it as inevitable, but he'd hoped things would turn out differently. *Because of Audrey.* Even though she hadn't given him any indication she wanted to continue things, if he stayed they'd at least have a shot.

A shot he wasn't sure she wanted.

"What about it being a Chicago show? You said you'd see how the pilot performed before making a decision on the show traveling."

"We had a show set in Chicago that premiered last month, *Windy City House Hunt*, and it's underperforming. Our highest rated shows are the ones that travel to different locations. Viewers like seeing what real estate is like in different parts of the country."

"I understand what you're saying, but—"

"You have such a higher profile now thanks to your social media," Valerie said. "Take that and combine it with you traveling around the country, restoring these historic homes, and you have a better chance of people wanting to watch every episode."

She'd obviously thought through any possible objections he could have before they got on this call.

After years of living in Boston due to the grueling

schedule for *Retro Renovations*, he was ready to spend more time at home with his family. But he wanted the show, too. There had to be a way he could have both.

"I'm not sure how I feel about the constant travel," he said. "I wanted to be in Chicago so I could be closer to family."

You'd be closer to Audrey, too. It didn't matter. He might be falling for her, but this thing with her still had to end. That was what she wanted. He'd respect that, no matter what happened with the show.

"We could set up the production schedule so you get a few weeks at home between episodes," Valerie said. "I think it's great that we're kicking the show off in Chicago. And no promises, but maybe we could have it come full circle and end the season with another Chicago episode."

They talked about how the schedule might work. While she spoke, he considered her idea. If he could give his show its best chance at success by traveling around the country, and the producers could work with him on scheduling...

Wait. There were no ifs here. This wasn't a choice. If this show failed, it was back to the family business. Back to not doing what he wanted. HomeTV had him at their mercy, and Valerie knew it. The fact they would work on his schedule was a gift. He should be grateful they wanted the show, and do what he could to make it a success.

Valerie ended the call by saying someone higher up at the network would send the contract to his agent and copy him on the email. Contracts and negotiations were his least favorite parts of the job besides promotion. But the hard part—the part where he had to hold up his end of the deal and deliver high ratings and buzz for the network—was over.

His new show had officially gotten the green light.

He'd pulled it off. No, *they'd* pulled it off. Audrey was a huge part of this. He sent her a text to let her know, and she responded right away.

Audrey: Congratulations! That's so exciting!

Luke: It wouldn't have happened without you agreeing to help me out. Thank you.

Audrey: I got something out of it, too. But you're welcome. She put one of those winky-face emojis at the end of the text.

He was about to pocket his phone when another text came through.

Audrey: I'm taking you out to celebrate.

Right, because he should be celebrating. Their plan had worked. All he had to do was sign the paperwork. He got to do something he wanted, for no reason other than he wanted to do it. When was the last time he'd had that?

Sure, he'd have to travel, but he could have Chicago as his home base. Buy his own place. Be close to family.

He was getting everything he wanted.

Almost everything.

He'd just have to get used to not having her around.

Luke and Audrey had very different ideas of the word *celebrate*.

Hers involved going out for dinner and drinks. Maybe seeing a movie or doing karaoke if she felt like staying out late, which she did approximately four times a year.

His was listening to a Bruce Springsteen album and eating Portillo's in his truck.

She tried not to judge. The local fast-food chain did have good crinkle-cut fries and milkshakes. And she was always down for some Springsteen.

There was a crowd inside the restaurant, and neither of them wanted to deal with that. After working most of the evening, she needed peace and quiet. They went through the drive-thru and parked in the lot to eat.

"Are you sure you don't want to stop for a celebratory drink somewhere after this?" she asked, digging into the bag of food.

He shook his head and lifted up his milkshake. "This is my celebratory drink."

She laughed and tapped her cup against his. "Cheers, then. To your new show."

They both took a drink while Bruce sang about dancing in the dark. Audrey ate her fries and kicked off her shoes. Ahh, she'd been waiting for that moment all night. Sweet relief. She wiggled her toes. Being on her feet for hours was the only part of the job she didn't like.

After they'd spent a couple minutes eating, she said, "When do you start filming the other episodes?"

"I'm not sure yet. The producer told me today they definitely want the show to travel to different places, so I'm waiting to hear where and when."

"That sucks," she said, flattening her tone, trying not to sound too disappointed. "I know how much you wanted to stay here."

He wasn't just leaving in a few weeks—he was *leaving*-leaving. Going on the road and not coming back.

Not that it made a difference. She'd always known traveling was a possibility for him. She got involved with Luke knowing he might be leaving, knowing all they could have was a fling. That's what made their arrangement so perfect.

For some weird reason, her heart sank anyway.

He shrugged. "They're willing to adjust the production schedule so I can come home between filming episodes. I'm still going to move back."

Her stomach gave a little flutter of hope. Which made no sense. If he moved here, that didn't change anything. Relationships weren't part of her business plan. They couldn't be. She'd enjoy what time they had left and get it all out of her system by Labor Day. That way, she could spend the fall crushing her goals and setting more goals for next year. She'd already bought next year's planner and was ready to put it to use.

"I'm excited for you." What else could she say? She *was* excited for him. He'd gotten what he'd wanted. They both had.

"Thanks. And hey, I'm excited for you, too. It seems like you're getting bigger jobs, like the thing tonight."

The awards ceremony she'd shot tonight for a nonprofit was a definite step up. It paid well, too.

"I am," she said. "Oh, and I forgot to tell you I booked a wedding for next summer. My ex once told me I'd never make it as a photographer, and I have one thing to say to him now." She raised a middle finger.

In general, she avoided letting Neil take up space in her brain. He wasn't worth the time, energy, or effort. But tonight, after finishing her biggest job to date, she couldn't help it—she had to bask in proving him wrong.

Luke shook his head slowly, like he was trying to process what she'd said. "He told you that? That you'd never make it?"

"He did."

"What kind of boyfriend says something like that?"

"A shitty one."

"Wow. What an asshole."

"That was the worst one, but he also liked telling me photography was a hobby and not a 'real job,'" she said, making air quotes around the words.

He'd also told her if they ever got married and had kids, he expected her to give up her "real job" anyway. He wouldn't even allow her to make the choice. That had been the final straw.

"What did he do for work?" Luke asked.

"He worked in finance. I have no clue exactly what he did, but he loved bragging to people that he made tons of money."

Luke took a bite of his sandwich and rolled his eyes. "Sounds charming."

"He was, at first. I met him on a dating app, and when we were messaging, he said all the right things."

"What about when you met up?"

"We had a decent first date." She hadn't seen any red flags. Nothing about him made her want to run in the other direction. "I was attracted to him, and he wasn't awful. It wasn't until things got serious that this other side came out. But I'd heard horror stories about guys who were so much worse, and I thought, 'At least he's not a total piece of shit.'"

"He sounds like one to me."

"Trust me, I know that now."

"How long were you together?"

"A little over two years. When I dumped him a year ago, he got angry, called me a bitch who only cared about her job, and walked out. That was that. He never contacted me again."

Luke made a noise full of anger and disgust, something that came from deep in his throat. "Does he still live in Chicago?"

"He doesn't. I unfriended him everywhere, but a few months ago he popped up in my People You Might Know thing on Facebook. Apparently he got a job in New York."

Luke crumpled the wrapper from his sandwich into a ball and tossed it into the empty bag. "Good riddance."

"Seriously. I can't believe I let him make me doubt myself." She paused before the next part, worrying at her bottom lip with her teeth. "When we first started dating, I'd been doing a lot of planning for how to start my own business. I put my dreams on hold because of him. Because he made me think I couldn't do it."

She would never, ever put her dreams and goals on hold for anyone again. Especially a man.

"It's easy to let people get in your head," he said. "They tell you a story about yourself and make you believe it's true."

She let herself sit with that for a minute. In the silence, Luke looked over at her, his face cast in shadows from one of the lights in the parking lot. He reached over to brush his thumb over the knuckles of her left hand. They stared at each other, still not saying anything. His gaze on her was soft. Reverent. The way you looked at someone you loved.

Her pulse pounded in her throat. No. They weren't—he couldn't.

"I'm glad you decided not to believe him anymore. That you went after what you wanted," he said.

"I decided to write my own story."

"You did. I feel lucky you let me be a part of it for a little while."

His voice was as soft as his stare. She should turn away. Stop the warmth that rushed over her the longer they sat together like this and the longer he looked at her like that, saying things he shouldn't.

She repeated, "For a little while" and gave him a quick kiss, pulling away before he could bring her in for something deeper. "We should get going. We've both had a long day."

He cleared his throat and put his hands on the steering wheel. "You're right."

She'd broken whatever spell had fallen over them. He started the truck and they headed in the direction of her apartment. The entire ride home, his words circled through her thoughts. She controlled her own narrative. She decided who got to be a part of it and how.

Was there room for Luke in her story? Could things be different this time if she let a man into her life?

She was getting too far inside her own head. She needed to slow down. Everything they'd shared—all the looks, all the touches, all the moments of connection— had her considering the impossible.

When he turned onto her street, she said, "Can you just drop me off tonight? I'm exhausted."

He nodded once and said nothing. In front of her building, he let her out of the truck with a flat "good night" and waited until she got inside before he drove away.

Something had shifted, but that was fine. Everything was fine.

But if everything was fine, why did her heart hurt so damn much?

Chapter Twenty-Four

Things got weird last night.

Audrey shared her past with him, and Luke said too much. If he had to bet on it, her reaction wasn't only about what he said. All those feelings he'd been trying to push down probably showed on his face. Like the one that said, *I think I'm falling for you.* Or the one that said, *Let's try this for real.*

She'd pulled away. Asked him to take her home. Didn't want him to come inside, even though he'd spent almost every night there these past couple weeks. He dropped her off and went home, where he spent hours lying awake, wondering how he let himself get in this deep.

Audrey had been clear on what she wanted from the start. She was his fake girlfriend turned regular hookup. She owed him nothing. He had no business wanting more from her.

His heart still demanded he try.

But what was the point? She was writing her own story, and he didn't have a role in it. He'd been up until three in the morning, trying to imagine a future where she'd want him in her life, a way they could make this work.

There was none.

Maybe I can change her mind.

He wasn't going to be that kind of guy. The type who thought he could wear a woman down and into a relationship with him. Audrey told him what she wanted and had certainly made herself clear last night. He would honor that.

He was leaving at the end of the summer, anyway. Even if she wanted a relationship, it would be hard to keep it going long distance. This was exactly why he should have listened to that voice in his head at the lake house when it told him not to start something with her. That getting involved would be a bad idea given the circumstances. That no matter how much he thought he could keep it casual, it was easier said than done.

Fuck, what he wouldn't give to have some shit to hammer or some walls to knock down. Too bad the project at the Victorian was almost done. Today an assistant producer was interviewing him for talking heads—segments of him talking to the camera. It wasn't his favorite part of the job, but it was easy when there weren't constant retakes. He had a teleprompter in front of him, and he still fumbled the words. Even after getting some much-needed caffeine in his system, he couldn't get his act together.

Last night did a number on him.

He prided himself on his professionalism on the job, in treating the producers and crew well and respecting their time. He hated that he wasn't on top of his game today. So when Katie, the assistant producer, suggested breaking for lunch early, he told her thank you and made himself scarce, desperate to regroup.

At lunch, he pulled up his email on his phone. The name at the top of his inbox was one he hadn't seen in a while: Mateo Suarez, his *Retro Renovations* cohost. He and Mateo had been friendly, but they didn't hang out aside from an occasional drink or dinner while filming.

I've got an event coming up for my new foundation and was wondering if you'd be interested in taking part...the email started.

Done. He was there. And hey, if Mateo had a fancy event, maybe he'd need a photographer for it. He'd follow up later.

Below Mateo's email, he had a new message from Valerie. His stomach dropped. What did the executive producer want now?

Hi Luke,

I hope everything's going well! My assistant producer told me you're ahead of schedule on the renovation and wrapping things up. How would you feel about using the extra time to help us scout locations for upcoming episodes? We'd love your input.

Best,
Valerie

Well, that was a relief. He wrote back and said he'd be happy to. How much work could it be? When they scouted locations for *Retro Renovations*, he would look at listings they sent him and offer opinions. The network had location scouts, people who did nothing but find houses and go check them out, who made the final decisions.

His phone chimed with a reply. Wow, she was fast. She'd sent a link to a listing for a house in St. Louis.

That's a quick flight from you if you want to check it out in person. We could have one of our location scouts meet you there. I know this is fast, but how's this coming weekend look for you? Bring Audrey along—just think of how much your fans would love seeing the two of you on a flight again! I know I would. :) Ask her and let me know if she can make it, too.

He growled at his phone. Hadn't they gotten enough out of him? Couldn't he be done with this social media bullshit?

A week ago, he would have welcomed a weekend away with her. After last night, it wasn't a good idea. He needed to put some distance between them before he fell even harder. Pull back on the number of nights he spent at her place. Stop spending time with each other's families. Put an end to the social media posts now that they'd both gotten what they wanted out of the arrangement.

Not seeing her at all was out of the question. He wouldn't go that far.

Despite his need for distance, pushing back on Valerie's request wasn't worth it. Audrey worked most weekends. Saturdays were one of her busiest days.

He'd get out of this easily, but he still had to ask her. Unless he made up an excuse or a lie and told Valerie that Audrey couldn't make it.

Nah, he couldn't. He'd told enough lies this summer. His Irish Catholic guilt was already in overdrive.

That night, after a million hours of talking to a camera, he went out to the back deck and called Audrey. He didn't want to put the request in a text, and this way, he got to hear her voice. Trying to figure out someone's tone in a text could be tricky sometimes.

After they talked for a couple minutes about their days, he said, "I just found out I have to go to St. Louis this weekend for work."

"St. Louis? What do they have you doing there?"

"Looking at a house with one of the location scouts from the network." He drummed his fingertips on the deck's railing. It was a muggy night, the air thick with a coming storm. "Would you want to come with me?"

He heard some shuffling, like she was flipping through papers. "Hmm. I *am* off this weekend."

Oh, shit. "You are?"

"I blocked it off in my calendar a while ago. I had a feeling I'd need some time off."

He shouldn't have asked. He should have made up one more lie, told Valerie that Audrey couldn't make it, and dealt with the guilt later. "If you'd rather relax at home, you don't have to come."

"I want to. It'll be good to get away. And…" She trailed off. Her voice got quiet. "We don't have a whole lot of time left."

At the reminder, his resolve crumbled like an old brick wall. They had less than a month before he had to leave. What good would distance do now when he was already half in love with her? He was kidding himself if he thought he could get rid of his feelings by spending less time together.

"Luke?" she said. "Are you still there?"

He rubbed the center of his forehead, trying to ease the throbbing there. "Yeah. You're right. We don't have a lot of time. Let's enjoy it."

They'd have the whole weekend together. Probably staying at a nice hotel, based on the accommodations HomeTV had put him up in before. One with a huge bed in the room, chocolates on the pillows, and a fancy restaurant—the kind of place with lots of mood lighting and dark wood. Romantic as hell.

He was screwed.

He didn't tell Audrey about Valerie's request for a picture until they boarded their flight to St. Louis. After she'd agreed to go on the trip, he forgot to ask. By the time he remembered, he figured it would be easier to say something in the moment.

Audrey pursed her lips. "Did she say you had to take a photo and post it?"

"No. She said something like fans would love to see us on a flight again, and so would she."

"But she didn't actually say, 'You must take a picture.'"

Where was she going with this? "She did not."

"Here's an idea," Audrey said, shifting in her aisle seat to get a better look at him. "Let's have a weekend without social media. No posts, and no pictures we'll share publicly."

What. The. Fuck. "But you always want to post stuff."

She sighed, briefly closing her eyes before opening them again. "I don't want to have to worry about it. I want us to enjoy this weekend."

The real Audrey must be missing somewhere, because this didn't sound at all like her. If she didn't care about social media, that must mean—

"You came on this trip just to spend time with me?"

She tilted her head to the side and gave him a look, quirking her lips and raising her eyebrows. "Yes?"

"You mean to tell me you're not going to make one Instagram post this entire weekend?"

She laughed. "Is it that unbelievable that I want to hang out with you for no other reason?"

After she pushed him away the other night, kind of. "I'm surprised, that's all."

"Well, believe it. We have three weeks left, and I'm not going to spend time worrying about social media." She smiled at him then, so radiant he lost his breath. "I like being with you, Luke."

Okay, then. She wasn't thinking two steps ahead about what they could post to get the most likes and comments. She wanted to be here with him just to be with him.

"I like being with you, too," he said.

He wasn't half in love with her—he was tumbling head over ass toward the real thing.

You're still leaving in a few weeks.

Leaving didn't have to mean never talking to her again, did it? If she wanted that, by all means, he'd leave her alone. She might not, though. The way she looked at him, the way she said she liked being with him—hell, the fact she was here on this flight with him—made a tiny pulse of hope flicker somewhere deep inside.

Take a chance, it said. Ask her if she'd reconsider. If there might be some way, and their time together didn't have to end.

The plane started to back away from the gate.

She nudged him with her elbow. "It's too bad this flight is too short for cheese plates."

He chuckled and gave her the world's quickest kiss.

Yeah, he was a goner.

Chapter Twenty-Five

Audrey had come to St. Louis because of a list.

The night they had that moment in the parking lot, she'd sat on her bed, her heart still hurting, and opened the notes app on her phone. Why she hadn't thought to make a list before then was beyond her. Lists solved everything. They helped her process her thoughts, narrow down ideas, and gave her a deep sense of satisfaction.

At the top of the list, she'd written a note to herself: *Use the time left with him to evaluate whether or not this continues. No social media?*

If she wanted to figure out whether they could work after this summer, she needed to do it away from Twitter and Instagram. Away from the pressure of performing for their followers, along with the pressure of worrying about her and Luke's careers. She wanted to enjoy being with him these next few weeks without all the other garbage.

This weekend was the perfect way to do that. So she'd said yes.

Then it turned out he probably only asked her because his producer wanted a picture of them on the plane. But he'd been genuinely pleased, in a disbelieving sort of way, when she'd proposed a social media–free weekend.

She couldn't fault him for wanting to bring her along for the 'gram. They'd been doing it for the 'gram for over a month now.

Dear God, she was becoming the kind of person who said *the 'gram*. All the more reason to take a break from it.

After they arrived in St. Louis, Luke went to look at a house while Audrey stayed behind at the hotel. She'd booked herself a massage at the spa and had to be downstairs in fifteen minutes. Until then, she looked over the list. Specifically the pros, because there were way more of them than the cons.

1. You like him a lot.
2. You enjoy spending time with him.
3. He's not Neil. He's shown you that over and over.
4. He's supported you in everything.
5. You've spent the entire summer basically dating him (even if it was fake), and your business hasn't suffered.
6. When you think about never seeing him again, your heart does that weird clench thing and your throat closes up. That has to mean SOMETHING.
7. The sex is amazing. Incredible. Excellent. Mind-blowing.

Goose bumps spread over her arms at that last one. Sexual chemistry wasn't everything, but it played a big part. She had to put it on the list.

She scrolled down. The cons: He'd somehow hold her back. They'd have to do long distance. She'd have to be a public figure's girlfriend for real, and deal with the attention even when it didn't benefit her.

She tapped a finger against her lips. Surely there were more cons. She didn't need to dwell on them now, though. Best to put her phone away and start the phone-free and social media–free weekend before the massage for maximum relaxation. Before she did that, she fired off a quick message to the group text.

Audrey: Hey, I wanted to let you guys know I'm here. I'm turning off my phone for the rest of the weekend.

Natalie: Staying busy? *peach and eggplant emojis*

Grace: You forgot the water droplets.

Audrey: How could you, Natalie? I'm disappointed.

Natalie: No one even likes the water droplets!

Natalie: Anyway, I get worried when you turn your phone off. Remember what happened last time?

Audrey: ???

Natalie: You went viral.

Audrey: Which I didn't know until you two told me.

Grace: Stop trying to scare her into leaving her phone on.

Natalie: I'm not trying to scare her! I'm just saying we'll have to keep an eye on Twitter this weekend now that she's famous.

Audrey sighed and typed, I'm not famous, and you definitely don't have to do that.

Natalie: You know I'm still going to do it, right?

Audrey: Yes. She put a red heart next to the word.

Grace: Enjoy your weekend, and seriously, don't worry about it. How many times can one person go viral?

She didn't know, but she sure didn't want to find out.

"Okay, put your hand underneath... No, like this."

"I've never done this before. I don't know what I'm supposed to be doing."

Audrey reached out and readjusted Luke's hand on her camera's lens. "If you want to take a picture, you need to learn how to hold the camera."

"What about this wheel thing?"

He rubbed his thumb around the edge of the mode dial. The action shouldn't have been erotic—he was touching a camera, for crying out loud—but damn, it was hot combined with his other hand cupping the lens.

"You're a beginner, so shoot on auto," she said. "Don't worry about the other modes."

Everyone else at the hotel's rooftop bar took photos of the view with their phones. The two of them were doing the no-phone thing, so she'd brought her DSLR. She would get better pictures with it, anyway.

"Are you sure about me using this?" He lifted the camera, feeling its weight. "It looks expensive."

"It was, and I'm sure. You asked me to show you."

He ducked his head. "Because I wanted to take a picture of you."

A tender, perfect ache spread through her. "Okay," she said softly.

She stood next to him, showing him how to use the viewfinder to frame the shot and what button to press to take the photo. He smelled delicious, like laundry and soap. She inhaled his scent, barely resisting the urge to bury her nose in his shirt. She'd never wanted to do that with anyone else. Then again, no one else's detergent and soap had ever served as an aphrodisiac—at least not to this degree.

"Think you got it?"

"Yeah. I was intimidated by all the buttons, but it doesn't seem that hard."

She went over to the railing to pose. With the city and a spectacular sunset behind her, the shot might be profile photo worthy.

Luke waited for a couple passing by to get out of the way. He lowered the camera slightly and gave her a crooked grin. She tried not to swoon.

Once the coast was clear, he raised the camera to his eye again and said, "I'm taking the picture now. At least I think I am."

She laughed. The shutter clicked a couple times. Luke looked at the camera's screen, rubbing his hand over his mouth like that could hide his smile.

He beckoned her over. "How are these?" He turned the camera toward her.

In the images, she was laughing, her face bright and happy, cast in the sunset's golden-pink light. Either one of these would be a great new profile pic. At the same time, they were too special to share right away. He'd photographed her as only he could, the way only he saw her. There was care and intimacy in these photos. Something special, just for the two of them.

"They're perfect." She smiled at him. "Do you want me to take your picture, too?"

He lifted the camera's strap over his head and handed the DSLR back to her. "Nah. But we could take a picture together."

"I'm not letting anyone else touch my camera," she said, clutching the camera tight against her body.

"Can you take a selfie with that thing?"

"It's not easy, but we can try."

After a few attempts and way too much laughter, they got a halfway-decent shot. With that done, she turned the camera off and slid it back into her bag. They went to sit down, nestling themselves into a corner booth and ordering drinks. She rested her head on his shoulder like it was the most natural thing in the world. He wrapped his arm around her. They stared out at the view of the famous arch, only a few blocks away.

"I can't believe this summer is almost over," she said. "Back when you got on that flight in Boston, did you ever think it would turn out like this?"

The rumble of his laughter echoed in her own chest. "Definitely not. I'm guessing you didn't, either."

"Hell no." She lifted her head from his shoulder to look in his eyes. "Even with everything"—she waved her hand, like the motion could encompass the fake relationship, going viral multiple times, and all the rest— "I'm glad it turned out this way. Thank you. For your help. For everything."

"I hardly did anything. You were helping me while you started a business. That's impressive. You should be proud of yourself." He gave her a quick kiss. When he pulled back, his fingers lingered at her jawline. He dropped his hand to take hers. "I'm proud of you."

Happiness flowed through her at his words. She'd accomplished something huge. With how fast things moved and how busy she'd been, she hadn't taken the time to let the realization settle.

"I made a lifelong dream come true."

"You always knew you wanted to be a photographer. I remember you saying that at dinner with my family."

"Since I was seven. I had this toy camera that took instant pictures, almost like Polaroids. I took it everywhere with me. I'd have all my pictures, and I'd make books out of them." She smiled, remembering *Audrey's Big Book of Pictures, Vol. 1*. She'd followed it up with volumes two through ten. Her parents still had the books at their house.

"I got my first real camera in high school," she continued. "I wanted to get a degree in photography, but my parents—as supportive as they are—said when it came to school, I had to be practical. Get a degree in something I could fall back on."

"Did you?"

"No. I got a degree in photography and a practical job. Which led to another practical job, and telling myself, 'Someday.'"

"You made it happen, though."

She sipped her Moscow mule. "I wonder if I could have done it on my own."

"What do you mean? You did."

"I mean, without you. Using the opportunity from…" She glanced around at the crowd, and at the group in the booth next to theirs. "You know."

He shook his head. "You saw a way to achieve your goal, and you took it." His voice was forceful, his words full of conviction. "You were strategic as hell, and I've admired that about you from the beginning."

Were those tears prickling at the backs of her eyes? Shit. She swallowed and sat up straighter. Gave him a wink. "I told you if you were getting professional advancement out of this, I was, too."

"I'd say it worked out well for the both of us." He threaded his fingers with hers and rested them atop her thigh.

Yeah, but what happens next? She wasn't going to worry about that. At least not right now. Why worry when she ultimately decided what happened? If this summer had taught her anything, it was that she was in charge of her own destiny.

She stared at the man next to her. More and more, she wanted him to be a part of it. She had three weeks left to decide. The time would go by fast. When an ache spread through her this time, it was for an entirely different reason.

Wow, this evening had gotten heavier than expected. She picked up a menu from the table and handed it to Luke, then picked up another one for herself. "We should eat something. I don't know about you, but all I've had since we got off the plane is a granola bar I found in my purse."

They got some food and sat there enjoying each other's company until night fell and the mosquitoes came out. That was her cue to get the hell inside.

"Let's head back to the room," she said, standing and holding out her hand for him to take.

His eyes turned heavy-lidded. He took the hand she offered and stood. "Good idea."

In the elevator, they were alone. He turned toward her. Took a step closer. He moved her hair away from her shoulder, brushing his fingers against the nape of her neck. Her pulse thudded in her throat.

"Can I tell you something ridiculous?" she said.

He nodded.

"I used to travel a lot for work, and I always had this fantasy about making out with someone in a hotel elevator."

His lips quirked up. "A stranger? Or a specific someone?"

"Usually a stranger. Someone I met in a bar or something. I thought it would be hot."

It had never happened. She didn't go around making out with strangers or picking up people in bars. *You only pick up people on airplanes.*

He moved closer, until mere inches separated them. "I'm happy to indulge you. Even though I'm not a stranger."

"We can pretend."

He slid a hand into her hair, tilting her head back, and lowered his mouth to hers. She sighed and melted against him. He gave her a sweet kiss, but it had an edge to it, too. The stroke of his tongue promised filthy, sexy things. If he wanted to take her right here and now in this elevator…

A chime sounded and the doors opened on their floor. She almost did that thing people did in movies and on TV where they pressed the emergency button to stop the elevator. Knowing her luck, though, she'd do it wrong and the fire department would show up. She reluctantly pulled away. They would be kissing again—and doing a lot more—in no time.

After they exited the elevator and headed toward their room, she fumbled in her purse for the keycard.

"Here," Luke said, pulling his own key from his pocket and waving it in front of the door. He pushed the door open with one hand and grabbed her hand with the other, pulling her in after him.

She yelped and laughed. The door slammed shut behind them. His arms circled her waist and he stared down at her. She slid her hands over his chest. He wore a light blue button-down with the top two buttons open, exposing the skin of his throat. She'd been eying that spot all night. She toyed with the next button on his shirt and opened it, then the next one. Now she got a peek at his chest hair. Perfect. The sight of it made her warm all over, made her want to lick her way from his throat to the center of his chest as she undid more buttons.

Before she could do that, he kissed her neck. She shivered.

"Tell me what other fantasies you have," he murmured against her skin.

Oh my God. "Hotel-specific ones, or any fantasy?"

He huffed a laugh and pressed another kiss to her neck. "Anything."

"I'm pretty vanilla. My fantasies aren't scandalous."

"They don't have to be."

She twisted her fingers in his hair as his lips moved down her neck to her collarbone. "I always did want to fuck in a hotel room with the curtains open."

He raised his head to look at her with his mouth open. His pupils were completely blown. "That might be a little scandalous."

"We don't have to—"

"I didn't say that to shame you."

Her cheeks burned. "Oh."

"I want to know what you want. And I want to give it to you."

In that case… She put a hand in the center of his chest and walked him backward into the room. The curtains were open. A tall lamp in the corner of the room provided dim light. They were on a high floor, and the room was still pretty dark, even with the lamp. No one could see anything, but that worked for her. She wasn't ready for full-on, bright-lights, curtains-open sex. He could give her a taste of it, though.

She stared at Luke. His breaths came in sharp bursts. "I mean it, Audrey. Show me. Let me give you what you want."

She wrapped a hand around the back of his neck and kissed him until they were both breathless. With shaking hands and fumbling fingers, she opened the rest of the buttons on his shirt. The anticipation, the need for him, made her heart pound and her control shatter. She burned for him.

They pulled away from the kiss to undress. Shoes got kicked aside. Shirts and pants came off, flung in different directions. When she was down to her bra and panties, she climbed onto the king-size bed in the middle of the room. Luke moved to join her, but she held up a hand.

Her gaze lingered on his boxer briefs. The sight of his erection against the fabric made her pulse throb between her legs. "I want to watch you take those off."

He didn't look away as he hooked his thumbs in the waistband. Slowly, he tugged the underwear down his lean hips. She bit her lip and pressed her thighs together.

She wanted to see all of him. Everything. How had she seen him naked multiple times and still hadn't gotten a good look at his ass? It *was* one of the finest asses in America, after all.

"Maybe you could turn around," she said, using one of her fingers to draw a circle in the air.

He raised his eyebrows, but a smile lingered at the corners of his mouth. He turned around and moved his hips from side to side, doing a little striptease before lowering the fabric the rest of the way.

Wow. He had a perfect butt. Round and tight and muscular. No wonder there were entire Tumblr accounts devoted to GIFs of all the butt shots from *Retro Renovations*. She got up on her knees and scooted down the bed toward where he stood. Perched there, she rested her hands on his shoulders and slid them down his back.

She couldn't believe she was about to ask this question. "Can I squeeze it?"

"Yes."

They both burst out laughing at the same time. She'd touched his ass before, usually when she was trying to pull him deeper inside her, but not like this. She took the cheeks in both hands and gave his butt a squeeze. Very satisfying. Like a perfectly ripe peach. Her mouth watered.

She slid her hands up to his shoulders again. Leaning in, she kissed a tiny mole on his right shoulder. She left another kiss at the nape of his neck.

"You can turn back around." Her voice had gone all breathy.

Humor still etched the corners of his mouth. "You surprise me sometimes."

"In a good way, I hope."

She wound her arms around him. He was gloriously naked and deliciously hard.

"Always in a good way."

His mouth dipped to meet hers. He lowered her to the bed and covered her body with his. She arched toward him, straining to get closer. He took off her underwear, then her bra. When her breasts spilled out, she brought her hands up to cup them and tease her nipples.

She was totally shameless, and she didn't care. He did that to her. He made her want him this bad. She rolled one of her nipples between her thumb and index finger.

He groaned and tossed her bra to the floor like it had personally offended him. "Watching you do that is going to kill me."

He skimmed his hands up her sides and lowered his head to the breast she wasn't touching. A gasp caught in her throat. He licked her nipple gently, then caught it between his teeth. Flicked his tongue over it.

Watching her was going to kill him? Wanting him was going to kill her.

She dropped her hand from her breast and allowed him to take over. He kissed both breasts and played with her nipples until she couldn't take it. Soon she was rocking her hips and saying, "Please" over and over again.

"Tell me you what you need."

"I want your mouth on me." She loved the way he made her express her desires out loud. "I want to come on your tongue."

With a smile against her skin, he kissed his way to her stomach. Lust wound its way through her. She spread her legs and let her hand follow the path Luke's kisses had trailed down her body. Her fingertips pressed to her clit, seeking relief, finding herself wet and slick. She was one big nerve ending, throbbing and pulsing and needing him so badly it made her want to scream.

He used his broad shoulders to spread her open further. Caressed her thighs and kissed the soft skin there. He took her hand, moving it away from her clit.

"I got you," he said.

With his hands on her hips, he brought her toward his mouth. He started slow, licking and tasting her, using his tongue to work her up until she begged. The lust that had wound through her earlier tightened its hold. So good, but not enough. Not anywhere close to enough. Not yet.

He knew her body. He knew how to get her where she needed to go. He'd just take his sweet time getting her there.

Time slowed down and sped up all at once. He'd bring her close and pull her back. She let the sensations rush over her, tried to sink into how good it felt instead of focusing on the finish line. When he finally gave her the direct stimulation she craved, she was wrecked.

A sound came from her throat she didn't even recognize. The orgasm crashed over her with a shimmering rush of pleasure. Her back arched and her toes curled into the mattress. She shuddered and whimpered as he brought her down from the high with his mouth and fingers. Once it was over, she lay there dizzy and panting. Waiting for the world to right itself again.

Luke kissed his way back up her body until they were face to face. He smiled down at her like he knew he'd given her one of the best orgasms of her life. Now she wanted to do the same for him. Not that orgasms were a reciprocal thing, but holy shit. If he could make her come like that, she wanted to make him come twice as hard.

"Now tell me what you want," she said.

"I want to fuck you." He gave her a lingering kiss. She tasted herself on his lips and got turned on all over again. "Do you want that?"

"Please."

More. That was all she wanted. She was greedy for him.

He got a condom from the nightstand and rolled it on. A moment later, he positioned himself between her thighs and entered her. The sweet stretch of him made her hold her breath.

"Okay?" he asked.

She let out the breath and wound her legs around his waist, pulling him closer. "Yes."

His slow, steady thrusts matched the kisses he gave her as they found a rhythm together. He moved a hand between them, touching her clit and applying the exact kind of pressure she liked. The sounds of their breaths and skin slapping against skin filled the room. He buried himself inside her and pressed his forehead to hers.

She didn't want it to end.

Not just this moment, but everything. His smiles, his kindness, his encouragement. His quiet steadiness and comfort. Her time with him.

A tingling sensation started in the back of her throat. Shit, she was not going to cry. Not now.

He raised his head, and their gazes locked together. Oh, wow. The way he looked at her—no one had ever looked at her with that much tenderness. Like she was special and cherished. Her heart expanded in her chest until it felt like it might burst.

I love you.

She didn't say the words, but she didn't have to. They were in every touch and stare and kiss. They were in the way their bodies moved, in how he ground against her, making her whimper. In how he whispered in her ear, telling her how beautiful she was and how much he wanted to watch her come.

She was so close, almost there, hovering near the peak for so long she became convinced she'd stay there.

"I can't. Not again." She shook her head. "You should finish."

He growled. "If you think I would ever finish without making you come first…"

He flipped them over so she was on top. Whoa. The depth and the angle changed everything. She rocked her hips and moaned.

"There you go," he said, rubbing his fingers against her clit while she writhed above him. "I wish you could see how you look right now. So beautiful."

He surged upward to capture her mouth in a kiss. That was it. She tensed and shook, an explosion of sensations rocketing through her. Luke held on to her waist, thrusting into her until his hips jerked and he went still. She gasped and sagged forward in his arms as the last of her aftershocks faded.

A few minutes later, after they'd cleaned up, she got under the sheets and went straight into his arms again. He pressed a kiss to her temple and wrapped himself around her, his front to her back.

"That was amazing," he said, kissing her shoulder. "You're amazing."

She tangled her fingers with his where they rested on her arm. "So are you."

His breathing evened out as he fell asleep.

She stayed awake. Reality took the opportunity to intrude into her thoughts.

All of her carefully crafted plans had fallen apart: The fake relationship. The rules. Keeping it strictly physical. Keeping her heart out of it.

She'd done the one thing she swore she wouldn't do.

Now she had to decide if she wanted to give them a chance for real.

It desperately and resolutely ignored the
the adrenaline. Familiar. Forgive it mostly it swelled
to find its. to the he
Still having trees my night the work out
Now, the end is prick they entice gathering
while he had

Chapter Twenty-Six

Fourteen hours later and thirty thousand feet in the air, Luke made up his mind. He was going to ask Audrey to be his girlfriend. His *real* girlfriend.

Getting out of town and away from social media provided all the clarity and certainty he needed. The past day and a half had been special, but last night was perfect. He glanced over at the seat next to him, where she sat with her nose buried in her Kindle. Every time he looked at her, his pulse picked up speed. Every time she smiled at him, it was like a jolt to his system. Like parts of him he didn't even know were asleep had begun to wake up, because of her.

He loved her. And after last night, he wanted to believe she loved him, too.

He still had to think through what that meant moving forward. They'd have to talk about what happened next. Make a plan. Audrey loved plans. She would be on board.

Three weeks was more than enough time. Until then, he would spend as much time with her as he could. Show her how good they could be together if they gave this a shot. This weekend had provided a taste of what things could be like, but she might need more. Some time out of the cocoon they'd been in before she made a commitment.

That cocoon burst moments after their flight landed at O'Hare.

Audrey pulled out her phone once the plane began its taxi to the gate. For the next couple minutes, the device didn't stop vibrating with new notifications. He turned his phone on out of habit. The same thing happened. Notification after notification filled the lock screen.

What could have happened while he'd been away? He'd kept his phone on do not disturb and had it set up so only calls from his family could get through. They hadn't contacted him. Anything else wasn't important.

She paused in scrolling through her messages to glance at him. "Your phone is blowing up, too?"

"Yeah. I guess we're more popular than we thought."

"This isn't normal for a weekend away. This is—" She went back to her texts. Her face went white. "Oh, shit. Look."

Without another word, she handed him her phone. On the screen was a screenshot of a tweet posted after midnight last night. It had a thousand likes and a couple hundred retweets.

My roommate has a friend over who's a publicist for @ HomeTV. She said #TwitterBae is A PUBLICITY STUNT for @LukeMurphy's new show! Omg.

His entire body went ice cold. How—the publicist in the tweet had to be Jessica. Why would she tell someone that? And why did her friend's roommate think this was okay to post?

He read the tweet again. "Where did you find this?"

"Natalie sent me screenshots. Keep swiping."

I'm in my bedroom but I can hear everything in the living room. Publicist has had a few glasses of wine and she's telling ALL the secrets. They might not even have been dating for real. He only asked her out because the producer asked. All the pictures? All the cute dates? FAKE.

And another one: Remember when #TwitterBae was on the Kiss Cam? Publicist set that up. I can't believe this! The world is a dumpster fire, and they were the only thing giving me hope! :(

"People make up stories for Twitter all the time," he said. Dread roiled his stomach.

You made up an entire relationship for Twitter.

And now everyone fucking knew.

"It has to be real." Audrey leaned toward him, her voice dropping to a whisper. "No one would know about this besides your publicist and producers. And they set us up for the Kiss Cam? What the hell is that about?"

His head spun. He gave her phone back. "We need to do something."

His phone buzzed with an incoming call. Valerie.

Audrey peered over at Luke's screen. "Who's Valerie?"

"The executive producer of my show." He sent her to voicemail and swallowed a string of curses.

"You need to talk to her, and a publicist. Not the one from the tweets."

Would Jessica even have a job after this? She was probably mortified. While he didn't want her to lose her livelihood, she should have known better than to spill all their secrets after a couple glasses of wine. Especially when someone she didn't know could overhear.

"I can't now. Not here."

"Absolutely not," Audrey said, sitting up straight and placing her hands in her lap. "As soon as we get off the plane, we'll order a car and go to my place. You can call Valerie back, and we'll figure out how to handle this."

"How are you this calm right now?" The rush of adrenaline made his hands shake, and his chest was tight, like he couldn't get enough oxygen. "You realize both of our careers could be threatened by this, right?"

At the mention of her career, her hands clenched into fists. Her gaze darted around, like she had to check no one in the seats around them was listening. Still, she kept her voice low and measured.

"I do, but let's not be hasty. This person doesn't have a ton of retweets or followers. I don't know if it has enough traction yet to merit some big response. That's why we need to talk to the people from the network who are trained to deal with these things."

"Tweets go viral quickly. We both know that. How many retweets does it have now?"

"I'll look." With a few taps in her Twitter app, she found the actual tweet. She winced. "It has a lot more."

The plane pulled up to the gate. He wanted to throw up. Everything he'd worked for would be taken away. Everything they'd done this summer would be for nothing. Valerie's call was probably to tell him they didn't want the show anymore. He hadn't had the meeting yet with his agent to go over the contract. Without his signature, could they rescind the offer?

He wasn't a lawyer, but he knew the answer to that question.

"Hey." Audrey took his hand and looked into his eyes. He gripped her hand like some of her calm would transfer to him the longer he held on. "We'll figure this out together, okay?"

They had to. He couldn't lose this opportunity.

And he couldn't lose her.

Screw thinking things through. Even if everything else got taken away, he needed Audrey in his life. He would do whatever it took to keep her there, to show her he wanted to be with her.

They just had to get through this mess first.

Between the time they left the airport and a Lyft dropped them off at Audrey's apartment, Twitter had exploded. Someone started a hashtag called #FakeBae. He couldn't stop reading the tweets, which popped up one after another on his phone screen.

@LukeMurphy is a liar. I'm never watching him again.

He's not just a liar, he's a fraud. Faking a relationship for publicity? That's pathetic.

If he'll lie to us about having a girlfriend, what else is he lying about? Is he even an actual carpenter?

I wonder if the initial tweet about meeting her on the plane was real. Maybe that was made up by the producers, too.

Valerie had told him the network still wanted his show, but it didn't matter. His career was imploding in real time. He had to do something.

"You're doom scrolling," Audrey said. "Put the phone down and wait for Claire to send you a statement."

He'd gotten off the phone with Jessica's boss, the network's head of publicity, ten minutes ago. She said she'd have a statement over to him in twenty, and that yes, Jessica was still employed, but they were "dealing with the matter internally." He wanted to talk to Jessica and ask her what the hell she was thinking. His anger and hurt at her betrayal simmered on a low burn while he waited for the email. He got up and paced Audrey's small kitchen, clutching his phone.

"I should tweet something. People aren't going to trust a statement. They'll know I didn't write it."

She pressed her lips together. "I don't know if that's a good idea. What would you say?"

He tapped the button to compose a new tweet. Maybe he'd send it, maybe he wouldn't. He had to see what the words looked like on the screen. It took forever to write two short sentences. His thumbs kept pressing the wrong keys.

"This." He handed her the phone.

She took it and read the message aloud. "'It might have started out fake, but it's real now. I love her.'"

In the ensuing silence, his heart thundered in his chest. Audrey stared at the screen. Her lips parted. She drew in a shaky breath.

What had he been thinking, handing her his phone? She wasn't supposed to find out from a tweet. He should have told her over a romantic dinner, or while he held her in bed. Something better than this. She deserved that. Instead, she had to read the words in a hastily composed response to his fans.

Finally, she blinked up at him with a dazed look on her face. "You love me."

She spoke with wonder in her voice, not disbelief or confusion. Okay, that was good. He could work with that. He dropped into the chair next to hers and scooted it closer, until their knees were touching. Gently, he removed his phone from her hand and set it on the table.

"I do," he said, taking both of her hands in his. He rubbed his thumb over her knuckles. Waiting. Hoping. Wanting her to say it back.

Words alone might not be enough. An impulse surged through him, unrestrained and reckless. A way they could make this work and be together, even though he had to leave. This wasn't the best time or situation, but would it ever be? If he waited too long, he might miss his chance. It was time to put it all on the line.

Show her you want to be with her.

"I love you. And I want you to come with me."

She tilted her head to the side. "Come with you where?"

"On the road while I film the new show."

She jerked backward and yanked her hands out of his grasp. "How could you ask me that?"

"I—"

"No." She stood, her chair scraping against the hardwood floor. She took a step away from the table. Away from him. "I have a business, Luke. One that I've worked hard to build. I have clients who are booking me months in advance. I can't drop everything to travel around the country with you and—and do what? Just be your girlfriend?"

"You can do photography anywhere. You could always fly back here for bigger jobs."

She rolled her eyes and threw her hands in the air. "I'm sure I can build a great client base moving from city to city every month. What about my clients here? Do you know how much money I'd lose?"

"You wouldn't have to worry about money. I'd help. I'd take care of you."

Her eyes widened. "I don't need you to take care of me. I can take care of myself."

This kept getting worse. He'd fucked up. Badly. "I meant—"

"I don't care what you meant. I'm not your family. I don't need you to step in and save the day."

She was not going to bring his family into this. "Hey. That's not fair."

"Neither is asking me to abandon my business to follow you around."

"Did you ever consider my career is important, too?"

"I never said it wasn't," she said with a little sniff.

He dragged his hands through his hair. "I'm lucky I still have an offer after this latest shitshow. Considering I haven't signed the contract yet, they could still decide to pull it. Then what?"

"Someone else will hire you to do a show for them. Or you can go work with your cousin. You have options." She shook her head. "I don't."

"You just think you don't. If your business doesn't work out, you could go get a real job."

She reared back. Her mouth fell open. "Wow."

Shit. "I didn't mean—I meant you could go back to doing what you did before—"

"Believe me, I understood you perfectly." She lifted her chin and gave him a look that speared him right through the heart. "You don't think I have a real job. If you did, you never would have asked me to come with you."

The words landed right in his gut, as heavy as a punch and just as painful.

"You have no idea what it's like to build something on your own," she said, her voice cracking with barely restrained anger. "And now, because of this mess, I might have to do damage control to save it. I don't have people to write statements for me or tell me what to do. Because I do everything myself. I made my dream happen, and I don't give a shit whether you think it's real or not."

He stared at the floor. "Sometimes, the dream doesn't work out, no matter how badly you want it or how hard you chase it." He knew that firsthand. Baseball had been everything—until it wasn't. "Sometimes your plans have to change."

She didn't let him get another word out. She marched over to the front door and opened it. "Get out."

He stood and walked over to her. "Audrey."

When he touched her elbow, she shook him off like a bug. "Do not make me cause a scene. Leave."

He picked up his duffel bag from the floor and stepped over the threshold. "I'm sorry. None of that came out right. Can we—"

She slammed the door in his face.

He stood there staring at the closed door like she'd change her mind. Like she'd let him back in to apologize and explain. After a minute, a sob came from the other side of the door. His heart shattered to pieces.

He placed a hand on the wooden frame. "Please. I messed up."

"Go away."

His shoulders sagged. It was over. She wanted him

gone. He'd ruined whatever chance they had. He was as bad as her ex.

"I know you're still there," she said. "My friends are coming over, and if they see you, they will murder you on the spot."

He didn't doubt it. He turned away with regret building in his throat.

And then he walked down the stairs and out of her life.

Chapter Twenty-Seven

After Luke left, Audrey slid down to the floor and sat there so long her butt went numb. She couldn't move even if she wanted to.

He was gone. Less than twenty-four hours ago, she'd realized she loved him. And now it was over.

She drew her legs up to her chest and rested her forehead on her knees. A fresh round of tears started, this time accompanied by a rush of anger.

He'd asked her to choose between him and her business. It went against everything she knew about him. Since the day they started their fake relationship, he had been nothing but supportive and encouraging. This whole time, she'd never doubted his belief in her. She'd trusted he meant it.

In the end, he was exactly like Neil. Putting his own career first. Telling her she didn't have a real job. Expecting her to drop everything for him.

Before their fight, she'd been ready to give Luke a chance and try this for real. It was good they argued and got everything out in the open. Relationships weren't compatible with her goals. By showing her who he really was, he'd saved her from making a huge mistake.

Natalie's and Grace's voices echoed up the stairs. She

swiped at the corners of her eyes with her shirtsleeves. A key slid into the lock on the door.

"There's something against the door," Grace said, trying to push it open. "Audrey? Can you let us in?"

She shifted to reach up and turn the doorknob. With a sniffle, she scooted away so they could enter.

When Grace opened the door, she took one look at Audrey and said, "Oh, geez. Nat, this is bad."

Natalie peeked over Grace's shoulder. Her expression went from concerned to murderous in a second. "Where is he and what did he do?"

They stepped inside and closed the door behind them. Grace had a pizza box, and Natalie held a grocery store bag. Audrey hadn't eaten much since last night, but she didn't want food. She wanted to sit here until the rest of her went numb, too.

Natalie extended the hand that wasn't holding a bag. "I don't know how long you've been sitting there, but come on. Couch. Food. Water."

Grace went to set the pizza box down and came back with some napkins. "You look like you could use these."

More tears fell. All summer, she'd lied to them. Now they knew the extent of her deception. Yet when she sent an SOS text, they came here at a moment's notice because that was what they did for each other. She'd lucked out in the friend department. They were the best.

"Thank you for coming," she said, dabbing at her eyes and sniffling. "I can't believe you're not mad at me. I've been lying to you for over a month."

Natalie snorted. "We kind of figured it out."

"What? How?" Audrey finally took Natalie's extended hand. She let herself be pulled to her feet and led over to the couch, where she flopped into a heap in one of the corners.

Grace stuck a glass of water in Audrey's hand. "Remember when you told us at the beach that you were 'helping each other'?"

"We've both read that fanfic multiple times," Natalie said with an exaggerated eye roll. "A relationship that conveniently benefits both of your careers? Do you really think you could have fooled us? Hell, I think Grace wrote one of those fics back in the day."

Audrey laughed, but her laughter quickly dissolved into more tears. "It was right after the trip that things started feeling real."

Her friends enveloped her in a hug. She took their comfort, even though she didn't deserve it. The day she met Luke, she'd reminded herself getting involved with someone would hold her back from going after what she wanted. She should have listened to that voice in her head. How could she have been so naïve?

"Now tell us what he did so we can destroy him," Natalie said, pulling back from the hug. She might not look threatening, but Audrey had no doubt Natalie could destroy Luke if she wanted to.

She balled up the napkin she'd used to wipe away her tears. "I told you the producers want his new show to travel around the country, right? He asked me to go with him. Because according to him, I don't have a real job." She crunched the napkin in her fist.

Both of her friends groaned and swore. She waited for them to finish before she continued.

"Since I don't have a real job, of course I can give up everything to follow him around. He said I didn't have to worry about money because he'd take care of me."

She still couldn't believe it. The same Luke who liked that she was a go-getter and was disgusted by her ex's behavior thought she wanted to be taken care of. That she'd be fine with leaving her business behind for a man.

"You can take care of yourself," Natalie said. "You're a bad bitch."

"I don't feel like one right now."

"I think being in touch with our emotions makes us stronger." Natalie slung an arm around Audrey's shoulders. "Luke can't handle a bad bitch."

She swallowed hard past a lump in her throat. "He's been so supportive all summer. I really thought he was different."

"You don't need him," Grace said. "You're kicking ass on your own."

"I don't know how long that's going to last after this. What if my livelihood is threatened?" Panic consumed her, making her dizzy. "What if all people see when they search for my name is this stunt? Will they even want to work with me?"

"The last time I checked, it looked like most of the tweets were calling out him and the network," Natalie said. "Not you."

"Give it time. The internet loves tearing women apart."

She'd been lucky so far. Something told her she wouldn't be this time. And then what? She couldn't go back to planning meetings and conventions. Not after getting to do what she really wanted with her life. Not after starting a business and working for herself. Finding an office job and dealing with another boss like Gary was her worst nightmare.

She grabbed a fresh napkin and wiped her eyes again.

"I don't think I can talk about this anymore. We should eat."

They had to reheat the pizza, which had long since gone cold. She managed to eat something, not that it helped her feel any better. She would feel like shit for a while, probably. But that was okay.

Bad bitches always got back on their feet.

Chapter Twenty-Eight

Walking away from Audrey was one of the hardest things Luke had ever done.

Three days ago, he left her hurt and angry, crying on the other side of the door. Now when he was alone and things got too quiet, he heard her broken-sounding sob playing on repeat in his head. Every time, it destroyed him all over again.

He would never forgive himself.

In the moment, he'd only thought about what he wanted. He didn't consider her needs at all. He asked a driven, successful woman to give up everything she'd worked for and dreamed about for years. He took her love for granted and figured—what? That she'd pack it all up and be content to let her business take a backseat to his show?

As if that wasn't enough, then he'd really gone and fucked it up.

Of all the things he could've said, he'd told her she could get a real job if her business failed. He hadn't consciously channeled her ex, but it didn't matter. The impact was exactly the same. The shock on her face and steel in her voice replayed in his head during those mo-

ments alone, too. In a matter of minutes, he'd ruined the
best thing to happen to him in his entire life.

He didn't deserve her.

With the work at the Victorian mostly done, he threw
himself into projects around Mom's house. He cleaned
the gutters. Did some yard work. Refinished the back
deck. He was out on the newly refinished deck that evening when the sliding glass door opened.

He jerked his head around. Erin stood there wearing a purple Hockey Is for Everyone shirt and holding
a six-pack of beer.

"What are you doing here?"

"Hello to you, too," she said, closing the door behind
her. "Mom called me."

"I told her not to bother you."

"She said, 'Your brother is heartbroken and won't
talk to me,' so I figured I better get my ass over here."
Erin plopped down in the chair next to his and handed
him a bottle. "Talk."

He accepted the bottle and popped the top off.
"Thanks, but I don't have anything to say."

"Then I'm going to make you talk."

"I'm pretty sure that's not how it works."

She put a hand on his arm. "Luke." She stared at the
side of his face until he turned his head to look at her.

"I appreciate you coming here, but I'm sure you and
Chloe had plans. You don't have to stay."

She scoffed. "I'm not leaving. Do you really think
I'd leave when you've been there for me my entire life?
When Dad died and later, when I came out—at the hard-
est and toughest parts—you were there supporting me.
Let me be there for you for once."

Ah, shit. He swiped his other arm across his eyes.

After everything that happened with Audrey, he hadn't cried. He'd beaten himself up, not slept, and barely ate, but he didn't cry. Tears didn't come easily for him.

Erin wanting to be there for him was what finally did it.

She stood and bent down to put her arms around him. He cried into her shoulder and let her rub his back. The last time he'd cried like this was when Dad died. That was a different kind of hurt from losing Audrey, but they both hit him the same. The wrenching pain in his chest, the guilt and regret, the hurt that felt like it would never go away—the feelings were identical.

When he pulled away from Erin's embrace, she squeezed his shoulder before sitting down again. "Do you want to tell me what happened?"

"I faked a relationship for social media and ended up falling in love."

"I got that from the tweets."

After he left Audrey's, he'd sent the tweet he showed her. He liked it more than the network's prepared statement, which lacked any emotion. The PR people weren't pleased, but he didn't care. He didn't owe them anything after Jessica went and messed everything up. Every time he thought about what she did and how her friend's roommate tweeted about it, a surge of hurt and disbelief hit him all over again. He'd at least gotten an emailed apology from Jessica, who said she was on a probationary period with limited access to the network's stars. He hadn't replied yet. He needed time to process before he said anything to her.

So no, he didn't care that the PR team rewrote their statement as a general one from the network and put it out on the HomeTV social channels. They could do whatever they wanted, but he needed to speak from the heart. That meant letting people know how he felt about Audrey.

His tweet didn't make #FakeBae go away. It didn't even smooth over most of the damage. Fans were still pissed, the network was still pissed, and his life was still a mess.

When it became clear he wasn't going to say more, Erin sighed. "Why did you break up?"

"I told her I loved her and asked her to come with me."

"She just started her own business. How did you expect her to do that?"

"I don't know." He shrugged and took a drink. "I figured she could do photography anywhere, and she could come back to Chicago for big jobs. When she mentioned she had clients and could lose money, I said I'd take care of her."

Erin winced. "You did not."

"I did. That's not even the real kicker."

She raised her eyebrows.

"I said if her business doesn't work out, she could always get a real job. You can imagine how that went." He still couldn't believe he'd said that. What a dick move.

Erin groaned. "You really fucked it up."

"Hey, I thought you were here to provide support."

"Part of being a good sibling is being honest."

"I know I fucked up. In the moment, I thought, 'I love her and I want to be with her, and the only way that can happen is if she comes with me.'"

"I get that. But…"

"But what?"

"You pulled some patriarchal 'I'll take care of you' bullshit, and that's not cool." She shook her head.

"I didn't mean it in a 'you're a woman and I'm a man, traditional gender roles, I'll take care of you,' kind of way. I meant 'I love you, so of course I'll help if you need it.'"

"That's not what she heard. It's not what I would've heard in that situation, either."

"I know that now."

"And no offense, but your definition of taking care of someone usually goes way beyond other people's. I think you need to get over this whole protector thing you've got going on," Erin said, giving his arm an affectionate poke. "Audrey can take care of herself. So can Mom and I."

"Mom basically told me the same thing a few weeks ago."

You did your part. It's been eight years. It's past time for you to start living your life for yourself.

He'd tried to start living life for himself and ended up with a broken heart and a contract he couldn't bring himself to sign. His agent hadn't stopped calling, texting, and emailing. She said they needed to get the document signed before the internet turned on him again and the network execs pulled the offer.

He still hadn't responded.

Erin swung her legs over the side of the chair so she could face him. "Both Mom and I are telling you we don't need to be taken care of, and I bet Audrey said the same thing. If we need you, we'll tell you. But you don't have to make sacrifices for us anymore. Go do what you want."

"I was trying to, with the new show. That was the first time in a long time I was doing something for myself."

"Yeah, but I bet you're planning on giving most of the money you make to us."

He shifted his gaze away from hers.

"You don't have a financial obligation to us," she said. "Maybe right after Dad died, you did, but not anymore. You've done a lot. Way more than you had to. I mean, you took the *Retro Renovations* job to help pay for my college education. I'm grateful for that, but you didn't have to. I could have gotten scholarships or financial aid."

"They might not have covered everything, and I didn't want you to have student loan debt. I saw a way to take care of that burden for you."

Her expression softened. "It made a huge difference. I can't thank you enough for it. But you don't have to take on everyone's burdens. You don't have to help everyone, or fix everything."

"I'm always going to want to help you and Mom."

"I know, but you don't have to be so intense about it anymore. Do this new show, and use the money you make to buy a house or do something nice for yourself. We're okay. Trust me."

That had been the plan. Do the show, buy a house, and spend time in Chicago when he wasn't working. Since he left Audrey's apartment, that plan had stopped looking so appealing. Everything in his life was less appealing without her in it.

What if he forgot about the plan and stayed? Would things be different with her then?

"I don't want to sign the contract."

Erin choked on the sip of beer she'd just taken. "What are you talking about, and where the hell is this coming from?"

"If I'm in Chicago, then we both get what we want. I don't have to leave, and Audrey can keep growing her business here."

If he stayed, he could prove she came first. Show her he knew he'd made a mistake when he said those things and walked out her door.

"I thought it was over with her." Erin coughed. "Now you're going to walk away from the show and hope she takes you back? Dude."

"I need to show her that she's important to me."

Erin tilted her head to the side, considering. "Can I give you some advice? You've risked a lot for her already. Confirming those rumors and going against what the network wanted you to post took guts."

"I might have risked a lot, but I still hurt her. I told her I was sorry, and she slammed the door in my face."

"You hurt each other. You had a fight, and you both reacted badly. That said, I don't think either one of you has to give up everything if you want to be together."

He stared out at the backyard. "What you're saying is it doesn't have to be all or nothing."

"Exactly. Also? She's the one who kicked you out. The ball is her court now if she wants you back. You can apologize all you want, but it's not up to you."

"I still don't know what to do about the contract." He rubbed at his chin. Aside from wanting to show Audrey he cared about her, did he want to sign for himself? What if there was another reason he was dragging his feet?

"Would being on TV make you happy?" Erin asked.

"I don't know anymore." He didn't want to give up the show, but after this summer, he was ready to be out of the public eye. Not permanently, but for a while. He needed a break from being a top-trending topic. On the other hand, he wasn't eager to go back to the family business, either.

It doesn't have to be all or nothing.

His choices didn't have to be between HomeTV and the family business. He could have something separate, something that belonged to him. Maybe he could take a page from a smart and successful person who always went after what she wanted.

"I think I have some decisions to make."

Chapter Twenty-Nine

Bad bitches always got back on their feet, but that didn't mean getting back up again was easy.

Over the past four days, a hollowness had settled somewhere near Audrey's heart. Some mornings she didn't want to get out of bed. More than once she woke up to emails from reporters asking if she had any comment. She deleted the emails and moved on. After several days, the reporters moved on, too. There was always another viral sensation to write about.

For her own mental health, she'd temporarily locked her social media after blocking some trolls. She stayed away from Twitter. She stopped checking Instagram, too, which sucked. That app was usually a refuge.

One night, her loneliness and desperation had her reaching for her phone when she couldn't sleep. She looked up Luke's Twitter account. The most recent tweet at the top of his timeline was from the day of their breakup.

It might have started out fake, but it's real now. I love her.

She burst into tears. After she told him to get out, the last thing she thought he'd do was press Send on that draft. But he had.

An ache bloomed in the center of her chest. He hadn't posted HomeTV's statement. By going against the network's wishes, he'd put his career on the line.

For her.

She wiped her tears away. He may have publicly declared his love, but that didn't change the fact he'd asked her to give up on her dreams. She had to stand firm. For years, all she'd wanted was to start her own business and leave her day job behind. No one would make her give that up.

Not even the man she loved.

She'd made the right decision. Time to stop doubting herself and move on with her life. The pain would go away eventually. She'd stop missing him, stop having dreams about that perfect weekend where he told her he was proud of her. That he admired her. Those were lies. If he were proud of her, he'd never have said the things he said during their fight.

The next morning, the ache was even stronger. How much longer would she have to suffer before she got over him?

She forced herself out of bed. After grabbing her phone from the nightstand, she headed into the kitchen. While she waited for the coffee to finish brewing, she pulled up the email app on her phone. A message toward the top of her inbox made her pause.

Mateo Suarez. Where did she know that name from?

She tapped the email and started reading.

Hi Audrey,

I spoke to Luke last week, and he gave me your email address when I mentioned I might need a photographer for an upcoming event. He highly recommended you and had a lot of great things to say about your work. I looked at your website and have to agree with him. My foundation is having its inaugural fundraiser next month and I was wondering if you'd be interested in shooting it.

I've put a link below to the foundation's website. Check it out and don't hesitate to let me know if you have any questions. I look forward to hearing from you soon.

She clicked the link. Ah, now she knew the name. The real estate agent from *Retro Renovations*. She scrolled through the webpage. Mateo's foundation worked to find safe, affordable housing for people in need. Not only was it a wonderful cause, but if she took this job, it would be a huge boost to her profile.

And Luke had recommended her for it.

Nope, not dwelling on that. She'd be a fool not to take the job, even if the person who recommended her for it broke her heart. There was nothing wrong with using her connections to get ahead. She wrote back to Mateo, thanking him for reaching out and letting him know she was interested.

Later that day, she met up with Natalie and Grace for dinner. Well, dinner and margaritas. Natalie told her she needed to get the hell out of her apartment and lured her to the restaurant with the promise of buying her drinks.

She took a sip of her margarita and looked across the table at her friends. "I have some news."

Maybe if she shared the news about this big job for Mateo's foundation, they'd both stop giving her that look. The one where they frowned and tilted their heads to the side, their eyes full of pity. She hated it.

"Did you hear from Luke?" Grace asked.

"No." A wave of sadness crashed over her. She pushed through it. "I got an email this morning from Mateo Suarez—"

"The way that man wears a suit is the only other reason I've ever watched *Retro Renovations*," Natalie interrupted. "But yes, go on."

"He started a foundation and its first big fundraiser is coming up. It seems like a big deal, and he wants me to shoot it." She shrugged and used her straw to poke at the ice in her drink. "Even if I only got the job because of Luke, I couldn't pass it up."

Grace grabbed a chip from the bowl in the center of the table. "How do you know you only got it because of Luke?"

"Mateo said he talked to Luke last week. He recommended me and gave Mateo my email address. I guess he said a bunch of great stuff about my work."

"Last week. Before you broke up," Natalie said.

"What does that have to do with anything?"

Natalie rolled her eyes. "Uh, it has a lot to do with everything."

"He recommended you," Grace said.

"And he spoke highly of your work."

They couldn't be serious. "Did you miss the part where Luke asked me to follow him around the country and told me I could get a real job? What happened to you two wanting to destroy him?"

"You fought and he said some things." Natalie picked up a chip and waved it back and forth, dismissing the question. "His actions are more important." She popped the chip in her mouth.

Were they?

She took a chip for herself and broke it in half. "He

said some things, and they keep making me wonder if he's the person I thought he was. If I can trust his actions."

"Who did you think he was?" Grace said, her voice gentle.

She stared off into the distance. The weight of missing Luke pressed down on her, right in that hollow place near her heart. Her eyes filled with tears. She pressed her fingertips to the corners of her eyes, like that would do anything to stop the tears from falling.

"I thought he was kind and decent. I thought he supported me. He told me he was proud of me and that he admired me. He said the way I'd built my business was impressive."

Natalie pursed her lips. "Do you think he was lying?"

Audrey dabbed at her eyes with a napkin. "If he wasn't lying, how else could he turn around and say what he said? The 'real job' thing, the idea of having to give up my dreams—that's my biggest trigger, and he hit it."

"Maybe you hit his, too," Grace said.

Had she?

Oh, crap. She had.

He took care of people. Look at what he did for his mom and sister after his dad died. What he still did for them. At the moment when his career was in jeopardy and everything was falling apart, he'd clung to the one thing he knew how to do. Taking her with him was his way of trying to show her how much he cared. That didn't excuse some of his comments, but it did put things into perspective.

"I think I did," she said slowly. "And he responded by saying the one thing guaranteed to make me go off."

"What I'm getting from this conversation is that you

both fucked up," Natalie said. "Now you either fix it or you don't."

Grace nodded. "He's not Neil, telling you that you were never going to make it. Luke's actions do matter."

"He recommended you and it sounds like he talked up your work," Natalie added. "Would he do that if he wasn't proud of you? If he didn't want you to succeed?"

Audrey rubbed the stem of her glass between her fingers and mulled over their words. Although Luke had said bad things—to be fair, they'd both said bad things—he didn't have to recommend her to Mateo. All summer, Luke had shown her he supported her and took her work seriously. A bad fight, a social media disaster, and knee-jerk reactions from both of them didn't change that.

People said crappy things in stressful situations all the time. Things they might not mean, or things said out of fear. They'd both been terrified. They hurt each other.

She had to try to talk things out with him. She couldn't go through the rest of her life wondering what could have been.

"His actions say my work matters, and that I matter, too," Audrey said. "I don't know what to do now, though."

Natalie picked up her margarita glass and glanced at Audrey over the rim. "Talk to him. Work through your problems. Decide if it's worth trying again."

That made things sound easy. A three-step plan for getting back her former fake boyfriend. But after everything that happened, this might be the rare moment where a plan wasn't enough.

"What if he doesn't want to hear from me?"

Grace heaved a weary sigh. "He'll want to hear from you. He loves you. I'd be really surprised if he's not as miserable as you are right now."

"He hasn't texted me once."

"You kicked him out and slammed a door in his face," Natalie said. "I wouldn't text you, either."

"That's an even bigger reason to think he won't want me to contact him."

"I swear it's like you're looking for reasons to keep being miserable," Grace said. "All you have to do is try to start a conversation. If he doesn't want to talk, you'll know."

They both made good points. Audrey dug in her purse for her phone. "I'm going to text him now."

"Are you sure you want to do that after half a margarita?" Natalie said.

"If I don't do it now, I'll talk myself out of it."

Audrey unlocked her phone, pulled up a blank text, and started typing. I miss you.

Should she add something else to the message? She didn't know what to say. That would have to be enough for now.

"There," she said, setting down the phone. "I did it."

Natalie leaned in, straining to see Audrey's screen. "What did you say?"

"I told him I miss him." Her throat got itchy. She better not cry again. "That's good, right?"

"It's a start, and a start is all you need," Grace said.

Three dots appeared underneath her text. She snatched up her phone from the table. "Oh my God, he's typing something back."

Grace smirked and took a drink. "Told you."

The dots disappeared, then came back. Disappeared again. The cycle repeated twice before the screen went dark.

"Sometimes phones do that when the other person is

taking a long time to type a response," Natalie said. She and Grace gave each other nervous looks.

"I'm not going to keep sitting here, watching dots on a screen and praying he texts back." Audrey tossed her phone back into her bag. "I hate this." She drained the rest of her margarita.

At least she'd tried.

Chapter Thirty

"You have to write the perfect response," Aidan said. "Like, 'I was wrong. You're a queen and I'm not worthy of your beauty and immense talents. Please forgive me.'"

Luke stared at his cousin. "I'm not writing that."

"I dictated the perfect text to you, and you're not going to use it?" Aidan shook his head and muttered, "Hopeless."

An hour ago, Aidan arrived unannounced at his doorstep with a pizza. Things were fine at first. Aidan could be annoying sometimes, but he was a decent person. He cared enough to show up here with dinner, although his kindness didn't extend to allowing Luke to watch baseball. Instead, Aidan put on that baking show Mom and Erin were obsessed with. He was already on his second episode of the evening.

"That meringue is incredible." Aidan whistled. "Look at those peaks."

Luke let him talk about meringues and shit because it meant Aidan stayed out of his business. Or he had, until Audrey texted a couple minutes ago.

"Your response is—it's a lot, man," Luke said. "I'm not trying to scare her."

"My advice hasn't steered you wrong yet."

Luke glanced up from his phone.

"Don't look at me like that," Aidan said, leaning back in the recliner. "I give good advice. I helped with your Insta game, didn't I?"

"This is a lot different. If I get this wrong…"

Aidan reached over to clap a hand on Luke's shoulder. "You're not going to get it wrong. Now, okay, I'll admit my suggestion was a little wordy. You're not a wordy kind of guy."

"I'm really not."

"Your response needs to be authentic to you."

Luke tossed his phone on the side table. "I'll think of something later."

"And leave her waiting for a response? Don't do that."

Yeah, he didn't want to leave her waiting. She took a chance by texting him. He'd take a chance of his own and text her back. He picked up his phone. This didn't have to be hard. He was overthinking it.

I miss you, too.

It was the truest thing he'd ever written. He missed her with everything he had. Missed her so much it was like he'd gotten punched and couldn't breathe.

He hit the send button.

"What did you say?" Aidan asked.

The retort was on the tip of his tongue: *Mind your own business.* It was easy to be an asshole when you were hurting. Aidan had come over here and tried to help; the least Luke could do was share this with him. He'd kept so much bottled up inside for so long. Audrey showed him it was okay to let people in sometimes.

Even if it backfired in the end.

"I told her I miss her, too."

Aidan rubbed his chin. "Simple. Straightforward. I like it."

"Hopefully she texts back."

Luke picked up his phone to check the screen, even though the device was right there. He would have heard it vibrate if she replied. She used to respond within minutes to most of his texts. This time, the screen stayed dark. He turned his attention to the TV but kept glancing over at his phone like he might catch her response the second the screen lit up.

Aidan kept side-eyeing him but didn't say anything. After a few more minutes, he pushed down his recliner's footrest and stood. "She might have put her phone away, or maybe she's out. Why don't we go do something else?"

"Like what?"

"Show me the renovation now that it's all done. I haven't been at the house in a while. You still have the keys?"

"Why do you want to see it?"

"I'm trying to get your mind off things," Aidan said, sounding more exasperated than Luke was used to. "Since I guess that's not clear."

Oh. Okay. "Yeah, I still have the keys."

He grabbed them and his wallet, then stuck his phone in his pocket, too. Just in case. They walked down the street to the Victorian on the corner. Luke let them inside and flipped on the lights in the entryway.

"I'm gonna go check out the upstairs," Aidan said. "Wanna come with?"

Luke waved him on. He needed the alone time.

He'd worked hard on this house. Poured everything he had into it. He didn't get attached to projects, but he'd been attached to this one from the start. Pretty soon it would go on the market. This might be the last time he saw the inside.

Walking through the first floor, he didn't stop for long in each room. Until he reached the dining room and the bay window with the view of the garden. The first time Audrey came here, she said she'd put a bench there and use the space as a reading nook.

So he'd made her one.

The built-in bench was the last thing he did at the house before finishing the renovation. She would never get to use it, but that spot was hers.

He couldn't stay in this room, not with memories of her everywhere. After taking a picture of the bench with his phone, he went to the living room. His favorite room. The crown molding and fireplace had been a pain in the ass to restore, but he'd loved every minute. Working on this house, he got to remember what it was like to put his heart into something. To put in passion instead of only sweat. What would it be like to do that all the time?

The back of his neck prickled. He *could* do that all the time.

An idea began to take shape. Something that would upend all the plans he had at the start of the summer. A way to do something he wanted instead of changing his life and leaving home yet again. He could make the safe, expected choice. Or he could try something new.

It was scary as hell. But sometimes the things that scared you the most were worth the risk.

He peeked at his phone. Still no response. He swore under his breath and went to catch up to Aidan. If he told Audrey about his idea, what would she say?

No question, she'd tell him to go for it. She always went after what she wanted.

It was time he did, too.

By the time he and Aidan closed the house's front door behind them, he knew what he had to do.

"You did a nice job," Aidan said once they'd reached the sidewalk. He stuck his hands in his pockets and smiled. "I did, too."

"Thanks for your help."

"I think that was the first time you didn't say something like, 'You only did the cabinets.'"

"I was a jerk. You helped a lot. Even if sometimes I thought it was just so you could get on camera."

"I'm not denying the world the opportunity to see this face."

Luke laughed for the first time in days. Aidan gave him a goofy grin. They started back toward home.

"When's the big premiere?" Aidan asked. "You know our moms are gonna want to have a watch party."

Here was his opening. "There's not going to be a premiere. At least not for a while. And not on HomeTV."

Aidan stopped walking in the middle of the sidewalk, forcing Luke to stop, too. "What the hell are you talking about?"

"I'm not signing their contract." Damn, saying the words out loud felt good. "The last thing I want to do is leave Chicago again."

"Is this about Audrey?"

"This is about me and what I want. I want to stay here."

Coming home for a couple weeks at a time wasn't what he wanted. He'd still be gone most of the time. Away from his family.

Away from her.

He swallowed past a lump in his throat before continuing. "I finally looked at the contract with my agent. We reviewed the one for the pilot, too. There's a clause that says if HomeTV passes on the pilot or if I reject the terms of their contract, I get to keep the rights to the idea. I can shop it elsewhere." He'd missed that the first time around.

"Whoa. Seriously?"

"Yeah. I'm not going to sign." His heart beat faster. He was really doing this.

"What about the pilot?"

"If they pass on it, it's mine. But if I say, 'Hey, I'm not signing the contract for the series,' technically the pilot is still theirs." His shoulders heaved as he sighed. "I don't know. My agent is trying to work something out."

Aidan's mouth opened and closed. He said "huh" a couple times before he managed a complete thought. "What happens next, then?"

"I want to go back to my original idea. Find old houses in Chicago I can restore. Maybe pitch it to a streaming service that'll let me have more creative control than HomeTV."

"And won't ask you to be in another fake relationship?"

"I mean, yeah. There's that, too."

Although if HomeTV had never asked him to be in a fake relationship, he wouldn't have gotten to know Audrey. They would have taken that picture together at the animal shelter and never seen each other again. Because of the network's deal, he'd ended up falling in love. He wouldn't take that back, regardless of what had happened between them.

He'd faked a relationship for an opportunity to have

something he wanted. But it turned out HomeTV couldn't give him what he longed for. Home, and family, and a chance to make things right with Audrey. His only choice was to walk away. Otherwise, he'd get stuck again, settling for the next best thing.

Fuck that. He was done settling.

He would always help his family. Helping others was part of who he was. But he didn't have to sacrifice everything at the expense of his own happiness. He could go out and do what he wanted, not because of his family or because of what a network wanted him to do. Audrey had left him with an important lesson: If you wanted something badly enough, you needed to go for it.

He slid his hand into his pocket and rubbed the edge of his phone.

"She text you back yet?" Aidan asked.

Luke took out his phone and pressed the button to light up the screen. "Not yet."

"I guess you'll just have to wait."

If there was a chance for them, he'd wait as long as he had to.

Chapter Thirty-One

I miss you, too.

Those four words had been burned into Audrey's brain since she first read them last night. The rush of joy over getting a reply—*he missed her, too!*—was quickly muffled by anxiety. What did she say now? She'd almost texted Grace and Natalie but stopped herself. Whatever she said next had to come from her, not someone else. Her friends had helped enough already.

By the next morning, she still hadn't come up with anything. The cursor blinked in the text box, waiting for her to type something.

Starting a conversation was easy. Fixing things? Not so much.

She'd already wasted too much time staring at her phone. The perfect response wasn't going to materialize out of thin air and appear on the screen. With a sigh, she stuck her phone back in her purse. Her potential client was due to arrive at the event space any minute.

The building didn't look like much from the outside— it was an old factory across from the Metra tracks on Ravenswood Avenue—but inside, it had high ceilings with timber beams, huge windows, and exposed brick. Nice hardwood floors, too. If Luke were here, he'd want to know if the floors were original. She laughed and sniffled at the same time. He was such a nerd about that stuff.

God, she missed him. What else was she supposed to write to him besides an endless loop of *I miss you's*?

She stared out the windows at the surrounding buildings and the trees blowing in the breeze. All she needed was a soundtrack of acoustic emo songs to make the scene complete.

"I'm sorry I'm late."

Audrey startled, turning around. A tall woman in a purple dress and high heels stood in the doorway. She had a huge leather bag on her shoulder and long, dark red hair cascading over one shoulder. She had the best hair Audrey had ever seen. "You must be Lauren."

"I hope I didn't keep you waiting," the event planner said.

"Not at all." Audrey pasted on a smile. At least she hadn't cried this time, like every other time she thought about Luke. "It's nice to meet you in person. Why don't we walk through the space and you can tell me more about the gala?"

First she got hired for Mateo's fundraiser, and now she had this meeting for another charity gala. Look at her, still thriving after the latest Twitter debacle. After she and Lauren checked out the main room and chatted about the charity—a foundation that funded arts education—they headed downstairs to tour the rest of the building.

"We hold this event every year, but this is the first time we're not having it in a hotel ballroom," Lauren said once they'd finished exploring the first floor. "We wanted to try something new, and go with a new photographer, too. I thought you'd be great for this."

"Thanks. How'd you find me?" Ha, like she didn't already know. Before she could stop herself, she said, "Let me guess—Twitter? Instagram?"

Lauren pursed her lips and shook her head. "I'm not too active on social media. Are you well known there?"

Audrey held in her laugh. "Um, sort of." That was the biggest understatement she'd ever made.

"I found you the boring way. I googled Chicago photographers, and there was your website."

"Oh. These days I just assume…" She trailed off, not voicing the rest of the thought. *That people only know about me because I was one half of a viral sensation.*

"I liked your work. You did some other event recently, an awards ceremony for a nonprofit? I thought the way you shot it was different, but in a good way," Lauren said, coming to a stop next to a high-top table where she set down her enormous purse. "They weren't the usual, boring 'here's a bunch of people at a party' or 'here's someone getting an award' kind of photos."

That awards ceremony happened the night she and Luke had celebratory milkshakes and she got freaked out by the depth of his feelings for her. Those feelings—his love for her—had been written all over his face.

Audrey swallowed past the emotion building in her throat at the memory. "I'm glad you liked them."

Lauren tilted her head to the side like she was trying to think of something. She tapped her fingers on the table. "There was a vibrancy to your photos. You have a way of capturing people in the moment and in their best light. Literally and figuratively."

"That means a lot to me. Thank you."

"You're welcome." Lauren beamed at her. "I'm looking forward to working with you."

"Likewise. This is such a great space. I'm excited."

Lauren said she'd follow up via email, and they parted ways. Audrey walked down the street to her car with Lauren's compliments echoing in her head.

People had to like her photos to hire her, no matter how they found out about her. No one wanted to pay for crappy pictures they'd hate. But here was someone who didn't know about her brief moment in the spotlight. Who didn't know about Luke. She'd gotten this job on her own merits. Lauren wanted to hire her because she was good at what she did.

Sure, the fake relationship gave her fledgling business a boost, but she could do this on her own. Now she had proof.

Before she kicked him out of her life, Luke would have been the first person she told about this job. He'd be so proud of her. She took a deep, shaky breath and got in her car.

Would he still be proud of me now?

She had goals and plans, dreams and ideas. No one would make her give them up. For a long time, she assumed she'd have to if she was dating someone. When Luke had asked her to go with him, he brought all of those old fears to the surface. It didn't matter why he asked or what he felt. All she heard was *give everything up for me.*

He'd screwed up, but it was in a moment of panic.

The Luke she'd gotten to know this summer—the man she'd come to love—would never expect her to give up everything. At the beginning of their fake relationship, he said he'd do whatever it took to help her. He followed through on that promise. Everything she asked him to do for her, he did. He went above and beyond.

He'd talked her up to his former costar. He'd helped her get her biggest job to date with Mateo's fundraiser, even though now she knew she didn't need him to get ahead. Her work stood on its own. Today, she'd seen that in action.

During their fight, she'd jumped to conclusions instead of talking things out. The choice didn't have to be between pursuing her goals and being in a relationship, his career or hers.

She could have what she wanted. He could have what he wanted, too. Committing to someone didn't mean she had to abandon her dreams.

Trying this for real would take compromise on both their parts. It wouldn't be easy for either of them, but she owed it to herself to try. She took out her phone and opened up their text thread.

Can we talk? she typed. Her thumb hovered over the send button.

After he left her apartment, she wouldn't even listen to his apology. Would he want to hear hers? Was missing her enough?

She had to go big.

And she knew exactly how to do it.

Chapter Thirty-Two

When you wanted to fly somewhere cheap at the last minute and needed two seats next to each other, you had to take what you could get.

Cleveland it was.

She wanted to go big. Sending Luke an email with a plane ticket and *I was hoping we could talk. Up for another cheese plate?* less than twenty-four hours before the flight's departure—that wasn't just big. That was ludicrous.

And she might pull it off.

He'd written back, *I'll be there,* but he had to be wondering what the hell she was up to. They could talk without getting on a plane. Sometimes, though, you had to pull out all the stops. She'd never made a big romantic gesture in her life. If everything worked out, this would be her first and last.

She sank into her seat on the small regional jet. Her stomach turned over. What if he didn't show up?

He would. If he said he was going to do something or be somewhere, he followed through. That was her Luke, strong and steadfast to a fault.

She closed her eyes and breathed. One deep breath in. Hold it for seven seconds. Let it out. Repeat. Her heartbeat slowed. The jitters she'd had since she left her apartment that morning began to fade. She was still a bundle of nerves, although not as tightly wound as when she first arrived at the airport.

Trying not to run into him in the terminal had been its own adventure. She'd ended up in the fancy airport lounge, taking advantage of the elite flier status she'd gotten from her old job while she still had it. In the lounge, she downed a free mimosa and stuck an entire to-go cheese plate in her tote bag. They sure as hell weren't flying first class this time around.

She took another deep breath. A second mimosa would be nice right about now.

She was still doing her anxiety breathing exercise when a deep voice said, "Hey, I'm in the window seat."

Blinking open her eyes, she tilted her head up. Luke stood in the aisle, gazing down at her with an unexpected softness. Her throat grew tight. Tears welled up behind her eyelids. Oh, God. How did she still have any tears left in her body after this past week?

A weird half sob came out of her mouth before she spoke. "You're here."

"I said I would be." He gave her a nervous smile. "Can I sit with you?"

She brushed away an errant tear with the back of her hand and got up to let him into his seat. Once she sat down again, he reached over and swiped his thumb over her cheek.

"Hey," he said. "You okay?"

She nodded. Another tear slipped out. "I slammed a door in your face."

"I know. We both messed up that day."

It was only a week ago, but it felt like a lifetime. "I'm sorry I freaked out."

"I'm sorry I said that thing about getting a real job. That was uncalled for," he said, his voice full of regret. "I never should have asked you to leave with me. I should have thought about the way you'd interpret it, but I wasn't thinking. All I could focus on was how much you mean to me. How I could show you I wanted to make this work. I went about it all wrong."

"So did I." She took one of his hands in hers. "We should have talked about it. But I thought you were asking me to forget about my dreams and give everything up. You asked me to make a choice between you and my career. That's my worst fear."

He shook his head slowly and glanced at their joined hands. When he looked at her again, he had a pained expression on his face. "That's not how I meant it, but my intent doesn't matter. I was wrong, and I hurt you. I'm so sorry."

"I hurt you, too. You were trying to show me how much you loved me in the best way you knew how, and I flipped out."

"I understand why. And you're right, we should have talked about it. Worked something out where we did long distance or you came to visit me when you could. But I was scared. It felt like everything was falling apart. I was trying to hold on to you."

"I know that now," she said softly.

One of the flight attendants walked by, reminding everyone to buckle their seatbelts. They let go of each other's hands long enough to buckle up. Once their seatbelts were fastened, she turned to him again.

"We can figure out how we're going to do it, but I

want to try this for real." She fought back another wave of tears. "I love you."

"I love you, too."

He leaned in and cupped her face in his hands, giving her a gentle kiss. Her heart ached at the sweetness of it, at all the love he poured into it. She kissed him back with everything she had, hoping he could feel all of her love, too.

After he broke the kiss, he rested his forehead against hers. "We don't have to worry about figuring things out. I'll be in Chicago."

Wait, what? She moved her face away so she could look in his eyes. "They're going to let you do the show in Chicago? Did you change the producer's mind?"

He shook his head. "I didn't sign the contract."

Holy shit. Her eyeballs almost popped out of her head. "Why not? Please don't tell me it was for me. I would never want you to give up the show for me."

"I came to a decision on my own. I thought about what would really make me happy and what I really wanted. I decided to go for it." He swallowed, his Adam's apple working in his throat. "I learned that from you."

Her insides turned to mush. "What will make you happy? What do you want?"

"I want to be home. I want to be with you, and with my family."

"But the show…"

"I'm going to pitch it somewhere else. Somewhere that lets me make the kind of show I want to make, where I want to make it."

"You deserve that," she said. "I'm proud of you."

He reached for her hand, and she slid it into his. "I'm

proud of you, too. If I've ever given you a reason to doubt that, I'll do everything I can to make you believe me."

"I believe you." The only reason she'd ever doubted him was because of her own fears.

Their gazes locked together. She couldn't believe she'd almost lost him. For the longest time, she thought her goals were incompatible with love. Then she went and fell for her fake boyfriend, even though she'd tried hard not to. She'd drafted half a page of rules and made Luke agree to them. She'd put up walls between them, both metaphorical and pillow-based. She'd done everything she could to keep herself from falling.

He'd captured her heart anyway. And she'd captured his.

They smiled at each other when the plane began to back away from the gate.

Breaking the rules was totally worth it.

Luke looked at her with a raised eyebrow. "Cleveland, huh?"

"I needed a short, cheap flight for my big romantic gesture." She lowered her voice and leaned in close, like they were in on a secret. "I can't take it out yet, but I have a cheese plate in my purse."

He laughed. "What kind of big romantic gesture would it be without one?"

Epilogue

One year later...

Luke wasn't one for parties, but then again, the viewing party hadn't been his idea. He was only responsible for what would happen afterward. His stomach did a backflip. It had been doing that off and on all day. His nerves would settle down soon. He just needed to get through this part first.

"Who's ready to watch me in my starring role?" Aidan said over the din of laughter and chatter in Luke's living room. He waved the TV remote above his head.

Audrey raised her hand. "I am."

Aidan used the remote to point at her. "I knew there was a reason why I liked you better than my cousin."

"Will you press Play already?" Luke grumbled.

Aidan chuckled and started the first episode of *Renovation Cousins*, which had premiered today. His cousin deserved credit for making the show more entertaining than Luke could have on his own. Last year, when Luke brought the idea for the show to a new streaming service, Aidan had helped refine the pitch and come up with the title. Which he made sure everybody knew.

Their friends and family grew quiet as the episode

began. Luke tightened his arm around Audrey's shoulders. She looked up at him with an encouraging smile. Watching himself on TV never got less weird. This time, though, he was proud of what he'd created. For one thing, there weren't any gratuitous shots of his butt, even if Audrey missed them. In the future, he'd have to work in at least one for her.

He looked down at her, returning her smile. He was so proud of her. Her business was thriving and had recently been featured in *Chicago* magazine, bringing her another wave of clients. She kept busy running between photo shoots and events, but he knew she wouldn't have it any other way.

"I can't believe that's what this room used to look like," Audrey said as he walked through the Victorian's living room on the TV screen.

Mom beamed at him from across the room, where she sat in a side chair. "The transformation is amazing, isn't it?"

"It is," Audrey agreed.

"When you started the renovation, I had a feeling you were going to end up living here," Erin said. She and Chloe were curled up together on the loveseat, both happy and glowing. "You've always loved this house."

He'd had a feeling he would end up here, too. From the time he was a kid, he'd been drawn to the house's arches and stained glass. After renovating it, he couldn't bear seeing it get sold to someone else. Once filming wrapped and the house went on the market, he had to put in an offer. Now it was his.

When he moved back to Chicago, he wanted a home, one he could grow into. And he knew, down to the depths of his soul, that he wanted to grow into it with Audrey.

He took a deep breath to calm his nerves and pressed a kiss to the top of her head. They'd only been dating for a year, but when you knew, you knew.

Later that night, they stood at the front door together, saying good-night to the last of their guests, which included Audrey's parents and best friends. Audrey gave Natalie a hug, and then Grace. Both of them knew he was going to ask her. They'd come with him to pick out the ring. After he waved goodbye to them, Aidan walked up behind him and clapped him on the back. "Quality party, man." He nodded at a covered plate in his hands. "I took the last of the mini sliders, if that's cool." Without waiting for a response, he bounded out the door and down the front steps. "Thanks for having me!"

Some things never changed.

Audrey closed the door and leaned her back against it. "That was a successful watch party, but I hope you never host that many people again."

"Especially people who are food thieves."

She rolled her eyes, but they were full of affection. "You weren't going to eat those anyway."

"Okay, true." He put his hands on her waist. Now that it was only the two of them here, his heart beat faster. "Can I show you something?"

She tilted her head and gave him a wary look. "Yes?"

"Come with me." He took her hand and led her toward the dining room.

"Why are we going in here?" Her footsteps slowed. "Oh."

Natalie, Grace, and Aidan had been the last to leave for a reason. Luke had needed help to pull this off. In Audrey's reading nook, they'd strung up white fairy lights across the bay window and clipped pictures to them.

The lights illuminated her face as she let go of his hand to walk farther into the room.

She glanced at him over her shoulder. "What is this?"

He stuck his hands in his pockets and followed her. She stepped closer to the window.

"Are these pictures of us?" She pressed a hand to her mouth. "Ha, there we are at the conservatory." She peered at the rest of the photos. There they were at the animal shelter, at the bar, at Wrigley Field, and on the hotel rooftop in St. Louis. One from this summer's trip to the lake house. A photo from the day he'd closed on this house. "Most of these are from last summer. Why did you—"

He slowly guided her to sit on the bench and sat down next to her, taking her hand again. "Audrey, you're the most amazing person I've ever met. You're strong and smart and brave. You accomplish anything you set your mind to, and you don't let anyone stand in your way." He swallowed hard. He could do this. "You inspire me every day. Because of you, I finally decided to take some risks and go after what I want."

He had a throw pillow next to him. With his free hand he reached behind it, where he'd hidden the ring box. He pulled out the box, careful not to drop it. His hand was trembling.

She gasped and shouted, "Are you proposing?"

He smiled. "I'm not done with my speech."

"Yes, please continue saying nice things about me." She sat up straighter.

"So I'm taking another risk right now," he continued, opening the box. Inside was a white gold band studded with tiny diamonds, with a bigger stone in the center.

"I love you, and I want to spend the rest of my life with you. Will you marry me?"

Her eyes filled with tears, and she nodded. "Yes."

With his own throat growing tight with emotion, he slid the ring on her finger. She threw her arms around him and buried her face in his neck. He held her close. He was so lucky to have her in his life.

They stayed like that for a long moment, until she pulled back and pressed a soft kiss to his lips. "I love you," she said.

"I love you, too."

He wiped tears from her eyes, and she wiped them from his. He reached behind the throw pillow again, pulling out another small box. This one was longer than the ring box, slimmer, and less heavy. "I have one more thing." He handed the box to Audrey.

"What's this?" she asked, taking it from him.

"Open it."

She tilted her head to the side and wiggled the top off the box. "A key?"

"A key to this house," he said.

Audrey sniffled. She looked up from the box to meet his eyes. "You're going to make me cry again."

"I want this to be your home, too," he said. "As long as you're okay with it, I don't want to wait until we get married for you to move in."

"Of course I want to move in," she said softly. "I'm here so often, it feels like home. Ever since you showed me this house for the first time, I've loved it, too."

That day was still clear in his mind—walking her through the house, showing her this room and this nook for the first time. Back then, they'd been wrapped up in getting likes and sharing as much content as possible.

These days, they mostly stayed quiet on social media, except to promote her business and *Renovation Cousins*. They both needed a break after last summer. Their viral fame had been fleeting, like summer itself, but in the end, he was glad they'd done it. Glad they had all the memories and love that surrounded them now.

"It's hard to believe it's only been a year since then," he said. His gaze drifted to the pictures hanging on the windows.

She stared at the photos, too, shaking her head. "You know, it's funny. In most of those pictures, we were falling in love and we didn't even realize it."

"But now we know."

She glanced at her ring, moving her hand from side to side and watching the diamonds twinkle under the fairy lights. When she looked up, she met his eyes. All the love he felt for her was reflected back at him.

"We do." She grinned at him. "What do you say about taking one more picture for social media? For old time's sake?"

He pulled her into his arms and laughed. "I'd say that's a great idea."

* * * * *

Acknowledgments

I've wanted to be a published author since I was five years old, so it's surreal to finally be writing the acknowledgments for my debut novel. I'm one of those people who always reads the acknowledgments—I like knowing who's behind the book and getting a glimpse into the author's life. A lot of people helped make this book possible, and I owe them my endless gratitude.

Chicago-North Romance Writers, I don't think I ever would have finished a book without you. I'm grateful for your support, as well as your critiques, which have made me a better writer. I've learned so much from all of you. It's been an honor to serve as your co-president, and I'm excited for our future. Thank you for everything.

Thank you to my friends in the Panera Supper Club. Your friendship, encouragement, and brainstorming—and our group text—kept me going, especially during the pandemic, when I wrote the bulk of this book. Thank you to Kelly Farmer, Kayla Kensington, and Shannyn Schroeder for beta reading. Your insights were invaluable, and your love of this book means so much to me. Thank you also to Jody Holford, whose critique of my first chapter made this book so much stronger and helped get it submission-ready.

Thank you to everyone at Carina Press, especially my awesome editor, Mackenzie Walton. Your editing gave this book the final polish it needed to truly shine. Thank you to Kerri Buckley—I'll never forget the day I got the email from you that said Carina wanted to publish my book. I was beyond thrilled you and Mackenzie loved Luke, Audrey, and home renovation TV shows as much as I do. This is a dream come true.

To my agent, Eva Scalzo, getting an email from you saying you wanted to set up a call is one of the best moments of my writing career so far. I appreciate your guidance, your insights, and your thoughtfulness. Thank you for believing in me and my book.

This book probably wouldn't exist without my friend Daria Hoey, who helped me brainstorm when I first got the idea for this story. Your enthusiasm for my early chapters gave me the push I needed to keep writing. Thank you for being one of my first readers, and thanks to you and Laura for your friendship, support, and the many delicious home-cooked meals. I'm so glad to have you both in my corner.

To Sarah Mulhern, it's hard to believe we've known each other for twenty years and have been reading each other's writing for that long. Thank you for being one of the early readers of this book and for always supporting my writing from the time we were both teenagers writing fanfiction. Your kindness and support mean everything to me.

To my family, I'm so grateful for you. Thank you to my parents, who are both teachers and instilled in me a love of learning and reading. They encouraged my writing from a young age and still have the first stories I ever wrote. They also understood I was an indoor child who wanted nothing more than to read constantly, and they did their best to keep me supplied with books.

My mom took me to the library every week as a child and encouraged me to read diversely. I have to give a special shout-out to the Carnegie Library of Pittsburgh, which is one of the best library systems in the country. Thank you to libraries and librarians—you are doing important, vital work to transform people's lives.

Thank you to Grandma, whose main concern was whether my book was "risqué" and was proud to learn the answer was yes. Thank you to my brother, Matt, and my sister-in-law, Elsie, for believing in me and cheering me on.

Last, but certainly not least, thank you to readers. If you picked up this book, thank you for taking a chance on a debut author and giving me the gift of your time. More than anything, I want my books to bring people happiness, and I hope this book did that for you. I can't wait to share more stories with you.

About the Author

Julie Hamilton has been writing stories for as long as she can remember. She fell in love with romance novels during the summer between quitting her newspaper job and starting grad school, when she realized she was looking for a love story in every book she read. She writes contemporary romance with heat and humor that features characters chasing after their dreams—and finding happily ever after along the way. A Pittsburgh native, she now lives near Chicago.

To connect with Julie, visit her website at juliehamiltonauthor.com, follow her on social media, or sign up for her newsletter.

Twitter: twitter.com/JHamiltonAuthor.
Instagram: instagram.com/juliehamiltonauthor.
Newsletter: http://eepurl.com/hzvLsX

A pro hockey player learns that home is where the heart is in the first novel of a delightful new series from USA TODAY *bestselling author Alicia Hunter Pace.*

Prologue

Hell on Earth.

Pro hockey defenseman Jake Champagne understood the meaning of the phrase, but had never lived it until that March day at the end of his second season with the Nashville Sound.

He woke to the sound of pounding and the smell of hockey stench. At first, he thought the pounding was in his head but, as the fog cleared, he realized someone was intent on getting into his hotel room. When he opened his eyes, the first image he saw was a blurry half-empty bottle of Pappy Van Winkle bourbon. No wonder he couldn't see straight. He was usually a beer guy, but special nights called for special liquor and last night had been spectacular—though not in a good way.

Oh, no. Not at all. After hoisting the cup two years in a row, his team had gone four up and four down in the playoffs. Plus, it was cold here in Boston and he hated the cold, hated the snow. You wouldn't catch any snow on the ground in March in the Mississippi Delta—or any other time either. That was just one of the things he missed about home.

The pounding on the door became more intense just as a warm body rolled over next to him.

Hellfire and brimstone. It was all coming back now, and that was where the hockey stench was coming from. She was wearing his nasty jersey, had insisted on wearing it while they made love. He laughed under his breath. *Made love.* Ha.

He pulled on his sweatpants and caught sight of the clock as he crossed the room. Five forty-one freaking a.m.! The team plane didn't leave until ten o'clock. He was going to kill somebody—probably Robbie. His best friend most likely hadn't been to sleep yet. The last time he'd seen him, Robbie'd been doing shots with a redhead, the companion of the blonde in his own bed. He jerked open the door. "What do you want?"

Not Robbie. It was Sound staff member Oliver Klepacki, who frowned at the tone of Jake's voice. "Sparks." He used Jake's nickname.

Dread washed over Jake. This man was not in the habit of knocking on hotel doors at this hour. In fact, from the looks of him, he had just rolled out himself. "Sorry, Packi. Is something wrong?"

"You need to call your mother."

After closing the door, Jake reached for his phone with shaking hands. He'd turned it off last night, even before coming back to the room with his latest charming companion. Not wanting to talk to anyone who might want to commiserate over the loss to the Colonials or the minutes he'd spent in the penalty box because he'd showed his ass on the ice for no good reason, he'd taken the landline phone off the hook.

But that seemed small now. Something bad had happened. Christine Jacob Champagne was a Mississippi Delta Southern belle who took breakfast in her room every morning at eight o'clock. She spoke to no one before then. In any case, she wasn't the type to hunt down her grown son like a dog who needed his worm medicine.

He didn't call right away. There had to be a clue on his phone, and he couldn't take another breath without knowing if his dad and sister were okay.

Fourteen missed calls, five voice mails, and six text messages later, he knew. His uncle Blake—the man who had put him on skates at four years old—had had a heart attack.

And he was dead. The texts and voice mails hadn't said so. His mother would never leave that in a message, but he had to be. Otherwise she wouldn't have hunted him down in Boston at this hour.

He started to call, but paused and looked down at the woman in his bed. His mother would probably know she was here, would probably be able to smell her through the phone. He went into the bathroom, quietly drawing the door shut behind him before he dialed.

"Darling boy." Christine answered immediately.

"Uncle Blake?" he said.

There were tears in her voice. "I know how you loved him."

Loved. Jake hadn't realized that he'd still held out a miniscule bit of hope until his mother spoke in the past tense. He had known before he even made the call, but—at the same time—how was it possible?

"So hard to believe…only forty-seven…" Christine's voice trailed off.

"Forty-six." Jake was very sure of that. Jake had been four and Blake twenty-five—just the age Jake would be come October—when Blake had moved to the Delta to work at Champagne Cotton Brokers. Not long after, he had married Christine's younger sister.

"Forty-six," Christine said. "You're right, of course. Would've been forty-seven in June."

Would've been. Cruel words.

There were things he should be saying, questions he should be asking to prove he wasn't an asshole. "Aunt Olivia?" He said the words, but his thoughts were on himself.

In a land where football was king and baseball crown prince, Blake had taught Jake to skate by standing behind him, hands on his waist. Blake claimed trainer walkers that beginning skaters typically used to steady themselves encouraged bad posture and technique.

"She's resting," Christine said. "At least I hope she is."

"I hope so, too." The words were hollow. *Hope* wasn't much of a word right now.

Blake had showed him the movie *Miracle on Ice* and bought him a souvenir 1980 U.S. Olympic Hockey Team puck. At the time Jake didn't understand that the puck had not been in the actual game—or for that matter, that *Miracle on Ice* wasn't actual footage of the famous Soviet/U.S. match, or that the game had been played years before his birth. And later it didn't matter. By then, the puck was his constant companion and good luck charm.

"Adam and Nicole?" Jake asked after his two teenage cousins. Even after Blake and Olivia had children, he had not forsaken his bond with Jake.

"About like you'd expect," Christine said.

But what was that? How did anyone know what to expect?

Expect. Things would be *expected* of him by people who seemed to instinctively know the correct behavior for every situation known to man. "Naturally, I'm coming home." For the first time today, his voice sounded sure and strong.

And suddenly, that was what he wanted, all he wanted—to be home in Cottonwood, Mississippi. He wanted to drive down Main Street, past the bakery, the hardware store, and the drugstore that still had a soda fountain. He wanted to go to the house that been home to three generations of Champagnes, sleep in his childhood room, and smell the bacon and coffee that Louella had made for his family every morning for thirty years. He wanted to take his grandmother to lunch at the Country Club and hit a bucket of balls with his dad.

But Christine was talking, interrupting the flow of his thoughts. "No, Jake. No."

"I don't need to wait until morning," he assured her. "I won't be too tired to drive. I'll pack a few things and get on the road as soon as I can. I'll get into Nashville around noon and be home by bedtime—well before." Certainly in time to stop at Fat Joe's and pick up a sack of famous Delta tamales.

"No, Jake! Listen to me." Christine began to speak very clearly as if she were speaking to a child. "Do *not* come home. We're all flying out tonight to Vermont. You need to go there."

"Vermont?" Did they have tamales in Vermont?

"Yes. You *do* remember that Blake is from Vermont, don't you?"

"Well, yes, but…" Of course he remembered. Vermont was the whole reason Blake had played hockey as a kid, the reason he'd taught Jake to love hockey. But it didn't make any sense. Cottonwood had become Blake's home.

Christine seemed to read his mind. "He has—*had* family there. His father is unwell and unable to travel under the best of circumstances. The funeral will be there. You need to go to Vermont. We've reserved a block of rooms."

So, no home. More cold weather. Probably snow. But there would be people from home. That was something.

"Who's going?" he asked. "Besides y'all, Olivia and the kids?"

"About who you would expect—your grandmother, your sister, Anna-Blair and Keith, your aunt—"

"Evie? Is Evie going?" He cut her off. The mention of his godparents, Anna-Blair and Keith Pemberton, naturally led to thoughts of their daughter.

"No," Christine said. "She can't get away from work."

Evie had opened a pie shop in a fancy-pants section of Birmingham, Alabama, a few years back. There had been a time when she would have—pie shop, or no pie shop—crawled over glass to get to him if he needed her. However, that was before he'd let life get in the way and hadn't bothered to take care of their friendship. But he couldn't think about that right now. He had to get to Vermont.

"Okay, Mama. I'll go there from here. Text me the particulars and I'll book a flight. Or rent a car and drive. Yeah. Probably that." It would be faster, and not nearly as annoying as dealing with a commercial airline.

"All right. Text me your ETA when you know. Your dad wants to talk to you. I love you, Jake."

"I love you, too, Mama."

"Son!" Marc Champagne's big booming voice was the next thing he heard. Jake could tell in that one spoken syllable that his dad was driving this heartbreak wagon, bossing everyone around, and making them like it. He couldn't fix it, but by damn, he would make it go as easy as he and his money could. If Marc had his way, he'd probably move Olivia and the kids into the Champagne ancestral home.

"Hello, Dad."

"This is bad business, Jake. Bad."

"As bad as it gets," Jake agreed.

"Listen." Marc always said that before he said something important, even when the person he was speaking to was already listening. "I'll buy you a plane ticket back to Nashville from Vermont."

Jake opened his mouth to remind his dad that he could afford his own ticket. But that wasn't necessary. Marc knew how much the Sound paid him.

"Sure, Dad. Thanks." Jake hung up and walked back out to the bedroom. He needed to get that woman— Meghan, if he recalled correctly—out of here. Goodtime girls had no place in bad times.

It was when he put out a hand to shake her awake that he saw it—the glint of gold on the ring finger of her left hand. Just when he thought he couldn't feel any sicker, his stomach bottomed out. Since his divorce two years ago, he'd taken raising hell to a whole new art form, but there was one line he had never crossed: he did not sleep with married women.

"Hey." He poked her shoulder.

"What? Stop!" When she jerked the covers over her head, he saw that the ring was not a wedding band after all, but some kind of little birthstone ring that had turned around on her finger. He didn't feel much relief in that. He hadn't asked, hadn't even thought about it. That was a first. And if he had been willing to cross that line, what was next? His eyes darted to his bedside table. He was relieved to see an open box of condoms there, though it didn't negate the panic and shame coursing through him. But this was no time for self-refection. "Hey, Meghan." He pulled the covers off her head. "You have to wake up."

She opened one mascara-smudged eye, seemed to consider, and decided to smile.

"Hello there, Southern boy. Come back to bed."

"I can't."

She sat up. "Sure you can. I want to see if you speak Southerner as good in the morning as you do at night." She ran a hand up his thigh.

"No. Really. You've got to go." He moved her hand.

"Why? What time is it?" She frowned and picked up her phone. "What the fuck! Do you *know* what time it is?"

"I do. I'm sorry. But you have to go." He was repeating himself, but apparently it was necessary.

She pouted. "I thought you liked me."

"I did. I do. But you still have to go."

She threw her legs over the side of the bed. He thought he had won, but she was relentless. "All right," she said with a sigh. "I'm just going to jump in the shower. Why don't you order breakfast? I've never had room service before."

And he was done trying to trot out his Mississippi Delta Cotillion manners—not that he'd been very successful. "And you aren't going to have it now." She didn't deserve it, but he was out of time, out of patience, out of everything except the raw feelings marching through his head and heart. He reached for his wallet and peeled off two hundred-dollar bills. "Buy yourself some breakfast and an Uber."

Meghan looked at him like he was a snake recently escaped from a leprosy colony. He couldn't blame her. She had signed up for a little uncomplicated fun and had woken up to a complicated man in a complicated situation.

When she didn't say anything, he peeled off another hundred. "Ubers are expensive."

"*You* are an asshole," she said.

He nodded. "I am that."

She snatched the money from his hand, gathered up her clothes and boots from the floor, and stomped to the door. With her hand on the knob she turned and hissed, "I'm keeping this jersey."

He nodded. "Please. I want you to have it." It was a good thing it reached her knees because apparently she couldn't stand him another second, not even long enough to put on her jeans.

Understandable. He couldn't stand himself.

Jake needed concrete evidence there was a time when he didn't drink a six-pack every night and sleep with women who were more interested in his jersey than in him—needed to remember a time before he'd lost so many pieces of himself that he didn't know who he was anymore.

He didn't want to be a man Uncle Blake would have been ashamed of.

But if things didn't change, he was going to become the kind of person that everyone hated as much as he was beginning to hate himself. He loved the Sound, loved his teammates, but it would be easier to start over somewhere else with people who didn't naturally assume he was going to raise hell.

His scalp prickled at the thought.

Start over. Leave Nashville.

Leave the Sound? Maybe he ought to. The team had enough heavy-hitting veteran players that he was still the new kid in town. It would be years before he skated first line in Nashville, and who knew if he had years?

Blake certainly hadn't.

Jake picked up his phone again and dialed his agent, Miles Gentry, who answered immediately, despite the early hour. "Jake! I was just—"

"Trade me," he blurted out.

"What?"

"Trade me. Hopefully to somewhere I can skate first line. But it *has* to be a place where I don't have to buy a snow shovel. I don't care where. California. Texas. Florida. Arizona. Just get me the hell out of Nashville."

"Are you sure about this?" Miles asked.

"As sure as the fact that death is coming for us all."

Miles was quiet for a moment. "How do you feel about that new expansion team down in Birmingham? The Alabama Yellowhammers."

Right. He hadn't considered the new Birmingham team. It was still in the South—and Evie lived there. Maybe he could get their friendship back on track. Those were pluses, but the team was an unknown quantity. "Talk to me," Jake said.

"They've asked about you. I was waiting until the playoffs were over to tell you."

"Playoffs aren't over. Just over for the Sound—and me."

"Semantics," Miles said. "So—Alabama. Brand-new state-of-the-art practice facility. Drew Kelty is the head coach." Jake didn't really know him other than by name, but Kelty had plenty of pro hockey experience—as a player and a coach. "From what they said, I would think first line is an excellent bet. Any interest?"

And Jake said something neither he, nor any other Ole Miss fan, had ever said before. "Roll Tide."

Chapter One

Five months later

Evans Pemberton considered the dough on the marble slab in front of her.

What was wrong with pie in this country was the crust. No one made quality crusts anymore or thought about which kind of crust went best with what pie. Butter crusts were wonderful with fruit pies, but too rich for pecan pies. Savory pies needed a sturdy crust, but it was important to get the right balance so as not to produce a soggy mess. A bit of bacon grease gave crusts for meat pies a smoky taste, and Evans liked to add a pinch of sage for chicken pot pies. Crumb crusts had their place, too.

As did Jake Champagne, she thought, as she gave the ball in front of her a vicious knead. And his place was now apparently *here*. He was going to land in town any day, any hour.

He hadn't spoken to her in almost three years. Sure, back in March, he had texted to thank her for the funeral flowers she'd sent when his uncle died and apologized for not making more of an effort to keep in touch. According to her business manager, Neva, he'd also stopped by the shop a month later when he'd come to Laurel Springs to sign a lease on a condo, but Evans had been in New York taking a mini puff pastry course.

She didn't know why she was thinking about him anyway. Who knew if he would even try to contact her again? He had abandoned her once after a lifetime of friendship. There was no reason to think, despite the text and drop-in, that anything would change.

"You're looking at that dough like you don't like it," said a woman behind her.

"I don't." She turned and handed her friend, Ava Grace Fairchild, an apron and chef's hat. Ava Grace was no chef, but Evans had given up on trying to keep her out of the pie shop kitchen, so she'd settled on doing what she could to make Ava Grace acceptable should the health inspector make a surprise visit to Crust. "Though I suppose it's not so much that I don't like it. I don't *know* it."

"I thought you knew every dough." Ava Grace tied the apron over her linen dress and perched the hat on the back of her head so as not to disturb her loose chestnut curls. She looked like a queen dressed as a chef for Halloween.

"I don't know this one." Evans placed her hand on the dough. Normally, she wouldn't think of putting her warm hand on pastry dough, but this was a hot water pastry so it was warm to begin with.

Ava Grace slid onto a stool and crossed her long, perfect legs. "What makes this one different?"

"It's for a handheld meat pie with rutabagas, potato, and onions. The crust has to be sturdy but not tough. That's tricky." She gave the dough another vicious slap. "They're called Upper Peninsula pasties, from Michigan."

"Never heard of them," Ava Grace said.

"Claire has, and she wants to feed them to the new hockey team on their first day of training camp tomorrow."

Ava Grace's mouth twisted into a grin. "For a silent partner, Claire isn't very quiet, is she?"

Evans laughed. Ava Grace would know. Claire was her "silent" partner, too. "Well, she never promised to be quiet."

"That's a promise she couldn't have kept. Why is she so set on these little pies?"

"You know as well as I do that Claire doesn't have to have a reason, but she says most of the team is from up North, so we should give them some Northern comfort food."

Evans had not pointed out to Claire that not all hockey players would associate these pasties with home. She knew of one in particular who would need barbecue pork, hot tamales, and Mississippi mud pie to make him think of home. Claire wasn't an easy woman to say no to, even if Evans had been willing. Saying no had never been Evans's strong suit, which was why she was catering this lunch when she just wanted to make pies.

Evans had thought it would be years before she could fulfill her dream of having her own shop, until Claire had taken her under her wing. Now Crust was thriving.

The old-money heiress had excelled in business, and successfully played the stock market rather than living off her inheritance. A few years ago she had decided to help young women start their own new businesses. Evans and Ava Grace were two of Claire's girls, along with Hyacinth Dawson, who owned a local bridal shop.

"Claire must really like hockey," Ava Grace said.

"I don't think it's that, so much as she likes a project and loves the chase." Claire was one of several locals who owned a small part of the Yellowhammers. Her uncle and nephew had been the ones to bring the team here, but Claire had quickly formulated a plan to turn Laurel Springs into Yellowhammers Central. "She knows a bunch of rich hockey players are going to live and spend their money somewhere and she wants it to be here." She had convinced the owners to build a state-of-the-art practice rink and workout facility in Laurel Springs, renovated the old mill into upscale condos, lobbied for more fine dining and chic shops, and turned the old Speake Department Store building into a sports bar and named it Hammer Time—all to welcome the new team.

"It looks like she's getting her way," Ava Grace said. "Everywhere you look there's a gang of Lululemon-wearing men in Yellowhammer ball caps."

"We should be thankful for them," Evans said. "Sponsoring our businesses was part of her master plan to make the area appealing to the team. Had to be."

Ava Grace pulled at one of her curls. "I'm sure she knows what she's doing. I've lived here all my life, and I've never known Claire to fail," she said wryly. "At least not yet." Of the three businesses Claire had backed, Ava Grace's antique and gift shop was the only one losing money. Claire insisted that was to be expected in the beginning, but it was still a sore subject. "Anyway." Ava Grace clapped her hands together like she always did when she wanted to change the subject. "Hockey in Birmingham. Hockey people here in our little corner of the world. I've never even been to a hockey game. Have you?"

And here it was. She'd never mentioned Jake to anyone in Laurel Springs, not even Ava Grace and Hyacinth, who were her best friends. And she was loath to do it now. What if he ignored her as he had the last few years?

"I have. A guy I've known all my life is a hockey player." She wasn't about to mention that he'd been the best-looking thing in Cottonwood, Mississippi—plus he had that hockey-mystique thing going for him in a world where most of the other boys played football and baseball. "His parents and mine are best friends, so we went to a lot of his games when I was growing up. After college, he went on to play for the Nashville Sound, but he's going to play for the Yellowhammers now."

Ava Grace widened her eyes. "Really? He's coming here?"

"If nothing has changed since the last time I talked to my mother. I haven't talked to him in a while." Technically not a lie—condolence texts didn't count as talking.

"Is he married?"

"Not anymore." She slammed her fist into the ball of dough.

Ava Grace's eyes lit up and Evans knew what was coming. Ava Grace was all but engaged and was always looking for romance for everyone else. "Is this an old boyfriend?"

"No! Of course not." She hadn't meant to sound so vehement.

Ava Grace narrowed her eyes. "You never went out with him a single time?"

"No. Never entered my mind." If she'd been Pinocchio, her nose would be out the front door. There had been this one time at a holiday party—for just a fraction of a minute—when Evans had thought he'd looked at her differently, when she'd been sure that Jake was finally going to ask her for a date. But they'd been interrupted, and the moment had passed. To this day, she never saw a sprig of holly or heard a Christmas bell without the memory of the humiliating disappointment slamming against her rib cage, driving the breath out of her.

"It's a new day," Ava Grace said. "I grew up with Skip, and look where we are. It could happen for you, too."

"Not likely." Evans floured her rolling pin. "A couple years back, my cousin Channing married and divorced him in the space of about seven months in the messiest way possible."

"Wow." Ava Grace raised her eyebrows. "Your cousin just up and stole your man, easy as you please? Why, you must've been madder than a wet hen!"

Evans shrugged. "He wasn't mine." She clenched her fist and the dough shot up between her fingers. "I doubt he would be open to romance with another Pemberton woman. Not that I would—be open to it, I mean."

The words had barely made their way out of her mouth when one of her assistant bakers ducked into the kitchen.

"Evans, there's a guy here to see you."

She stilled her rolling pin.

"I think I conjured up a man for you." Ava Grace laughed and removed her cap and apron. "See you tonight at Claire's house."

"Right." It was mentor dinner night with Claire, something they did every few weeks where Evans, Ava Grace, and Hyacinth gave reports and swapped advice.

Ava Grace nodded. "I'll just slip out the back."

"Who is it, Ariel?" Please, God, not the rep from Hollingsworth Foods—a regional company that provided frozen foods to grocery stores. According to Claire, they were interested in mass-producing her maple pecan and peanut butter chocolate pies. So far, the rep had only tried to contact her by phone and it had been easy enough to elude his calls, allowing her to tell Claire that she hadn't heard from them.

Ariel shook her head and played with the crystal that hung around her neck. "I don't know."

Evans sighed. Of course she wouldn't have thought to ask. The female hadn't been born who was more suited to her name than Ariel—ethereal, dreamy, not of this world. But she could make a lemon curd that would make you cry.

"All right." Evans reached for a towel and wiped her hands. As tempting as it was to follow Ava Grace out the back door, she supposed it was time to deal with it. "Will you cover these and put them in the refrigerator?" She gestured to the sheet pans of oven-ready meat pies.

Ariel nodded. "I'll just get the plastic wrap." And she floated to the storeroom.

Evans still had a few meat pies, then peach cobblers to make for the Yellowhammer lunch tomorrow, so the quicker she sent him away, the better.

She hurried through the swinging door that led from the kitchen to the storefront—and looked right into the eyes of Jake Champagne.

Eyes.

He had eyes all night long and possibly into the next day. Big, cobalt blue eyes with Bambi eyelashes. They weren't eyes a woman was likely to forget even if he turned out to be a man she had to walk away from. Still, Evans had thought the day was done when those eyes would make her forget her own name. *Evans. Evans Blair Pemberton*, she reminded herself.

Jake widened those eyes. That was a willful act. She was sure of it because she'd spent years studying him— so she knew what it meant when Jake Champagne went all wide-eyed on someone. He understood the value of those eyes and the effect they had on people. When he widened them, he was either surprised or angling to get his way. This time he was surprised. If he'd been trying to get his way, he would have cocked his head to the side and smiled. If he wanted his way really bad, and it wasn't going well, he'd bite his bottom lip.

Speaking of what he wanted—what in the ever-loving hell was he doing here? She was pretty sure he had not gone to work for Hollingsworth Foods.

"You look great, Evie." She was suddenly sorry she'd studied him. Knowing he was surprised that she looked great wasn't the best for the ego.

Besides, she didn't look great. Her hair was in a messy ponytail, she was wearing an apron covered in flour, and any makeup she'd applied this morning was a memory. She only looked great compared to the last time he'd seen her—at the Pemberton family Thanksgiving two years ago, when she'd been coming off a bad haircut and sporting a moon crater of a cold sore. That had been five months after his wedding and two months before his divorce. Now, three years later, he could still send her on a one-way trip back to sixteen.

"Hotty Toddy, Jake!" Why had she said that—the Ole Miss football battle cry? Neither of them had gone to Ole Miss, though most of their families had. They were fans, of course, but she didn't normally go around saying *Hotty Toddy*.

"Hotty Toddy, Evie. That's good to hear in Roll Tide country."

She stepped from behind the counter and the awkward hug they shared was softened by his laughter. Though she didn't say so, he really did look great—however, in his plaid shorts and pink polo, he looked more like a fraternity boy on spring break than a professional hockey player. Jake's eyes might be his best feature, but he was gorgeous from head to toe. His caramel blond hair was a little shaggy and his tan face clean-shaven.

They came out of the hug and she looked up at him—way up. He was over six feet tall to her barely five feet four.

"It's good to see you, Evie."

Evie, rhymed with *levy.* He'd christened her that—probably because it was easier for a toddler to say than Evans. "Only people from home call me Evie now," she babbled.

He raised one eyebrow and his mouth curved into a half smile. She'd forgotten about that half smile. "I *am* from home."

He had a point.

"Would you like some pie? I have Mississippi mud." His favorite. The meringue pie with a chocolate pastry crust and layers of dense brownie and chocolate custard was one of her most popular. She glanced around to see if one of the round marble tables was available. Though it was after one o'clock, a few people were still lingering over lunch, but there was a vacant table by the window.

"No, I don't think—" He stopped abruptly and narrowed his eyes. "Yes. I would. Can you sit with me? For just a bit?"

Of course she could. She was queen of this castle. She could do whatever she wanted. But did she want to? Ha! What a stupid question, even to herself.

"Sure." She might still be making cobblers at midnight, but that was nobody else's business. "Joy?" She turned to the girl behind the counter. "I'm going to take a break. Can you bring a slice of Mississippi mud and a glass of milk? And a black coffee for me." She met his eyes. "Unless you've started drinking coffee."

He looked a little pained and she wondered why. "No. I still don't."

He held her chair before sitting himself down in the iron ice cream parlor chair opposite her. What had she been thinking when she'd bought these chairs? Apparently, not that hockey players—let alone this hockey player—would be settling in for pie. He looked like a man at a child's tea party. She laughed a little.

And in that instant, with the sun shining in the window turning his caramel hair golden, Jake came across with a smile that lit up the world. Good thing she'd packed up all those old feelings, right and tight, when he'd gotten involved with her cousin. Her stomach turned over—a muscle memory, no doubt.

"What's funny?" he asked.

"I was thinking I didn't choose these chairs with men in mind."

"You don't think it suits me?" He leaned back a bit. "Maybe you could trade them for some La-Z-Boys."

"Not quite the look I was going for."

He looked around. "So this is your shop? All yours?"

"I have an investor, but yes. It's mine."

She loved the wood floors, the happy fruit-stenciled yellow walls, the gleaming glass cases filled with pies, and the huge wreath on the back wall made of antique pie tins of varying sizes. Five minutes ago, she'd loved the ice cream parlor chairs. She probably would again.

"I knew you had a shop." He looked around. "But I had no idea it was like *this*. So nice."

You might have, if you'd bothered to call me once in a

while. Evans bit her tongue as if she'd actually spoken the words and wanted to call them back. Instead, she packed them up and shoved them to the back of her brain. Jake was here. She was glad to see him. That was all.

"I've had some good luck," she said.

His eyes settled on the table next to them. "You serve lunch, too?"

"Nothing elaborate. A choice of two savory pies with a simple green or fruit salad on the side. I would offer you some, but we sold out of the bacon and goat cheese tart and you wouldn't eat the spanakopita."

He frowned. "Spana-who?"

"Spanakopita. Spinach pie."

He shuddered. "No. Not for me, but I'm meeting my teammate Robbie soon for a late lunch anyway." She knew who Robbie was from *The Face Off Grapevine*, a pro hockey gossip blog she sometimes checked. They called him and Jake the Wild-Ass Twins, though they looked nothing alike. For whatever reason, this Robbie was coming to play for the Yellowhammers, too. Jake went on, "He's been in Scotland since the season ended and just got in this morning. We're going to a place down the street."

So I'm only a pit stop. "Hammer Time. Brand-new sports bar for a brand-new team."

He nodded. "I hope Hammer Time is half as nice as your shop. You obviously work really hard."

"I do. But I don't have to do it on skates." She held up her chef clog-clad foot. Why had she said that? Belittled herself?

He laughed like it was the best joke he'd ever heard. Ah, that was why. She'd do anything to make him laugh. She'd forgotten that about herself.

"Here you go, Evans." Joy set down the pie, milk, and a thick, retro mug decorated with cherries like the ones on the wall.

"No pie for you?" Jake picked up his fork.

She sipped her coffee. "No. I taste all day long. The last thing I want is a plateful of pie. Are you sure you want that? Aren't you about to eat lunch?"

"I want this more than I've wanted anything for a long time." He took a bite and closed his eyes. "Other people only think they've had pie."

If she never got another compliment about another thing, this one would do her until death. "Mississippi mud is a hit in Alabama."

"Don't tell her, but this is so much better than the one from your mother's bakery."

No kidding. Anna-Blair Pemberton was all about a shortcut. "If she'd had her way, I'd be back in Cotton-wood, making cookies from mixes and icing cakes with buttercream from a five-gallon tub."

Jake laughed a little under his breath. "My mother might have mentioned that a time or six."

"No doubt." Christine Champagne and Evans's mother were best friends. When Evans had deserted her mother's bakery after graduating from the New Orleans Culinary Institute, it must have given them fodder for months.

"I, for one, am glad you're making pie here." Jake took another bite. "There's something about this…something different. And familiar." He wrinkled his brow. "But I can't place it."

Evans knew exactly what he meant, and it pleased her more than it should have that he'd noticed.

"Do you remember the Mississippi mud bars we used to get when we went to Fat Joe's for tamales?"

"Yes! That's it." He took another bite of pie. "We ate a ton of those things, sitting at that old picnic table outside. Didn't Joe's wife make them?"

"She did. I got her secret and her permission to use it. She used milk and dark chocolate, and she added a little instant coffee to the batter."

He stopped with his fork in midair. "Coffee? There's coffee in here?"

Evans laughed. "You've been eating Lola's for years without knowing." She reached for his plate. "But if you don't want it…"

"Leave my pie alone, woman." He pretended to stab at her with his fork. "Those were good times."

"They were. We did a lot of homework at that picnic table."

He grimaced. "Well, it wasn't the homework I was thinking about. I'd have never passed a math class without you."

"Oh, I don't know about that."

"*I* do." He shook his head and let his eyes wander to the ceiling like he always did when he wanted to change the subject. "What about the beach this summer. How was it?"

The question took Evans aback. Jake hadn't been on the annual Champagne-Pemberton beach trip since Channing came on the scene. She was surprised he even thought about them anymore.

"Sandy. Wet. Salty," she quipped. "Like always."

He grinned. "Must have been a little *too* sandy, wet, and salty for you. I hear you only stayed two days."

"Lots to do around here." She gestured to the shop.

He let his eyes go to a squint and his grin relaxed into that crooked smile. "Too much sorority talk?"

"I swear, it never stops." She slapped her palm against the table. All the women in that beach house—Evans's mother and two older sisters and Jake's mother and younger sister—were proud alumnae of Ole Miss and Omega Beta Gamma, the most revered and exclusive sorority on campus. Addison, Jake's sister, had recently made the ultimate commitment to her Omega sisters by taking a job at the sorority's national headquarters.

Jake took a sip of his milk and chuckled. "I hear you. Especially with rush coming up."

"It's like being in a room full of teachers who won't talk about anything except test scores and discipline problems. You just get tired of it." But it was more than that. Legacy or not, Evans would have never made the Omega cut had she gone to Ole Miss instead of culinary school. She wasn't tall, blond, and sparkly enough. She loved those women—every one of them—but she had always been a little out of step with them. Plus, living with all that sparkle could be hard on the nerves.

Jake laughed. "Well, they have to do their part to keep Omega on top, where it belongs."

"Sorority blood runs deep and thick in Mississippi," Evans said. "Sisters for life."

Jake went from amused to grim. "I don't think Mama and Addison feel very sisterly toward Channing anymore."

Channing had, of course, been the poster child for Omega. "For what it's worth, my mother and sisters don't either." *And I don't feel very cousinly toward her. Not that I ever did.*

He shrugged. "I've moved on—not quite as fast as

she did, of course. Miss Mississippi, hockey wife, music producer wife, all in the space of eight months. I suppose you've heard she's pregnant?"

"Yes." The baby would probably have mud-colored eyes like Mr. Music Producer, when it could have had the bluest eyes in the world. Baffling.

"But I'm better off," Jake went on.

She studied his face and decided he meant it. "I'm glad you know it. You're better than that, Jake. You deserve better."

Jake looked at his pie, and back at her again. "You remembered my favorite pie and that I'm not a coffee drinker?"

Thank goodness for the change of subject. "How could I not remember? You always asked for Mississippi mud pie when you came into the bakery at home."

He took a deep breath. "I'm glad to see you, Evie."

"I'm glad to see *you*," she echoed. And she was. But something was niggling deep in her gut. It seemed Glad and Mad were running around inside her, neither one able to get complete control. She beat back Mad and embraced Glad. It was impossible to control most emotions, but mad wasn't one of them. She had always believed that if you didn't want to be mad, you didn't have to be. So what if he'd only come to see her because Crust was near his lunch spot? They had history. That was what was important. And he'd been through a lot: divorce, Blake's death, a new town and team, and—well, she didn't know what else, but wasn't that enough?

"I probably don't deserve for you to be glad to see me, but I appreciate it." Oh, hell. He was going to try to get negative now, just when she'd talked herself into a good place. She would not allow it. The only thing she was better at than turning out a perfect puff pastry was turning a situation around.

"Why wouldn't I be glad to see you?" She smiled like she meant it, and she did. Everybody always said you had to clear the air before you could move on. As far as she was concerned, that was way overrated. Sometimes it was better to just let it go. Saying yes when others might say no sometimes made life go smoother.

"Let's not pretend I don't owe you an apology." He cocked his head to the side and widened his eyes. What was the point of that? She'd already forgiven him.

"Jake, there is no need for all of this."

"There is. I haven't been the friend to you I should have been. I guess when I met Channing, I didn't think about anything except her and hockey. I know I texted that to you a few months ago, but I wanted to say it in person." He lifted one corner of his mouth. "I did come by before I took Olivia and the kids to Europe, but you weren't here."

"I was in New York."

"I know. Please say you forgive me."

It would have been easier to downplay the whole thing and say it didn't matter. But no one was going to believe that, so she did the next best thing. "It's in the past. Our friendship goes back far and deep. It can withstand a storm or two." The truth of that lightened her heart.

Jake looked relieved, happy even. Maybe she did matter to him. "I shouldn't have let our friendship slip away—let you slip away."

The hair on the back of her neck stood up. *Slip away?*

With that, Mad slammed a boxing glove into Glad's face and a foot on to its fallen body.

Why had he had to go and say that? She hadn't *slipped away.* She had gone kicking and screaming. It was true that she hadn't contacted him for a month after *that Christmas*—the Christmas of Channing—but wasn't she entitled to that, considering how things went down? And he damn sure hadn't bothered with her.

Evans had been home from culinary school for the holidays, and Jake from the University of North Dakota. They hadn't seen each other since summer, so they'd filled their plates with Anna-Blair's fancy canapés and found a corner to catch up—though catching up wasn't really necessary, because back then they talked and messaged each other at least three times a week. But they laughed and talked and she thought she'd finally seen the spark she'd felt for twenty years reflected in his eyes. He almost confirmed it when he said, "You know, Evie, my fraternity spring formal is going to be in New Orleans, and I was thinking that—"

But she'd never know for absolute certain what he had been thinking. Maybe he wasn't going to invite her. Maybe he was only going to ask her for a ride from the airport or advice about where to get the best gumbo.

Channing's family seldom made the trip from Memphis to Cottonwood and never for Christmas—but they had that year. And Channing chose that precise moment to sail in, looking like Vogue and smelling like Chanel. Or maybe it was Joy. Who the hell knew? It damned sure wasn't vanilla extract. Whatever it was, Evans had gotten a good whiff when Channing swooped in and hugged her—something Evans could never recall hap-

pening before. Of course, Channing had never walked
in on Evans in conversation with someone who looked
like Jake before either. "Well, cousin, who do you have
here?" Channing had asked. Evans had introduced them,
and then it was all over but the crying.

And Evans had cried—for a month. But what purpose
would it serve to go into all that with Jake? It was over.
It didn't matter—except it did. Strange that it only oc-
curred to her now that if Jake had been planning to ask
her to the dance, maybe it was because she was going to
school in New Orleans anyway—convenient.

"You know, Jake, I didn't slip away." She took down
her ponytail and put it back up again. "I didn't go easily." After that month had passed, she'd batted back the
humiliation and put on her big girl panties. Still, no matter how many times she'd called or texted, he never had
time for her. Even if he answered, he was somewhere
else. The next time she'd seen him had been in New Orleans the morning after that dance, when she'd met him
and Channing at Brennan's for breakfast. Channing had
brought the nosegay of white roses and succulents that
Jake had bought her for the dance and held hands with
him under the table. Evans had cursed herself for saying
yes to that breakfast invitation, when she should have
said no. It wasn't the first time, and it wouldn't be the
last. "I fought for our friendship."

The moment the words cleared her mouth, she was
sorry. He'd apologized. What more did she want? Jake's
face went white and he put his fork down. Understandable. He probably didn't want to eat any more of her pie
after what she'd said. Why hadn't she just left it alone?

"I'm sorry. I shouldn't have said that," she said hur-
riedly.

"Why? It's true." There was real hurt on his face.

"Nonetheless. You apologized, and I wasn't gracious about it. And after all you've been through. It's behind us. Let's move forward."

He looked skeptical, but nodded. "That's all I want. And you've been gracious to forgive me at all." Eyes wide. Head cocked. Lip bite. "I'll make it up to you."

He had never, as far as she could remember, had to get to the lip biting with her before. "There's nothing to make up."

He picked up his fork again. "I disagree, though it may not be possible. But I will say this: for a while there, I forgot what was important. After the divorce, I forgot my raising. But after Blake… It made me stop and think. I won't forget again. I'm going to be a better man—a better friend."

He covered her hand with his, and her heart dropped like a fallen star.

"We're good." What was wrong with being convenient anyway?

Then he nodded and smiled like he was pleased. Pleasing Jake Champagne had once been her life's work.

She supposed she was glad she had finally accomplished it.

Don't miss Sweet as Pie *by Alicia Hunter Pace,*
available wherever books are sold.
www.CarinaPress.com